The Creation Series
Volume Three

While the Ashes
Rise to Life

As the body withers and dies,
When the soul ascends to the highest heights,
While the ashes rise to life.

By Crystal Wolfe

THE CREATION SERIES: VOLUME THREE

Cover Design by Crystal Wolfe
Interior Design by Crystal Wolfe
Typography by Crystal Wolfe
Edited by Donald Hart, Amber Pearson, and Crystal Wolfe

May 27th, 2023

Revised Edition

Original Edition: *As the Ashes Rise to Life*

ISBN-13:
9781954258051

Library of Congress Control Number:
2023934433

A United World Press
New York, NY

WHILE THE ASHES RISE TO LIFE

THE CREATION SERIES: VOLUME THREE

WHILE THE ASHES RISE TO LIFE

Book Reviews

This book has changed my life. It opened my mind and imagination in a way I've never experienced. The adventures are unparalleled—totally different than in any other novel I've read. No matter what your preferred genre is, the author's writing style is so beautiful and riveting that anyone would enjoy reading it.

While the Ashes Rise to Life carries the most visionary and original of stories and characters, delving into the mysteries behind the family lines in the Garden of Eden, delving into the secrets of the waters and deserts in a way that has never been done before. The book explores the inner workings of people and places, taking the reader where other writers dare not go—and with an artistry that is nothing less than prolific and profound.

The way the viewpoint shifts from different character's perspectives, moves the story forward powerfully and compellingly. At times I was at the edge of my seat while reading this. The depth of this story, and the depth of these characters, are both soulful and heartfelt. This author has a wonderful way of making the reader *feel* the emotions, and understand the reasoning, of each character. The many viewpoints on display can be laugh-out-loud funny, and are at the same time deliciously psychologically satisfying because the truths revealed are pure genius.

There is a book of magic and healing in what can only be considered a work of art. This enchanting novel is nothing less than a masterpiece that will leave you breathless, gasping for more...

—Darmar Publishing
New York, NY

Combining the genres of fantasy, action, adventure, mythology, spirituality, and psychological realism—Crystal Wolfe's third book of The Creation Series, *While the Ashes Rise to Life,* has continued the theme of adventure, interwoven with eloquent insights and depth. The imagery is fascinating and engaging as the lives of characters take unexpected turns—from unique ocean adventures, to desolate desert extremes, to hidden acts of betrayal, to seaside beauty, harmony, and love.

Throughout the book, Wolfe continues to explore the various effects of trauma in certain characters—from healing and forgiveness, to rage and abuse—in a way that brings depth of understanding. As the characters experience raw moments of pain, heartbreak, and grief, they are transformed by it. For without pain there can be no depth of growth. Yet, intertwined throughout, there is an unending seed of hope and love. It is clear that the refiner's fire is not without intent.

Wolfe's writing style is suspenseful and captivating, I believe anyone could relate to it, and become engrossed by it. You don't have to be a fantasy and science fiction fan to enjoy reading this book. I couldn't put it down. I highly recommend this book to anyone who is open to experience adventure in a totally unique way; anyone who is curious how trauma and loss affect us differently, and ways to overcome it, through transformation.

—Integrated Wellness Strategies

A spiritual fire seems to spark from these pages, an awakening of truths tapping into the very soul of the earth. The dialogue can be humorous, with the characters differing voices and viewpoints, then suddenly pulsate with startling insights into the human psyche.

Somehow this story opens the eyes and senses, compelling the reader to see what lies beyond the veil of life and death, urging us to recognize the unity of everyone on earth, challenging us to feel and understand one another, and to remember not just our Fall in the Garden of Eden, but also, our original innocence.

THE CREATION SERIES: VOLUME THREE

—A United World Press
New York, NY

This book is dedicated to…

A lifelong friend, childhood director, fellow actor,

and eternal optimist, Donald Hart,
who was the first to tell me about
"The Legend of the Selkie."

And…
Every person who has known the taste of defeat, the
grief with no solace, the suffering without end, and yet
has found the strength to rise again.

Table of Contents

The intensity of the desire in her heart combined with the mighty determination of her will, until the purposeful clarity of her imaging grew so strong the pulsating in her body became a whirring tornado from inside her eardrums and organs. Her body shifted, transforming before her own eyes. Soft skin and supple flesh molded into a much smaller, slithery form, with gleaming silver skin.

"*She who bears the raven mark*
Shall be the first to fall and rise again.
From fire and coal, out of ashes and shadow
She returns more than whole in the resurrection."

I closed my eyes of gleaming sapphire. With a single flap of my wings, the fire burst forth from my body, and consumed me, until all that was left of me in the nest I had built of aromatic woods, was ash.

As they sang, I touched my silver horn to Jonlin's crudely constructed grave, turning it into a hallowed monument of epic proportions. The magic of my horn turned the gravesite into a memorial.

The light and happy bride she would have been, with curled hair and big doe-eyes full of hope for the future and all of life itself, behind a white veil between childhood and full-blossomed womanhood, was now a dead dream. She had crossed the dark veil, and gone over to the side of the living dead.

Thus, through forest and shadows, by the dying light of the setting sun, he wordlessly led Darlillyth to the daughter she had believed for centuries was dead.

Shadonai took the box the boy handed her, and with a great many spiraling counter clock-wise motions she threw Varawynn's ashes into the brewing cauldron moving now by itself. It spit and smoked as the ashes dissolved into the fiery cauldron.   Page 103

Beautiful dreams were born and lived in a moment. A lifetime's worth of joy and love and beauty was encompassed in the first moment's step into the light, and countless more lifetimes of joy and love and beauty were to be lived for her, the Light of God, guided forth into eternity. The life she'd lived as a mere shadow slipped away like a distant memory, as an eternity of light and love was begun.   Page 124

Some animal instinct, more or less than human, brought her through the fields of heather to the waves beating the rocks and cliffs. As she walked to the edge of the cliffs late one evening with the water and full moon calling out to her, she stood staring down into the water's murky depths. Suddenly she didn't want to go back to the campsite any longer. She wanted to plunge into the depths of the sea.   Page 133

Watching in wonderment as the Sirens approached the ship and the men pulled the Sirens onboard, my brain couldn't remember, for the life of me, the end of this legendary tale. It didn't entirely matter as I was about to find out.   Page 155

Galloping across the endless desert sands, Eliju and his dream-to-end-all-dreams of riding a wild stallion from dawn till dusk, until the beating sun set, was fulfilled. And the feeling of wild freedom spent itself again and again. The culmination of Eliju's heart and spirit found release in the self-same spirit of freedom he and the stallion shared.   Page 175

As life no longer had him in it, she was prepared to make some questionable choices in her pursuit to have and to hold some part of Eliju, the object of her love and obsession. Even if whatever she gleaned of his was not freely given, she came to the desert prepared to steal it...   Page 189

Aldoran yanked the sea shell souvenir from the small pack on his side and pierced the sea monster with the sharpest end of it. The creature, all mouth, howled again. Yanking some seaweed up by the roots that were flowing around them, riding atop the waves of the water, he deftly wound the long, thick seaweed around the creature's two front teeth, pulling with all his might as it screamed.

Page 205

Rushing across the desert plains and away from the shadowy Jinn pursuing her, there was no outrunning the desert creature. As demons they could move a legion in a breath. Her heart constricted in fear. *What can I do? Where I can turn? There's no way to get away from it.* So, she did the only thing she could do…she just kept on running.

Page 224

It was as if the sun exploded in the darkness, as shooting stars fell from the sky and the whole darkened world was flooded with blinding, burning light. The hard and rocky, scorched ground basked in the glow of the bursting sun and falling stars, the world around them fell apart as it came to life.

Page 244

Donning my human form for my seal skin, I transformed right before the woman and babe into the seal. As the seal, I lay my fin upon the baby's forehead as Sara leaned the baby down for me to reach. In the sea's sonar language, which sounded very different out of the waters, I offered the child a blessing in the form of a prayer.

Page 258

In the midst of the pain of the worst of our fears coming to fruition, in the middle of the worst, the most impossible of circumstances, we have even then, especially then, a choice; to let life break our hearts, crush our spirits, and destroy our souls or to learn to endure our hardships by the guiding light of love.

Page 278

Crying out in her dreams his beloved name, she reached for him from amongst the shadows. He was shouting something, but she couldn't hear his words. All she could make out reading his lips was, "Don't, don't, don't, *don't do this…*" Was the ghost of Jonlin trying to keep her from a life of happiness…or warn her about a life of misery?

Page 292

Blind and faithful, without logic or reason, unconditional and gently imperishable like the inextinguishable flame of hope, dimly burned in his spirit. An inner knowing that there was more to life than this, that the world held more than this dungeon, kept him going.   Page 301

Epilogue   *The Battle for Souls*

The angels fought on their behalf, the human prayers empowering their every blow, and protecting them like a shield for the battling of souls on the sides of Good versus Evil, in the Eternal Conflict, the Eternal War between pride and humility, love and hate, vengeance and grace. Only God knew the souls that would be saved, and those who would be lost, condemned to the shadows of darkness forever.   Page 316

Explanation of Symbols:

~ ~ ~ = Break in Time

* * * = Change in Character

~ *** ~ = Change in Character and Time

Note: Scenes that are italicized are from the past.

The powers that be began to create:
    The first one, goodness, created a soul with bones.
    The second one, forbearance, created a soul with sinew.
    The third, joy, created a soul with flesh.

The fourth, peace, created a soul with marrow.
The fifth, self-control, created a soul with blood.
The sixth, kindness, created a soul with skin.
The seventh, gentleness, created a soul with hair.
The eighth, faithfulness, created a soul with form.
The ninth, wisdom, created a soul with eyes.
The tenth, divinity, created a soul with love.

– The Creation of Man

Prologue
The Legend of the Selkie

4th Millennia B.C. in the Celtic Isles—

In the land of the Celtic isles, along the banks of a silvery sea shore, a shape shifter took ungent into a potion, a liquid herb aiding the Celts in the magic of metamorphosis. It was a full moon night in early October—the powerful Harvest Moon of transformations.

Shards of memories like rays of light peeking through tree leaves flooded her mind, coming in scattered scenes of words and touch in non-sequential order so as not to overwhelm her heart. Powerful feelings evoked from the memories drowned her, eclipsing all hope. Crying up at the moon with a howling wolf's haunting cadence, the priestess sent up into the night the desperate uttering of a prayer, for an easing of the pain of her unrequited love.

Into the darkness of the sky, as she cried, a longing and desire overtook her, to escape into the sea. The longing and desire grew so strong a pulsating began beating inside her body. Willing an external armor to protect her vulnerable, aching heart, she envisioned a thicker skin to bear more readily the waves of the sea. As the image clarified inside her inner eye, she felt her body tingling from inside out, as her fingers and feet shook and throbbed.

The intensity of the desire in her heart, combined with the mighty determination of her will, until the purposeful clarity of her imaging grew so strong the pulsating in her body became a whirring tornado from inside her eardrums and organs. Her body shifted, transforming before her own eyes...

Soft skin and supple flesh molded into a much smaller, slithery form with gleaming silver skin. With awe-struck wonder, she realized she'd become a seal. Her amazement over the transmutation and her gratitude to leave behind her life as a human, and bear alone the loss of love she'd so coveted was overwhelming, but she embraced the transfiguration as a unique gift from the gods. A gift that was offered to her in payment for the unfairness of her treatment, and the greatness of her need to escape the memories that plagued her mind.

Without a glance behind her, she dove into the waters, ready and willing to discover the secrets of the sea, and forget for a time the troubles of her life on the shore. In time, she grew to miss certain things about her life as a human...the deep green grass above the jagged cliffs, the heady scent of the endless fields of heather, the relieving cleansing of the rain on her supple, fleshy body, the movements of her muscles as she ran, the curve of her hips into the small of her waist, and the blossoming rounded angles of her chest. By donning her seal skin on and off, she was able to return to land or sea. In this way, she had the best of both worlds.

There were times when possessive men, greedy for her enchanting beauty, would steal her seal skin in order to keep her on land with them. Imprisoning her for want of control over her fluid grace and one-of-kind charms, these men did not love her, nor did she hold any sympathies for them.

Such greedy men do not know what true love is. Love for them was earthly and selfish. Always she found a way to outsmart these manipulatives, grasping men, stealing back her seal skin and escaping, back into the sanctuary of the sea.

Then, free once more from the empty lust of the men of the earth, she yet was imprisoned by the pain of lost love still burning in her own lost and wandering heart, the memories repeating over and over in her tortured mind. Sometimes she wondered if she would ever be free from the grip of love that still tormented her, even as the years passed, even as she lived a life independent of men. She also lived a life independent of love.

Her seal's song sounded out a haunting melody from the deep hollows of the dark night of her soul. The melody came from the core of her, from the marrow of her being that ached with the depth of her pain.

Sweeping over the waters, upon the fog over the Celtic Isles, breathing a life of its own, it is what solidified her seal's form, what caused men to fall in love with and desire her so instinctually, and what gave name and shape to what she had become. It was the song of her soul, and of the creature she had become—

"The Song of the Selkie"

"My God is the God of Broken Dreams
My God is the God of Broken Things,
And that's why God chose me to be
Queen of all the pain unseen.

Into the sea of emotions, I drowned,
Rising from the depths, with a hard-won crown.
Thus, I became the Queen of the Sea,
And all women betrayed by love, shall be my legacy.

The gods transformed my body,
As an escape for my soul,
And I have found solace in the depths of the sea,
In the beds of lost treasures and broken dreams.

In the songs that I sing, I find an easing of my pain—
The power of my voice gives me power over what I cannot change—
Though my song is the essence of the shattering of my soul,
In the waters, as the Selkie, I am whole.

Some are the Queens of family and birth—
Some are the Queens of fire or earth—
Some are the Queens with castles and Kings—
For some are the Queens given beautiful things.

But I, I am the lone Queen of the Sea:
The haunted, haunting Queen of the Lost and Broken Things.
A creature of the waters singing of all the Broken Dreams.
I am the first woman seal. I am the Selkie."

After singing her bewitching melody upon a desolate stone rock at sea, the original Selkie dove once more into the waters, swimming with her fluid, inhuman movements into the depths of the water's endless mysteries. Her adventures would eventually lead her back to herself, to the realization that what she sought, had lied within her all along.

Time passed, and as often happens with magical creatures, Selkies became a thing of legends. But Celtic women who are in great pain and in great need, with the aid of ungent, Harvest Moon magic, and the haunting call of the first woman seal, were guided in the metamorphosis of the Selkie. They were led by a higher calling, to drown their sorrows in the sea, becoming the enchanting Sirens of ancient myth, who swim, and sing away their suffering.

She was the first Selkie. She was the first woman to transform her body through the pain of her soul. She knew there would be others— other Celtic women suffering from the pain of lost or unrequited love, who were destined to follow in the path of transformation. She would help them to find that magic in themselves that turned pain into beauty, and destruction into the evolution of body and soul.

Chapter One
Secrets of Ancestry

Over two thousand years ago in the Emerald Isles—

"Keep up boy!" I shouted. From every angle, the waving wands of the sorcerers shot burning rays of curses, missing us by mere inches.

Close. Too close. The curses and magic were everywhere. We were surrounded on all sides. I was numb and terrified at the same time. How could we escape their wrath?

Though it was midday, the sky above us prematurely darkened. As those around us were killed, falling dead to the ground one-by-one, I kept pulling my son away from the battle. As the blood from the bodies shamed the earth, the sky itself darkened with clouds of red: an omen of death and destruction.

"I'm trying father," he whimpered. "I'm going as fast as I can!"

"Stop your belly aching, and be careful with that box, boy!" I shouted again, for there was no time for patience now, and what the boy carried was vital to our futures,

Little Arseth, barely five-years-old, was doing his best to keep the pack on his slight shoulders, but it kept slipping off as we ran from the wizards and sorceresses who were pursuing us. Arlillyth let out a low moan, the poisonous bite from the serpent beginning to do its work.

"Between the two of you," I growled. Merlin's beard, I knew the child was trying, but I couldn't get us and the sacred objects to safety all by myself! Or could I? Perhaps the child was just holding us up. I looked down at my son with narrowed eyes.

Arseth's warm brown eyes filled with tears. His fear and exhaustion overwhelmed me, for they reminded me of my own. His knees buckled, as he struggled not to collapse. My heart beat painfully in my chest as I looked at him. He's only a boy...

"Give it here," I relented, taking the pack and lifting it as quickly as possible onto my own broad shoulders. This is no place for him. He isn't old enough or strong enough yet for battle. I should send him away, away from the danger, until we can come and retrieve him.

So, I took hold of my son, shaking him to make him stop and listen to me. Yanking him by the arms, I picked him up, to set him straight down in front of me. Staring into his eyes intensely, I knew he'd be too intimidated not to listen and obey. "Run as far and as long as you can to get away from here, Arseth. Wait for Arlillyth and I to come and get you."

"Yes, father," agreed the small boy obediently, caked with dirt and grime, a small smile of gratitude playing at the corners of his mouth. The boy wants to get out of here. Good. This is confirmation I'm doing the right thing.

"Take this vial, and drink it once you get far enough away from here," I continued, hastily shoving him a potion from inside the pack. An arrow shot into Arlillyth's shoulder, and her blood splattered over the chest and face of the small boy. Arseth's face exploded with the tears pouring from his eyes, his tears mingling with her blood.

"Go! Now! Get away from here before you get yourself killed!"

As Arseth turned to go, I grabbed the child up and into my arms. I allowed myself one moment, just one, to kiss and inhale the smell of the crown of my small son's head, the smell of mud and grass stains, and the terror of the insecurities of youth filled my nostrils…that and a faint whiff of the boy's mother, like warm amber in the golden light of sunset. My own eyes filled with unbidden tears that I impatiently blinked away, as I roughly pushed the boy aside. This was no time for tears, damn it.

"Be careful boy," I said as my voice broke. He must learn…he may only be a little boy, but he must learn fast how to become a strong man in this hard world.

In a voice imposing and booming, I added, "You better be careful—or you'll have ME to answer to!" Growling at the boy in warning, my face contorted fearsomely.

Arseth nodded emphatically, taking off past the battle raging around us. Running as fast as his short legs could carry him over the hills; he ran and ran for what seemed like days. He ran blindly, as the tears fell down his cheeks, far beyond the hills and into a valley, beneath a horizon of high majestic mountains.

* * *

Leaning back against a tree to catch my breath, I chugged down the potion my father, the great wizard Vorseth, had given me. Suddenly I couldn't remember who I was, where I was, why I was here…or how I'd gotten here. Disoriented and shaky on my feet, I stumbled around like a drunken man. Out of nowhere, a dark figure appeared on the horizon. As I stared at the dark shadow moving towards me, fear overcame me. Slowly its shape and form emerged…

* * *

Slowly I inched myself a few paws from the small boy, staring at me defiantly, trying to look stronger and braver than he was. Familiarity filled my senses. Recognition was my instinct. It was as if fate itself was staring me in the face. We looked at each other for a time that felt as long as the chilly winter nights.

I would take him to the tribe where he would be safe. I would stay with him until I understood these impressions.

* * *

As the wolf slowly approached me, I feared the wild creature wished me harm, until a powerful sense the wolf was there to guide and help me reassured me. The wolf nodded, as if it understood my fear, and wanted to comfort me. It shook its head, looking up into the mountains. I sensed the creature wanted to lead me somewhere up that mountain range.

I don't know why, but I let the wolf guide me. I instinctually trusted it. Besides, I had no sense of direction about where to go, or what to do. Taking me a few miles up the mountain, the sound of *reveling and the smell of mutton soup with vegetables and hot apple cider seeped the air.*

Drums were being beat. Songs were being sung. Men were smoking pipes and tobacco, and the smoke from them wafted through the air like rising fog. Women were cooking over the open fire, and their children were dancing around the flames like wild spirits from the otherworld.

It was a small nomadic tribe celebrating and feasting around several small fires, with one massive fire in the center of the festivities. The wolf had let me into their midst...confused, displaced, and covered in blood...

~ *** ~

After dumping Arlillyth's lifeless body off in the far recesses of the caverns, I carefully engraved symbols of ancient Eden magic on the cave walls, for protection. After a few hours had passed, I cautiously stood in the mouth of the cave, looking out at the sea. Listening intently to the sound of the waves and water, my ears were perked like the ears of a wolf, for any signs the battle was still raging on.

I heard no shouts, no cackling of fire or flames, and yet it seemed unwise to leave the protection of the caverns so quickly upon entering in. I was worried about Arseth, but I knew it was better to wait then to inadvertently bring more danger upon us both.

Fluffing up the scrolls of the Prophecy, and other magical items from the pack, into what would do as a pillow, I managed a few hours of sleep on the hard and rocky cavern floor. By morning's light, I guessed they'd be searching for me and my son. So, I waited another day.

Most people don't like to wait. I had cultivated patience long ago, in the quiet stillness and isolation which were necessary for study, and to write the Prophecy. Patience was also necessary to make the Prophecy come to pass. Cities and temples weren't built in a day—though they could often be destroyed in a night.

By the next morning's waking light, I sneaked out of the shadows of the cavern's protective darkness. Furtively moving from tree to tree, and up to the rock wall, my movements were like the spry, intuitive movements of a silver fox, a trickster or thief.

Warily looking about, me, making my way, steadily and carefully, to where I'd said goodbye to Arseth, somewhere a raven was cawing in the distance, and a vibrant bird streaked through the sky. Ravens and birds were a good sign I was on the right track.

It took me three times as long to get back to the battle scene, as I was going much more slowly and round about then when two nights hence, I'd rushed through the terrain with Arlillyth on my back. Arlillyth…a pang of sorrow beat in my chest for her death, but I dismissed and detached myself from the feeling almost as quickly as it had come.

No clouds obscured the full force of the sun and the day's heat. The cloudless sky unnerved me. Clouds and darkness were much safer to travel in, shadows much safer to hide amongst. The day was calm, and the sky was clear, but my mind was full of concerns and doubts.

I traveled for several hours more, miles past the battleground, and up into the foothills beneath the mountain range, then up to the top of the mountain peak. A strange pounding filled the serene skies. Just for a moment, the sound of drums beating in loud exaltation, reverberated in my mind. Then at last I saw him—my son Arseth in the midst of the exaltation—my son the cause of the exaltation.

"A gift from the gods!" shouted the chief of the tribe, with his elaborate headdress of vibrant feathers like the exotic bird I'd seen streaking through the skies in the valley, ruffling about him, as he moved his body up and down emphatically.

"But he must have a family! He can't have come from nowhere!" A concerned tribe member spoke up.

"The boy was covered in blood—his kin could well be dead, and if they're not, it may be best they never find him," said the chief's wife protectively. "Who knows the evil the poor child has had to face—and only as big as a small sparrow yet."

* * *

I caressed the little boy's shoulder, already feeling as if I'd bore him. Instinctively, the poor boy grasped my hand tightly in his, giving my hand a sharp squeeze, begging safeguard from the divided tribe.

In my heart, I vowed to protect the lad. I wouldn't let anyone hurt him again. I was the chief's wife after all, so my opinions held weight.

"Little boy, where did you come from?" I asked him softly. "That's all they want to know." Secretly I was hoping he wouldn't say. I couldn't have explained it, but I wanted to keep this child. Truth be told, I already loved him as my own.

* * *

Dropping her hand, my son kneeled. With one hand on the wolf, and one hand on the ground, the boy closed his eyes, and made a deep humming noise. Pushing the palm of his hand into the ground, fire came down through his fingers to the ground. The flames burst forth, bursting forward, as if thirsting for the air, swiftly turning into a roaring, but contained fire.

The wolf looked at Arseth as if he was perfectly cognizant of his actions. As they exchanged glances, the boy knew the power of the fire he'd started was not from him. The wolf had lent him its power when he touched him, so that the tribe would not only accept him, but revere him.

* * *

I lent the boy my fire magic. I understood the tribe and how they thought. If the boy was made to do something special, the tribe would want to keep him. I wanted to keep him too. He was my person. And I was his.

* * *

The tribe gasped, awestruck. "He's of the Okawana! He's magic!" I, the chief of this exalted tribe, declared. "He is MY son, a gift from the gods, a god-child given to me to raise, teach, and learn from as my own!"

Parental love shone from my eyes. My wife gleamed. "He is a god of fire, and the answer to our prayers! The gods have listened! The gods have answered! The gods have spoken!" The gods were so good to bring this magical boy, and his special wolf, into our midst, just when we'd needed them and their fire magic most.

"What then shall we call him Chief Black Bear?" the tribe demanded to know.

* * *

There were so many things I didn't understand. How had I performed fire magic? The wolf had appeared at my side, when I'd needed him most, as if he'd always been there. And yet, like me, he'd seemed to wander out of nowhere. It was the wolf who had allowed me to do the fire magic. I knew that. But why did that seem to impress the tribe so much?

The chief grinned, as a light from inside his mind and heart illuminated his face. "I know his name!" he exclaimed with a triumphant BOOM on his drum. I couldn't remember my real parents at all, and I looked up at the chief in awe. Would this formidable man really become my father?

The chief's wife pulled her long, braided hair about her nervously. I felt my face soften as I looked upon her. She was good and kind. I knew she would protect me. I knew she already felt a motherly protection over me.

"Wandering Wolfe! That is his name!" the chief cried, "And his wolf companion shall be called Flint, for he is the spark that has ignited the boy's flames!" The Chief's declaration was met with raucous cheers from the crowd.

I was overwhelmed. Numb. I couldn't remember my past at all, but now I had a place to call home, a place to belong. I accepted my new life without question. It was my fate to be raised by this Chief and his loving wife. They would become my new parents. I had no idea who I once was, but I knew now that I was Wandering Wolfe.

* * *

The fire magic had lulled the protesting tribe members into submission. Shamanic tribes were always swayed and subdued by elemental magic they couldn't explain. It was as predictable as the tides. But the name they had given to my son Arseth…Wandering Wolfe…it took me a little by surprise.

I watched my son Arseth, now called Wandering Wolfe, on the outskirts of the tribe, as a day of partying in honor of my son ensued. I watched, and I reflected.

Would it be better for my son to remain here, where he would be untouched and untainted by any outside influences? Where he would be safe from those who knew of his innate powers, and would only twist them for their own use?

There would be people looking for him. But they would be looking for him as Arseth, son of the illustrious warlock Vorseth. No wizard or sorceress would be looking for him as Wandering Wolfe. His new identity would protect him from those who wished him harm.

I thought over my questions and concerns, and pondered the future of my son here for the rest of the day, as I watched my son and the nomadic tribe from a distance. Yes, for now, at least, leaving him here would be best, I decided. I would send for him when the time was right, when he was older and ready to be taught, and circumstances were safer.

I watched my son until the sky darkened and he was gathered up into a tent to sleep, and could be seen no more. Only then did I allow a moment of sadness to send a crack down the walls of the strong fortress guarding my heart.

"Oh, Arseth, when will you learn who you really are, and where you come from?"

Shaking the memories of Arseth's ancestors and true legacy from my mind, I whispered, "You will learn of your inheritance and your ancestry when the time is right, my boy. We shall all have to wait for that time."

A gentle breeze wafted through the trees around me. The sweet smell of flowers filled my nostrils. Even in the night, there was a feeling of light and peace here. The tribe was strong and colorful. They would teach the boy their own kinds of magic.

This is a nice place for him to grow up. I'm doing the right thing. He's safer here…that's what I told myself.

I was not the kind of person to make a decision and later torture myself with useless doubts over it, so when I turned my back on my son, I didn't look back. I wasn't meant to raise my own son, but I would raise Arlillyth's daughter, the little girl Darlillyth.

I would teach her, mold her, and shape her, as I would have done with my son. Hastening in the obscured shadows back towards the castle, I recalled a verse of the Prophecy that took me by surprise—for I'd written what had just happened, long ago:

Son of prophet, wizard, warlock
Wandering to a tribe,
Lost at battle, found unawares
By people not of his kind.

Raised by wolves, born of sin,
Born of blood unseen,
Dirty, lost and orphaned boy
Becomes companion to the King.

Learning of his purpose through his father,
Unknowingly the trickster leads him
To the uniting of the chosen fourteen
In a path of predestined wanderings.

Damned from birth by ancestral sins
And the secrets of his mother's origins,
He holds the magic of immortality
From dark and evil family blasphemies.

Unwittingly, he shall live apart from his kin.
He shall wander most of his life

Ignorant of the secrets of his ancestry,
So that he may become the redeemer of his family line.

As I turned my back on my only son, I knew I was turning my back on the man the boy Arseth would've become in my care. It gave me pause to consider what kind of man Wandering Wolfe would become. Back to the castle I went, back to the child Darlillyth, who had just lost her mother and needed my care, now more than ever before.

* * *

The mysterious warlock was coming back to the castle, but where was his son? What had happened to my mother? He seemed to be coming back to the castle unaccompanied. I was only a few years old, but I felt it. I felt her loss. He didn't have to tell me. They were gone.

Arseth was my best friend. My mother was the only one who could protect me from my father. If she was gone, I feared what my life would become. The great wizard Vorseth returned to the castle, only to confirm my worst fears.

Arseth was gone. He didn't offer details on that, but I imagine it would be hard to discuss the death of your own son.

My mother was dead. Killed in the battle of magic, fought by the greatest magic wielders on the earth. My mother was forever lost to me. Young as I was, I knew that the future was full of darkness for me, without a mother to protect me from the evil that lurked in those around me, like a snake with baited breath, just waiting for the perfect time and opportunity, to strike.

* * *

Cradling the little three-year-old Darlillyth in my arms, I felt the crack in my heart splinter further, deeper, thinking of this child, and how she'd lost her mother only a few nights hence. Darlillyth's father was a violent man, the Egyptian God and King, Amen-Ra. Arlillyth had done well choosing her mate for his power and influence, but his soul was as corrupted and unfeeling as a snake's.

Cruel and abusive to his daughter from birth, his treatment of her grew pronouncedly worse the day Amen-Ra took for himself a new wife, soon after Arlillyth's death. Shortly after they'd wed, they had a child, Prince Mardavian. After his birth, Darlillyth lost all rights to an inheritance within the family line. Yet she was the one who had inherited all her father and mother's magical gifts and abilities.

By the time I sent for Wandering Wolfe, he was almost full grown. I was pleased by how well the tribe had raised the boy. Indeed, Mardavian and Darlillyth had not faired nearly so well under Amen-Ra's influence. Guiding the hurt and embittered girl to the kind and protective young man my son had become, I orchestrated their romantic relationship, manipulating their love and days together, until at last their passion was consummated— with Shadonai as a subsequent result of my meddling.

I took a baby from a peasant family in town, who was glad of having one less mouth to feed. Its death was unimportant in the grand scheme of things. It didn't take much gold to buy the baby or their silence.

Amen-Ra was enraged by the birth of the baby. I hid Shadonai in the dungeons, and brought Amen-Ra the peasant babe. Wandering Wolfe and Darlillyth watched in horror as Amen-Ra tore the innocent babe apart. I knew in that moment, Darlillyth decided to sell her soul to the Devil, and to become a part of the darkness.

She invited the demons in, for the vengeance of the little girl her father had killed. A little girl that shared the blood of both her brother, Mardavian, and her lover, my son.

Wandering Wolfe continued to be honorable and true. For that was how he'd been raised.

Unbeknownst to any of them, their daughter lived. I quietly buried the peasant baby in an unmarked grave, in the place of my grandchild. I brought my real grandchild, Shadonai to her new home with Elijah and Ruth when she was only two-days-old.

They were a Jewish couple, exiled to the remote and Isolated island of Skye, for their exploration of the occult. The Jewish magic and wisdom of numbers, the Kabbalah, was the one magic Shadonai did not inherently, genetically possess. With that, her range of power would be unparalleled. She would need the power of the Kabbalah to defeat the Chosen One of the race of Israel.

Passed down from generation-to-generation, this couple would counter-balance Eliju's future parents, Kenneth and Tamara, long before they were even conceived. Karma comes full circle, and sometimes we tip the scales of favor before the scales are tipped to what is owed.

I knew my son would never understand or condone my actions. There was too much of his mother in him. It would be difficult for him to understand that sometimes tough decisions were required in order to further human evolution. Sometimes to save the masses, we must sacrifice the few. Sometimes it better for them not to know it. Sometimes it easier for a mind to grasp the whole picture, if the images come one-by-one, piece-by-piece. For to see the whole, all at the start, is too overwhelming to the senses.

Elijah and Ruth were killed by King Mardavian. Shadonai had no idea why they'd been killed, but it created a rage inside her against the King, her own father—unbeknownst to her. It murdered her soul, when her parents were murdered.

Of course, I knew why they'd been killed, as I'd put the idea into King Mardavian's mind myself. It was all just a part of the Prophecy, and they were just the inevitable causalities of fate.

When Shadonai was left all alone, after her surrogate parents were safely dead and buried in the ground for many years, Shadonai at last began to question why with the passing of years she never aged.

That's when I came to her, when she was confused and vulnerable, searching for answers. I told her what she needed to know. I taught her the things she needed to learn. I kept the true reason for her life hidden, until the bitter end. I hid my true intentions under lock and key.

Meanwhile, I fed Darlillyth lies and twisted truths about my son, now called Wandering Wolfe. In her rage, she had his whole tribe killed by her brother's hands. With Wandering Wolfe's tribe safely out of the way, my son could focus on his true destiny, unfettered by his adopted family and the mundane rituals and practices of the nomadic tribe that had raised him.

I was the puppet master, and Darlillyth pulled the strings. She was the mastermind behind her brother's exploits, while I fed her half-truths to further the agenda of the Prophecy.

I well understood how people are more susceptible to manipulation when they are alone in the world. So, when I visited my son who was living alone where his tribe had once been thriving and growing, and which now stood empty and desolate, Wandering Wolfe was more than willing to listen and believe anything I had to tell him. This was when I first showed him and explained to him in greater depth the Prophecy, and where he fit into it.

At first, my son was hesitant to believe what I had to say. But as I spun him yarns with shades of truth, showing him the aged parchments of the Prophecy with lettering of sparkling gold, like slivers of the sun on paper, the more my son bought into it. There was a familiarity in the scrolls that Wandering Wolfe couldn't understand, stemming from the boy Arseth he had once been.

Laughing in my mind, I wondered how my son would react to learn I was his father—and that the beauty of the poetry and the Prophecy which so enticed my son was written with the Elven blood of gold. These were scrolls he'd once viewed as a very little boy, and that's why they seemed so familiar.

What would he think to know his grandfather was Seth, son of Adam and Eve, and his grandmother was the first woman in the Garden of Eden, Lilith? What would he have thought if he knew the secret mysteries of his mother's origins? How would he react when he finally learned the truth…about himself?

That he was born immortal from the line of both the first woman in the Garden of Eden, Lilith, who had eaten of the Tree of Immortality, and of the Line of Adam and Eve, who had eaten of the Tree of the Knowledge of Both Good and Evil. And that he was the only person on earth whose blood from both lines flowed throughout his veins, forever.

Though I surely was the puppeteer in the epic play of our lives—there were others in the play, other unseen hands guiding our actions, with an agenda of their own…

~ ~ ~

Twisted bones and marred skin, long willowy hair of silver, once a vibrant golden auburn. Beauty and scars, within and without. "*Where is our son?*" *my wife, Arra, whispered.*

"*He's safe.*"

"*Where?*"

"*A wolf found him wandering in the hills where I left him during the battle, and led him to a nomadic tribe, into safety. He is the boy's companion now, Arra. The tribe saw the birthmark of the wolf on his shoulder and gave him a new name—Wandering Wolfe.*"

"*A wolf?*"

"*Yes, my love.*"

"*So, our son has become the companion of a wolf—the ancient mystical creature of loyalty and spiritual truths of the ancient earth and elemental magics.*"

"*The boy put fire on the ground with his fingertips in front of the tribe. They are calling him a god.*"

"*And so, he is. Fire, hmmm…warmth to the earth. Bright flame, wanderer, mysterious wolf. But did the fire power come from him, or from the wolf who shepherds him? Arseth never started a fire before…I am not so sure this creature is merely a wolf. What does this all mean?*"

"*It means that the Prophecy has begun, my dear. And our son is a big part of it. He is a part of both of us. He has your warmth, and my brilliant mind, which detaches me from unreason.*" *Vorseth hesitated, before adding,* "*Your sister Arlillyth is dead, as the Prophecy foretold.*"

"*All is as it should be.*" *Her voice broke, and her hands shook. Vorseth's eyes saw her grief, and his hands caressed her back, to ease her anxieties.*

"*I shall raise Darlillyth, and strangers shall raise Arseth.*"

"It always seems to be strangers who raise the Chosen Ones…"

"We were all strangers once," he reminded her.

"Like once we were all brothers and sisters."

"Not so very long ago…"

"Not I…I always stood alone. And I will raise neither boy nor girl, neither daughter nor son." Her voice was heartsick.

"Only you, Arra, could bear so nobly this pain."

"Only me," her voice shook. "Only I, who was born with the pain of everlasting isolation and exile. Born cursed."

Vorseth reached out his hand, and took her small, pale hand in his own. "I love you," he whispered. "You're beautiful. You will always be beautiful to me."

Arra's amber eyes burned in the face that had been permanently scarred, but Vorseth's love-lit eyes only saw her as the beautiful carefree girl he had first met and fallen in love with long ago. It is strange how both love and hate can blind the eyes.

Squeezing her hand in his own, with his left hand, he guided her face to his chest. Resting her head against his chest, his heart beat in her ears, his heart that beat for her.

"Hate is what damaged my face and broke my bones," she whispered. "But at least hate comes from the same deep well as love does."

"Yes," Vorseth murmured, "I understand your meaning. It is indifference that makes the real difference."

Tears fell down her crinkled cheeks. "Like my mother was…indifferent. And that made all the difference."

"You're beautiful," Vorseth assured her again.

"The Prophecy…"

"You know I shall make it all come to pass…for you, my love."

"For him, Vorseth, for him. For our son, little Arseth, now Wandering Wolfe. You shall bring him back when he's old enough, and teach him our ways, won't you?" Vorseth nodded softly, then bent down his head and kissed Arra's lips, wet with tears.

She closed her eyes. She reached her hand up to caress his hair and neck. In that moment, time stood still, as time always will, for those whose love is true.

~ *** ~

Chapter Two
Mordorn's Warning

In the Celtic Highlands, where Within the Genesis of Time Volume Two of The Creation Series left off—

"Varawynn!" Eliju cried, throwing his body down on her scattered ashes. "NO, NOT VARAWYNN!" Wandering Wolfe came down beside him, as close as a shadow.

Mordorn's warning flashed through my mind. Something clicked. I hadn't understood his message until now. Maybe there was a way...a way we could still save her.

"Quickly—who has a container we can put her ashes in?" I asked urgently, pulling my long, blonde hair into a pony tail so that my hair wouldn't collect any of Varawynn's remains.

Alondria pulled from the folds of her dress the ornate jewelry box Eliju had given her on one of his sacred holidays. "I do," she said, swiftly handing me the box.

"Please help me gather her ashes into this box," I instructed Eliju gently. I could see in the defeated way they were gathering her ashes to be scattered in her homeland into the waters of the Isles of Apples, they didn't see any hope in the situation. How could I blame them? If I hadn't been a witness to magic all my life— and Mordorn hadn't shared with me that part of the Prophecy, I would feel defeated too.

"What are we going to do?" Eliju looked up at the Shaman, as he was gathering the ashes of Varaywnn scattered on the ground. "What are we going to do without Varawynn? We only have twelve now. Twelve! How can we go on without Varawynn *and* Jonlin? I thought you said the Prophecy foretold one of us would be sacrificed—not TWO!" Pounding his fist into the ground, after dumping a clump of Varawynn's ashes into the box he'd made himself, his anger and grief were palpable.

"We're not going to be without Varawynn," I insisted. Eliju stared at me incredulously. "What do you mean, Pharean?"

"We can use her ashes to bring her back to life."

"Are you serious? How do we do that?"

"Yes how?" Wandering Wolfe asked more warily.

"I don't know exactly," I admitted, as Eliju guffawed. "But I've been told we'll find the way. My friend, and the symbol of my birthmark, the great-horned owl, Mordorn, came to me when Aldoran first found me, and told me this verse of the Prophecy:"

> *"She who bears the raven mark*
> *Shall be the first to fall and rise again.*
> *From fire and coal, out of ashes and shadows,*
> *She returns more than whole in the resurrection."*

"Death is not always the end of life. There must be a way to bring Varawynn back to us, and we have to find it." I tenderly gathered the last small piles of Varawynn's ashes into the ornate box Eliju had crafted, with my delicate pale fingers.

"If we can do that for Varawynn, can we do the same for Jonlin?" asked Alondria, a glimmer of hope shining in her eyes.

"No, we can't. I'm sorry, but the Prophecy was about Varawynn…about ashes brought to life and her raven birthmark. Jonlin was foretold by the Prophecy as the sacrificial lamb, and I'm sorry…"

I heard my soft voice trail off almost to a whisper, as I looked at the lovely princess with her big doe eyes so full of sorrow. Biting my lower lip to keep myself from crying, Alondria looked away. She knew if she held my gaze, she'd burst into tears herself.

"Who would know such dark magic as resurrecting the dead?" Illumina asked.

"Undoubtedly Darlillyth would," answered Ileona.

"She wouldn't help us of course—she's the one who cursed Varawynn to ashes," Eliju sighed.

"Who else would have the ability?" Luquinn piped in. He seemed a practical fellow—always looking for the solution.

My eyes wandered over to Aldoran. His face was cut and already bruising, and his hair was mussed from the fighting, but his war wounds only made him more dashing than ever. In the midst of all this death and tragedy, I felt my heart stop for a moment as I looked at him. He was, of course, eyeing his sister, probably worrying about how well she was going to cope with Jonlin's death. Not well from the looks of it.

"Shadonai," murmured Wandering Wolfe. His voice stirred me from reverie.

"Who?" Eliju asked.

"Shadonai," he said a little louder. "Is my daughter with Darlillyth."

"What?" the group in unity exclaimed. A glimmer of something cold and dark passed across Eliju's eyes. Jealousy.

I couldn't understand why he would be jealous of that. His expression registered in my brain, but I shut it away for later. Before I fell into sleep, scenes like this would enter my consciousness, and a supernatural insight would come like a sudden flash of lightening, to explain what I had seen. This had happened to me many times before, enough to know when to expect it.

"The seed was split two ways. My daughter has two fathers. She bears the blood of both King Mardavian and myself."

"Wow," said Luquinn, "and I thought my family was messed up."

"I only found this out a couple months ago, as I was on my quest in the maze. So of course, I want to find my daughter anyway, but I think she could help us. I think she's the only one who *could* help us."

"That makes sense," Silvandrin, the infamous black unicorn acknowledged, with a flip of his silver mane.

"But who shall lead us? How shall we find her?" Illumina asked, with her own graceful flip of long, shimmery blue hair. I almost expected Ileona to rush into our midst to do her own hair flip, and insert herself as the center of our attention, but Mordorn came down flying into our midst at just the perfect time.

* * *

Of all things, a great-horned owl zoomed down to us from the sky. We all stopped talking to watch its elegant descent. There was something so majestic and awe-inspiring to see a bird in flight.

"I will guide you. My name is Mordorn," said the owl with fiercely burning eyes, in his dark furry head. There was nothing humorous about his tone, as he disheveled his feathers, and ruffled his head with dignity. His bearing and attitude compelled instant respect. "Shadonai dwells in a small hut in the woods on the Isle of Skye. I shall lead you there."

My heart soared like an eagle in flight over a mountain crest on the horizon. Unbidden tears flooded my eyes. I was so afraid I'd lost my daughter again, after just finding her. "Thank you." The idea of seeing my daughter—getting to *know* my daughter, sent my morale soaring at a time when otherwise I would have been devastated by the loss of the members in the group.

"And what about Jonlin?" asked Alondria, with a violent thrust and pulling of her silky long curls. I was afraid she wasn't going to take his death very well.

"What about him?"

"Are you so sure we can't bring him back to life too?" she asked Mordorn.

The owl shook his dark head gravely, his large sulfuric eyes blazing with glints of sad knowing, like dying embers without the hope of rekindling.

"Why *her* and not *him*?" insisted Alondria. "Why Varawynn and not Jonlin?"

"He was foretold to be the sacrifice, Alondria," Pharean repeated gently.

"Oh, my goodness, the damn Prophecy again!?" she shouted furiously. "The Prophecy is not a holy work! We should NOT be putting so much stock in it!"

"Alondria!" her brother started, concerned over her sudden anger.

"What are we going to do with his body?" she demanded, ignoring the group's shocked faces.

"Take him home I suppose," answered her brother Aldoran. "After all, that's the only proper thing to do…bring him home for his family to bury him."

I nodded. That made perfect sense. Aldoran was such a nice, sensible young man—not to mention a fierce warrior. We were quite fortunate he had joined us on our crusade.

"Of course, you're right about that, it's the proper thing to do," Alondria nodded. "But WHY did the Prophecy say he had to be sacrificed? Why can't we even TRY to bring him back to life as well?"

"Well, what is it you expect us to do?" Eliju countered impatiently. "We're not happy he's gone, but Mordorn said there's no hope to bring him back to us…"

"He's not gone, he's DEAD!" Alondria screamed. "He's dead—because of YOU! Because of US!"

"I know."

* * *

Eliju's face looked flushed and pale. I had never seen Eliju look so guilty. I felt sorry for him. Of course, I'd only known him as long as Jonlin. My thoughts shuffled back to the day we'd met in that little tavern in Hebron. How long had it been? Over a year, but not quite two. Felt like several lifetimes ago.

I was a little surprised Alondria was acting this way. She was the calm one usually after all. Maybe it was worse for her because she'd been in love with Jonlin. I hadn't even realized that until now—but Jonlin and Alondria had loved one another. Still, his death wasn't Eliju's fault. Jonlin *had* died protecting him—but he would have done so for *any* of us.

"Good. I'm glad you can at least admit it. He was the best of all of us, and yet Varawynn will get to return to life and our broken group. SHE will be resurrected and not HIM?"

"I didn't decide that, Alondria!" Eliju shouted. "The Prophecy did!"

"The Prophecy, the Prophecy, the Prophecy—it always comes back to that ridiculous Prophecy!" she hurled back at him defiantly. "All our lives are governed by *the Prophecy* and what it foretold for our lives! Have we no free will to make decisions for ourselves?"

"Of *course*, we do, Alondria! And Jonlin *chose* to sacrifice himself for *us*—for *me* and for *you* as well! For all us! For all the good we have yet to do!"

"I wish it had been YOU to go!" she raged out-of-control. Even placid Luquinn looked aghast. Alondria had always been the peacemaker of the group. In her grief, she was full of rage.

"Alondria, please…" I pleaded with her in my voice. "Please don't say such things to Eliju."

Aldoran put a restraining hand on his sister's shoulder. "You don't mean what you're saying, my sister. You're speaking from your fresh wound. Let yourself heal a little first before you talk to Eliju."

"These wounds will NEVER HEAL! He stole my destiny! With Jonlin gone, all my hopes, all my dreams, all that my life SHOULD HAVE BEEN is gone! Time will only make my wounds cut deeper. I will never have love, and love is the meaning and purpose of my life…*was* the purpose," she sobbed, hurling her words at us like weapons. "I have no purpose now."

"You loved him?" Eliju started, shocked. I guess he hadn't figured that out yet…

"Yes, of *course* I loved him! I still love him! And we were destined to spend our lives together…so now my life is lost. There is no comfort. There is no consolation."

The tears on her face fell heavily, then stopped as suddenly as they'd fallen, drying quickly. Her face turned as grey and dim as the bones of a skeleton. A look of futility came down like a veil over her face. Her grief was intense and frightening. She was in a place all alone, a place we didn't know how to reach her.

I longed to help her. I cared. But what could I do? Perhaps another soul retrieval would help her, but the wounds were surely still too fresh—and Alondria wouldn't have even let me try right now. Eliju's face was full of guilt and sympathy he didn't know how to show, concern she wouldn't have let him show anyway. Alondria clearly wasn't going to let any of us even *try* to help her. She was beyond grieved over losing Jonlin. I felt terrified we were going to lose her too.

"Alondria, please, stop this course of thinking," Wandering Wolfe interjected, trying to be the voice of reason. "Please don't see what happened this way…"

"Why because the Prophecy told you I shouldn't?" she quipped viciously.

"No, actually the Prophecy claimed you would behave this way after Jonlin's death. That you would lose your way and leave us for a time…" She blinked.

"No," Wandering Wolfe continued sagely, "I'm asking you not to do this because this isn't the right attitude to take, my dear. You say you believe in free will—then show us where the Prophecy has gone wrong. Rise above your pain and loss, my child," Wandering Wolfe challenged her gently.

"I am not your child," she answered so coldly, it didn't even sound like her voice. "Regardless of the damned Prophecy, I'm taking the attitude I wish to take! There is nothing left for me now…without Jonlin and the hope of love, what else does my future hold, but pain and loneliness?"

"And that's just what the Prophecy said would be your reaction," Aldoran said kindly. "We're asking you to use your free will against what the Prophecy foretold right now, Alondria."

"We understand your pain, but please don't give up," Pharean whispered so softly, you had to lean toward her to try and catch her words on the wind. We were each trying in our own way, to think of what we could say or do to help her.

"The Prophecy can be sent to hell in a hand basket for all I care, and by God, nobody better ever mentions those cursed scrolls to me ever again! Now who shall accompany me in bringing Jonlin's body home to his kin?"

It was so silent, we could've heard a pin drop on the soft grass. No one said anything for quite a while. I think we were all too afraid to speak after her outburst. "May I have that honor?" Luquinn asked her humbly, from the shadows cast by the dreary grey green sky. His eyes always followed her, and her expression visibly softened as he watched her anxiously.

"Yes, you may Luquinn," she answered him readily, taking his offered hand. "Thank you." It seemed he would be the only one of them she would let in. "And shall no one else venture with me back to Jonlin's home to give him a proper burial after he died for us?"

"If it pleases you, we all shall. I don't want to speak for everyone else, but it's the only proper thing—for all of us to pay our respects to the lost member of our group, who died to protect us. He deserves our time and respect for such a noble sacrifice, and I truly am sorry, Alondria. I wish it had been me too," Eliju said pitifully. "Who really knows if Varawynn will come back to us? I wish I hadn't lived either."

Alondria's face further softened. She almost looked like herself again—almost. Alondria was typically such a kind and fair person. I had always so admired her, as the perfect woman. I even hoped for a daughter just like her someday. How I wished she would be fairer to Eliju!

* * *

"But what about Varawynn's ashes? Shadonai is so close; shouldn't we go to her first instead of going all the way back to the desert, and then back again?"

I had been silent during this entire exchange. I'd been thinking about Varawynn, and determining how we would bring my favorite person in the group back to us. The girl had always looked up and admired me so. She was almost like my daughter, certainly my friend.

We had only just scattered her brother's ashes in the Isle of Apples. I'd be damned to bring her ashes back to the Priest and Priestess so shortly after they'd lost their son.

"How proper is that?" Alondria practically screamed at me. Aldoran put his hand on his sister's shoulder again, trying to restrain her. Had she lost all sense of propriety? The girl was losing it. Usually, I would have put her in her place—I let no one speak to me that way. But considering the circumstances, I thought I'd let this one slide.

"Yes, it *is* out of our way," Wandering Wolfe concurred. Before Alondria could yell at him again, he added quickly, "But Jonlin went out of his way to help us—he died for us, our group. He died so that we might go on, and do what we've been called to do. So even though it's out of our way, I think we should bury our dead before we go to Shadonai, and see what she can do to help us resurrect Varawynn from her ashes."

"Bury the dead before bringing the dead back to life," Mordorn agreed, nodding his fury head approvingly.

"Even if Shadonai is so close..." I murmured irritably under my breath, thinking people were being a little insensible right now. Of course, I cared about Jonlin, of course I was sorry he was dead. He was a sweet kid, no question about that. But...I never would have admitted it out loud, but I had found the overly sensitive bard rather annoying at times.

"Yes, of course we'll all go," Illumina assured Alondria. "We *want* to go. We all loved Jonlin very much, dear heart." She smiled at her sympathetically. I looked away, so no one would see the impatience and frustration on my face.

"Back to my homeland," said Eliju, "back to the desert. But this time we're going back for altogether different reasons."

"Do you remember that's where we met, Eliju?" quipped Shadow Rain. "And where we met Jonlin?"

Eliju eyes filled with tears, which of course made Rain's eyes fill with tears too. Humans and their emotions. Rather inconvenient as a general rule, if you asked me. Not that anyone ever did. I blinked away the wetness in my own eyes impatiently.

"Let's go then. Right now!" Rushing ahead of them, Alondria led the way back to Hebron, back to the beginning.

* * *

Chapter Three
The Origins of the Phoenix

Celestria tended to come and go. So, it wasn't a huge surprise when she stayed behind, as the rest of the group headed back to the home of Jonlin. They could only hope that she would meet them along the journey, or at least for the burial of their beloved friend, the Bard of Hebron.

~ *** ~

While the rest of the group headed south, I flew back to the battle scene we'd just left, back to the crater where the star had fallen from the sky, leaving a deep indentation in the earth. I felt an aura of galactic power on that spot, with a force field protecting it.

There was something in that crater, something I was meant to find or see. So, I went back to explore it, curiosity lifting my wings through wind, carrying me swiftly forward. For this fallen star was something I had never encountered before, and I was eager to explore it.

The mass of the star that fell from the great sky above the earth had created a tunnel. My senses told me to enter in. Without a second thought, or any hesitation, I dove into the energy of the dark mass, passing through the invisible forcefield effortlessly.

This told me what I already knew—that this hallowed ground had been waiting for me. There was something here for me, meant for me, something that I had been called to do. I didn't know what that calling was, I only knew that I must trust my instincts, and fall into the crater with the same sure descent of the falling star which had created it.

As I dove into the tunnel, I felt time and distance interchange with the speed of light. Through the warp drive, the speed of light was broken. This was a wormhole, bending time and space, transcending it.

I flew into the heart of it, into the whirring zooming propelling me ahead. As fast as I was moving, I felt everything around me standing still. Somehow, I was frozen, fixed, even while I was moving so fast. The speed of light was the fastest any signal could travel, yet somehow, I had tapped into an elemental power, riding a beam of light through a tunnel, traversing and defying, time and space. Time was relative.

The force of gravity was the result of the way mass warps space and time. The more mass squeezed into a region of space, the more spacetime was manipulated, and the slower everything around it became.

Squeezing in enough mass, the spacetime became so warped that even light cannot escape its gravitational pull, forming a black hole. I moved towards the edge of the black hole, its event horizon, and was compelled by a pulling, to go forward into it.

In the spacetime continuum I zoomed through eleven dimensions. There was a dimension of time, three on earth to be moved through, then there was seven more, small and invisible. I used the spatial dimensions to move through all the dimensions.

I did this through the wormhole that was formed at the event horizon of the dark mass that was formed by the star that had fallen from the sky unto the earth. It was a phenomenon that formed a passage between two separate regions of spacetime, in the background of the supermassive black hole. The gravitation conditions this had caused was a source of negative energy so strong, it kept the wormhole open and visible to me.

My quest through the Tunnels of the Past and Future, had helped me to view my mistakes with greater perspective. Now I knew there was something more for me to do, something that would alter the past. Last time

I traveled through the tunnel to the past, as a mere observer. This time when I went through the worm hole, I would participate in it.

In the tunnels from my quest, I had gone from either end, but what lay in between was a wormhole, which would propel me faster than the speed of light into the eternal NOW, not as bystander of time, past and present, but to insert me into time itself, in order to make the conscious choice to *change it.*

Only I knew the history of the earth. Only I understood how devastating the mistake had been for humans and animals to eat of the Tree of the Knowledge of Both Good and Evil. So, I was the only who could have gone through this tunnel. Into the essence of time itself, to alter it forever.

Anyone else would not know how. Anyone else would not know what to change. Anyone else would make a mistake. It only took one action, or rather inaction, just one moment, to change the course of history.

I knew that my mistake was to eat of the apple at all. After Eve gave Adam the apple from the Tree in the Garden of Eden, so upset with the curses from God, she seduced and manipulated all the animals to partake of the forbidden fruit, so that they would be cursed too. Out of jealousy and spite, she had cursed us all.

In the original Garden of Eden, in the previous origin of time, I had eaten of the apple, cursing myself, and causing the death of my mate, Astori. The consequence of my curse was the loss my voice, and the subsequent death of my mate. In return, I witnessed the history of the earth for thousands of years as an immortal from the beginning of time.

Now I was going to be given a gift. I was going to learn how to manipulate time, and rectify my mistake. I was going to go back in time, and choose to not partake of the juicy forbidden fruit.

A change in time such as this could mean dangerous consequences for history. I knew that better than anyone else, having been made a witness to it. Yet I saw now what I hadn't seen before: my quest had been intended for me to change the history in the origin of time, I was meant to become something else...something more...which would affect the outcome of our troupe, and perhaps even the world.

Somehow, I knew that I was the key—of both the creation and the destruction of the earth. Before I could destroy, I would have to learn how to create, to go back to change, transform, mutate, heal, and become...something *more* than I had been created.

So I went through the wormhole, what I now recognized as a tunnel passing through time, with the speed of light, back into the past. This time, I knew I would change my future, altering my fate. My quest had only begun.

~ ~ ~

I watched Eve from a distance, covered in ill-fitting clothes she had unsuccessfully tried to sew together, in the most arcane of ways. It was shortly after the fall of mankind, and Adam and Eve had learned of their nakedness.

Eve tried to make crude clothes for herself and her mate. She was restless, bored and exhausted all at the same time. "Why should we be so punished, Adam? Why do the creatures in Eden get to continue on, as if the world hadn't stopped, hadn't changed, forever?"

Adam was a man of few words, and he put a hand on her shoulder, caressing her hair. He was also a man who knew little of tenderness, but Eve was so unhappy. To be honest, so was he.

The knowledge they'd so coveted, had been gleaned by the partaking of the forbidden fruit. But knowledge had turned out to be a burden that separated them from their Creator. He felt that burden as keenly as his wife did.

"What if we didn't have to be alone in our burden?" Eve turned to Adam. "What if the beasts of the fields and forests, and the flying creatures of the air, could share in our curse?"

Again, Adam said nothing. Only shook his head. What good would it do to share the burden that weighed them down?

Eve thought it would do some good. It would make her feel better not to suffer alone. So, she devised her plot to make each of the animals partake of the apple, thereby simultaneously gaining knowledge, whilst losing their original innocence.

Eve hadn't learnt her lesson. She did not repent. She was angry and resentful of her plight on earth. She missed paradise. She missed her life being simple, and easy.

Jealous of the freedoms the other creatures in the Garden enjoyed, I watched her giving the apple from the sacred tree in the Garden, to the deer, to the eagle, to the wolf, to the ox, even to the lowly mice that scurried across the plains. She ruined them all. She stole all their voices.

For in the beginning, in paradise, in the luscious Garden of Eden, before our fall, all animals had the use of our voices. We could all speak in the beginning of time. In the gaining of knowledge, our kind had lost the ability to share knowledge. I realized that sharing knowledge, in order to help others, was what turned knowledge into wisdom and truth, altering it from a curse into a blessing.

Finally, Eve came to me, after tricking the other creatures in our land, with her spinning lies, that I had once believed. She approached me with the forbidden fruit to tempt me, just as she had done with Adam, and all the other birds and animals in paradise.

The serpent had partnered with Eve. He had put this awful plot into her mind. He had given her the idea. Eve chose to go through with it.

But this time I denied her. I was the only creature in paradise who denied Eve, and did not give in to her temptation, her lies and *manipulations. I at least was able to retain for all birdkind, the ability to sing* **and speak!**

As I was the only creature that resisted the temptation, I was rewarded. I heard His voice from the high heavens, amongst the clouds—"Death has no power over you, because you resisted the temptation of the forbidden fruit." Now the Angels of Death could not take me. I was beyond the shadow's reach.

I lived many years of peace, before I sought the cosmic fire to destroy. But not before I sought the justice of Eve...

I watched Eve manipulate man, starting with the first man, Adam. The curse of man did not change her. She was still the same woman as before. Only worse. With the Knowledge of Both Good and Evil, she developed more subtle ways to manipulate men to get what she wanted.

Of course, not all women were like Eve, or even Lilith. Some women were pure at heart, and they were often manipulated by men. Men could also be manipulative.

Purity was one of the rarest qualities in humanity. It needed to be protected, defended, cherished, nurtured, and ultimately, chosen. Innocence was often destroyed by the darkness, for the darkness is attracted to the light. Light overcomes the darkness, but too many people once pure, succumbed to it, once the struggles and challenges of life set in. Every time a person chose to do good, even after they'd endured an evil act against them, that purified and cleansed what evil had sought to claim.

All qualities were really developed through choices. The consistent attempt toward kindness, especially after deep suffering, created a soul and heart that could stand the test of time.

This quality of purity was so rare, but I knew I had seen it in both men and women throughout time, and I knew I had felt it in each heart of the Chosen Ones. I knew the day would come when I returned to the place and time where we had lost our beloved Bard of Hebron, and the raven girl who was turned to ashes by the wicked sorcery of Darlillyth. But for now, I had to follow through on my new fate...

~ ~ ~

One day Eve and Adam got into an argument. Their faces flushed with anger, Adam shouted, "If not for you and your feminine whiles, we would still be in paradise! I would not have to toil to till the earth, plant, water, and work so hard to make things grow! You ruined my life, and the lives of all our offspring!"

I entered into the scene, flowing low enough to meet Eve's face, and stare into her bright brown doe eyes. How could such sweet, refined features bear such a selfish heart within?

"And you destroyed our kind too, knowing full well what you were doing!" Adam continued his tirade.

"I didn't eat the apple alone, Adam! Maybe if you weren't such a foolish coward, you could have convinced me not to!" Eve lashed back.

"But it wasn't I who convinced the other creatures in paradise to eat of the forbidden fruit—you tempted them to commit that sin on your own!"

"So what if I did? I don't regret it! Why shouldn't we all suffer with the knowledge of the good and evil that is such a burden?"

"Because if you were good, you would have borne that burden alone!"

I finally decided to come forth from the shadows, deciding not to be a coward myself, and confront the selfish woman head on. I flapped my wings angrily in her face. Eve could see how angry I was. She recognized that I was the only creature who had stood up to her, but I had still lost my mate, Astori, because of her evil trickery.

Eve laughed ruefully. "So that you and your mate could have lived happily ever after in the Garden of Eden? I was never happy with my mate, even in paradise! Why should anyone else be satisfied? Why should you be happy when I am not?" She stared me in the eyes, then tossed her beautiful mane of brown hair back haughtily.

The rage hit me hard. Adam's face and eyes were red and bulging. I knew he felt the rage too. Adam was indeed a coward, and an idiot, but he did have some semblance of a heart. Eve's spite boiled my blood. I felt like I was going to burst from my skin, I was so angry.

I became woefully overheated. I thought I might have a heart attack. The fury ate and burned me up. Where was God? Where was Justice?

Suddenly my body exploded. In a burst of light and flames, I was reduced to a pile of ashes. Yet I still felt alive in spirit. I watched Adam and Eve as they stared at my ashes, awestruck Adam was horrified and dumbfounded, while Eve laughed ruefully. They both believed me to be dead.

Eve's curiosity had gotten the best of her before, when she ate of the forbidden fruit. She laughed to herself now, and got down on her knees to pick up my ashes, and put it into her pouch. She wanted to keep my remains in her satchel, as a constant reminder of her victory.

In the spirit realm, I continued to watch as she gathered my ashes. Suddenly she screamed, "What's happening to me?"

My ashes burned her hands. Then my ashes became embers. The embers became flames. The flames became an all-consuming fire that burned the wicked woman, Eve, from head-to-toe, alive.

She screamed in rage and fury, bested again by the only creature who had ever resisted her charms. Adam reached for her, as the flames consumed her totally. They exchanged a moment of regret in their eyes. "I'm sorry," he called out to her. "I don't know how to save you."

The flames continued to consume her, as she screamed in agony. Minutes passed as the fire quickly ate away the surface of her skin, turning it black and charred. The sounds of agony that came from her no longer sounded human.

With her last bit of strength, she whispered, "I'm sorry too, Adam...for being so selfish. I wish I could have been..."

"It doesn't matter anymore," Adam told her, as he stood a few fit away, totally inept and unable to do a thing to save her. The nearest stream was a quarter mile away. There just wasn't enough time even to try.

As the flames almost exploded from her body, they said their last words to each as one, "I love you." In her last moments, at last she fully understood the heartbreak she had wrought over the earth, for her own family, for her own life, throughout time, and throughout all the ages to come. At last, she felt regret.

In the last moment before the flames utterly consumed her, Adam reached out his hand for her, with tenderness and regret, as the flames burned the last of her skin, captured the last of her life, feeling in his own chest, the last of her beating heart.

Though they had been made for one another, they had been ill-matched in many ways, but they'd loved each other in their own way, in the shadow of the light of God's love. Here on earth, where love was merely a reflection, love often failed to do what God intended. For God had never intended our differences to divide us, but to complete us.

Adam stood for a long time, contemplating what had just occurred, knowing that nothing would ever be the same. Until at last, he bent down to kiss the ground where his wife Eve had been consumed by fire, into mere ashes.

He had now lost two wives. The second was created from him, borne from his own rib. So, he felt her absence and her loss more keenly than Lilith's exile, who had also been ill-matched to his temperament.

He began to wonder if God had had a purpose for his union with these women, so very different from himself. He began to reflect that perhaps they'd been created to offer him what he himself lacked. Perhaps union was not all about being like-minded, but about becoming whole.

He drew a circle in the sand, and began to realize what it meant—why immortality was a circle, and infinity was two circles, like two completely different people who shared their lives in unity.

He slowly gathered the ashes of Eve into a crude pouch he made from an uneven cloth, and laid her ashes on the graves of their children. In this way, in her death, she would always remain with the children she'd bore him, who had died because of the Fall.

~ ~ ~

My ashes killed Eve. This was a part of my purpose in returning to the past. It was her destiny to fall at the touch of my ashes. Her touch on my ashes turned her to cinders, my ashes killed the mother of All. Upon Eve's death, her offspring, and the generations of her ancestry, were free of her power and control, but not of the curse she had wreaked upon races of man and animal and magickind, until the end of earth's time, and a new world of peace and plenty was begun. Until a new paradise in new heavens was created...

I was not exactly dead. But you couldn't say I was exactly alive either. In this netherworld, I saw Varawynn's brother Aengus. He came to me, and he said, "For my sister I was glad to lose my life, so that she might live..." He was like a ghost, or an apparition, but his words were alive, his words stuck in my head, and would haunt me until I understood their meaning.

Like Varawynn and Ileona, I hung in the balance of the in-between, not fully dead, but also not fully alive. Then after three days' time, as time passed like an eternity, I felt a call to return to earth, to life.

Three days hence, from the ashes and flames, I came forth again. This was the first time I wondered if I could ever be killed.

I was not the same Celestria as before. My plumes were different now. The sapphire and emerald had become the color of my eyes. My red, orange, and yellow flames remained. I discovered that I now had powers that made me immune to fire.

I was growing tired of the paradise that was lost when my wrong actions resulted in Astori's death. The death of Eve was my recompense, and the recompense for all the innocent lives she had altered, she had cursed. That burning hatred inside me for Justice was met by the last quiet whimper of Eve. Only a uniquely magical creature could have destroyed her. Now there was nothing left for me in the place where I had sprung.

I wished to leave the Garden of Eden. After I left, I explored the earth. I traveled across countries, across continents, over lakes, and oceans, and forests, and mountains. I traveled the world. A thousand years passed. I held in my mind, the memories of my life as the Bird of Eden, and also as my new fate as something more.

After a thousand years of new history, from the history of the earth I had once known, before entering the tunnel and crossing through space and time, allowing me to rewrite history, and change my fate, I began to long to return. I began to long for the beginning. Yet I did not return to the Garden of Eden. Instead, I flew to the Gardens beyond Eden, to a place so like where I was born, and yet had never been.

I went where the first woman, Lilith, had been exiled, along with her children from Adam, and her new kin from the Fallen Angel, Samyaza, who was her mate. There, I found a holy tree, in one of the sacred spaces of a temple, belonging to her son with Adam, Amen-Ra.

I turned that holy tree into my home. I built a nest among its branches. Looking up at that familiar landscape beneath the awaiting sky, I felt peace. I found comfort with Lilith and her kin. I liked Arra, her daughter from Adam, and became close to Amen-Ra.

Still, I missed Astori, and I wanted to go and be with him. I wanted to cross time and space for the last time, and fly into the heavens, to find eternal rest with my mate.

So, I built a special nest upon that sacred tree, and prepared myself for death. I used frankincense, myrrh, and cinnamon twigs to build it, whose earthy scent wafted beyond the temple gates, into the open sky. As I built my nest, for my final resting place, I sang of love and longing for what never could have been. Sure, I had gone back into the past and regained my voice, but there was nothing I could do to bring back Astori.

I waited until sunset. Amen-Ra rode his chariot across the sky, bursting onto the hallowed ground where I rested peacefully. He heard my song, and was drawn to listen. When my song was finished, he resumed his journey. A spark fell from the sky. A burst of colors exploded in the night.

I closed my eyes of gleaming sapphire. With a single flap of my wings, the fire burst forth from my body, and consumed me, until all that was left of me in the nest I had built of aromatic woods, was ash.

My brightly colored plumes of red, orange, yellow, and purple, now lay as grey dust. All my bright colors were reduced into ash. Again, I burned myself alive, in a spiritual explosion of soul.

Again, I was alive in the netherworld. Three days later, I was reborn from the ashes. God's words came back into my mind. I began to understand what creature I had become, and I sang a new song, "Phoenix Rising"…

In a moment, with one fated mistake,
I lost my voice and I lost my mate.
We were the only two God made,
But He restored my voice to me,
To save a raven girl destined to uncover mysteries of the sea.

I knew the history of the world,
I'd witnessed the lifetimes of many souls.
Then in my quest, God made me whole—
Returning to the Garden of Eden where I lost it all,
Where our kind had lost paradise in the Fall.

This time I denied the fruit Eve offered me—
The apple of the knowledge of both good and evil.
For I had learned the lesson of wisdom the hard way.
Still, I lost my love, Astori, on that day,
But I found my voice, and new powers to heal and save.

I flew alone to the place in paradise where I lost my mate,
I would bring the judgement down upon Eve's sure fate.
She, who caused the fall of man and creatures alike:
My ashes would burn her alive,
With the fire and flames of the knowledge
That she was the reason for the fall of all kinds.

I learned my ashes and tears could also be used

WHILE THE ASHES RISE TO LIFE

To bring the dead back to life,
I learned that I could never die,
I learned why God had allowed me to return.
Because not all beings evolve and learn.

Armed with the knowledge of how
To change my fate,
My voice was regained,
And I shall change the world
With my fire and flames.

I rise with the sun,
And die with the night.
I am consumed in a blaze,
I am risen from the ashes into the skies.
I am reborn throughout time and space.
The loss of my mate, is a constant reminder of my mistakes.

Blessings are released on those
To whom my shadow falls,
Where the shadows meet the light,
My duty guides me to cross time and space,
To help those who, like me, have fallen from grace.

I was created to consume the world in fire,
In the destruction of its own making,
For I know the undoing of mankind,
I have seen the history of all kinds,
So, in my presence, none can tell a lie.

Constantly evolving and transforming,
Constantly morphing and mutating,
Constantly changing and evolving,
As the symbol of resurrection and immortality,
I know the end is only the beginning.

The Bird of Eden burns deep within my soul,
To remind me of the history of the earth I know.
Throughout space and time, I fly,
Resurrected endlessly throughout time.
As the immortal Phoenix, I shall never die.

I had special powers as the Phoenix. I remembered my life as the Bird of Eden throughout time, simultaneously understanding the changes I'd made to the future, which were the catalyst to my transformation.

I felt a different kind of calling now, different than the urge to burn myself alive every five hundred to a thousand years. I felt it was time to go home. Back to the time and place where I had decided to go back and change history.

So, when the third time came, I burnt myself alive. When I awoke after three days as ashes, I was back to where I'd left off. Back to battlegrounds where the star had fallen, the crater which had virtually ended the battle that had claimed the life of the Bard of Hebron, Jonlin, and the Priestess from the Isles of Apples, Varawynn.

Some deep wisdom occurred to me. The worm came from the apple. The worm was a part of the curse of all birds. After we ate the apple, we were cursed to eat the bugs that preyed upon the apple, rotting it from within.

I alone knew what history had been before my transformation into the Phoenix. Now I alone knew the difference. With the death of Eve, a new order of womanhood was possible.

I had altered from the Bird of Eden, into the original Phoenix. With my new powers, I would be an even greater asset to our group of Chosen Ones.

My powers were unparalleled. I was even more unique as the Phoenix, then I had been as the Bird of Eden. But even immortal creatures can be killed. Even magical creatures have their weaknesses. I had learned in my travels that my fatal flaw was iron. So, in the battles and wars, I was careful to evade the fatal blow of the iron's hot sting.

WHILE THE ASHES RISE TO LIFE

My first ashes had killed Eve. Yet my ashes could be used to bring the dead back to life. From the ashes I was reborn, every five hundred to one thousand years I was resurrected. This was why no one had ever heard of the Bird of Eden, except those who had known me as such. But as those from the beginning of time, and their ancestors, died off, I alone would remember our story, and how we had changed our fate, by changing our name.

The Bird of Eden had become the Phoenix. This was my new name. This was my new destiny. This was my new beginning, and I suspected that I would have the final word, in the end...

~ *** ~

Chapter Four
The Burial of the Bard of Hebron

From the Celtic Highlands to the Deserts—

In silence, we journeyed back to the deserts of my homeland. Days and weeks passed with little to no communication, in deference to Alondria's deep grief. I was thinking a lot about the first time I saw Jonlin. Well, I'd heard him before I'd seen him, really.

He'd been playing a lullaby on his instrument, singing a haunting song. The beautiful melody had drawn me to him. I'd known right away that he was very special, humble and kind. I wondered if I would die with as much honor as Jonlin had lived.

I remembered the first time I'd seen Varawynn too. It had been recognition at first sight. Maybe love at first sight too. A pang of guilt overcame me, and I hoped that it was not too late to tell the Celtic Priestess how I felt about her. I was praying for a miracle.

* * *

I could only think of Jonlin. There was never a moment when something didn't remind me of him…a comment he'd made about the sweet fragrance of a flower, the way he loved the highland mountains, the songs he used to sing on our travels to brighten the days along our journey, the way he'd loved my homeland of Andorra, the way I'd known he loved me, even without words. I was overcome with regret that he'd never gotten to love me, or tell me how he felt, though I believed if we'd have been given the chance, we would have spent our lives together, in the bliss of true love.

I carried his fiddle on my own back, and when it got too heavy, I allowed Luquinn to carry it for me. The regret I carried was a heavier burden than anything I carried on my back. It weighed on my heart. It hurt deeply, the loss of what might have been…

Why hadn't he shared more of himself with me? Why hadn't I asked him more specific questions about his past? I didn't even know his parents' names. Jonlin, "the Bard of Hebron," was the man of my dreams. Why had God taken away the chance for me to tell him how much I loved him?

All my secret dreams of love tucked away in the hope chest in my soul…were in the cherished dreams of a future with Jonlin. Now that future was lost—no, it had been stolen.

Hope was gone. To live a life without love? Impossible. Unthinkable. Unbearable. The grief I felt over Jonlin's death was like my constant shadow. I would live as a shell of what I once was…and what I might have been.

* * *

I wished Alondria and I could bond in our shared grief, but instead she was cold and distant with everyone, especially me. Why couldn't we do anything to comfort her? Were we so woefully inadequate? How could we get her to see things from another perspective? What would become of us without her? She was the very heart and soul of our group—especially now that Jonlin was gone.

I saw her brother Aldoran try with her, as we all did, but she was unreceptive to any and all attempts to comfort her, seeming to resent our very lives, maybe even her own life…when Jonlin was soon to be buried beneath the ground.

I wished now I'd paid more attention when we were in Jonlin's home—to his parents and siblings, their names and all they'd said. How could I have known how close we would become?

Close enough that Jonlin had died protecting me. Dear, sweet, faithful Jonlin. Somehow, he'd had such a way of being the strongest and gentlest of us. He'd been a peacemaker like Alondria. Now the peacemakers were causing our division: Jonlin, by his death, and Alondria, by her response to it.

* * *

Did Alondria believe she was the only one who missed Jonlin? Did she believe think his death did not matter to us? Did she think she was the only one who had lost someone special and kind? I had lost my best friend. He had always come right to my side when he sensed my emotions overwhelming me, as they often did. Eliju had lost the closest thing to a brother he'd ever had. We'd all lost our steadfast moral compass, the saint among us, who always knew and did what was right.

What about Varawynn? Did Alondria even stop to consider her loss? Yes, there was still some hope that we could bring her back…but still. I hated to even think it, but it seemed to me that the princess was being a little selfish.

I was often accused of being selfish myself. Maybe it took one to know one. Or maybe I was being too hard on her. Yet where once she was the first and only person to go into the source of love and light, into the source of life itself, now she was barely able to even be civil to Eliju.

Eliju strived so hard to be patient with her. He treated her with the utmost respect. The gods know he'd never treated me that well. Out of respect for Jonlin, he tried to never meet her resentment and anger, with impatience.

He didn't know her well enough to know how to reach her in her grief, and we all felt that if her own twin brother couldn't comfort her, what could we do? Best leave well enough alone, we thought, after her continued passive aggression and sudden outbursts of rage. Let time do what our efforts can't. Doesn't time heal all wounds?

This too would pass. At least we hoped it would, and soon.

* * *

Little did they realize the unwavering steadfastness of Alondria's loyalty, and that to be left alone in her grief was the worst thing possible for her healing. I understood that.

I remembered the damage my father's absence had done on my mother. So, I did my best to remain by Alondria's side, when the other members of the group deserted her. I wanted to believe they meant well, but I couldn't help but resent their absence on her behalf. Few things were as reprehensible to me as abandoning someone in need.

After a few days, something unexpected and colorful broke through the sky, and our morose moodiness. Wait, was that Celestria? It was as if her feathers had turned to flames.

Mordorn descended upon us too, his feathers ruffling out about him prestigiously. "Celestria is now the Phoenix," the owl informed us, with his stately air. We really didn't know what that meant, but we had a feeling we would be finding out.

~ *** ~

After several weeks, we were back where we'd started. Back to where the first members of the group had banded together. Nearly two years had passed since Eliju and I had met, and the first members of the group had come together, and been inside this hut.

Jonlin's childhood home was small, but neat. It was going to be very difficult to come into the warmth of it, and deliver to them this tragic news.

We all stood for a moment at the threshold, gathering ourselves before knocking on the door. Alondria seemed especially nervous—she wasn't exactly meeting Jonlin's parents under ideal circumstances. Still, she wanted to make a good impression. She straightened her skirt, tidied her hair, and pinched her cheeks. She nodded to me to go ahead and knock on their door.

* * *

Who could it be? We weren't expecting company. I looked at my husband in surprise. "Can you get it, honey?" he asked me, engrossed as he was in his book. We were humble people, but we surely loved knowledge, for knowledge was a good foundation for wisdom.

"Of course, dear," I said, quickly going to the door.

I felt something then, like a sudden lightning strike to my heart. It was a foreboding, a mother's intuition, that whoever waited outside did not have happy news to offer us. So, I hesitated for a moment before opening the door.

Wandering Wolfe's face was about the last I expected to see. For a minute I stood there with the door open, trying to place him.

Then I happily guided them across our warm, bright threshold, with the fire burning merrily in the hearth. I was so excited at the prospect of seeing my son again. I cheerfully smiled at Shadow Rain and Eliju, recognizing and calling them by name.

My husband almost reluctantly marked his place in the novel, to stand and greet them, but of course, my noble husband was nothing if not respectful. Though my husband and I had never met the rest of the group, something in the Princess Alondria's somber countenance gave me pause. My eyes roved around the room, noting Jonlin's absence, and then coming to rest once more on Alondria's face and eyes, suddenly flooded with tears.

"Oh no, not Jonlin," I heard myself utter, as if watching myself from a distance. I was overcome with weakness, falling into my husband's sure embrace. "Not our sweet Jonlin."

We had lost our younger son, Jacob, years before. Now to lose Jonlin was just too much! To lose that talent was a sin, that beautiful, God-given gift he had for music and song. To never hear again his voice, or the way his hands instinctually knew the way of any instrument he picked up. To never see again his gentle smile, and the way he had of comforting those around him, like the silent warmth of the sun on a cold winter's day. Oh, no, not Jonlin.

Alondria glided across the room, reaching out a hand in comfort for a mother's grieving heart. I saw something in her face, in the way she moved. I noticed something in her. I felt an emotion in her.

She had loved my son.

I knew it. I knew it in the same way I had known that my husband and I would be married someday—even though at the time we were both betrothed to someone else. I knew we would wind up together, and love each other all our lives. The heaviness of Alondria's broken heart encompassed the room. Everyone could feel it.

Some kinship of knowing passed between our eyes. Something in the pressure of her hand, let me know without words that Jonlin was gone, and that the girl had loved my child. I knew in the sweeping of her hair, the graceful poise of her bearing, and the angelic sweetness in her mien, my son had loved her too. I could suddenly see all that would have been, if he had lived. I pulled Alondria into my arms, holding her as if she were my own daughter.

* * *

I watched my wife holding on to the girl Alondria, and felt myself struggling not to choke up myself. I didn't know what to do or say. So, I waited.

After a few moments passed, the shaman Wandering Wolfe cleared his throat. "I am so sorry for your loss. Dear Jonathon and Elizabeth, we want you to know that your son died to protect us. His death was a sacrifice for our lives, and we shall be forever grateful for it. We are in your debt, now and always."

Then my worst fear was true. My son was gone. It was difficult for parents to bury one child. Jonlin would make two children my wife and I buried.

"Your son was a wonderful young man," Silvandrin boomed from the corner. "His conduct and behavior would have made you very proud." I was taken aback by Silvandrin's appearance—who had ever heard of a black unicorn?

What was described to me as the "the Lady of the Lake," a very pretty blonde lady, piped in. "You raised him well," Ileona added with bowed head, with a subtle respect and reverence I'd wager she didn't often bestow on just anyone.

"He was everything I wish I could be. I want you to know he has inspired me to become a better man, and to treat others better in his honor," Eliju's voice faltered.

Now I was a practical man. But to hear that your son had inspired others to become a better person, was just about the best thing you could ever hope to hear said about him. I felt the tears lodge in my throat, making it hard to respond.

"He was my best friend," the girl named something Rain said, in-between strangled sobs. They were all so young. So young and innocent to experience such loss. You looked at people with youth, and you wished they would never have to grow up, that they would never have to experience things like death, and the losses throughout life which changed them. The world called it maturity, but too often, it was loss of innocence and hope. I found myself often hoping that the young could spend a lifetime in ignorance of the evil in the world…but we all must face evil, and greet death in the end.

"I loved him with all my heart," Alondria whispered, as a shroud of darkness descended over her face.

* * *

It was as if my sister's angel face went pale, and all her rosy life seemed to lose its bloom before our eyes. It was as if a shadow fell across her form like a veil falling between the loving spirit, she had once been, and the half-alive shadow of herself she had become.

She was no longer the person of the light we'd known and loved. No one knew and loved my sister better than I did. Not even Jonlin. It was Jonlin she was grieving now, and the life she would have had with him. Our childhood past together didn't seem to matter now, in the wake of the future that was gone.

The light and happy bride she would have been, with curled hair and bright doe-eyes, full of hope for the future, and all of life itself, behind a white veil between childhood and full-blossomed womanhood, was now a dead dream. She had crossed the dark veil and gone over to the side of the living dead. I who knew her best, and who was so skilled with the sword, and so witty with words, who had shared with her the loss of our childhood friend, Oric, felt useless to alleviate her pain—so apart and outside of me, so deep to the core of what I knew would hurt her—the loss of love that meant life itself to her.

"And he loved her," I told them with a significant look to Jonlin's parents, as I put my hand over my sister's back, and stroked it. I gently pulled at her curls, as was her own nervous habit. I knew that my caresses would calm her nerves, at least for the moment. Sending her light and healing energy through my touch, I lifted her spirit up in silent prayers. I prayed during this heart break that she would find peace.

I remembered how we'd spoken alone, as we were getting closer to Jonlin's home town, about his quest in the Land of What Might Have Been, and earlier still, when Alondria had first met Jonlin. She'd confessed to me, after Jonlin was gone, that the reason she'd been so quiet was because she'd sensed he was her true love.

She hadn't wanted to talk to me about it at the time. She had been uncomfortable with her feelings.

Jonlin's father, Jonathon, nodded with understanding at all our words of love. "At least he is with his brother now. That will make him happy. One day we will all join them. I have faith that we shall be together again, in a far more beautiful world, a land without suffering...the land without end."

So, this was where Jonlin's unwavering faith had been born. His parents were clearly true believers.

Wandering Wolfe again cleared his throat, and coughed. Clearly, the faith of Jonlin and his family made him uncomfortable.

"We've brought Jonlin's remains back to his homeland. We thought it proper he be buried with the kin from his homeland," Wandering Wolfe gently informed them.

"Thank you; this is just what he would've wanted. We'll bury him next to his little brother, Jacob. His other brother, Matthew and his sisters, Rebecca and Rachel, shall be heartbroken to lose another brother, but what's done is done, and we're grateful to know our son died honorably, to protect those he loved."

"Though his brother's death was not his fault, he always blamed himself for it. In a way, I think Jonlin would have been satisfied with his death being a sacrifice, as an atonement. We know him. The way he thinks, this sacrifice would be like making amends for his brother's loss. Please, do not feel any guilt over his death."

* * *

I was filled with gratitude for their kind words; after all, he had died trying to protect me, but they were looking at Alondria. Wandering Wolfe nodded, and we let Jonathon and Elizabeth make the preparations for their son. We went to the tavern from the last time we were in town, booked a few rooms, had dinner at the restaurant downstairs, then tried to get some sleep.

The next few days were a blur. We took one step at a time, but nothing felt real. Nothing seemed to matter anymore.

Finally, the moment of Jonlin's funeral came. Jonlin's family, friends, and various neighbors, gathered together. A hole was dug up near Jacob's small grave. Their local minister officiated over the proceedings. This was the first time I heard the sermon of a Christian.

* * *

As his pastor, I knew Jonlin like no one else did. The boy had been a natural servant of God. Music was his ministry. I would miss hearing that heavenly music in our church. I'd had hoped after his quest, he would return to us. I would miss hearing his voice.

God, in His infinite wisdom, had not wanted it thus. I had learned long ago that we must submit to God's will, even in our deepest grief and loss. So, I searched for words to comfort those he'd left behind.

"The Lord is my shepherd; I shall not want.
He makes me lie down in green pastures,
He leads me beside the still waters,
He restores my soul.
He guides me in paths of righteousness
For His name's sake.
Yea though I walk through the valley of the shadow of death
I shall fear no evil; for you are with me.
Your rod and your staff,
They comfort me.
You prepare a table before me,
In the presence of my mine enemies.
You anoint my head with oil;
My cup overflows.
Surely goodness and mercy shall follow me
All the days of my life.
And I shall dwell in the house of the Lord forever."

I threw a handful of earth into the wind, and onto the open grave. "Ashes to ashes, and dust to dust. Peace for the one we lost, and peace for the ones you left behind. All that burns returns to dust, but love remains as ashes."

"You lived a good life, Jonlin. When God called you to a noble cause you willingly left your simple life to serve the greater good. You died for a cause that was greater than yourself. You sacrificed yourself for your friends, like the perfect lamb of Jesus Christ. Dying to protect those you loved, as Jesus died for his love of all of us."

"You lived your life by the 'Way of the Cross,' Christ-like in your burden of suffering. Your loving spirit embodied 1 Corinthians 13:4, 'Love is patient, love is kind. It does not envy, it does not boast, it is not proud. It is not rude, it is not self-seeking, it is not easily angered. It keeps no records of wrongs. Love does not delight in evil, but rejoices with the truth. It always protects, always trusts, always hopes, always perseveres…'" Oh yes, surely this passage embodied our sweet Jonlin. But now we must find the strength to persevere without you."

I looked pointedly at Alondria. I could see she would have been perfect for Jonlin. There was something about the girl that made a man feel like he could do anything.

"His music was anointed by God, and could have brought such beauty and healing to the earth," I continued. "But we mustn't lament what is done, dead and gone. It is wrong to question God's plan and will. Better to appreciate the time we had with Jonlin, and his songs that touched us all."

"We must not allow the love we had for Jonlin to embitter us, for this cannot be what God would want from us," I continued. "Now more than ever before, when our circumstances are challenging, and our hearts are broken, we must find blessings in our life to be grateful for."

"We must not harden our hearts by the pain of what we are experiencing, but soften our hearts in obedience to God, with the trust that even death and pain is a part of God's plan, and can be used for our good, and for his glory. We must acknowledge the spiritual realm, where the battle for souls' wage between the principalities."

"We must also recognize that by and through the spirit, we are never separated. The love of God, and the love of those who have gone before us, is closer than our own breath, and not even death can alter that love. This can give us a peace that passes understanding, if we allow it to. Please bow your heads with me now in prayer."

"Dear Father, who art in heaven, hallowed be your name. We do not understand why you took this dear boy from the earth, which was so uplifted by his music, so soon, but we put our trust in your plan, we surrender our lives to your purpose, and we believe there is a reason for this suffering."

"We ask for you to grow our hearts and strengthen our minds now, beyond what we thought was possible. We ask for peace in knowing that Jonlin is in a better place, and that someday we will be united with him there."

"The tree with the deepest roots on the earth is the Shepherd's Tree. The Shepherd Tree has roots go nearly two hundred and fifty feet deep. May we all follow the true shepherd, and may all the painful things we endure deepen our roots, so that no matter what harm befalls us, no matter how difficult the circumstances we face, our faith, and our hope, and our love shall not waver."

"Though it hurts to love, after losing such a great love, we choose to love the others around us even more, with a Godly love, like the love Jonlin displayed for us while he was with us on this earth. For who among us embodies the qualities of Christ better than he did?"

"And so, we thank you for his life, and the beautiful testimony of his death. We thank you that the people he died to protect yet live, to accomplish great things with their lives, which will honor him."

"We cherish our memories of him, but we do not let it ruin our love of him and others. We ask you, father, to give us the power to do this, give us your holy spirit, fill us with your divine presence, so that we may forgive this grave loss, and continue moving forward. We ask all this in your precious name, and in your heavenly name we pray for your will be done on earth, even as it is in heaven. Amen."

Alondria told me after the service, she felt as if the prayer and my sermon were meant just for her. Shadow Rain and Eliju told me that too.

"A mark of a good minister is how his sermons speak to all his flock," Jonlin had once said to me.

Oh, God, I would miss that dear boy. I would send that energy of love I had for him into the prayers for the rest of the people in the group, to give them strength in their journey, to save us all.

* * *

After the minister said his beautiful prayer, the singing began. A choir of voices sang Jonlin's favorite hymns, sang the songs of his they knew he loved best. As they sang, I touched my silver horn to Jonlin's crudely constructed grave, turning it into a hallowed monument of epic proportions. The magic of my horn turned the gravesite into a memorial fit for a king.

Jonlin's simple grave was transformed into something truly spectacular. Composed of white marble, and engraved with the words of the Prophecy, written in thousands of tiny, sparkling diamonds, I whispered these words, as I created this place of honor for "the Bard of Hebron,"

> *"Bless the sacred sacrifice*
> *Of this reverent, gentle soul,*
> *Who taught us by his death*
> *The love that Christ has shown.*
>
> *His name shall be immortalized*
> *For many years to come,*
> *His life shall be a testament*
> *That even in death is God's will done."*

A porcelain angel looking a lot like Alondria, with delicate, fine features, guarded his grave. A second stone angel knelt before the grave, hands clasped in prayer, with a face as lovely as a star, and wings outspread, as if she would soon take off into flight.

Alondria placed her hand on my back, with gratitude for the gift I'd given to Jonlin. We all loved Jonlin. I wanted to give the boy something special in his death, for all those who loved him to remember him by. Even now, when Alondria was full of rage and bitterness over losing the man she loved, she was still the only human who was pure enough to touch me, even though I was a cursed unicorn of black and silver, who had lost long ago, the innocence of my white and gold.

* * *

I was so touched by Silvandrin's lovely memorial to Jonlin, as well as the anointed words of Jonlin's minister, who clearly knew him well. Then as the crowd of Hebron continued to sing Jonlin's songs, Illumina lifted her arms into the sky, as if in signal.

A hundred of the elves' illustrious white doves, the messenger birds of the sea, flew amongst us. As the sound of flapping wings sent a current of air through the crowd, I shivered, feeling as if Jonlin's breath was on the softness of my bare shoulders.

As one of the songs came to a close, I could have sworn I felt Jonlin's kiss in the curve of the nape of my neck, and his fingers wiping away the cold tears on my cheeks.

I felt him. I could have sworn I felt him. As if he were still alive. As if he was right there beside me.

I heard his voice among the gentle swooshing of the white doves' wings. I heard his voice once more in the crowd, singing the words he had written, in the melody he'd once sung.

I hear his voice whisper, *"Believe in love."* I spoke back him, somewhere in the deepest recesses of mind and heart. *I can't, not without you.*

Then I heard his answer, coming from within the depths of my soul. "Please go on. Go on without me."

I can't. I won't.

"Don't lose who you are because of me. Move on, Alondria. Carry on my love. Be the light."

I can't, I won't. Who I was is being buried in the ground here with you. Don't you see? They buried all my love when they buried you.

Then I turned away from his voice, and I turned away from his caress, and I told myself it was all just in my imagination. The darkness that I felt all around me, convinced me of the lie that Jonlin's spirit wasn't here in that moment, that I could never move forward, and that I may as well have died with him. They may as well have buried me alive. Because all I was now was a ghost, haunting and haunted.

The darkness seemed to sweep down over me, surrounding me on all sides. As my tears overflowed in the emotion of his loss, my brother Aldoran took my right hand, and Eliju took my left.

* * *

Caressing firmly the birthmark of the cross in her left palm, I felt her dainty hand warm my own. A sense of rightness passed over me, to be able to touch her and comfort her in this moment. I admired and revered her, so far above me, as she was in her ancient wisdom and childlike innocence, so astoundingly beautiful, as a direct descendent of the muses, with such a unique and perfect blend of everything a person ought to be.

Profoundly sorry for the loss of the kind Jonlin, as I looked into Alondria's eyes, I wanted her to see the infinite gratitude I felt too, in Jonlin's faithful sacrifice. Wanting to prove to her, above all, that Jonlin had not died for nothing, that his death fueled our agenda in a way it hadn't before, making my desire of noble pursuits and ideals far more real and treasured then they'd been before. The quest, and this whole journey, felt more *real* now.

With Jonlin's death, I was determined to become a better man. I was determined to help Alondria to heal. If we did accomplish whatever we needed to, and if I was meant to become the king, I was determined to lead through service, first and foremost. I desired to serve her, Alondria, the girl who had lost everything when she lost Jonlin, above all others.

* * *

Without words, I understood that for Eliju, Jonlin's death had not been for nothing. His sacrifice would make him a better man. I knew he would always be working to live up to his memory. But for me Jonlin's death had brought only pain and grief. I found nothing positive in his death. The only silver lining for me, was in death itself. For in death, we would be reunited.

So, I longed for the grave, like those who are dying long for life. It was consuming my every thought. It was becoming my dearest hope, my only hope. My life had become a death, and death in my mind now was life...

Jonlin's white monument encrusted with silver sparkling diamonds, stood out in the dull desert sands, like the light of a lighthouse over the sea on a moonless, starless night, eclipsing the little grave of his brother, whose grave his lay beside.

Bowing his noble head, Silvandrin gently touched his horn to Jonlin's little brother Jacob's grave too. With the tap of his horn, the grave enlarged, transmuted into the same white marble as his brother's. It was a smaller monument, but still composed of sparkling diamonds on white marble like Jonlin's. Silvandrin was so kind. He didn't leave it at that.

Another porcelain angel statue appeared, with one hand resting on Jacob's grave, and one arm reaching up toward the sky; her face staring up into the heavens, with a look of such light and holiness, the whole group was transfixed on the glorious expression on the angel's face: *hope*.

Jonlin's parents leaned against one another, gaining comfort and strength from each other's embrace. That kind of love was rare. That kind of love was natural, what God had intended everyone to have—a marriage of love that grew deeper over the years.

Beth merely had to move her hand, to find her hand in his. She had merely to sniffle, before Jonathon's arms reached out around her. They could communicate with one look, with a single word…a story, an idea, a feeling, in reference to a lifetime of love. A simple gesture was enough to say what a thousand words could never articulate.

I looked at them, full of pain and loss at the love I'd never have, and could have had with the son they buried. Walking up to Jonlin's parents, I brought my hands to theirs, entwining myself into their embrace. Without words, as Jonlin's parents held me, I knew they understood how much I'd loved their son, and would loyally, faithfully, and fiercely love him still, all the days of my life.

* * *

We longed to tell her to let him go…to live her life, and to move forward would be a greater honor to our son. We wanted her to live her life fully, rather than to live her life as if she were dead and buried with him. Yet we knew enough of life and love, to let it be. If it was Alondria we were burying, we knew our son would feel the same way. Jonlin would never have moved on from her.

It is unkind and false to say to those who grieve that love will come again. For some it won't. Not everyone is capable of a half-love, or a half-life. For these rare people of a highly loyal breed, their love is buried with the one they lost, or the love that has forsaken them. Some cannot let go of love, when it is deep enough that it not only defines them, but brought them to life. For with love, comes a greater awakening than the moment of our first breath, when our eyes opened to our first dawn.

I had felt that awakening with my husband, Jonathon. Alondria had felt it for Jonlin. What would I have done if Jonathon had been taken too soon? At best, I would have lived my whole life on the surface, never really knowing the depth of love I had missed out on.

We grow the most with others. I had grown and changed over the years with Jonathon. My love had grown and deepened so much. I never would have known such a deep, devoted love was possible at the beginning our romance. Not everyone is capable of such a deep, abiding love

Beyond infatuation, spending your life with someone, was a love far above any other. I was broken-hearted that Alondria may never know that kind of comfort, of going to sleep next to the one you love, and waking up to have them there, beside you still. The deepening of love over time, over decades, was sacred.

Just as Jonlin had been unwilling, or unable, to let go of the guilt of his little brother's death, Alondria was unable to let go of her love and guilt over his dying to protect the Chosen One, Eliju, who was clearly in the throes of a lot of guilt and regret himself.

Of course, we understood Alondria's desire to live for Jonlin, yet there were others who needed her that she would neglect in her faithfulness to the one who had passed on. It was hard to breech such a topic so soon after Jonlin's death. Further still, we had not the right to tell Alondria how best to grieve, or for how long. But we were worried about how grief would alter the sweet and loving princess. For healers were often able to help others through their pain, and not themselves.

When the children of the light succumb to the darkness, the whole world darkens. We could only hope and pray that the angels who fought on behalf of Alondria's soul, would pierce through her mind and her heart, the simple truth that love never dies.

~ *** ~

Chapter Five
The Seeds are Split

The idea of seeing Shadonai bringing Varawynn back to life, when my own true love lay buried beneath the desert sands, tortured me. So half-way back to where we'd started in Caledonia, I announced, "I'm going home." I couldn't be with them anymore. They all just reminded me of Jonlin.

"You can't go. We need you to help find Shadonai," said Luquinn instantly.

"You can't just leave the group—" Eliju started.

"Please don't disband the group, Alondria," Pharean beseeched me meekly. "We all love you and Jonlin. We want to be there for you."

"Please understand, I can't be here—with all of you right now," I insisted firmly. My usual nervous habit of playing with my hair had taken on such a compulsive turn, my hair had been coming out. My hands were trembling, as I continued pulling at the glossy curls, yanking and twisting them viciously around my shaking fingers.

They all looked at one another helplessly. It was hard for them to deal with me. I could tell.

"I need this. Please. I can't be here anymore. With all of you." Shadow Rain and Eliju looked at one another feebly. They'd been becoming closer friends; out of necessity if nothing else. They talked a lot about me I knew, trying everything they could to pull me out of myself. They loved me, and felt they had failed me. I knew the truth was, I was failing them. But I couldn't turn off my feelings.

Wandering Wolfe stared at me warily. "There's nothing we can do to change your mind is there, Alondria?"

"No."

Nodding, he gave me his consent to go. I was both grateful and hurt at the same time.

"I will relent, only if I am permitted bear her place in her stead," Aldoran spoke up quickly. I was shocked. My brother would take my place in my stead? I felt instant resentment well up in me. I was betrayed by my own twin brother.

It still didn't matter to me as much as losing Jonlin. Luquinn stared at Aldoran wide-eyed.

"I would agree to that," said Eliju.

"And would you?" Wandering Wolfe asked me.

"I don't care," I lied. "I just want to go home."

"I will accompany Alondria back to her homeland," Luquinn stated resolutely. "Since her own brother wants to take her place here."

"We mean no harm," Eliju insisted. "I want Alondria *and* Aldoran to stay with us, but if Alondria's mind is set, and none of us are helping her—"

"Then you are tired of trying, and will just let her go? I see," Luquinn glared at them all on my behalf. He felt the same as I did. Their release of me, and Aldoran's staying, was a clear betrayal.

"Stop it Luquinn, that's not what Eliju is saying. He wants what's best for her. We all want what's best for her," said Wandering Wolfe defensively.

"Leaving someone in need, and alone, is the worst thing you can do to them. Believe me, I know, my father did just that to my mother. It destroyed her."

"I know this isn't what you want, but I think it may be best for us all to go home," Shadow Rain suggested. "At least for a while."

"But what about trying to resurrect Varawynn?" Eliju demanded.

"Some of us can go with you, and try to bring back Varawynn, Eliju," Pharean suggested. "And some of us can go back to our homes."

"I want to go home to my tribe," said Shadow Rain. "We can't fulfill the Prophecy right now anyway. We need time to grieve and heal."

Eliju glared at her, "Traitor."

She shrugged, "I'm sorry, Eliju, but I'm grieving Jonlin hard too. And I'm homesick."

"I thought we were finally getting closer," Eliju lamented.

"Until Varawynn comes back to life, and Eliju, I really believe she will."

"It's not like that, Shadow Rain. I wouldn't cast you aside! I really appreciate—"

"She is no more a traitor than you are Eliju," Luquinn interrupted, putting a protective arm over Alondria's slim shoulders.

"I need to go on my own journey," said Ileona. "I need some time on my own too." She'd been very quiet for a long time. Ever since her quest. Something had happened that she'd been stewing over, but I really didn't even care enough to ask her about it.

"Ileona, how could *you* not come with us to help Varawynn?" Eliju stuttered incredulously. "You knew her all her life."

"Eliju, I have complete faith Varawynn will be resurrected, with or without me. For now, I have things I need to accomplish on my own, which will eventually help us to complete our mission."

"I'll still come with you," Pharean assured Eliju.

"As will I," said Aldoran.

"Of course, you know where I stand," said Wandering Wolfe.

"We're going to come with you too," Illumina and Silvandrin said together.

"But it isn't right," Eliju insisted. "It isn't right for us to disband. It isn't right we were all there for Jonlin's burial, and not for Varawynn. Luquinn is right too. It isn't right for us not to be there for each other right now, and I *want* to be there for Alondria!"

Luquinn's hardened expression softened slightly. He still didn't always like the Chosen Boy that much, but he was beginning to realize more and more he was well-intentioned. I also believed Eliju was well-intentioned.

"It's been almost two years since we started this journey. Two years of traveling ten to fifteen miles a day, except for the six months we were held in captivity. For some of us that time is shorter, but for all of us I'd wager we're weary, and we want to rest and spend some time with our families for a little while before we travel on and on again. I don't even like traveling as much you do. It doesn't come as naturally to all of us as it does to you, Eliju." Shadow Rain told him, trying to explain how most of them felt.

"Eliju, I'm in agreement with you and Luquinn," Wandering Wolfe acknowledged. "But I do *not* think we can control the needs and desires of others. I also feel it's only fair to take other people's feelings into account. I'm sure Rain's not the only one who's tired of traveling."

"But what about the Prophecy?" Pharean asked. "We thought we were fighting King Mardavian, but we were wrong. Darlillyth is the one who's behind much of his conquests."

"I'm starting to think the enemy lines are blurring, Pharean. I'm not quite as certain now who our real enemies are. There will come a day, and soon I believe, when we will all be united once more. We still all desire to fulfill the Prophecy, I hope..."

"But I think we need some space and time to deal with and heal from the traumas we've faced. The loss of

Jonlin has affected us all. Shadow Rain has a family to go home to, and a tribe that needs her. Ileona has to go on her own journey right now. We all have to grow in order to defeat the evil we will inevitably face. Unfortunately, I think right now some of us will grow better apart, than we would by remaining together," Illumina said reasonably.

* * *

Sadly, after much argument, the group came to agree. And so, the group dispersed, knowing there would come a day they would reunite. I knew where each member of the group was at all times. I was the Watcher, the Ever Present One, and simultaneously, the Ever Absent One.

Hence Ileona set off for the desert; Illumina and Silvandrin stayed with them, Flint was here and there, and I of course was here and there and everywhere, coming and going without being much seen, like a shadow. Always present, and yet never really present. Abstract and obscured. I was never a part of the core group. I was a loner. I was round and about, not often getting involved in the day-to-day activities and conversations. The Bird of Eden, turned Phoenix, flew above us, sometimes with the group, but often flying off alone.

Shadow Rain just couldn't bear to stay with Eliju. She knew how much he missed Varawynn. She knew she was bound to come back to them. She couldn't handle even the idea of the look on Eliju's face when she did. It had nearly destroyed her to see the way he looked at Darlillyth.

Rain cared about Varawynn. They had become friends. She wanted her to be okay. But she still didn't want to see Eliju's expression when and if she was resurrected.

Alondria willingly submitted her place to her brother, and went back to Andorra with Luquinn, while only Aldoran, Pharean, Flint, Wandering Wolfe and Eliju were searching for Wandering Wolfe's daughter, Shadonai, in hopes of resurrecting the ashes of Varawynn. If they were unsuccessful, they would return her ashes to her homeland, allowing her family to perform a death ritual for their daughter the way they'd recently done for their son.

It is strange how something as good and pure as loyalty can become twisted if taken to the extreme. Alondria's loyalty was born with Jonlin's life, and was sealed with his death. No one could make her feel otherwise. Yet Pharean was right when she said her attitude had been foretold by the very prophecy Alondria had so radically denounced:

She shall leave behind her destiny,
As for a time the group retreats
For she is unable to imagine a life
Without the one who fulfilled her dreams.

She, of withering shadows once of the light,
Broken by the darkness,
Shattered by death, forsakes her own destiny,
For the pain of a loveless life.

She is nothing without her everything.
Without love, for her there is only suffering,
No silver lining can brighten her life,
There is nothing now for her but despair and strife.

For a time, there is only anger
There is only pain
There is only the loss of an endless,
Fruitless winter of the love that was taken away.

Then from the broken pieces
Of his body buried beneath the ground
Life emerges, and love from her heart
Brings her back to the light.

Graced by the goodwill of her love,
As if from the grave
He reaches out his hands,
To bring her back a perfect love again.

In perfect time,
To consecrate a new love of her life,
And from the death of life
Her crown sits once more upon her downturned face.

And upon his head,
The One who for so long loved her in silence,
In the dark deepness of the night,
Unspoken tenderness comes like a lullaby.

What once might have been,
And what now shall never be,
Meet at a crossroads,
As a new love reminds her of what is yet to come.

Something bitter had taken root in Alondria's soul. It would be some time before the group would feel again the sweetness of her loving spirit, or her golden smile of God. I, who knew the Prophecy so well, was assured that someday she would return to her true self. Her beautiful smile would be even more powerful because it would be tempered by the shadows and tears of silver, and the refining warmth of amber's ancient wisdoms, learned best through suffering.

WHILE THE ASHES RISE TO LIFE

They had no idea when we disbanded that it would be nearly eighteen years before we'd be together again. I knew, but revealed nothing.

~ *** ~

Chapter Six
In the Shadow of God

Shadows merge with darkness dancing
Life and death go to the fray
Warlock, Shaman, Sorceress, brother,
Die to bring life from death this day.

Sing they bird of raven and woman
Sing they sister and brother
Sing they the song of life and death
Back from the glimmering ethers.

Shadows falling from the grey light dimming
Shining as a beacon into the night
To resurrect the raven girl to life
The Shadow of God must be sacrificed.

"It is time for them to find each other. Lead them Vorseth. Bring them together. Let them meet before they have to say goodbye."

"Arra, I'm not sure she's ready. She is more impatient than ever."

"She is only impatient because she senses it is time. Besides, sometimes actions propel us to do things, and become things, which would not have been possible otherwise."

"That is true. But I shall miss her. Who shall be my student now?"

"The boy; the boy of your other scholar. Take care of that one now, Vorseth. His own time is coming soon."

"Yes, Arra, I know you're right. We must ultimately let what was written, and what we decided long ago, to come pass."

"There is no altering the course of the constellations now. Our destinies are written in the stars, in the moving of the heavens. Upon the sands of time, we measure our lives in the finite moments that make up who we are. As surely as the moon controls the tides, so the Prophecy's words must be taken into account."

"At the appointed time the Shadow of God must be sacrificed. From birth it was decided…"

"By a greater power we bow to. We must get out of the way of destiny…"

"So that the way of truth may be found."

"For some—"

"For her—"

"For all—"

"From birth her destiny was the grave."

~ ~ ~

October—

"Where have you been this time, Vorseth?" I demanded. "Always, always, always you are disappearing! Why must we continuously have the same conversation? Again, and for the last time I ask you, *where have you been?*"

The old warlock hesitated before finally answering me in a significant tone. "Why don't I take you there?"

It took a lot to surprise me enough to reveal my inward feelings. But I'm fairly certain my poker face was registering shock. It took even more to take my breath away, but I was speechless. Vorseth had never been an open book, and as a general rule he never offered up his knowledge or secrets easily. Wordlessly, I nodded.

* * *

Thus, through forest and shadows, by the dying light of the setting sun, through the tunnels underground, and secret passageways, on a trail just past the neighboring forest, I silently led Darlillyth to the daughter she had believed for centuries was dead. It was a strange feeling. I could feel the anticipation in the air. Even now, when the time had come, it felt uncomfortable for these secrets to come to light.

The small hut stood small but proud, aglow with the rich hues of fall's golden sunlight. The day was cold, and the sun would be setting soon. I couldn't help wishing that Arra was here, to see with her own eyes, the Prophecy coming to pass.

* * *

Something was pulling at my heart. Something that had pulled at me for a long time was unraveling itself. I knew wherever Vorseth was leading me would provide an answer…the answer to a question I had never dared to ask, a question I had never dared to hope for, outside the security of my own mind.

I wouldn't ask Vorseth where he was taking me. I didn't want to demand answers like I usually did. Something inside me intuitively knew. No words needed to be spoken, to know that all answers lied within the walls of this quaint hut we were coming to, laden with the heady scent of heather and lavender.

* * *

I knocked on the door. Two taps, then seven taps, then two taps again—our special code.

* * *

A girl…a woman, perhaps, who looked like a girl, with straight black hair, wearing flowing skirts of coarse grey, and eyes as shiny as two silver coins, opened the door to stand before us. Her roving, observant eyes missed nothing, as they quickly took in the woman before her. Vorseth took my hand, guiding me inside.

* * *

Before the hot and raging fire in the hearth, Darlillyth and Shadonai, mother and daughter, stood at last together. No explanations were wanted or necessary for them to know the truth. Standing face-to-face, they drank each other in, like fine wine in elaborate goblets of cobalt blue crystal.

For Darlillyth, seeing her daughter come to life, gave her life a new purpose. Hope and joy had been buried for so long—as long as she'd believed her daughter was dead. I could see it on her face. I hadn't seen that look in her eyes in so long. Since she was seventeen, and her daughter had been taken from her—by me. It had all just been a matter of due course. Matters of the Prophecy.

* * *

Never wanting to hope since…to dare to dream that my daughter could be alive, tears came into my eyes I had no concern about hiding; grief so evident it hurt my heart to look at her directly, just like looking directly into the sun. My words were thick when I managed to say, to ask for her name… "My daughter…"

* * *

"I am Shadonai, the Shadow of God." Studying my mother's face hungrily for signs of her feelings, finding a perverse pleasure in the pain in her eyes, I murmured, "My mother…what is *your* name?"

"Darlillyth, of the House of Lilith, the original Woman in the Garden of Eden," she murmured through her tears. At last, we knew each other's names.

* * *

She was smart and intuitive. We understood each other without effort. Spontaneously pulling my daughter into my arms, the tears poured down my face like water floods a river from a breaking dam. For many moments we held onto each other, learning of each other through the depth of our unspoken feelings.

* * *

For many moments more I watched as they tore away each other's layers of masks till they got to the core—to the raw emotion of their feelings. Studying their similarities, comparing their differences, reading the emotions behind the expressions, analyzing over and over every nuance and shade of each other's souls, as exhibited through the eyes and the angles of the face. They were like mirror images in a dirty mirror—not exactly identical, but uncannily alike enough to make one do a double take.

Clearly, they were cut from the same cloth: fine, black, and composed of sleek silk. They shared the same jet-black hair, the same phoenix eyes, the same slightly angular face, and dramatic, sharp curves. More so even than their looks were their thoughts, the way they expressed their feelings, the alluring confidence of their walk, and the personalities that were more in sync then the moon orbiting the earth.

They had the same way of projecting hardness, when they were achingly vulnerable inside. They hid behind their cool exteriors, an otherworldly sensitivity of heart, and highly attuned perception of social interactions that was unable to be taught—for them it was mere instinct. Beneath their magnetic charisma, they shared the same leaning toward ruthless cruelty, ignited most fiercely by kindness, even more so than by hurt— and not because they did not want kindness, but because they did.

I, who knew both of them better than anyone else, could tell you the motivations behind every action they took. Their first reaction to hurt or kindness, was the same—to destroy the person who bestowed it. For both love and hurt ignited their fears, revealing their vulnerability to themselves...that which could be endured least because it made them more open to hurt, and thus must be ripped out of them by violence to others.

Now staring into each other's eyes, one set silver, the other black as burning coal, their very sameness set them at ease with one another other, so very much the same, they felt they could at last be themselves, without the judgments and misunderstandings they often encountered in others. There was a part of me, call it the sentimental, weak side of myself perhaps, that regretted keeping them apart for so long.

* * *

"Mother—Darlillyth, I never thought, I always wanted..." Smiling through my damp eyes, a sudden lightning bolt struck my heart as I thought about Benoni locked away in the dungeon. "I always wanted to find you," Shadoan managed to finish.

"If you only knew how I've agonized...how I've suffered over you...the way you were taken from me..." I whispered.

"How *was* I taken, Mother?" Shadonai slipped her hand into mine, all of sudden all of eight-years-old, and more fully human than she'd ever felt before. Just as suddenly, I felt like that young girl again, whose baby girl was wrenched away from me by my father's hands, to be killed.

But I couldn't tell her that. I couldn't tell her the truth. Nothing would hurt her so much.

* * *

A shadow passed across her face. "I don't know if you want to hear that story." Darlillyth's hand was shaking as she removed my hand from her own. I didn't understand the reason for her sudden aloofness.

"I do. I do want to know," I insisted.

"Well, I don't know if I want to tell it!" Darlillyth snapped. My eyes glinted like sparked flint. I felt the fire in my spirit burning. "I need to know, Darlillyth. I think I have a right to know."

* * *

I was sure she'd noticed the switch from Shadonai calling her mother to Darlillyth. "I'm sorry," Darlillyth apologized immediately.

Darlillyth never apologized. She knew her daughter calling her by name was meant as a punishment. It was exactly what she would have done herself, if she were in her daughter's place.

"Then tell me," Shadonai demanded, the dangerous tone ignited. I stood away and apart from them, but watched them sitting together by the fire. I wasn't even sure they were aware of my presence.

Darlillyth took a deep breath and moved away from Shadonai, to sit in the tiny window seat at the end of the room. Staring out into the woods, as her daughter had done so many times, throughout all the years of her life, for a moment they exchanged their souls.

Darlillyth felt the years of isolation and loneliness, as Shadonai learned of the years of abuse her mother had endured. I felt their souls exchanging back and forth into each other. To understand the things they shared, the way they differed, and the life they'd lost, they went into other's minds and memories.

"I would have wanted to protect you from this. You insist now to hear what happened to you. I'm afraid once the story has been told you shall wish you'd never heard it. But I've learned the hard way that the truth is like a dead body at sea—inevitably it will rise to the surface. The truth persists inside us, until we're forced to speak it…to release ourselves from the burden of bearing the weight alone."

"And what is the truth, mother?"

"I never knew my real mother either, Shadonai. We have that in common. She died when I was only a few years old. I was raised by my biological father, and a jealous, resentful stepmother. I grew up with their child, my half-brother, King Mardavian."

Shadonai inhaled one long, deep breath. "King Mardavian killed the parents who raised me. I have dedicated my life to finding you mother, as well as to tracking, and killing him."

"He is already dead. He was killed by a girl named Varawynn."

"He was? When?"

"Not long ago. In a battle in Caledonia with the Chosen One. She is one of the fourteen."

"Where is this girl? I must thank her."

Darlillyth fidgeted. I knew she was reluctant to share all this with her. "She's dead too, Shadonai."

"Dead?"

"Yes, dead."

"How?"

Hesitating, she admitted reluctantly, "I killed her."

"Why?"

"It's very complicated. Mardavian was—he was more than my brother, Shadonai."

"What was he?" We were getting to the most difficult part now. She was worrying how Shadonai was going to take it.

"My father abused me in many ways, my daughter," Darlillyth continued telling the sad story of her childhood to her daughter. "My stepmother beat me and said such cruel things. She hit and whipped me countless times. And my father…since I was young, only a child, really, would come down the hall, come down the hall and, and…"

Darlillyth just looked at her then; communicating in the uncanny way they had through the eyes, without the use of words, that expressed the emotions of the soul. She didn't want to have to say it out loud…that her father had raped her throughout her childhood.

Shadonai gasped and drew her mother's hand back into her own. "Oh, mother!" A strange emotion crossed her heart, like a sudden cloud obscuring the sun, or rather, like a light coming out from behind a cloud. Was this compassion on Shadonai's face? I'd never seen it there before.

"And some years after it started, my brother, my half-brother, Mardavian, came into my room late at night too, after my father was done with me."

"Ohhh….no…how horrible…"

"About this time Wandering Wolfe came to us, to study with us, and to be mentored by Vorseth," Darlillyth continued. "Bear in mind, my daughter, that my experience with men in the world had been limited to my brother and my father. Wandering Wolfe was very good to me, very kind and courteous, so very different than the other people, the other *men* I had known."

"He was the first person who made me feel like he saw me…you know really *saw* me." A soft, sweet smile played and curled at the corners of Darlillyth's lips. A happy light of remembrance transfigured her features into the look of a young girl's first taste of love. I had guided my son to Darlillyth. I was glad he had given the Queen at least a little happiness.

"So, you loved him then?" Shadonai interrupted her reverie.

"Yes, as much as an inexperienced young girl can." Her face and voice hardened as quickly as it had softened.

"I'm sure you've realized, Shadonai, that we are not

fully human. I've taken it to understand that my mother—your grandmother—mated with a Nephilim, and ate from the fruit of the Tree of Life. Thus, we are by blood immortal. I am two thousand seventeen years old. *You* are two thousand years old, born one day before my birthday. In a few weeks you shall be *exactly* two thousand years old, on November 16th. My birthday is on November 17th."

"And my father Wandering Wolfe? Mustn't he be an immortal as well?"

"That is clear…but distinctly unclear is it not? That is what I'm trying to explain."

"I don't understand."

"Neither do I—it is evident that Wandering Wolfe must be more than human for him to have been alive this long, but what he is I do not yet know. You are an immortal in more than one way, Shadonai…in three ways, just that I know of."

"In *three* ways?"

"My brother hadn't stopped coming into my room when Wandering Wolfe and I stole under a canopy of leaves along a riverbank, my daughter."

"What are you *saying*?" A sense of urgency made her voice come out squeaky, like a door knob that needed oiling.

"The seed was split among two men…is this creature foe or friend? The truth is hidden well from them…"

"What are you saying?"

"It can happen. Science dictates—"

"WHAT ARE YOU SAYING?"

"Wandering Wolfe is not your only father. King Mardavian was your father as well. It was your grandfather who demanded your death. Vorseth was the one who carried it out…or who I thought had. Vorseth must have switched the babies…because…because I saw the cold, lifeless blue baby with my own two eyes.

That's the real reason I started hating blue. Blue to me was always the color of that baby I thought was you...and now...now—"

"Now I know what I always feared the most is true. *I am an abomination*—the bastard child of a brother who raped his sister."

"Her half-brother and your half-father."

"Right, his half-sister, my half-father. What difference does that make?"

"And a man who loved you since before the day you were born; who loved me too at one time. Wandering Wolfe."

"And a grandfather who wanted me dead the day I was born! The worst part is that he was right. I should have been killed from birth."

"It's not your fault who your fathers are."

"How do you *know*? How do you know for sure?"

"Because Wandering Wolfe's eyes are reddish-brown, and my eyes are black and Mardavian's eyes are grey, and so are yours. And because when you smile, it's with that crooked smile that belonged to my brother. You also have the same walk and cleft in your chin as Wandering Wolfe. I see them both in you."

"Of course, to be certain, I also performed a spell when you were in my womb to see who your father was. I knew before you were even born that the seed had been split two ways, and you were the girl of that Prophecy. So you see, I knew the truth before you were even born, and I still wanted you. I still loved you. For you are more mine than theirs anyway."

Turning and walking away from her mother, Shadonai grabbed a small bucket from the kitchen, and puked out the wretchedness of the truth. Afterwards her face looked like the white grey of a ghost. "You were right...you never should have told me this."

"I'm so sorry. I've lied to people all my life—I

didn't want to lie to you."

Her shaking hand gripped the side of a half-empty glass of water on her desk. "I'm the one who should be sorry. Every time I smile...you must see the man who raped you. You must see him in my eyes."

"No, Shadonai, no; I see you when I look into your eyes. You are not your father. Even if you bear a resemblance to him, that doesn't mean you are anything like him inside."

"Oh, but I am...I am like him." Shadonai dropped to her knees, all the color draining from her face now. Her shaking hand dropped the glass Darlillyth caught and set aside. Some mother's instinct she'd thought she'd lost the day she believed they'd buried her baby girl in the ground, made her kneel beside her grown baby girl, and take her up into her arms.

"It isn't your fault, my girl. None of this has anything to do with you. You were innocent then, and you are innocent now. I loved you then, and I love you now. To me you will be, *we* shall always be...pure. They can't take that away from us."

Shadonai's ethereal soul had now indeed been exchanged with her mother's. She'd withdrawn too deep inside herself to be reached. So many years before, her mother had done the same thing, for the sake of love for her. Now Shadonai did so for the guilt and love over what had happened to her mother, of which she was the result. She felt as if she were the physical manifestation and consequence of her mother's abuse.

* * *

A plan as twisted and perverted as my birth formed in my mind. I now had what I'd always longed for most in my life...my mother's love. Yet in the finding of it, I'd learned to hate myself.

This plan I was forming in my mind would make things right. It would do what Vorseth should have done so many years ago.

Staring out into the woods, after my mother left, disappearing into the forest beyond my hut, and into the hidden passageways that would lead her back to her castle, my vacant eyes didn't see the wolf outside the windows; my ears didn't hear the question in his cries.

I no longer saw what I had once seen, or worried over what I'd once heard. All I could think about now was the answers in my mind, a way to end my mother's pain and erase all traces of King Mardavian, and his abuse of her.

I guess even the worst of creatures can feel love for something…someone, I thought with ancient bitterness. *No matter how twisted.*

It can't take away from the actions. It doesn't take away the consequences. Justice is like death—it cannot be stopped, and it is an inevitability. I may be an immortal, but death shall someday come for us all, as we reap the rewards or punishments of our lives. I am the balancer. I shall be the redeemer of my mother's suffering.

Inhaling the heavy scent of heather and lavender in the air, I savored the sweet taste of the wetness on my tongue from a recent rainfall. I savored the scent of the amber and jasmine of my mother. I savored the memory of her embrace, and her love. I savored the moment of love I had waited for, for so long.

Shuddering with the knowledge that King Mardavian, my sworn enemy, was also my father, my softened heart turned colder and harder than it had been before, when I thought of him. I turned away from the window, and walked to the fire, to sit and brood by the flames over my feelings, and the horror of the ugly truth.

~ *** ~

Chapter Seven
All the Scattered Pieces Whole

I wasn't sure I would ever be the same. Perhaps being the same wasn't the purpose of this anyway. Moving on for us might mean accepting the changes within, and trying to ensure that the changes were for the better. Moving forward might mean change, transformation.

Still, it took me by surprise just how much I missed Jonlin's calming presence, and the absence of Varawynn was like an abscess on my heart, festering and rotting my soul. Like a slow poison, it was slowly killing me to live without her.

I was realizing in her death, just how much I loved and needed her. Memories and visions of her were always on the surface of my consciousness, as if I were the ocean and she was the surface, always at the top of my mind...with her beautiful curly black hair, her glamorous green eyes that had an uncanny way of looking into my soul. The possibility of seeing her again is what drove me on so insistently, to find Shadonai.

I remembered the way the Celtic priestess looked when she'd come into my tent, the only time we had kissed. The dawning sun had been like a halo around the outline of her torso and hair, as she'd opened the flap to my tent. I remembered the feel of her skin on my hands, soft as rose petals. The tears she'd cried were like liquid diamonds, and just as precious.

How could Alondria ever come to accept Jonlin was truly gone, and there was no hope of reviving him? At least I harbored some crazy, far-fetched hope we'd be able to resurrect Varawynn, to bring her ashes back to life.

As far-fetched as the idea might be, it spurred me on and up each morning, and like a man possessed, I was determined to find Shadonai, and see if it was possible for such a thing as bringing the dead back to life.

~ *** ~

"We don't have all the time in the world to save Varawynn," I warned them, ruffling my feathers, and shaking my head. "We have only one week more before the allotted time to bring about her rebirth." Winter was now on the horizon. Months had passed since Jonlin's death. The November air had put a bitter chill in the air.

"Why didn't you tell us that?" Eliju barked, instantly losing his cool.

"Because it was right to take Jonlin back to his homeland, and certain things needed to happen first."

"What things?"

"Your group needed to be disbanded. This wasn't all about you either. Shadonai needed certain things to happen too."

"So, do you know where she is or not?" demanded Eliju impatiently. "As you just said, 'we have only one week more before the allotted time.'" The loss of Jonlin and Varawynn, had put an edge of sarcasm in the Chosen One. Just as bitterness hung on the words and expressions of Alondria.

"I already told you I know where her hut is," I cooed back testily, ruffling my feathers. "In order to prepare our spirits for this time, we must rest our flesh and fast before we find her. There a time for everything. Everything has a season under the sun. You need not fear or doubt, Eliju. Shadonai is very near. Trust me."

"As long as we get there before the time is up, I don't care if I'm hungry when we get there. We just need to hurry," said Eliju. "Are you SURE then, that we will be able resurrect her?"

"Nothing is ever certain," I answered the rash young man sagely. "But worry and doubt make the possibility even less so."

The odd motley crew grew closer to the edge of the Isle of Skye. The cursed black unicorn, the illustrious sea elf, the ancient Shaman, the simple shepherd, the scholar Pharean, raised by the famous philosopher, Ruminous, and descendent of the Essenes, the mystical royal line of the Jews, and Aldoran, the twin prince of Alondria, descendent of the muses were almost there. The edge of the waters was against the horizon. By sunset they would gather on the ferry that would help them cross over, onto the enchanted island of the Isle of Skye, isolated and far removed from the madding crowds.

~ *** ~

Meanwhile, Shadonai and the wizard Vorseth, brewed hot mint tea in a kettle on the hearth of the small hut she was raised in and had lived in all her life. They were in preparation too. In the corner of the open room where her small kitchen and living room were, she'd constructed an altar where herbs lined the box and Aengus' thigh bone lay like a prize across the top of the silver silk sheet.

"They'll be here soon, my dear," Vorseth assured her from the table in the center of the room. "The time has come." He fingered the small silver pouch in his pocket, to reassure himself it was still there.

Caressing Aengus' thigh bone, Shadonai merely nodded. Realizing Vorseth had been right all along, a peace and serenity had entered her spirit.

She recalled a particularly stormy emotional season over a year ago, when Vorseth had told her that when the time came, she would not have to go looking for them—they'd find her. Trust in him had since been redeemed, and she entrusted her life to him now. Unwittingly, she'd been groomed all her life for this one moment. It was her birthday—two thousand years hence, on November 16th, the Shadow of God had been born. Tonight, something special would occur in honor of it.

That night the long-awaited troupe was led by an owl to her door. It was meant to be. It was written in the stars when the stars were first woven in the sky by the creator's hands. It was discerned by the mind of Vorseth, the visionary who'd brought down into words, the knowledge of the stars.

Their fates were penned with the golden Elven blood by the hands of this ancient prophet. He was the puppeteer who had orchestrated this moment thousands of years before. Now a part of this ancient Prophecy was about to be fulfilled.

~ ~ ~

The small, but clean home felt oddly familiar to Eliju. The way the grey stones ran a spiral pathway up to the door. The fields of heather around the hut held the same scent from his own mother's home. For a moment the smell caught him so off-guard, and hit him so deep in his gut, he nearly lost his footing.

Clutching Varawynn's ashes protectively in the box he'd carved for Alondria tightly in his sweaty palms, he prayed unceasingly that this sorceress would be given a power unto God Himself, to resurrect this girl he loved.

Barely able to function or mumble a few monosyllables under his breath for days, all he could think about was seeing Varawynn again, and all he could do was try to have faith she'd be able to come back to life, back to him. His mind and heart were set on seeing her again, and in spite of his best intentions—his hopes were up. He could not hold back his excitement.

Wandering Wolfe, however, had other things on his mind. While the idea and hope of Varawynn coming back to life cheered and thrilled him; being with Shadonai again, apart from his quest, caused such emotion in him, he was barely able to function with the nervous joy and anticipation turning his stomach to butterflies. Wandering Wolfe was not used to such emotion, and it overwhelmed him. He didn't know how to handle himself.

Silvandrin, being less attached to Varawynn, and thereby more objective, wondered if Varawynn was resurrected, if she would be the same—and what the cost would be to Shadonai. As the time drew near, Aldoran too felt wary and nervous about the spiritual implications of such a resurrection. His hopes were beginning to turn into an ominous foreboding, for Necromancy was the darkest of dark magic.

As the group walked up the steps leading into the sorceress' home, they knocked on the door. Shadonai opened the door quickly, and ushered them in. Wandering Wolfe and his daughter locked eyes. This was no fantasy—this was reality. This was real. Shadonai had been alive all this time, all these many years: and Wandering Wolfe was reunited with the daughter he thought he'd lost.

As he looked upon her, drinking her in like a dehydrated man drinks water after being without it for weeks in the desert, his eyes welled up with tears. A soft shadow swept across Shadonai's flinty grey eyes.

Like the first soft rays of the dawn, they were the first rays of genuine light and love that'd ever crossed her features. Without question, it was clear Wandering Wolfe loved her and believed in her goodness, unlike

Vorseth who'd always taken her obedience and questionable motives for a given.

In spite of Wandering Wolfe's age and experience, there was something in him that still believed in giving the benefit of the doubt to all people. He still believed in the power of love conquering all, and being the redemption of humanity.

Shadonai found herself unexpectedly drawn to his belief in the basic goodness of human nature, as something she'd never before encountered—and the idealism and strength of character it requires to live up to those ideals.

His faith was not born from naivety. His faith came from experience, and it was tinged with the burning fires of many hurts, much death, and betrayals. As well as bearing witness to many surprising transformations from people that the world had written off as lost causes. His faith had been tempered by a refining fire, into an unshakable belief that anyone can be redeemed, if they choose. When faith is chosen after pain and suffering, it is a faith that contains the power to manifest miracles. Wandering Wolfe's soul contained that special kind of miraculous faith.

"We've come to see if you can...that is, if you have the power to resurrect this girl. That is, a member of the group of fourteen," Eliju stammered.

Shadonai broke eye contact with Wandering Wolfe. She looked as if she were just emerging from a reverie. The soft silver light left her eyes and her expression hardened, turning back into a dull grey. "So, you've come because you want my help."

"We've come because we need your help, yes," confirmed Wandering Wolfe, still staring into her eyes. "But you know I would have come for you anyway."

She met his eyes again and glowered. "What have you of her?" Shadonai demanded.

"We have her ashes, and I have a lock of her hair she gave to me before—well before she was burned," whispered Eliju breathlessly.

"This is your destiny," said Vorseth, stepping out from the shadows, to stand before them in front of the burning hearth.

"Vorseth!" Wandering Wolfe exclaimed. "*You!? You are alive too?*"

"Yes, Ar-Wandering Wolfe. It is I."

"You've been alive this whole time!"

"Yes."

"I can't believe it! How could so many of us be alive from so long ago?"

"Believe it, Wandering Wolfe. Many of those from the beginning of time walk the earth longer than the new souls birthed on this ancient earth, after the Fall."

Wandering Wolfe shook his head. "Eliju— everyone—this is the prophet who wrote the Prophecy. This is the man who tutored me so long ago, who I had believed was long dead." The group stared at the wizard, wide-eyed and astonished.

Shadonai looked sullen before them. "It seems as if you didn't know a lot of people were still alive, Wandering Wolfe, and you don't know a great many things."

"Yes, I suppose you are right, my daughter. But I can't deal with Vorseth, and everything I didn't know right now. We just need to know if you can you do this. We do not have much time left to us to try bringing this girl back to life. Can you resurrect this Celtic Priestess?" Wandering Wolfe asked directly, swimming in the pools of his daughter's pearly grey eyes.

"Yes, I *can,* but I don't know if I *shall* do it—yet."

"Please," Eliju's voice was full of pain. "We cannot go on without her. *I* cannot go on without her." It was his eyes...his blue green eyes that she suddenly realized were the eyes that had haunted her all her life. His eyes asked of her all that she had to give.

"Shadonai, I know it is in your power to do this, and I know it is within your heart to help us," Eliju said.

"Who are we kidding?" Aldoran interjected. "We're wasting our time with this black witch! Who is *she* to bring Varawynn back to life? She isn't God, and this isn't right!" All his hope and optimism were lost in the fear of what this dark magic would do to them, to Varawynn.

"Varawynn?" Shadonai's grey eyes caught the light once more, turning silver.

"Yes, that's the name of the girl we want you save, Shadonai," said Wandering Wolfe.

"Varawynn...please help Varawynn!" was Eliju's heart's cry.

"Varawynn...is this the same girl who killed King Mardavian?"

Wandering Wolfe's eyes widened with surprise. "Yes. How did you know?"

"A little birdie told me," Shadonai laughed ironically. "And the answer then is yes—I shall help you to bring this girl—this sorceress who killed King Mardavian—back to life."

At last she surrendered the struggle of self, and nodded at Eliju. "Her ashes and hair will suffice. I shall perform the ceremony now."

Spontaneously, Eliju rushed to her, picking her up and swinging her around the room in deliriously happy exultation. Wandering Wolfe looked pleased—Shadonai looked as ruffled as an owl awakened unexpectedly from its slumber.

Watching in awe as Shadonai set up the black cauldron and objects, her back as straight and stiff as a feline cat, Eliju was both excited and terrified by the proceedings. Her ritualistic way of setting things up, bore an eerie resemblance to the ritualistic ways of his religion. Meanwhile, Aldoran's conscience was tormenting him.

"Wait!" Sweat was pouring down Aldoran's face. "Are we sure this is right?" he asked again.

"Aldoran," Illumina warned. "Please just let it be."

"I'm scared, Illumina. Please let me voice my concern...I believe in magic, and that it can be bad or good depending on the intentions of the person using it, and if the petition to the source of that power comes from heaven or hell, for good or for evil." He paused. He was making some fair points Eliju thought.

"But Necromancy...the dark magic of death...which holds the ability of bringing the dead back to life. *Is this right?* Isn't the very nature of Necromancy evil? Will Varawynn be the same if we bring her back? Will she even still be...human? Jesus Christ came back from the dead...but should *we* try to bring the dead back to life ourselves? Even if we *could*— *should we try?* Isn't Necromancy—without exception—a dark art whose source of power is the Devil himself?" Aldoran whispered his last question.

"Aldoran, Mordorn said it was in the Prophecy," Pharean countered.

"But again, does that make it *right?*"

"You raise some good concerns, Aldoran," said Wandering Wolfe. "Let's look at intent. Shadonai has nothing to gain. Varawynn has done nothing wrong to deserve death. The Prophecy says her fate is to be resurrected."

"I am a descendent of Essenes, the mystic Jewish sect that taught Jesus to levitate and make wine out of water... I understand how to use the properties of energy to multiply," Aldoran said. "I understand how the stars and planets guide us, and act as a tool to understand one another. But this..."

Pharean countered, "There is nothing to fear in magic. Magic is just what we call things above the physical realm where we live. The manifestation of faith is miracles, a form of magic. You know that, Aldoran. What you said is right. I agree that normally Necromancy is a dark art. I also think there are exceptions. I'm sure most doctors could tell you about cases where someone they thought was dead suddenly sprang back to life. Look at Jesus Christ."

"I think we have to try," Elliju added. "For Varawynn's sake, don't we at least have to try? If she comes back as something sinister, as less than herself, we'll deal with it then. But in this moment, I want to allow Shadonai to try and bring her back to us. Regardless of what the Prophecy says, we need her, *I* need her." The determination in Eliju's voice, and in Pharean's logical words, alleviated most of Aldoran's worries, but only in part.

"It's going to be okay," Pharean's soft voice was soothing, like aloe on an open wound. "I really believe this is all going to work out for the best, and Varawynn is going to come back to us, good as new."

"I believe that too," Eliju proclaimed, with complete confidence.

Aldoran turned to face the Shaman. "And you, Wandering Wolfe? Do you believe that too?"

"I believe it too," he said, but there were worry lines crinkling in the corners of his eyes. Aldoran stared into Wandering Wolfe's eyes carefully. Then he closed his eyes and felt; searching inside himself for the answers, intuitively seeking, and asking himself the hard questions.

"We should ask *him*," said Silvandrin, which a nod to Vorseth. "The warlock who wrote the Prophecy himself."

Vorseth stood still before them, so still it was as if he were made of stone. A cutting shroud fell over them. The air felt colder, thinner somehow. "This is meant to be," he declared. "Varawynn shall come back just as she was. But the time is now. It must be tonight. By morning's light is shall be too late."

It seemed like days passed in the heavy silence, until the group as one nodded their assent. They were in agreement. Vorseth had pushed them over the edge. They were going to take the plunge, and hope it wasn't bait.

"May I continue then?" asked Shadonai, her hand half-raised to put a black candle etched with silver upon the hearth.

"Please continue," nodded Wandering Wolfe. Vorseth moved beside Shadonai to help her. A significant look passed from Shadonai to Vorseth, and then over to Wandering Wolfe.

It disconcerted the Shaman the way Vorseth sent her a glare, as if warning her to keep quiet about something, something in regards to him. He was worried now. Worried about Varawynn yes, but worried too about the ancient prophet who had first told him about the Prophecy...worried that Vorseth had been alive this whole time, and what that meant for the group.

How long had the wizard known his daughter was alive? Or had he always known? He was the one, after all, who was supposed to have killed her. Who was Vorseth to have lived this long? Who was *he*, Wandering Wolfe, to have lived this long? Not for the first time, Wandering Wolfe considered how slowly he had aged and how long he had lived. *How?*

Looking at the wizard, he remembered so much of his teachings. It was blatantly evident that there was still so much he didn't know—even about himself, and his origins. For the first time, he doubted his own ability to lead the group, but this was not the time to consider stepping down as their guide.

Setting aside his fears, he took courage, not that the end would justify by the means, but that their loving intentions would bring back their Varawynn, perfect and whole, and that nothing dark would come through his daughter that night. Putting his faith in his own blood pulsing through her body, he believed that something beautiful would come of this, like burning embers fanned back into flames.

He believed that Varawynn and Eliju were meant for each other, just as he was meant to be Shadonai's father. This was their second chance, and by God, and for God, and in the name of God, he was taking it.

The Shaman's warm brown eyes wandered to meet his daughter's clear grey eyes. In the exchange, was a passing of the understanding of souls. The Shaman's eyes filled with tears. The sorceress' eyes hardened like stone. Now he understood: his daughter was born and protected by Vorseth for just this moment. His daughter had been saved at birth to be a sacrifice on this night, on the night of her birth two thousand years ago.

Hours passed into the dark of night as Shadonai worked on potions, and setting up the cauldron, altar and hearth. Finally, she made the last finishing touches on the words in her spell. From the altar, Shadonai brought out a black velvet pouch. Pulling from the dark folds, a long thigh bone, she murmured, "This is the thigh bone of Aengus, Varawynn's brother."

"So, you're the sorceress who killed him?" Eliju demanded, at once relieved that it hadn't been Darlillyth, and repulsed to use the bones of Varawynn's murdered brother to bring her back to life.

Glaring hard at Eliju she answered, "Yes, you foolish boy, it was I who killed her insipid brother, and it is needed now in order to save your precious

Varawynn. Some people were born to die and be used in their death so that others might live. Just as some were born to suffer, and a few lucky chosen ones were born to live a charmed life, filled with much happiness."

Glaring fiercely back at her, Eliju said, "And how do we know we can trust you now? How do we know you haven't lured us here to kill us, like you did Aengus?"

Wandering Wolfe put a restraining hand on Eliju's shoulder. "We aren't trying to put you on trial here, Shadonai."

"Oh, aren't we?" Aldoran chimed in. "The end doesn't justify the means. Are we to believe she killed Aengus in preparation of this moment? She's a murderer and the daughter of Darlillyth, our deadliest enemy—the very one who killed Varawynn!"

Pharean reached up to Aldoran's shoulder, pulling him down to her level, "Be silent, be still," she whispered in his ear. Her breath in his ear sent shivers down his spine.

"And the daughter of your teacher as well," the Shaman said mildly. With a pointed look at his daughter, he added, "Who loved her before she was born, and loved her when he believed her to be dead, and will continue to love her no matter if she betrays us or helps us. Oh my dear, how I hope you will help us, Shadonai!"

She narrowed her eyes at Wandering Wolfe. "I told you I *could* and *would* help you, did I not?"

"Are you sure you know what you're doing?" Eliju worried.

"Silence now!" Shadonai boomed. "Let me do my work in peace. You may watch, but keep your silence. She's already dead, so what more harm can I do her? Hence, it's worth a try, but I need to concentrate. Let me focus on this ceremony in calm and quiet. Necromancy is no light matter."

"Nor is it much white magic," Aldoran mumbled under his breath.

"Silence *you!*" she barked, as she stretched out her arm and pointed her hand at his mouth, wherein strands of seaweed wound themselves around his face so that he couldn't speak. "I'm quite tired of your meddling. I warn you now, I will bind and tie you all up if you won't let me do this work without interference!"

Eliju would have liked to have made a snide remark about her "work," but he held his tongue, not wanting to wind up like Aldoran. Ultimately, she was right. Varawynn had been reduced to a pile of ashes. What more harm could be done to her? She was already dead after all. What more did they have to lose? Besides that, there wasn't much time left before Varawynn would remain a pile of ashes forever, without any hope for resurrection at all…

The dark sorceress worked carefully, meticulously, and with the mysterious movements of ancient arcane rites. She built a fire in the pit of her yard. Filling the cauldron upon the fire with potions with labels like "toad's eyes," "frog's feet," and "fairy dust," until at last the cauldron was filled.

Making strangely graceful movements with her hands, the signs and symbols she made were incomprehensible to the innocent young man's eyes. Her spell casting looked like a dance. Then at last she threw the bone of Aengus into the fire. Eliju held tightly to the multi-jeweled box he'd made for Alondria for Yom Kippur the year before, which was now filled with Varawynn's ashes.

Shadonai made a motion for the special box Eliju had carved for Alondria. Eliju hesitated once more. Necromancy was so dark. If this were successful how would Varawynn feel about them using her brother's thigh bone to bring her back to life?

This was the moment of truth. At last Eliju handed her the box, and the strand of dark curly hair he kept in his chest pocket, close to his heart. Any Varawynn, even an altered Varawynn, was better than none at all he decided.

Shadonai took the items the boy handed her, and with a great many spiraling counter clock-wise motions, she opened the box, and flung Varawynn's ashes into the brewing cauldron that now moved by itself. It spit and smoked as the ashes dissolved into the fiery cauldron.

"Emuna Emundra Eekor sorpeaRA!" she cried.

The air filled with smoke. With unnaturally swift, fluid motions, she raised her arms high above the cauldron. With her left forearm, she brought down her hands, close to the cauldron's bubbling brew, then with her right hand, she pulled from the pockets of her dark robes, a dagger glinting red with rubies against the cloudy sky.

Plunging the dagger onto her wrist, she bled into the spiraling brew, screaming wildly into the wind, "Bloodredra bloodredra shadownai tu for asendROR!"

The ashes rose from the cauldron into the musky sky, but after all these dramatic displays, the bubbling cauldron only spit back at her, as if in defiance to her will. She glared at her own concoction.

"What now?" she turned to her mentor, Vorseth. "What did I do wrong?"

"Nothing my dear," he whispered. "You simply lacked all the ingredients."

Then with a wide, dramatic flourish, he pulled from the folds of his robes, a hidden pouch. The group as one, gasped.

He opened the pouch, and declared, "This is a hair from King Mardavian's head. I took it after he had been killed by this Celtic Priestess. May his hair now bring back his murderer to life."

He took out the hair, and dropped it into the swirling, spitting brew in the churning cauldron. There was a colorful explosion from the cauldron as the hair hit the water, filling the air with a light scent of sandalwood.

Vorseth paused for dramatic effect before continuing. "And I think now it's time to reveal to the group just who stole Eleethion's horn so long ago. You didn't know it at the time, my dear, but the horn was to be used at this precise moment—to resurrect the Celtic priestess. In an ironic twist of fate, this horn of pure gold shall ensure that her humanity is intact when we bring her back to life."

Shadonai nodded, and the group watched in silence and trepidation as she went to her bookshelf. There was a secret space hidden behind three books she moved just so. There was a small safe she opened with a combination of six numbers. She took out something that was wrapped in silver fabric. Slowly, she unwrapped it to reveal the bright, glittering, magical horn that was taken from the unicorn Eleethion so long ago.

Then Celestria flew before them, out of nowhere, commanding their attention. "How in the fields of heather did you find us?" Shadonai gasped, as she began to shoo it away.

"Is that Celestria?" asked Pharean. "She looks so different."

The group stared at her, until Vorseth broke the silence. "She has transformed from the Bird of Eden, into the Phoenix, the bird of transformation and resurrection. She has come for Varawynn."

"What is a Phoenix?" Eliju asked.

Vorseth murmured, "You shall soon see. It is part of the Prophecy," and nodded to the sorceress.

"So, there is more," Shadonai whispered, staring at the Phoenix, the Bird of Eden had become. "Ashes to ashes, dust to dust, the ashes of an ancestor, and the ashes of the phoenix, shall bring the priestess back to life, but it shall take a little more time."

They watched as the bird built an aromatic nest of cinnamon twigs and myrrh. Then the bird clapped its wings together just once, and the group watched in horror as the bird took flame, burning itself to ashes above the spitting cauldron.

Although Celestria was the first Phoenix, the history she had altered when she'd killed Eve was now a part of history, which had turned into a legend over time. So Shadonai knew that the bird's ashes could help bring the priestess back to life. For sometimes the very same object used to cause death, can also be used to create life.

The group, who didn't know the story of Eve and the Phoenix, was shocked and dismayed, now afraid they had lost another member of their group. Shadonai laughed to herself, as she took a handful of Celestria's ashes, and threw them into the cauldron. Then she held up the golden horn, and with a dramatic flourish, threw it too into the bubbling cauldron.

A burst of light and fire and flames sprung up on the surface of the bubbling water. The flames licked the air, as slowly a body emerged. The group, as one, gasped and moved backwards. Through the fire, and *from* the smoke, and the flames, a form took shape, rising into the air thick with magic. The sorceress rose her hands once more and chanted:

> *"Bring back from death this girl,*
> *Bring flesh from smoke and shadows,*
> *Fill this cauldron with bones made whole,*
> *On this predestined night,*

We call the raven girl's ashes, to rise to life."

With the last words of the spell, Shadonai dropped the strand of Varawynn's dark hair into the concoction. From the fog and smoke, in ashes she rose, continuing to take shape and solidify into flesh. As the form rose, the details of Varawynn's face slowly appeared.

The gentle poutiness of her full lips, the long dark lashes of her emerald green eyes, the shade of her dark hair and the very fibers of its texture. Her hair looked so very much the same, Eliju longed to reach out his hands and caress her silken tresses.

Now fully emerged, they could see that her leg was no longer twisted back. Floating up above them and out towards them, gradually, from ten feet above them, she wafted back down to earth like a feather.

After several minutes, Varawynn moved a few feet on the ground, and in awe, she realized that she was no longer lame. The raven birth mark was still upon her right thigh, but now the birthmark depicted a flying raven with an open mouth, as if it were singing, to signify that the priestess had found her voice at last.

"Relaseo amondo, doDRA soHEDO!" Shadonai shouted, hurling her words toward Varawynn like an insult.

From the raven birthmark, her brother Aengus flew as a raven from her leg. The magic of the Celts, and their father, and the Priestess Dagda, their mother, lived on in their children. As Varawynn was brought back to life, from the bones and ashes of her brother, Aengus— so he too was brought to life, as a bird from the raven birthmark on her leg. From his thigh bone, her leg was healed, and she was made whole. She would never limp or use her cane again.

As the raven brother bird flew inside the hut and out, and in and out again, Wandering Wolfe stared at

Varawynn, a mix of hopefulness and trepidation waging war behind his eyes. Aengus kept flying outside, up and back, inside and around them. "Aengus!" Varawynn cried, choking on a sob. Her raven brother made cawing bird cries like a song, a haunting bird's cry of comfort for his sister. She sang with him, along with the cawing melody...

"We are alive and free.
Resurrected as whole are we.
From your thigh bone
Was I brought back to life

And from my thigh bone
You emerged as the raven
Of my birthmark,
Free to live and free to fly."

Varawynn is alive! Eliju's psyche screamed inside his skull. The group watched everything that was happening in awe-struck wonder. To hear her voice again...he felt as if he had died and gone to heaven.

Varawynn's body felt different. She'd never walked normally, and it felt strange for her left leg to work as easily as the right leg. The healing of her leg was an unexpected blessing, but something also felt different deep down inside.

Something sinister plagued her mind and heart. That is, she *was* fully human...*wasn't* she? She didn't feel bad or evil, but she felt stronger, more powerful perhaps? She wasn't sure what it was that was making her feel different, and it scared her.

Being able to recall the other world was disconcerting. She felt she'd not been judged, but held in an in-between, a waiting room, as if God had intended her resurrection. It *had* been in the Prophecy...and being dead for the past three months, and now having come back alive, able to breathe and think again, was disconcerting in and of itself.

From her first gasping breath back into the world on earth, she remembered what had happened right before she died. The pain of knowing that Eliju had been with Darlillyth during his captivity, and she was the one he loved, came flooding back to her, as fresh as if it had happened a second ago.

The world of the Beyond was as close to her as her breath; closer than her breath. Her life in death had been as real as this, and if Eliju couldn't love her back as much as she loved him, she wished she'd have stayed in the in-between, or gone on to whatever it was that existed in the afterlife, whether for judgment or paradise.

She'd studied there; studied about the water. Always fascinated by the Isle of Apples, the waters had soothed her growing up, and they'd soothed her in the in-between. She'd always both admired and envied Ileona, not just for her status in their community, but for being the Lady of the Lake, able to return to live in the waters at will. Indeed, the sea held its own hidden mysteries, and for some reason she longed now more than she ever had before, to uncover its secrets.

Varawynn's guilt over her brother's death, and the use of his thigh, which had helped to bring her back to life, dissolved as she saw him fly. He was so happy. Happier than he had ever been in life.

This was predestined. So many strange things had been foretold by the Prophecy. It was sometimes hard to make sense of life when everything seemed predestined. Sometimes things happened she couldn't explain—like her brother's murder. Now she understood there'd been a reason for that too.

Could there be a reason Eliju couldn't be with her? *No.* That was impossible. That idea was too much for her. People who loved each other should be together, but that didn't mean they always were.

Three days and nights passed. By the morning light, at sunrise, Celestria herself, as the phoenix, was resurrected. Her plumage of yellow, orange, red, and royal purple seemed more vibrant than before. Her eyes of sapphire seemed to shimmer with an otherworldly light.

We all knew that the phoenix's ashes, from its fiery death, had helped to stoke the embers of Varawynn's ashes back to flame, back to life. Just as the ashes from the bones of Varawynn's brother, who had been murdered, were used to bring the Priestess back without her lame leg, whole, and in perfect form.

Yet it still remained to be seen, if the powerful ashes of the phoenix that lay at the heart of Varawynn's spark of life, would transform the girl into more than she was once was, and if she now would be counted among the elite group of immortals...

~ *** ~

Chapter Eight
The Heart of Dark Magic

After the group left Shadonai's cabin, it was just her and I alone in the small abode, as it had been so many times through the centuries. "It was kind of you to protect me as a baby, Vorseth. I believe you meant well. I really do. But you should have let me die."

"Whatever are you speaking of mistress?"

"I am an abomination!"

"Shadonai…"

"The Shadow of God is what I am. I am the darkness cast by the shadow of a twisted love. I could never enter into the light. Now I shall never have the chance…"

"Shadonai…"

"The cast is set. God's will be done!"

"So, you know?"

"The ashes…the shadow…the bones…aren't they all the same thing? They're symbolic remnants of something once alive now dead—and you knew all along the price of bringing Varawynn back to life, didn't you, Vorseth?"

I merely glanced over at her, poker-faced, but my insides were churning. "When will it happen, Vorseth?" How much time do I have left?" There was no malice in her tone, which made me feel worse.

"Not much, mistress," at last I admitted.

"And you knew this was my fate all along?"

"Indeed," I finally consented, speaking honestly. I owed her that much.

"How long did you know?"

"Since the beginning—since your birth; before then, even." Shadonai shook her head, feeling foolish and blind-sighted. "Do I have time to speak to Wandering Wolfe and my mother before the end?"

I did not usually allow my emotions to push through to the surface, but this was the end. Perhaps just now, when I was losing my pupil, I could allow the guilt of her existence to enter my mind and heart. After all, she was my granddaughter. "You only have time to say goodbye to one of them."

Inhaling deeply, her eyes filled with tears. Her own emotion took me by surprise. She hadn't even cried when Elijah and Ruth had been killed. She had only been angry.

"I was not expecting this sadness and remorse from you—it almost makes it regrettable you have such a limited amount of time left. Our emotions, though they make life more difficult, reveal our humanity. Who shall you choose to spend the last of your time with here on earth, my child?"

"Why—how is it going happen?" she asked, avoiding my question.

"Your bones shall disintegrate over a period of twenty-four hours. By this time tomorrow, you shall be in ashes." She shuddered.

"Now who do you choose to spend your last day on earth with? Shall it be your mother—or your father?"

"Neither, for I have seen enough of them. The last thing I want is a bitter or sorrowful parting when I meet life's end."

"Then who do you want to spend your last day with?"

"Silvandrin—the unicorn who spared my life long ago, when I killed Eleethion, and took his horn."

I looked at her with calculating eyes, "An interesting choice."

"Why?"

"It's not very human."

"And I'm not very human, am I?" she countered back bitterly. "I'm not exactly normal having two fathers—one of which is also my uncle. Now shall I get to see Silvandrin, or should I sit at my window staring out into a world I never got to be a part of, in a life I've never gotten to live, as I was born and groomed for death on my last day, like I've done on every other?"

"I shall get Silvandrin and bring him to you right now," I replied calmly, though inside my stomach felt more nauseous than ever.

"Thank you."

I was not known to admit fault or express my feelings, but in these last moments, I too fought with the emotions in my heart. "I'm sorry, Shadonai."

"Are you? Wasn't this your plan? Wasn't this a part of your precious Prophecy? Wasn't I just saved by you as an infant to die for Varawynn in this moment? Have I not been just a pawn in the chess game of our lives?"

"It wasn't how I would have wanted it."

"Isn't it? Are you not the prophet who composed this prolific Prophecy, which seems to govern our every move?"

"Yes, mistress, but there is more to it than that."

"What more?"

"I wrote the Prophecy from a vision, you know that. I had no control over what I saw, what I wrote. I tapped into the Akashic Records, into the stars themselves, to write this Prophecy. So I do believe your sacrifice is part of a plan, a plan bigger than you, than me, than any us. It's bigger even than I, who foresaw so much and wrote down the Prophecy from a divine revelation, can conceive of. It is no more up to me who lives in abundance, and who dies as a mere babe—than it is in the control of anyone else."

"So now you're saying you weren't responsible for the other little baby you killed in my place?"

"All of this was predestined."

"I wonder about you sometimes, Vorseth. I wonder why it is I feel like you are still hiding things from me, and on the eve of my death no less."

"Only those who need to know the truth, who are a part of the truth, shall know it. There are many things we—you—don't ever need to know. Some mysteries even I shall never know."

"I would like to know the truth about myself at least, Vorseth. I would like to understand my own part in the Prophecy before I die. I am glad to die. It is justice. I only wish that I could have been given the gift of knowledge, the gift of understanding I have sought my whole life."

"You may yet learn what you want to know. I shall work on your behalf for this to come to pass," Vorseth promised her. "I'm going to bring you Silvandrin now."

"Thank you, Vorseth," she murmured, moving like a shadow to her well-worn window seat, and staring out into the forest.

She almost thought she heard the old warlock whisper, "I love you," before he turned to go, but she couldn't be sure, for he had never uttered those words to her before.

The wolf was not there tonight, and the loss of his howling, which had always seemed like a warning, or a question, made her feel more alone than the imminent moment of her death. She leaned her head up against the cold window pane, and let a few lonely tears silently fall.

~ ~ ~

It took only half an hour to bring the blackened unicorn back to Shadonai's door. "Shadonai...I knew there was a reason I kept you alive."

"You protected me, so I could later save your Varawynn. And because I saved her I shall die."

Silvandrin's eyes were like orbs of the moon, glowing luminescent like pearls. "I am so sorry."

"And I am so sorry about what happened to you— your blackened mane. You kept me alive when I killed the unicorn Eleethion. Thank you. I never had the chance to thank you."

"You are very welcome."

"And then I killed Varawynn's brother, and my mother killed Varawynn, and I used her brother's bone to resurrect her, and now I have to die to save her. Why Silvandrin? Can you tell me why my mother killed Varawynn?"

"I think it is because she loves Eliju."

"She loves him?"

"I believe so, yes."

"How do you know?"

"Sometimes there's a fine line between love and hate. Sometimes where there's deep love, deep hatred and jealousy make controlling people feel out-of-control. When love finally reaches them, this lack of control causes them to act out because they fear that love weakens them. Killing Varawynn took out Darlillyth's competition, and I think she believes it will make Eliju stop loving her, so she can stop loving him. Varawynn being alive shall be a secret weapon for us now—against your mother."

"I don't want to be used to hurt my mother. Do you understand? She's been hurt enough. I don't want Varawynn, or my death, to be used to hurt anyone."

"I understand."

"You once had compassion for me when I'd done nothing to deserve it. I am asking you to do the same for my mother now.

"I shall."

"Silvandrin—"

"Yes?"

"What else can you tell me about my mother and father?"

"I understand you wanting to know—but are you sure you want an answer to that right now, right before—"

"I die? Yes, I want to know right now. I've waited all my life to know about my parents and my blood family, and you know them both. Though I know you've seen my mother at her worst, I want to know about her."

Silvandrin paused, before his thoughtful response. "I am more objective in this matter than Wandering Wolfe, and I know much of what he knows in regards to her. I know there is pure evil in the world—I have looked directly into the eyes of it, and I can tell you that King Mardavian was evil. Your mother has done some cruel, unspeakable things...I do not believe they come from a place of true evil. I believe they come from a place of deep pain."

Silvandrin shook his mane and continued. "I realize that is no excuse for what she did, nor does it take away the repercussions, or the consequences. I also know you were the sorceress who killed Varawynn's brother, but I do not believe you are truly evil either. I believe you have been manipulated, and the truth has become twisted in your mind."

"I see not in color, but in shades of grey. There is no question some of your actions, as well as your mother's actions, have been morally irreprehensible. Yet I do not believe you did these things with the express desire to hurt—but for the power to further your agenda, stemming from an intense feeling of being out-of-control."

"You're right. It's easier than the pure in heart may suspect to step-by-step, inch-by-inch your way into corruption and compromise. But my mother..."

"You are very like each other. So, the questions you have about her can in part be answered by asking yourself the same questions."

"Better now than never."

"Better now than in the afterlife."

"Do you believe in an afterlife, Silvandrin?"

"I believe in THE afterlife. I believe that all of our actions, both good and bad, shall have an accounting for. I believe there shall come a day of reckoning, of justice for us all. It is inevitable." "I believe that too," said Shandonai.

The cursed black unicorn smiled at her sadly. "You resurrected Varawynn out of love, and nothing is wasted if done from love."

"Even those who throw their pearls to swine?"

"Do not pearls have an intrinsic worth, whether or not the recipient knows of their worth? Apart from their worth in money or trade, is there not an intrinsic value in their beauty, and the act of love in sharing them?"

"Just as—"

"Just as there has been intrinsic value in your own life, Shadonai, and in your mother's life. So, forgive her trespasses, and forgive yourself. In this way, God's will is done on earth, as it is in heaven."

"Thank you, Silvandrin. You have said enough to give me some hope."

"Safe travels now, my friend, on your journey into the afterlife, Shadonai. It is the most important journey of your life—the path into your death, where eternity awaits."

A shadow fell across her face, as shadows fell upon the walls and floors of the room. A heavy sadness entered in, as Silvandrin made to go. Then as the door opened widely into the hut, and Silvandrin stepped out into the dark night sky, Wandering Wolfe stood at the threshold, and entered in.

Unbidden tears filled Shadonai's eyes, as the shadows shifted, letting in some light. "I didn't want you here."

"But I wanted to come. I needed to. I had to say goodbye to my only daughter."

"How did you know?"

"I'd guessed it. Vorseth confirmed it. He came to me and told me to come here, to you."

They went to sit together before the hearth. The hot flickering flames lingered on the warmth of their skin. Shadonai's skin held a grey cast; her weight was falling off her like ice falls off a house in the first warm days of spring. She was diminishing before his very eyes. Vorseth had given her twenty-four hours, but it was only ten hours later, and the end was near.

Holding his newly discovered, and now dying daughter in his arms, Wandering Wolfe rocked and cradled her in his lap. Her closed and her bitter face took on a strange light as she looked at him—the first and only man who had ever truly loved her.

A light passed over her grey eyes, turning them once more to sparkling silver, with a tint of an inner spiritual light her half-father King Mardavian's eyes had never held. Her skin also turned pale and grey.

As she took her last gasping breath, a shadow passed across her face as she died, then her father's hand moved like a shadow over her face, closing her eyes. She died on her mother's birthday, November 17th.

* * *

King Mardavian's curse upon me in the tower when I had been his captive, came to pass in that moment. He'd cursed me to know the way of a woman's body but once, before she was gone. As I held my dying daughter in my arms, his last bitter curse was fulfilled, and another part of the Prophecy came to pass. The first time I held my daughter in my arms, who I loved with all my heart, was also the last.

* * *

He continued to hold and rock her as he cried. "Too short…there wasn't enough time. I had so much more to give, to love…there was so much more…to be shared…I wanted to learn…I want to teach…I wanted to know her, to love her, from the inside out."

The holy spirit of her shadow entered her father's soul. He felt a lifting in his soul. He felt a transformative power shift his perceptions.

He felt no bitterness or regret, he was only thankful in this moment to have met her, grateful she had lived. Grateful for her sacrifice, so that Varawynn could live. Thankful there was still Varawynn, and Eliju, and Shadow Rain, and all the rest, to be loved, and with them, there was so much more to be shared.

~ *** ~

Chapter Nine
Transformations

There she came in the in-between, in the ethers of soul and energy, where there was no time, only eternity. There, a feminine figure awaited her arrival. She had flowing amber hair, and her eyes burned. She was beautiful, and deformed. It was strange to see such a creature at the pearly gates, but she was the one with the answers.

"I want to know the truth," the Shadow of God spoke at the gates to the woman. "I still don't know my origins."

"You were the great-granddaughter in the line of Lilith and the Nephilim, Samyaza."

"And I was chosen to die?"

"Yes, because your line was corrupted. You could not mate and further contaminate the line."

"Because of King Mardavian's blood being my blood?"

"Wandering Wolfe too...he was related to Darlillyth."

"He was, but how?"

"Through me—I am the missing link in the Creation Story. I was floating in the belly of the first woman in the Garden of Eve, the first mate of Adam. She ate of the Tree of Immortality to save me, the unborn baby in her womb."

"The first woman was not Eve?"

"The first female was Lilith, Ra. The first Man was Adam. They were called Amanra or Amenra. Then when Lilith was kicked out of the Garden of Eden, there was Eve, Woman."

"So, who are you?"

"I am from the sole line of the first female and the first male, born Immortal, my name is Arra. My twin was Amen-Ra, and he is the father of Mardavian and your mother, Lilith. I am the grandmother of Darlillyth, and your great grandmother."

"What happened to you?"

"Adam hurt my mother. Later Adam hurt me."

"Why?"

"It's simple. People often fear most those who are different from themselves."

"Adam feared you, even though you were his own daughter?"

"Adam feared me because he could not see how we were alike. He could only see our differences, and that frightened him. Sometimes when people are frightened, they do ugly, violent things. Bullies are not born of power, but of fear and insecurity."

"What did Adam do to you?"

"Adam used the ashes of the Phoenix to permanently scar me. They were the same ashes it had used to kill Eve. He saved the ashes for many years. The first, and only time, I met my father, he used them on me."

The right side of her face, arm, and hand, were all strangely shriveled, and cratered by strange scars. He studied her closely. "So then how did you defeat him?"

"In the end, Adam's cowardice behind his bravado was his undoing. Eve knew how to play into his weaknesses and manipulate him. Lilith was glad to leave him. I understood his flashes of anger, and I got away from him in time to survive it. But not soon enough to not be damaged by it."

"Who is behind all of this? Is it you, Arra? Are you behind this…this Prophecy, or is it Vorseth? It seems to me that someone is orchestrating our actions, manipulating us like Eve manipulated Adam."

"There are many people working for the greater good, but there are those who think the end justifies the means."

"Like being born to die…that is an evil that justifies the means?"

"That is what some believe."

"Like Vorseth?"

Arra hesitated, her long flowing hair blowing in the wind. "Yes," she finally answered. "Like Vorseth."

"And you? What do you believe?"

"I believe that the way to an outcome is worth as much as the outcome itself—that the journey is as important as the destination. We are all important. Your life was important, Shadonai. It mattered. And your death, and how you died, as a sacrifice for the greater good, that matters too."

"How are you different from Adam and Eve?"

"I have the heart of man, so my soul is capable of the same pain and frailties. To have lived all my life with this human heart is difficult without the gift of a human death. In life, there is much pain. I have not the relief of death, for I was born immortal. With time, my love grows deeper, but I have not the knowledge to understand it. I live forever without the ability to understand what I am feeling and experiencing."

"You seem very wise and knowledgeable to me."

"I am not. I have just lived so long as to glean the wisdom from others."

"But not everyone chooses to learn, to grow."

"That I cannot disagree with. Unfortunately, there are always those who stubbornly persist in following the same false path. I am different, because I live as an immortal, transfigured by my father into a monster. Still, I love. More perhaps than those who are part Nephilim. Less perhaps than those who are fully human. My brother Amen-Ra and I stood alone, but Amen-Ra is long gone now."

"What happened to Amen-Ra?"

"He became a twisted version of the innocent brother I once loved and grew up with. He abused his daughter, your mother Darlillyth. For that, she killed him."

"Will she be punished for that? Will I be punished for killing Aengus?"

"Murder is a sin. Sin separates us from the Creator, from the God who is love. In love, there is no sin, there is only light. Acts of love and kindness, words of love, and great sacrifices, dissipate the darkness within and without. What you did to save Varawynn, cleansed and purified your soul on a core level. Nothing can separate us from the love of God. Nothing anyone does, no matter how evil, is without the opportunity for redemption."

She felt something within her lift. "And what happened to my grandmother, my mother's mother?"

"Arlillyth, my sister, was struck by the wand of a sorcerer."

"Whose wand struck her?"

Arra shook her head. "That I still do not know. Though I have suspected for a long while that my mother had something to do with it. And before she was struck, I believe she was poisoned by a serpent that bit her. I'm not sure which killed her, or if both did—the ray or the bite. Either way, as she died, she became an immortalized form of ash."

Shadonai shook her head. "So do you believe that this all leads back Lilith?"

"So much still remains a mystery, but I believe we are a part of great purpose, that all comes back to her...the Prophecy of the lines of Lilith. And somehow, somewhere, in some form...I believe she yet lives."

"And Vorseth?"

"He is my husband."

"And you and Vorseth are—"

"We are the parents of Arseth—known to you as Wandering Wolfe—your father."

"So you and Vorseth are my grandparents?" Arra nodded, "And Amen-Ra was my twin brother. There were two seeds in the womb of Lilith when she was thrown from the Garden of Eden. Amen-Ra is your grandfather, the father of Darlillyth and Mardavian."

"This is very complicated, but it all makes sense. So, you believe that the first woman in creation, Lilith, is still alive?"

"I don't know for certain, but that is my sense. Perhaps she still dwells among us, but in a new form. Perhaps it is another curse from God, or one of her spurned lovers."

"Can you explain why this is this happening? Why am I finally learning the truth, here in the afterlife? What is going to happen next?"

"We shall be delivered and redeemed. The Chosen Ones of the race of Joseph, the Children of the Light, shall lead us to the new heavens and earth."

"And what shall become of me now?"

"In life, you were the Shadow of God, Shadonai. What would the light be without the shadows? How would the stars shine without the night? How could man breathe without the wind? How could woman live without the warmth of the fire, without the cleansing of water, without the fruits of the earth? How could Lilith and Eve, and their descendants, live without the knowledge of our original innocence? How could man and woman live, conceive, and create, without each other?"

"Is the air greater than the ground beneath it? Are the simple ones who live, eat, mate, and die, easily, naturally, less important than the children who were born to lead extraordinary lives, and thus endure extraordinary loss? Are not great leaders and human monsters born of the same pain?"

"We decide which we way we go," Arra continued. "As you said earlier, our lives are about choices. You decided to be used for a great good, Shadonai. You decided to sacrifice yourself to resurrect another human life. What that human does with her life—good and bad, are in part your responsibility because you saved her. You share a part in her rewards *and* her consequences. Thus, every choice we make have eternal repercussions. Our rewards are not always bestowed to us in our lives on earth."

Arra continued, gesturing beyond the gates of heaven. "When you go past this state of in-between, then you shall have far greater answers about life than I can give you, and there you shall see for yourself, far greater rewards than mere words can describe."

Arra nodded to me. "Yes, Shadonai, you were born to die. So were we all, even those few Chosen Ones who are immortal. Our lives are a mere breath in the breadth of eternity. Your choice has determined for you, to live a lifetime of rewards far greater than anything the earth could have offered you. I encourage you to go forth now."

"Go forth? You mean…leave the shadows? Go inside, past the gates?"

"Shadonai, you lived on the earth for exactly two thousand years. Yet the last day of your life was the only day that you truly lived. It was on this day you learned what being human is: the compassion for your mother, the love of your parents. If you had had but one day to love, this one day would have been sufficient. Go forth. Now that you've had a taste of earthly love, you are able to experience a love far greater than any you could know on earth."

"I'm afraid...I've only ever known the darkness."

"I know how much you wanted the answers in life. I have come to give you the answers in death. Do not be afraid to go into the light. Do not be afraid to experience what you have never known before. Do not be afraid of the things you do not understand."

"Let the light encompass you—surrender to it. Surrender your will; surrender your feelings, all your pain and your fears, for perfect love casts out all fear. There is no fear in love. There is no fear in the light. So, release it. Your earthly chains no longer bind you. You have wings now. You can fly. You belong in the light."

Arra smiled at her granddaughter proudly. "I am here to proclaim that you have been given a new name. Lucis Adonai, you are now the *"Light of God."* You have redeemed your family line, *our* family line. Now the Prophecy that has governed all our lives can break open, like a rainbow breaks open across the sky. Beautiful things shall come from your death. Beautiful things have come from your life..."

Shadonai's dark energy shimmered as Arra spoke, becoming a bright light, becoming Lucis Adonai. The in-between of life and death had transformed her. Her hair was haloed in the light. A calm serenity had flowed into her. Wings sprouted from her back and lifted themselves with a great swoosh into the sky.

Beautiful dreams were born and lived in a moment. A lifetime's worth of joy, love, and beauty was encompassed in the first moment's step into heaven's light, past the shimmering gates, and countless more lifetimes of joy, love, and beauty were to be lived for her, the Light of God, ushered forth into eternity by an ancestor who still inhabited the earth, but whom God had allowed to rise, as a gift. She chose to stay at the gates of heaven to greet other newly departed souls and guide them into the light, as Arra had done for her.

The isolated half-life Shadonai had lived as a mere shadow slipped away, now a distant memory, as an eternity of light and love was begun. As Lucis Adonai, she not only let the light in, she became the Light itself.

~ *** ~

Travelling to the campsite after Varawynn was resurrected, was a little hazy and harried for everyone in the group. The first day at camp went by in a blur. Everyone was so excited to have her back the Priestess felt like a rag doll being pulled every which way.

She was starving once they'd made it to camp, so Aldoran and Eliju built a fire, and Wandering Wolfe killed a dying deer who'd pretty much laid herself down at his feet. Often animals came to the Shaman when they were close to death, as an offering. So, they roasted the venison over the fire pit along with some mushrooms they found in the woods. Varawynn ate ravenously.

"This ought to comfort Aldoran. She's still human at least!" Eliju said to himself.

Pharean made Varawynn tea as they waited for the food to cook. She barely remembered Pharean putting in the honey and steeping the tea in rose petals, deep in reverie. She knew the tea had come out airy and delectable, but the making of it, and the drinking of it, and the sharing of it was foggy. Pharean was in a daze himself.

Wandering Wolfe could vaguely recall hunting in the forest, the deer practically falling at his feet for him to kill and skin and eat it, but the cutting of it and the actual stabbing of its heart felt like the actions of another man from another life.

After a day or so of all of them acting and speaking in this haze, the cloud finally started to lift, and they began to ask Varawynn what had happened to her. Wandering Wolfe was not there. They didn't know it, but he was saying goodbye to his daughter. Illumina and Silvandrin were in the forest looking for vegetation to eat for their dinner, so the younger humans were on their own for the time being.

"Do you mind if I ask what it like in the afterlife?" Pharean asked Varawynn. Aldoran, Eliju, Pharean and Varawynn were huddled together around the fire, wrapped in blankets, the girls' heads covered in shawls. It was a frigid, cold twilight, and they were all ears waiting to hear Varawynn tell her story.

They were roasting the venison on the fire pit—the deer had been cut up and salted and cured so they could be eating it for a couple weeks—and it spit out its juices at them as if in anger. Aldoran got up to turn the meat. When at last Varawynn answered them, the somber inflection in her voice and her words made Aldoran stop his movements and forget everything but what she was saying, and the captivating way she had of expressing her thoughts.

"At first it was nothing. I felt nothing. There *was nothing*. As if all the universe was smoke and mirrors. Then slowly, I came to. I looked down at my ashes, at Darlillyth and all of you looking down over me. I could *see* your emotions and actions, but I was not a part of them. I was sorry to have caused you pain, but there was no way to bridge this invisible wall separating us."

"What did you do then?" Pharean asked her, spellbound.

"Then I went away…away from all you."

"But where did you go?" Pharean persisted, the boys too awestruck to ask anything at all.

"I went to a place of waiting, of holding, I guess. I didn't cross over into heaven. I think it was some version or part of the in-between. Some may call it purgatory. They told me I could go where I wanted to go, so I went to a place of learning. The knowledge there was incredible."

"What knowledge? What place of learning? And who are 'they?'"

"The angels. The angels told me. There are rooms with books, endless books. But books not like those on earth."

"How were they different?"

"I only had to hold them to read them. It didn't take so long to read, and I didn't have to use my eyes. It was more like how I use my mind."

"Whoa," said Eliju, his mouth half-open in wonderment.

"Sometimes a mentor, a soul, would come in and discuss the things I read with me. If I was confused, someone would always come in to help me understand. But mostly I was alone reading, learning."

"Did you meet God?" asked Pharean,

"No," said Varawynn. "I did not see God."

"What else did you see?" Eliju asked, taking courage and comfort in sitting beside her, and grasping and rubbing her hands in his. He couldn't believe how wonderful it was to hold her hands again. To see her face. To know her heart was beating, and she was ALIVE!

Varawynn threw him a grateful look. She was cold, and it meant a lot for her too when he held her hand. She still loved him blindly, relentlessly, unconditionally. "It was amazing there, Eliju! There aren't words to describe it. It wasn't heaven where I was, but it was still just wonderful...so much MORE than earth, more real, more colorful, more of everything!"

Aldoran smiled at her, and sat back down on the other side of Pharean. He was so glad everything had turned out all right. Clearly Varawynn was really back to them, good as new, and his fears were alleviated as he heard her speak.

Although Necromancy was a dark and evil art, Shadonai's act had been one of love and sacrifice, so it put a light of goodness on Varawynn's resurrection. Her life would always be tinged by the light of that love and that sacrifice.

"I saw the gates to heaven when I first left the place where all of you stood over my ashes," Varawynn continued. "The in-between was beautiful too though. It was like I was surrounded by a thick invisible wall that let nothing in—and nothing out. There were no memories of my life on earth. It was like I was in a cocoon of waiting. There was only pure love and peace and joy and hope. There was no sadness, or memory of my suffering."

"The whole universe was at my disposal to learn from and to study. I learned so much in the time I was there. I'm glad you took Jonlin home to bury him before you came back here to resurrect me because it gave me more time to learn things, so many things I'd always wanted to know. Things I may be able to use to help us along our journey..."

"I can't say I remember most of what I learned. It's like when you're in heaven it's hard to remember the physical plane of earth, and when you're on earth it's hard to grasp the infinite knowledge and love of heaven, but a few things have stayed with me."

"Can you share anything you learned there with us now?" asked Pharean eagerly, at the edge of her knees, eager to hear every syllable of Varawynn's words. Aldoran stood and started rotating the venison again, still smiling.

"I learned the properties of things, so many things, like fire and crystals. To know and understand an object or person is a tool necessary to manipulate them. I don't mean that in a devious way necessarily, although many do use knowledge for power and control. I am talking more of magic."

"To understand how to cast a spell on a horse, for instance, it is essential to know all about the horse, not just its habits in what it eats, but its motivations and the workings of its anatomy. Thereby fighting the horse or casting a spell on it will be that much more effective, by playing into the unique individuality and anatomy of that horse."

Aldoran shook his head. "Your experience sounds incredible, Varawynn. Do you know why you never fully crossed over?"

Varawynn nodded. "I was kept in that state of in-between, and I never went inside the pearly gates because I was never meant to die. I was always going to be resurrected. What I learned isn't bad, though knowledge can always be used for evil as well as good. What I was saying, or trying to say about magic, is that it's important to know the object before you do magic on it."

"If you use your understanding to manipulate others to do your will, that's equivalent to killing others to do your will. Not telling someone you are doing magic on them is equivalent to stealing from them. It's a violation. Something else I learned—in magic, the most important thing to know is yourself."

"That's true," Aldoran nodded. "That's true in war or swordplay as well. The first rule of combat: know yourself. Know your capabilities, as well as your limitations."

"That was my father Ruminous' first rule in philosophy as well: 'Know thyself, for from the self stems all knowledge of Man.'"

"The first thing in the Kabbalah I studied was my name, the meaning of my name, the letters of my name and the numbers of my name which make up who I am. The sound of my name and the meaning is there every time I speak it, or someone calls me by it, at least unconsciously the connotation is there," added Eliju. All four of them stared at each other.

"Everything is linked," whispered Pharean.

"Only most people don't realize it, or can't see it," agreed Varawynn. "And to understand how things are connected, gives us power. Power we could use for good or evil. It is up to us as individuals to seek that power and understanding, and to choose what we will do with it."

"Absolutely," agreed Aldoran. They all became very quiet, deep in their own thoughts and going over the concepts of their conversation.

The venison spit at them viciously again. They all jumped. Then they laughed. Aldoran got up to see if dinner was ready. It was. They ate their meal together, talking and laughing and telling funny stories about their lives. Wandering Wolfe still hadn't returned. Even so, the evening finished off light and merry, and they each slept well that night. Aldoran was beginning to realize that Varawynn hadn't come back the same as she had been—she was better.

~ ~ ~

The great-winged bird Roc swept down upon Silvandrin. "Ileona needs your help," it informed him, ever direct and clear. "You have the Prophecy of the Sphinx?" the great bird asked. The unicorn nodded.

"Ileona has taken the wrong path into the Arabian desert. You must enter from the southwest gate. There are ley lines which will take you to where the Sphinx guards the desert kingdom's gates. She has been waiting to leave her post, for the appointed time. A unique human creature needs her. You must inform her that this is the time. She will know how to find the Lady of the Lake. But you must find the Sphinx."

"But am I meant to be with Ileona in the desert?"

"No," answered the Roc. "I shall give you another assignment in the time of the group's disbandment. Find the Sphinx. Tell her to go to Ileona and then wait for further instructions from me. Illumina should go back to the realm of the sea elves after she assist you in the desert." As usual, the bird knew Silvandrin would follow his instructions and did not wait for his reply.

Its massive twenty-five-foot wing span sent a huge wave of wind back at the unicorn, as it flew away, who knew enough by now to brace himself against the backlash of the roc's current. In a few moments, the creature was gone, completely lost in the obscurity of the dark sky.

Illumina agreed to go with Silvandrin to the Arabian deserts to help Ileona, before she went back to her coastal home. Silvandrin agreed, and they immediately took their leave of the group without guilt or pause, knowing that Varawynn was okay.

~ ~ ~

Wandering Wolfe returned to the group after the last moments with his daughter, and after taking a day of rest and solitude. Her love spurred and carried him on. He hung on to his love of her, but he let go of the loss, and accepted her death as a part of life. He was grateful for and cherished every moment of his daughter's life that she had lived, and that he had shared with her.

Even so, it was clear to the old shaman that the Celtic Priestess was struggling with something. The dislike they had once held for one another had dissipated with her death, and resurrection.

"What is it, Varawynn? How do you feel differently?" Wandering Wolfe asked her, concern creasing his brow.

"It's hard to explain." The note in her voice left no further room for discussion, and they left it at that. The truth was, Wandering Wolfe harbored the same fears she did, and there were questions he had that he wasn't sure he wanted the answers to. Aldoran was reassured, but the Shaman was more worried than ever. He sensed she wasn't being totally honest with all of them. He sensed the change in her, more perhaps, than anyone else did.

Varawynn was keeping things from them, it was true. Her body was changing, growing smaller and hunch-backed. Her skin took on a slippery, silver sheen at night. Her skin was toughening. Inside her chest and stomach, she felt her organs relocating. These changes occurred within her a little bit more every day. The changes were getting harder for her hide.

Eliju touched Varawynn much more now, as if to reassure himself that she was really there. "I can't believe you came back to us," Eliju shook his head and said over and over again.

"I came back to *you,*" Varawynn would whisper, too softly for him to hear. But he felt it.

Varawynn herself was living in fear and constant dread. Something was happening that was frightening her because she didn't have control over it. She let everyone think she was fine. But sometimes her skin would shimmer and shift so unnaturally. She was afraid the magic which had brought her back to life was dark and evil, and she feared she was not as she had once been. Sometimes out of the blue, she felt her skin crawl.

"Are you feeling, okay?" Eliju asked her, several times a day. Nodding adamantly, she answered quickly, "Of course," but she didn't meet him in the eyes…in his beautiful green eyes haunting her soul, her life, her dreams and her nightmares.

"Eliju, Eliju, Eliju, I love you…" she murmured over and over again, every night as she fell asleep. Calling out to him in a cry from her soul, her love for him tortured her, and how she wished she haunted him too. Often, she wondered if he could hear her, wondered if he could feel her longing, deep in the night. Varawynn had been through so much in the moments of the in-between, that she felt as if she were a hundred years old when they brought her back to life.

One day, she took Eliju by the hand, bringing him into the forest. The green leaves around them were thick and plush, and it made her miss the vibrant emerald green of her homeland. "Did you miss me, Eliju?" she asked him softly, longing for words of love and a little tenderness.

"More than I can express," he told her with a smile.

She kicked a small rock with her slipper, breaking up some dirt. "How do you feel about me, Eliju?" she probed him.

"I care about you," he said instantly.

"But how much? More than anyone?" she wheedled.

"You're certainly at the top of my list!"

"What about that woman…the women who turned me to ashes? The way you were looking at her, Eliju…after what she did to me…?"

"Varawynn, Darlillyth is the woman I saw in the mirrors at the Crystal Palace. She is my future."

A hard knot caught in Varawynn's throat. "You're not telling me you love her, Eliju?"

"I do love her," he had to admit.

"More than me?"

"I have to be honest with you, Varawynn. I loved you since the first moment I saw you. I thought for a while that it was you who I saw in the mirror. But it was her, Varawynn. I'm sorry."

Varawynn stood from the rock she was sitting on, and walked away. Eliju was left there, full of regret in his eyes and heart.

~ ~ ~

"Did Shadonai use Necromancy to bring me back to life, Wandering Wolfe?" Varawynn worried. "I know what a miracle it is that I'm alive, and how lucky that I came back with a healed leg…but…I don't quite feel like myself anymore."

In this state of worry and fear, weeks passed by, and Varawynn's anxiety and restlessness continued to grow. Every day, especially every night when her skin grew leathery and grey, she longed to go to the cliffs, she longed to look out at the sea. Resisting the call of the sea every day, took a toll on her body. Her bones ached and throbbed all the time. She was afraid of what she was becoming. She was so afraid she was not herself anymore.

She realized one day that it was her skin, her bones, and her height that was changing—not her heart, not her soul. Even though it hurt, it was her love for Eliju that kept her strong, and it was her love for Eliju that made her feel like herself.

Whatever magic Shadonai had used to resurrect her, that magic had brought her body back whole, but her heart was still broken, knowing that deep down Eliju didn't love her. At least, not as much as he loved Darlillyth, the sorceress who had brought her down to ashes.

Knowing she was still herself, she began to accept her body's changes more readily. Finally, the skin on her face too became silver, and felt her body transforming into slippery skin in the night. It only happened at night, but slowly it was beginning to stay this way into the mornings as well. She began to avoid the group more and more. She felt like she had to. How could she tell them, worse yet, show them this *thing* she was becoming?

Some animal instinct, more or less than human, brought her through the fields of heather, to the waves beating the rocks and cliffs. As she walked to the edge of the cliffs late one evening, with the water and full moon calling out to her, she stood staring down into the water's murky depths.

Suddenly she didn't want to go back to the campsite. She wanted to jump, into the depths of the sea. She wanted to leave them all behind.

Listening to the crashing waves, to the healing ebbing and flowing of the tides, to the water swooshing over the rocks, her senses heightened, her body lurched forward, her soul was stirred by the guiding light of the pain in her heart. She felt her bones breaking within her body.

On the Full Cold Moon in December, as the air was growing colder, empowered by the ungent she'd taken in her tea before going to bed, she became the Selkie of Celtic legends, with the same heart-shaped face of Varawynn, the same probing soulful green eyes, the same wild black hair, uncurling in the wild wind.

Crying out into the sea, the song of her love and longing for Eliju, of unrequited love, was flung up and carried away on the breeze, in the blowing of the wind over the Celtic isles of her soul's home. Her song sounded out from the hollows of her pain, and was felt in the heart of the one she loved:

WHILE THE ASHES RISE TO LIFE

"I am the lover without a love
I am the faithful one who's lost her faith.
I am the nameless grave.

Hopes of the dream are nightmares to me.
Happiness is a gift that eludes me—
There is nothing left, but the dark, deep sea.

I am broken beyond repair,
My soul is scattered like leaves on the wind;
My body made whole, reshapes itself again.

Born under the sign of the changer,
Under the sign of the transformer,
With the heart of a dreamer:

I change myself
I reinvent myself
I lead myself

To drown in the deep blue sea,
In the furthest reaches of pain,
Where most dare not go, I choose to be—

Seeking to uncover the mysteries of the sea—
I dare to shape shift into a Selkie,
Unafraid of the drowning of the deep.

The Celtic Priestess on land—
The woman seal of the waters—
The haunting Siren of the sea.

I am the lover without a love,
The singer of wordless songs in hearts unsung,
Of the endless mysteries of the waters, I have become...

As she sang, Eliju came upon her. "Varawynn…" As she turned to him, he visibly withdrew from her. "What's happened to you?"

"There is nothing to fear, Eliju." He moved towards her, grasping her seal hand in his. "Why do you look this way?"

"I'm not dark or evil, Eliju. I'm still the girl I was…just MORE than I was before."

"How this possible?"

"My leg was healed. In the resurrection I was made whole, but when Aengus came out of my leg as the raven birthmark, my body, not my soul, but my body, has been transforming so that I am becoming both more…and less than human."

"What have you become?"

Letting out a cry, a scream that was both a howl and a song, she sang, "Through my pain I have become a creature of the land and the waters, a Siren, a seal, a Selkie. I can shape shift from human to Selkie by will."

"Then stay, stay Varawynn," Eliju beseeched her, squeezing her hand. "Even as a seal you are beautiful to me."

"No," she answered, backing away from him. He reached for her. "No," she said again, this time turning her back on him, and running as she had never been capable of running before, towards the water.

"Wait!" Eliju called after her.

Diving off the cliffs into the waters, with her soul's cry, she transformed fully in the descent into the waters. Her face, her hair was gone. Submerging herself into the sea, Varawynn was now fully transformed into the Siren Selkie singing her suffering.

Eliju reached out for her, as she dived off the cliffs of Caledonia, into the waters. Tears poured down his face, his eyes bright green with the pain of losing her again.

"Varawynn!" he screamed into the wind. "Don't leave me again! Come back!" The longing in their souls united like a thread, like a ray of light it connected them, even while she swam with the fishes in the sea, and breathed in the water.

"Please, don't go...I love you..." their souls whispered the same words to each other at the same time. "Please don't let me go..."

Deep in his mind, deep in the night, Varawynn submerged herself completely into the sea and her pain. Eliju imaged her as the broken girl, she'd once been, not this Selkie Siren she'd become. He missed the lame girl, the crippled girl. Hating that in her resurrection, she'd been reborn whole, now she could run from him, and now she'd become something he couldn't reach, gone to places he'd never be able to find.

Her soul was lost to him in the waters; he had no power to protect her. And he missed the sound of her voice, and he missed the devoted way she used to look at him, and he missed her stubbornness and her fierceness, her sweetness that sometimes turned to rage with the intensity of her sensitive feelings being hurt by his clumsy bluntness.

He could feel her exploration of the waters, and she could feel him staring down at the sea on the edge of the cliff. Thus, she knew after a time of waiting and hoping for her return that she wasn't coming back, and he and Wandering Wolfe traveled back to Haran.

She could feel their traveling, just as Eliju could feel her swimming in the waters in movements too fluid to be fully human. It was love that had kept her alive, and it was love that transformed her into something to escape it.

Eliju whispered, while falling asleep, "Varawynn, I'll always love you..."

She heard his words, and she felt the vibrations of his voice in the drowning of the deep, in the undulating currents of the ebbing tides, but kept moving forward, alone through the waters.

~ *** ~

Chapter Ten
Selkie's Tales of the Sea

These are some of the adventures and accounts of Varawynn as a Selkie, discovering the hidden mysteries of the sea...

Swimming through the depths of the water was frightening, exciting, and titillating simultaneously. The waters had always had a soothing effect, and been utterly intriguing to me. Now the secrets of the water were mine to uncover.

The first few hours beneath the surface were the most invigorating I'd ever known. I moved my body in the water like no human can on earth. Like a dancer or a gymnast flying through the sea, I felt free.

After I'd been resurrected, the use of both my legs had been an uncomfortable sensation. The flexing of my muscles as I ran had felt foreign, though my leg being healed was a gift. The way I swam through the waters as a seal was unfamiliar in the same way. Unfamiliar, but the most amazing sensation I'd experienced yet in life.

There was no comparison to the sensation of muscles grinding against bone on a hard, uneven surface in running, with the fluid, effortless feeling of gliding through the waters in swimming. Here in the waters, I was graceful, beautiful, so much more confident...

But after a few hours of pleasure in the exploration of these new sensations, from behind the vibrant hot pink coral, I sensed danger. My senses in the sea, as a Selkie, were heightened. A strange whirring vibrated from the coral reefs. I could *feel* the warning call from inside, from the fluid in my organs to the very marrow of my bones. As a Selkie, I made a moaning sound, calm and nonthreatening.

From beneath the resplendent multi-colored reefs, the menacing creature emerged. Throwing back a wave of blue hair and baring her teeth in the water with a menacing hissing, the wild-eyed sea creature was fiercely beautiful in her very fury. Even deep in the waters and completely on my own, I was more fascinated than frightened by the creatures of the sea.

From the stories of Celtic legends, I recognized the creature as a Kelpie, a malevolent water horse. I hadn't expected its strange, exotic body to be aqua green with long, thick curly hair that swept out past me like a curtain. Hissing once more, the Kelpie lunged at me, and I felt a moment of intense fear as everything went dark…

Upon coming to, I discovered myself lying upon a bed of thick, soft green moss, in a room surrounded with all different shapes and colors of sea shells. In the vibrating sonar language, I heard a voice, as clear as a bell to my seal's ears. I knew on land, with human ears, it would only be gurgled, strangled cries, but as a Selkie, I could understand the language of the ocean.

"The sea shells protect us from the monsters. The shells lock in the silence, and lock out the sounds of sonar."

I looked up. The beautiful Kelpie, with her glowing blue-green scales, gracefully swam towards me, with a fish in her mouth. Without standing on precedence, she nodded her head once and dumped the slimy fish into my mouth.

At first, I thought I would be repulsed by the raw fish, afraid of choking on its sharp scales, or get sick because of its slimy texture. But as a seal I did what seals do, as I had first learned to walk as a human when my leg had healed. I went for it.

Swallowing the fish down whole was foreign like the muscles of my legs in motion as I ran, and yet it was natural too. I instinctively knew what to do…how to eat the fish. I did it quickly because to my surprise I found that I was really hungry, and the fish tasted good.

The Kelpie nodded its head, and threw another fish my way. I caught it this time in my mouth, and swallowed it whole again. She threw me another, and I caught and swallowed it in the same way a few more times. On the fifth fish, I found myself chewing it, enjoying ripping the tendons of the fish, relishing the crunching of the scales beneath my surprisingly razor-sharp teeth, and the blood gushing down my throat into my stomach made my body feel warm deep within. It felt good.

"Thank you," I said to the Kelpie, not surprised anymore that as a Selkie I knew the sonar languages. "What happened back there?"

"You thought I meant you harm, didn't you?" said the Kelpie sadly. "No, no, no…it wasn't me."

"I'm sorry. I didn't mean any offense to you. I've just always heard that Kelpie water horses were evil creatures."

"As are some humans, but not all."

"That's true."

"You didn't see the creature coming up behind you, and I was trying to warn you."

"What was it?"

"A water dragon, the one monster all sea creatures fear." It hit me then like a high wave on a calm ocean—Kelpies were not evil—they were merely misunderstood. As I often had been as a human.

"Thank you, and I'm so sorry for misjudging you."

"I will forgive if you if you remember three things. First, the appearances of the creatures here can be deceiving. Beautiful creatures can be ugly and cruel within, ugly creatures can be helpful, but whenever you are in danger—go to the surface. The darkest creatures fear the air and the light. Secondly, remember that sea shells can be used for protection. Thirdly, you should be aware we are free creatures here, but there are still rules in the waters."

"What are the rules?"

"The rules are who eats who." I gulped, the fish digesting in my stomach squirming and churning a little. "There is an order here, of life and death, that must be respected."

"Thank you, I will remember that." The Kelpie nodded once more, and threw me one more fish, which I swallowed whole. Leading the way out of the hidden sanctuary of the sea shell room, she swam off without a word or a goodbye. I swam up and away in the opposite direction.

After being so deep in the waters for so long, my body and lungs craved the surface. Especially since the Kelpie told me the surface was a safe place away from the more dangerous creatures. Swimming in quick, deft movements, I followed the air bubbles up to where the wind kissed the waters. Gasping for breath, my mouth opened and inhaled the taste of the salty sea air. My tongue drank in the moist breeze.

Swimming to the nearest embankment, I flipped my seal's body up and around, making three perfect somersaults in the air on my first try! I flexed my fins. I danced on the rocks. I flipped a few more times, suddenly realizing that what I was feeling, I hadn't felt for a very long time: *joy.*

Not wanting to venture too far out yet, I swam to a blue lagoon near the murky shores. Diving in and out of the murky Celtic Isles, I saw more of the banks than I would ever have dared dream as a human. Beautiful blues and greens amid salty silver waters along shores of blonde and white, stretched themselves before me.

There was an endless playground of nature to be admired and explored.

Stretching out my fins, sunbathing on a sandy beach, I stared up into the sky and clouds in perfect bliss. Just as I was thanking the gods for this divine moment of timeless serenity—

SPLASH!!!
      BANG!!!!
           BOOM!!!!!
"AAAAAAAHHHHHHHHHH!!!!!!

Screaming bloody murder at the…thing that had emerged and belly flopped upon the surface of the water disturbing my *nearly* perfect moment—! "What the—"

The big, clunky creature looked like a log with thick green moss all over it. Turning its log-like body over, it inadvertently sprayed an endless stream of mucky water at me from its snout. As the sea monster finally spoke, in a sonar voice reverberating beneath the weeping willow trees and the moss hanging from them, above the canopy of the blue lagoon, it was all I could do not to dive away from the loud, booming voice reverberating in the waters.

Into the secrets
The secrets of the deep
Into the secrets
The deep and dark do keep
Come tell the secrets
Of the dark and deep
Deep in the sea
Where the secrets WILL keep

I was suddenly pulled and compelled toward the strange creature, as a moment ago I had been repulsed by it. There was an antiquated, ancient melancholy its words and voice quality that attracted me. "What sort of creature are you—foe or friend?"

If I keep the secrets
The Secrets that keep
Of the creatures dark and deep
Foe or friend?
Amongst the creatures of the sea
Then I am friend
For are not they
WHO keeps the secrets
The Secrets of the deep
A friend of the waters
And its mysteries?

"Who are you?" I spoke back it, in the same sonar language.

I am a secret
Legend like the Selkie
Of the lochs
Ness the mythic snake
Of days when
Dragons and dinosaurs
Roamed and ruled the earth
And THE sea
and soared through the skies
When there were so many more
Of our kind

"So, you're the Loch Ness Monster...errrr Loch Ness, I'm sorry. But you're telling me your secret is that really you were a snake, a mythic water snake in the days of the dinosaurs that lived after their fall, and the rise of man?"

You have gleaned my secret
My secret old and deep

Guard it well
Secrets were not meant to tell

"I won't tell anyone…but, may I get a good look at you? I've always dreamed of meeting the Loch Ness!" I was increasingly excited about my explorations. They were fantasies come to life.

And I always dreamed
of meeting a lady Selkie
silver shimmering and sleek
once a beautiful maiden
now a part of the secrets of the sea

Diving beneath the waters, I climbed onto the back of the Loch Ness, as the girl that I once was would have climbed a tree. It had dirty, thick hair that felt and looked a lot like seaweed, which I guessed often acted as a great camouflage against anyone who wished it harm.

Nestling my sleek seal's body into the nape of the neck of the Loch Ness, felt surprisingly comfortable. Though it was a cousin of the snake and dinosaur, it was a unique offshoot. Its body was lengthy and thick, like a long log covered by seaweed; its head looked like some version of a dragon, as did its tail, but when I pressed my body onto its back and heard the booming in its chest, I sensed it had the heart of a unicorn, kind and pure.

Kissing the Loch Ness on the crown of its head, I leapt and made somersaults on the gentle creature, and we laughed and played. Sensing it was more afraid of me than I of it, I teased it mercilessly for the sheer experience of for once being the holder of the power, and not the receiver of fear and rejection.

I spent a merry week in that blue lagoon. A merrier week than I sensed it had ever seen or would see again. Nessy had been alone for a very long time, and the ancient melody in her voice and her heart filled with loneliness and hopelessness, dark and deep, told a story in the sweeping of the seaweed canopies hanging from one branch to the next in the skies, once made to keep out the flying dragons, now all they kept Nessy from, were the stars.

"Will you ever leave here?" I asked the Loch Ness one day. "Why don't you seek your fortunes elsewhere, for the time of dragons and dinosaurs is long past."

And that is why here I remain

Nessy answered simply and honestly, but somehow, I still was disappointed. She must have sensed it for she added:

When the catastrophe occurred
That killed the majority
Of our kind
As the earth fell into the seas
And sea flew into the skies
As volcanoes and fires burned
The sea and the Icelandic icicles
Froze the birds in flight
I learned to value the simplest of things
I learned to value most
The gift of being alive

Of that time
And of those beasts
So few of us remain
That I cannot risk
That simple gift
This gift of life
I will not waste
Not when so many other Lives
were taken too soon

WHILE THE ASHES RISE TO LIFE

Burned and frozen
Bruised and beat
Fallen beneath the core of earth
Buried In the deepest darkest depths
Of the forgotten recesses of the seas
Hidden in unreachable crevices of desert caves
Are the skulls and bones
Of the most magnificent
Of the ancient beasts
So much more worthy
Of the gift of life
Then me
SO, IF I HAVE TO LIVE ALONE
THEN I AM STILL GRATEFUL TO BE ALIVE
IF I AM SOMETIMES LONELY
I ACCEPT THAT AND LET IT BE
For at least here in my blue lagoon
I am free

Still, I dream of dreams
That I am not the only loch ness
That remains
The day will come
When we will meet and mate
Or the day will come
When I must lose this gift of life
Either way I wait
In the dream of dreams
Of this enchanting blue lagoon
For the sea to meet me half way
For the birth of my dream of dreams
May or may not come true
Yet it is not up to me
To meet or make my fate
I will not choose: I wait

"But how will you continue on…after…surely there will come a time you will die. How do you intend to carry on the species?"

Swimming back and forth impatiently through a small stretch of water, I was feeling restless with her words and her unwillingness to even TRY to discover a solution more assertive than the passive pursuit of waiting, hoping for more, but not really *trying* or *living,* merely *existing.* It felt weak. It felt complacent. It seemed short-sighted.

If Nessy wanted to live, then surely, she would have to reproduce after all. For don't parents in some intrinsic, fundamental way, live on through their descendants?

And is this not a choice? I thought it in my mind, but I didn't say it. Perhaps a day would come when I would really try to convince her to be more courageous. But for now, I let the Loch Ness stay in her safe little cocoon in the blue lagoon.

Not too long after our conversation, I left the Blue Lagoon, and the secrets and sadness of the Loch Ness behind me, ready at last to encounter the deeper secrets of the ocean. For if the Loch Ness had taught me anything, it was that I couldn't wait for my fate to meet me. Instead, I would go out boldly and confidently in pursuit of it.

Swimming for days, I encountered nothing. Of course, in my readiness to explore the ocean's depths, I wanted to go some distance quickly, so I was swimming upon the surface of the water mainly, breathing in the salty fresh air, and resting and sleeping when need be upon the rocks. I had not yet explored the shores of the land beneath the waters…perhaps today…?

Then on the dawning of the new day's horizon, I saw a sight such as I had never imagined. The dolphins and the whales, two totally different species of water mammals, played—flipping and spraying each other, their smiles as joyful and innocent as the sight of a group of young children playing.

Watching at a distance, as a nonparticipant bystander several hundred yards away, it was soothing to witness them play the day away. It made me wonder if two sea creatures of different species could get along, why humans of different races could not.

As the sun dimmed, the sky filled with vibrant shades of purple and blues. I was lulled on the tides of the moving waters, to something beyond the playing and splashing of whales and dolphins, to a point of power of which had always fascinated and enthralled me growing up…

From the distance, a ship's proud mast dipped up and down with the waters and waves. My roving eyes, hungry for discovery and exploration, left the pleasantness of the playing whales and dolphins, for the proud, graceful movements of a ship.

Its white mast dipped and curved, flexed and opened, and dipped and dived as the air pushed through it. The mast itself was a dance with the wind. The ship was moving in a slow, graceful dance with the waters.

Its golden body was too heavy to move quickly, but from a distance of several hundred yards, it moved with movements as fluid as the dolphin dive through the waters. The dolphin's fins were as much made for water as that ship was made to sail it, and that mast was meant to soar through the skies, propelling it forward.

As I became more and more enthralled by the ship's ancient symbol of man's voyage across the wide seas; a song echoed from across the open skies. The once bright and cheerful day was dimming; it was just before the sun kissed the horizon and lost itself in love of the sea, as I had.

The song rang on, like a lullaby, as the sun dipped below the equator. Twilight blue and green dimmed the clear sky, but not the sparkling of the countless winking stars shining brighter as the light waned.

I heard the Sirens from a distance, singing to the sea, targeting the golden ship with the big, happy masts sweeping over the cold waters. The Echeneis, little sucking creatures, attached themselves to the ship in order to help and work with the Sirens in slowing the ship down, so that the men onboard would be more likely to become enchanted by the Siren's song. I saw how even if the men had *wanted* to keep sailing, the Echeneis wouldn't have let them.

As they sang the "Siren Song," I had a sinking feeling that something terrible was in store for all the unsuspecting men upon the ship, who listened…

"The ship that sails upon the waters—
Graceful, swift and sure,
Stands just past us, proud and pure.
Its sailors watch our flawless beauty.
Rising from the white, thick foam;
Hair long, shiny, and glossy,
Beckons them towards us, like a lighthouse, home.

They feel the calling of our enchanted beauty,
The sensual movements of our flesh,
And we take them down to the bottom of the ocean,
With the lust and desire, they feel
From the rise and fall of our every breath.
These sailors spend their useless lives
Searching for the capture of a beauty prize,
Seeking treasures in the leisurely life,
Killing in endless, drunken fights,
Using woman after woman
To satisfy their constant need, and untamed greed.

WHILE THE ASHES RISE TO LIFE

With no honor, no reverence, no respect for a woman's life;
We sing for their innocent victims to be freed.
We sing for justice, and sweet, sweet vengeance—
For the downfall of these wicked men,
Calls us ever through the waters,
To rise from the ocean foam, and destroy again."

The ship's wide mast dipped and dropped toward the waters, as the Sirens sang their seductive melodies. Clearly the captain was distracted by the singing, his shoddy steering a symptom of his lack of focus.

The sailors too were walking around in a daze. Their glassy eyes were haunted, obsessively searching for the source of the exquisite music. Believing such beautiful, ethereal sounds must be coming from some beautiful, ethereal creature. They were not disappointed.

Out at sea, like goddesses, their perfect torsos bewitched the sailors. Their untamed, wild curls, thick and silky like velvet drapes, swept back from faces of such exquisite perfection, the men were overcome by desire and lust, aching to touch them.

Their slim bodies were covered with voluptuous, impossible curves, with lips soft and subtle, eyes soulful and hungry, large with lashes as curled and feminine as their hair, complexions of unlined radiance bewitched the men as much as the haunting cry of their mating song. They were of all hair colors and all eye colors, and all skin colors, and they were all flawlessly beautiful, impeccably formed, with perfect-pitch voices...some sopranos, some altos, but all sang the melodies as melting butter, as soothing as the sound of the waves beating against the surf...

Watching from afar, to see what would become of the men, I wondered what the beautiful Sirens' true intentions were. I was nearly as bewitched as the men, as

I watched the graceful and refined movements of the Sirens, every motion a corporal visual delight. They were all so lovely, so deliciously delicate and feminine. But something made my eyes wander over them, seeking the Siren's leader, seeking the one who stood apart, and above the others.

She came forth, the last to rise from the waters. Her hair was like warm caramel with streaks of dark brown, amber and gold. Red sea shells covered the ample curves of her chest, and her necklace was elaborate red and gold strands composed of sparkling prizes from the sea. Her hair was neither brown, nor golden, nor red, nor black, rather, she was the perfect blend of all hair colors, even with strands of silver that did not age her, but only enhanced her ageless youth and vibrant beauty, and the dazzling aura of her presence.

With gentle eyes of violet, with a form so slim and slender, she was like the delicate violet flower itself. But there was strength in her form that was not as apparent in the others. She was in appearance, the most refined and unique of the Sirens, but certainly she was their leader too.

In that moment, I decided not to interfere in the proceedings. Though a part of me wanted to help protect the men, I felt as helpless as they were against the sheer, irresistible force of their beauty. Recalling the story of Ileona's mother and her father Merlin, I could understand the pull of beauty on the men, the way their beauty addled their brains, weakened their resolve, and deadened their logic.

Watching in wonderment as the Sirens approached the ship, and the men pulled them onboard, my brain couldn't remember, for the life of me, the end of this legendary tale. It didn't entirely matter though, as I was about to find out.

"Man overBOARD!" the first in command cried, as if the entirety of the men on the ship, including the captain himself hadn't been watching the Siren's approach to their ship since before sunset. The men held out their oars and arms to help the lady Sirens aboard the ship.

There were nine of them in total. Lenora was the name of their leader. With her lustrous waves and tresses of auburn and copper and gold, with her soft, unguarded eyes that pulled at one's heartstrings, with the shy false blushing of her cheeks, and the downward curve of her smile, and the lashes looking down and up at you becomingly, they were perfectly calculated charms to gather up the hearts of those who looked at her, with the impossible length of her fine lashes.

Her movements and looks were expressly designed to capture the heart of a man, like a captain's net captures the bounty of the fish swimming unwittingly through the waters, to be caught up, deboned, breaded and fried. She twisted her tiny waist, and with the stretching of her arms, she knew how to best show-off the sinewy muscles in her back and waist, and the allure of the large red sea shells on her chest, what they covered, and the ample dent in between them.

The Captain and Lenora stood facing each other, sizing one another up. The captain was a good man, who read the Good Book every night, and by dawn's first light. He knew the Good Book warned against beautiful woman with beautiful bodies who took men down wayward paths that lead to hell.

But in the sweet gentleness of those expressive violet eyes, he found it hard to believe. There was something so sweet and innocent about her, as if she were unaware of her beauty, and its heady effects on men.

He also found it hard not to look at her body, and apparent innocence. without an instant desire to make use of its utter perfection. He knew the pleasure of her body and kiss, would be beyond what he could imagine or ever attain again, for as long as he lived, as a poor merchant sea captain.

He knew her pleasures were worth more than the priceless gold and gems which were his cargo, and which kept his ship stable and steady. He knew he would have given it all up to her, if she would permit him to taste the supple softness of her swan's curved neck on his teeth, just once.

"*But what of pleasure?*" he asked himself. *Am I mere animal? Am I mere man after all, like my weak-minded sailors here, paying for a woman's body and soul, as if she were a dinner plate, an object to be bought and sold at will?*" A phrase in the Good Book came to his mind… 'I have bought you at a price,' sayeth the Lawd…'"

So though his loins ached for her, and his fevered sweaty brow, and his clammy, grasping hands longed to wrap themselves around her—to take her right there on the hard wooden floor beneath them in front of any and all, like an animal, he rose above the passion of his base desires, and opened his mouth to deny the pleasures she offered, for the sake of his soul. But not before a war cry sounded from Lenora's deliciously juicy, pouty pink lips—

"NOWWWWW!" she commanded, and as she made the command, the beautiful Sirens' faces and bodies changed to silver, their heads widening and elongating, their teeth lengthening and sharpening. Their shiny fingernails became claws they used to tear up the men's bodies with their hands and teeth.

The sailor's heads crunched, their eyeballs rolled, and their limbs were severed, before the men even had a chance to open their mouths in protest. Inhumanly fast, their claws and fangs gorged themselves on the male bodies, eating them alive.

I watched the scene at a distance. I watched as the Sirens swallowed limbs whole, like I swallowed fish whole, sometimes crunching the bones in their strong jaws to make it easier to eat, and for the pleasure of hearing bones break and tendons snap. The waves were eerily calm, and the night was as still as a grave, while I watched on in horror, the Sirens munching on the seafaring men, occasionally threw spare limbs out to the Echeneis in payment for their help earlier, in slowing the ship down.

The dark waves beat against the once proud golden ship, with its bright white masts. Now the masts seemed crestfallen with what had become of the men aboard its vessel. And what would become of it?

I watched for at least an hour more as the Sirens ravaged the sailor's bodies. Lenora, turning back into her more becoming form, told the other Sirens what to do. Pointing at the enormous bags of gold and the chests of precious gems, by her waving arms and fingers, it was clear what she wanted her fellow shapeshifters to do with it.

Viciously, violently they worked together, to throw the precious treasures out to sea. Not a single remnant, not a single finger lay behind from the sailors, only lines and splatters of blood on the sides of the front deck, and the floor was a carpet of red. Without the weight of the gold and jewels, or any sailors to steer it, and the captain to direct it, the life expectancy of the ship was tenuous at best.

Though it was only a mere vessel, a way to get from one point to another, something deep inside me pitied the ship her fate, and of course all the men who would never be seen or heard from again. That was the bittersweet blessing of being a sailor: you didn't leave too many people behind, to miss you when you were gone. If you were smart and wise and kind enough to know any better that is.

At the moment, Lenora looked like a crazed banshee, wild eyes and hair, her waves of hair becoming long curls entwining themselves into unruly spirals in the wind. *She can't be a total goddess if the wind undoes her hair like that,* I thought to myself, finding a bit of pleasure in the knowledge that her Siren form wasn't fully perfect. Although the truth was, she was even more beautiful with her thick, untamed curls. Actually, they looked a lot like the hair of my human form, Varawynn. I laughed at the snarky human part of me that'd formed the thought.

I suddenly realized that it was the *human* blood that allowed the Sirens to retain their youth and otherworldly beauty. And I was reminded of what the Kelpie had warned me: sometimes ugly creatures can be kind and helpful, and beautiful sea creatures can be dangerous.

The Kelpie had also taught me that creatures are individuals, just like humans. So perhaps there were some Sirens as beautiful on the inside, as their forms were on the outside. As I stared out at the lonely ship covered in the sailor's blood, I hoped so.

Standing at the helm of the ship, with her hands and palms open and wide in the air before her, four Sirens stood to the left of their leader Lenora, in a line. Four more gathered in an identical line to her right. The once calm, still night filled with thunder and electricity, as Lenora chanted in her lyrical sing-song voice, once light and lilting, now deep and full of power, a spell that pulsed the rains from the sky the instant their arms fell down to their sides.

"AnnoWA!" Lenora cried, as one-by-one, she again taking the lead, dove head-first back into the cold, dark waters. The storm raged for hours more, as the gallant ship was tossed and torn asunder. Its bright, bold masts bellowed out widely with every gust of the wind, with the crash of lightning too near...and BOOOMMM CRACKKK BANNGGGG BOOOMMMM!—an electric bolt of lightning pierced straight down its center.

The wood holding the masts up, toppled over each other, with loud CRACKS and KURPLANKS and SSSSWAAASH, until all that remained of the ship was its long, wide golden body's skeleton. Yet the storm raged on.

After another hour, the ship valiantly held out, its body cut and ripped and torn, yet it managed to retain its dignity keeping itself afloat atop the waters. It was noble somehow in its desperate attempt at survival. The Sirens still swam about it in the waters, wise not to go until all evidence of their work for the night was eradicated, as just another secret for the sea to keep.

Lenora lifted but one arm, with the ruby ring on her left hand amongst the waves, so subtly I almost missed it. Then her open palm closed, and she slowly pulled her arm into the waters. As she did, the ship sank in the exact same movements and timing of her arm and hand into the water.

Tears fell from my seal's cheeks, as I watched the last of the topmost mast disappear beneath the waters. In the stories of the musical Sirens bewitching sailors at sea, I now knew the true ending.

What remained of the ship would fall to the ocean's floor, along with whatever treasures still remained on it. All that was left of the sailors, was blood on the decks that would be washed away on its slow, but sure descent to the bottom of the sea.

With the Loch Ness, I'd seen how ugly creatures can be kind and pure. With the Sirens I'd witnessed how beautiful creatures can be treacherous. With the Kelpie I learned that there is bad and good in all races. These lessons of the sea I would always remember, in the uncovering of the secrets of the waters...

~ *** ~

Chapter Eleven
The Shepherd and His Stallion

In the desert town of Haran—

Wandering Wolfe and Eliju traveled back to Haran, living as they had in the beginning of their journey. Wandering Wolfe often slept outside, in the open air, when the weather was fitting. Eliju regularly joined him. They'd build fires, and talk into the wee hours of the morning, while the flames flickered and turned to embers in the pit.

Eliju and the Shaman weren't concerned about enemies in Haran anymore. Eliju now had fighting skills, a bow and arrows, and his sword to defend himself. Since they'd come out into the open, as two members of the elite group, there were bound to be enemies everywhere. At least they would be overcoming them together.

Eliju knew now there was magic in his blood. Though he wasn't sure about its origins, he hoped to learn more magic, especially in combat. The magic fighting of some of the others in the group had inspired him.

Over two years had passed since Wandering Wolfe had come to Eliju's home, taking him on a journey where he'd met the most amazing people and creatures he never could have imagined. He dearly loved them all. He especially admired the elves, and liked the dwarves. They were his friends. More than this, he considered them family.

He hoped it wouldn't take long for the group to come together. He hoped for forgiveness from Alondria, for playing such a major role in Jonlin's death.

Eliju worked hard, toiling to get his farm back in working order during the hot desert days. In the nights after the sun had set and the day's work was done, and a dry chill had settled over the land, Wandering Wolfe taught him Shamanic rituals and weapon training. Sometimes, Eliju taught him about the culture and traditions of his people. They discussed and studied the Kabbalah. They labored over Jonlin's Bible, trying to understand what had made the simple bard so great of soul.

Over dinner one night in the fall, going on one year since the group had disbanded, they discussed the members of the group, and the philosophies of life and death. "For every heart we break we pay a price," Eliju said sadly.

"But you didn't intend to hurt her, Eliju. Don't be too hard on yourself."

"My intentions may matter, but the result is the same. Varawynn is lost somewhere at sea, and there's no way I can reach her. I've broken her."

"No, you've transformed her into something more than human. Her broken heart is now a gift, Eliju," Wandering Wolfe retorted. "Sometimes it is in our suffering, we find the character to become what we were always destined to be."

Hesitatingly, he asked, "But how can you be so sure you don't love her, Eliju? Your feelings for her are clearly deep, and your actions towards her are so protective. No one can deny there was a kinship and attraction between the two of you from the start. How can you be certain she's not the one for you?"

Eliju looked out into the landscape of grazing sheep, and the small olive grove just beyond the hills, where some of his neighbors harvested grapes for wine. He knew this was the time to come clean and be honest with his friend. Yet he chose not to. Instead, he changed the subject. "I've always hated my parents for abandoning me. I wanted to be nothing like them. But when I met them in Avalon, I realized that my mother and I at least have one thing in common. We both have dreams and visions that come true."

"All my life I've dreamed of the woman who I would spend my life with," Eliju continued dreamily. "She had rich black hair and pale skin, but I could never make out her eyes. When I met Varawynn, I thought for a while that she was the girl of my visions. It took me some time to be sure. In the Mirrors of the Crystal Palace, there were two women with dark hair, like mirror images, but only one was the true love I'd always dreamt of."

"The day I met Darlillyth, the moment I saw her face, I no longer had any doubts or uncertainty. She was the woman who had haunted my dreams, and dominated the visions of my future all my life. She was the one I had been waiting for. Varawynn is so much like her, and Varawynn and I share so much in common, and have endured so much together. I can't deny that I love her too, but as a sort of shadow of the light."

"The source of the light of love itself, for me, is Darlillyth. I'm sorry. I know it's complicated and messed up, and you loved her once too. Yet I feel my soul is tied to hers. Inexplicably and utterly and irrevocably bound, and I can't really envision myself with anyone else."

Wandering Wolfe sensed there was something more, something Eliju wasn't telling him. He sighed. He debated pressing the boy, then decided that if Eliju didn't want to share everything with him, it was his prerogative. He would share it when he was ready.

"I know it wasn't easy to share this with me, Eliju, but I appreciate your honesty. For myself, I think Darlillyth was the shadow of the light, and the true light of love was found in my daughter, Shadonai, the

Shadow of God. If I am going to be honest with you too, my boy, I will admit that deep down I feel I failed her."

Eliju shook his head. "We all know it wasn't your fault. Even she didn't blame you. It was her choice."

"Shadonai's life…for Varawynn's resurrection," Wandering Wolfe's voice faltered, and Eliju put his hand on his mentor's shoulder, to lend him assurance, comfort, and strength, as the Shaman had done for him so many times before. For a handful of heartbeats, the Shaman couldn't speak, and all that was left unspoken was felt in the heaviness of the air around them.

"I don't want to sound unkind or uncompassionate of your feelings, Wandering Wolfe," Eliju said carefully. "But Shadonai did kill Varawynn's brother. So, it was fitting, in a way, that she sacrificed herself to save Varawynn."

The Shaman nodded. "Of course, spiritually I know you're quite right, Eliju, but my heart…" He placed his hand over his chest and took a deep breath.

Wandering Wolfe's agonized fiery brown eyes were wet and strained with guilt. For a moment, he went back in his mind, remembering Shadonai's last moments. He closed his eyes, and he was rocking her again, like a baby in his arms. Her eyes were silver, and she was smiling in a way she hadn't smiled in her entire life. He felt it, and he felt her—an overwhelming love that was as close as his own heart's beat in his chest.

When he turned to look back at Eliju, his eyes held a glint of his daughter's quiet strength, flashing with silver. Dismissing the memories of the ghost that haunted him, he looked at Eliju with the same fatherly affection he'd felt for Shadonai. More so even, if the truth be told.

Shadonai had known that he loved Eliju more, from the first moments of their encounter, in the maze from his quest. The Shaman had always had a special place in his heart for the shepherd boy of Haran. He always would.

"I think I understand, Eliju. But I know how much you love Varawynn, and I know how much she loves you. You need each other. I'm glad she's alive somewhere out there, even if she isn't with us."

"We do need each other. Every day without her is like I'm getting further away from myself."

"Do you need Darlillyth?"

"Yes, but in a different way. Darlillyth makes me a better man, makes me stronger. It's easier to be strong with her. It's like with Varawynn I'm me, and with Darlillyth I'm how I'd like to be, how I'm going to be. You're right when you say I need Varawynn. There's a constant ache in the pit of my stomach without her."

"I worry about what's become of her. There are mysterious dangers in the waters I won't let myself think about. I do love her, but I'm stronger with Darlillyth. I need to be strong. My feelings for Varawynn are more like a weakness. What I feel is, it's more like Darlillyth needs *me*, and her need for me makes me stronger."

"But to love someone like Darlillyth...is that not like a poison?"

"I don't see her like you do. I know you think my loving Darlillyth is a weakness, and maybe for you it was, but for me it's not. I know you see Darlillyth as evil, and how could you not after all the horrible things she's done? Killing her parents, and trying to kill our Varawynn were certainly not acts of good. But loving Varawynn, as good as she is, is a poison *because* of how much I need her. I understand that because of how impossible it seems to be able to live without her, I *have* to learn how to live without her."

The Shaman shook his head. "Sometimes I don't know if you are the wisest man I know…or the biggest fool."

"Do you think my visions are wrong? You don't believe me?"

"I didn't say that."

"Then what *are* you saying?" Eliju was getting riled up and impatient. People not believing in his visions were a trigger for him.

"I'm saying I don't think you see Darlillyth clearly, and I don't think you see Varawynn clearly either. Varawynn is separated from you, but I do not believe she has abandoned you. I do not believe she ever has, or will, or ever could, not even when she lay in ashes at your feet. But Darlillyth…the horrible things that were done to her, have twisted her and darkened her soul. I am afraid she will stop at nothing to destroy you."

"Why?"

"Because you are her competition, and because…you are right in some ways, Eliju. I think she loves you. More than she ever loved me. But she is too afraid to let love in, and that's why she killed Varawynn, hoping to destroy your love for her. For what she loves she must destroy."

"But she didn't destroy my love."

"And that's how your love for her makes you strong, and it's what gives you power over her. That's why I still believe you will overcome her, why I still believe we shall win. Love conquers all in the end."

"But how do you think I will conquer her? I don't want to hurt her any more than she's already been hurt."

"I don't know exactly what the outcome will be. I only believe through your love, the outcome will be in our favor. I don't want Darlillyth to hurt anymore either. Yet I don't know how we can get her to release her pain and anger, forgive, and move forward. I believe many people have tried to help her, myself included, and have failed."

"Well, how do people move forward anyway?"

"What?"

"Well, what's so good about moving forward? If Alondria never finds anyone she loves more than Jonlin, why should she move on?"

"That wouldn't be moving forward, you're right. Alondria needs to remember that there are other kinds of love, love of friends and family for example. She needs to love them too. She needs to value our love for her. We each have callings and a purpose for our lives— after all, that is, in essence, the Prophecy."

"She is meant to fulfill her calling, and help us fulfill the Prophecy. Everything that has happened is moving us forward. Sometimes just living, getting up every morning, and going on, is an act of endurance and faith, and can be enough to see us through until things get better."

"And Varawynn...Varawynn is drowning her sorrows in the sea. Will she ever return?" Eliju's breathless longing betrayed the emotions he was trying to hide, even from himself. The question burned again in Eliju's mind, that if he loved Darlillyth so much, why was it Varawynn he couldn't live without?

Wandering Wolfe paused, as if allowing Eliju to reflect on his feelings. "Indeed, she will return. Indeed, all of the troupe shall come back together. After some time has passed, after some of our wounds have healed, scabbing over to become scars. We shall find our way back to one another, Eliju. In the meantime, we must patiently wait, finding fulfillment in our simple work, in our seeking of knowledge and truth, and in silent contemplation and reflection."

Looking at Eliju fondly, the shepherd boy said nothing more. Only a sensation flashed through his body...a sensation of moving through the waters, in a body that couldn't be human...and the way Varawynn's curls felt a little like the curly fleece on the bodies of the sheep he loved.

~ ~ ~

From the long stretch of desert sands, a wild stallion ran towards Eliju, like a mirage of water on the horizon over a long empty stretch of desert, playing tricks on a man's eyes. Its black streaming hair was a fantasy come to life, like Eliju's birth mark come to life. The horse came right to him, as if it had been searching for him all its life too.

The wild stallion's eyes were amber globes of fiery passion. With wild abandon, it flung back its mane, and Eliju pulled himself onto its back. It happened so quickly, Eliju barely knew how it happened.

He rode the great beast in ecstasy, as claiming a wild stallion as his companion had always been his grandest wish. He caressed the broad black back of the horse, like other men caress gold.

Burying his face into the sleek darkness of its mane, burrowing his face into the nape of the horse's neck, he inhaled the deliciousness of its scent. Galloping across the endless desert sands, Eliju and his dream-to-end-all-dreams of riding a wild stallion from dawn till dusk, until the beating sun set, was fulfilled.

The feeling of wild freedom spent itself again and again. The culmination of Eliju's heart and spirit found release in the self-same spirit of freedom he and the stallion shared.

"YEEHAAAAW!!!! Eliju shouted up into the sky. "HALLELUJAHHHHH! FREEDOM!!!!!"

The stallion threw back its head and whinnied. Its regal voice was not like that of a regular horse. There was something almost human-like about it, as if it's neighs and whinnies were words. This wild stallion's call was low and deep, full of power and confidence. He was magnificent.

Eliju leaned down on the horse's back, pulling up his arms higher on the horse's neck, to give them more swiftness as they ran. Eliju knew his inner thighs and arms would be bruised to high heaven, and scraped raw when they were through gallivanting, but he was only looking forward to it as evidence that this long-awaited, long-anticipated and prayed for moment had occurred.

"Faster, faster, *faster!*" Eliju cried. In the next hours he learned the most comfortable way to ride bareback on a horse. He learned of positions he could take to help the stallion run faster. *This horse is going to come in handy one day*, Eliju thought to himself, *but right now I just want to think about how FUN riding him is!*

For another hour they raced along the desert sands, in and out of the silent olive grove and low hills, until the dark night obscured Eliju's sight. "Ah!" Eliju yelled, feeling a hand coming down on his back. Falling from the back of the black stallion, he collapsed to the ground in a heap. "Ah," he felt bruises on his arms from hands unseen.

"Varawynn..." he cried out, before losing consciousness.

When he came to, Wandering Wolfe was on the ground leaning over him.

"Varawynn...Varawynn is in danger," he murmured groggily.

"There's nothing we can do Eliju," the Shaman said sorrowfully.

"I love her, *I love her!*" he yelled into the horrible whining of the wind that sounded like his words and the aching in his heart. "I love her! And I'm supposed to let her go? Let her swim among the sharks in the waters?

Let her be in danger? Without me to protect her? Without me to defend her?"

"You love her?"

"*Of course, I **love** her!* And she's in danger! Someone's *hurting* her!"

"Someone's hurting her?"

"*Yes!* And I can't do anything to stop it!"

"Maybe there is yet something we can do for her."

"What?"

"Let's say a prayer for her, Eliju."

"Say a prayer? Not perform a ritual or drum?"

"No, I think we need to say a prayer for her, my son." Wordlessly, Eliju lifted himself to a kneeling position. The black stallion was gone, but Eliju barely noticed its absence, focused as he was on Varawynn. Perhaps people meant more to him that his dream black stallion after all.

Together, the Shaman and the shepherd boy knelt and prayed for a mighty power to protect the Selkie Priestess from whatever danger had befallen her, for a mighty power to protect her and all innocent from danger. Afterwards, they felt at peace, the way Jonlin had felt when he went by himself to pray and meditate apart from the group.

It was a quiet, gentle peace they felt that passed their understanding—that they could feel calm and grateful in the midst of Varawynn's trial seemed strange, but they already knew what the outcome would be. She would be okay. They were destined to be together again one day. When the time was right.

~ ~ ~

The years passed by, day-by-day, season-by-season and Eliju, Flint, and Wandering Wolfe stayed together. Flint, the wolf, and the black stallion came and went, and Eliju trained him slowly, naming him Jareth, after someone from the Holy Book belonging to Jonlin that he now kept hitched to his side in the small pack he carried with him. The pack consisted of three things: a small knife, a vial of anti-venom, and Jonlin's Holy Book with the drawing he had made of Varawynn long ago stored safely in its folds.

Now that Shadonai was gone, Eliju was the child, in Wandering Wolfe's eyes, he'd never had. To Eliju, Wandering Wolfe was the father he'd always wanted to have. They took care of one another, as the family each had never had, and always wanted.

Eliju learned countless Shamanic rituals, and Wandering Wolfe learned too of the sacred rituals, foods, and holidays of Judaism. They shared in each other's practices and beliefs seamlessly. In perfect harmony, they lived and loved each other. During the days they were both mostly busy. At night, sometimes Eliju would ruminate over his thoughts and feelings.

The shepherd rarely spoke to Wandering Wolfe about it, but he thought about Varawynn and Darlillyth often. Darlillyth, the woman they'd both loved, was a topic and conversation they'd made a silent pact to keep off-limits, since Eliju had first expressed and been honest about his feelings, as it always seemed to get them into an argument.

Eliju couldn't help but wonder if Wandering Wolfe thought of her as often as he did, or if he thought about her at all. For that matter, he wondered if Darlillyth ever thought about him. If he'd only known, his name was spoken from her lips every single day, using a term he never would have imagined.

Eliju also thought often about Jonlin, regretting how Alondria had taken his death, though he didn't blame her for it. He wondered if he'd ever see his parents again, and if he did, how much better or worse he would feel from the meeting. He wondered if he'd ever have the courage to kill his parents for abandoning him. Wouldn't that make him just like Darlillyth?

He worried over the Prophecy too. If they did come back together and were successful, he was foretold to become their king. If that happened, what kind of king would he be? If he killed his own parents that would set a precedence for the law that he wasn't sure he was comfortable making. Especially not after all he had learned in the Akashic Records.

Nor was he sure he was comfortable telling his people that what was good for the goose was not good for the gander, and he could do and be as he pleased, but they had better do as he commanded. If he chose to rule in such a manner, it seemed to him that he wouldn't be that different from King Mardavian himself.

Eliju learned a lot about Shamanism from Wandering Wolfe as the years passed. The growing they did was in the simple daily routine of duty, responsibility, and study. Their wounds were healed in the time of waiting, through repetitive actions, and the practice of knowledge they learned and shared. As the years passed, Wandering Wolfe learned much about Judaism, and together they learned much about the Christian faith of Jonlin.

As the Christian Word of God became a part of their vocabulary, they slowly changed together in learning about the God of love, and the simple beauty of quiet faith. The Bible was added to Eliju's morning and nightly reading of the Talmud and Torah, and Jesus' words illuminated the hut with a radiance, where before there had only been intense shadows of loneliness and sadness. Where before he'd kept his shutters closed and locked, now he opened them wide, to let the morning light in.

While waiting for the group to come back together, peace was found by the Shaman and his student, on the journey of the seeking of truth and the wisdom of life. And what true love is. They retained the tools and lessons from the religions they'd been born into and brought up in, but it was Christ who captured their hearts, and healed their souls.

~ *** ~

I'd grown up a simple farm boy, a simple shepherd who loved his flock. Now I was no longer a boy. I was becoming a man. I wanted a family, but that seemed impossible so isolated in my small hut, in such an isolated region of Haran.

I wondered if I would ever experience the simple pleasures in life, like love. The simple pleasures of husband and wife that others took for granted, were themselves complex and out of reach for me. As they had turned out to be for Wandering Wolfe, my mentor and father-figure.

I dreamed often of a daughter and son bearing my eyes of blue and green. Her eyes were blue and his were green. I did not know if these children existed in the future, or were perhaps wishful thinking on my part, but my dreams were as vivid as if they were right in front of me. As if I could reach out my arms and embrace them.

The memories of my children stayed with me, deep green eyes and blue, son and daughter both hidden away from me. I often wondered if they were all in my imagination. And yet their images could not be dismissed. It was as if my children themselves were calling out to me to find them. I wanted to be the father and have a relationship with them that I'd never had with my own.

Since I'd finally found my stallion, or rather, since my stallion had found me, my senses were more heightened, and I was more and more sensitive to the land itself. The world turned, and I felt it. I felt the burning of the fires, and the turning of the tides. I felt the young mountains beyond my home expanding. I felt the grass growing and dying, dying and growing, from season-to-season, from year–to-year, each day.

I felt the flowers blooming, never striving as they reached out and up towards the sun. They budded, blossomed, bloomed, flourished and died. Then they came back to life in the spring. I felt it all.

Opening itself with ease to bloom without malice or sadness at its inevitable end, fading into withered crinkled pieces of the vibrant beauty it once was, I felt the flower's fading and decay into the soil, as other flowers took its place and bloomed after it had decomposed into the ground, strengthening and nourishing the next flower's growth and blossoming. I began to understand more and more the circle of life and the importance of moving forward, with the seasons and time.

I became more observant to the ripe beauty of the earth enfolding itself before my eyes in the rhythmic movement of the wind. I began to recognize the constant transformations of nature itself, and how humans were also meant to be in a constant state of change, of evolution. In this way, I began to transform myself, from the inside out.

~ *** ~

Chapter Twelve
The Betrayal of the Chosen King

Among the nomadic Shiwanna Tribe, travelling to the desert town of Haran—

Back at the Shiwanna tribe, Shadow Rain tried to push memories of Eliju from her mind. Yet the more she tried, the more his image and memories of their time together filled her consciousness, leaving little room for anything else. Fantasizing constantly about things that'd never happened and were unlikely to, the idea of them never happening made her want to act out impulsively.

If he didn't love Varawynn, there wasn't a fat chance in Haran he would ever love *her*. It was about as likely as hyacinths blooming in the winter. *Well then,* Shadow Rain thought to herself, *by the gods of the clouds and skies and storms of my people I will* **make** *it happen.*

Neglecting her duties had become an everyday occurrence for Shadow Rain, though she never neglected the people of their tribe and their problems or concerns. Though happy and glad to be back among the people who were like herself, who respected and revered her, with whom she had nothing to prove, she yet would rather sit alone in her tent and fantasize about Eliju than do too much else. There was nothing for her to prove, so why not dream of claiming the one thing she knew she could never have…Eliju's love?

Sighing to herself, Shadow Rain turned back to the Medicine Man. She'd nearly forgotten he was sitting in her tent talking to her, lost as she was in her fantasies of Eliju.

"Dear Shadow Rain, it will not be long now before I retire. It will be you to take my place." His shocking words immediately brought her back to her senses.

"Already? How many years more? I don't know near enough yet, White Tiger! It's only been a few years since the group disbanded and I returned to the tribe! You do know we will probably come back together to complete the Prophecy at some point?"

"I realize that. We will just have to deal with your absence when the time comes. You know more than you think you do, Shadow Rain. I will be available for consultations, if you feel the situation calls for outside council."

"I'm questioning this timing, White Tiger. My destiny—"

"Your destiny with the Prophecy will take precedence, but in the meantime, we want you to take over as the tribe's spiritual leader. Soon. Time is of the essence. We must be in the moment. You know we support your fate, Shadow Rain, but you are also fated to become the Medicine Woman of the Shiwanna tribe."

"I don't feel ready, but I will accept the honor when you see fit, White Tiger."

"I will remain in the position for six moon cycles yet Shadow Rain. I know you will be ready when the time comes. You have six months to prepare." Nodding to her significantly, she knew she had no choice. As he left the tent, the softly flapping skin of the tent opening hit her like a slap on the face.

Only six moon cycles…just six months! *I just have to see Eliju again before—I won't be able to sneak away after I become Medicine Woman…duty, honor, responsibility, will take precedence. Oh, bother! Sometimes I'd just like to be like a horse—wild and free and only have to worry about myself!* She'd never felt such an urgent and wild need before. She wasn't like a horse. She was like the turtle on her stomach.

She was slow-footed. She wasn't quick-witted and outspoken like Alondria, or quick to swing into action like Aldoran. She liked traveling pretty well, but she needed her nest to come home to. But there was a part of her character, yes there was, that was as reckless as any other fool in love.

She wanted to see Eliju again; she was compelled to go to him. Now there wasn't much time. Shadow Rain had never felt such a desperate need, never known the obsession of loving one man above all others. But she idolized the Chosen One and possessively wanted him for herself, even if only for a moment.

In this weakened state, when she would have done anything to have him…anything that was at her expense even—or his; a well-timed knock beat on the ground outside her tent flap. "Who is it?" Shadow Rain asked, as she opened the flap to a stranger standing before her earthen abode.

From her fingertips, Shadow Rain could see she was a wizened old woman. From her long fingers and fingernails, she was what they called in the nomadic tribes a "Spearfinger—" a sharp-fingered hag with six fingers on each hand, coupled with sharp wisdom spewed without diplomacy or pretense. "I have been waiting for this moment for a long time," the hag said to her.

"Please come in," Shadow Rain replied, eager for reasons she sensed, but could not have explained.

The old women labored inside the small tent opening, sitting cross-legged before Shadow Rain.

"I know the desires of your heart, dear child," she told her. "I know what, or should I say *who* it is your heart is longing for. I know there's no dissuading you from having him. Since he is hopelessly disinterested in you, it will take the wily ways of a woman of experience to ensnare the boy into the night of passion you seek."

"I have no idea what you're talking about," Rain shrugged precociously, trying to seem dignified and proud, but her voice cracked.

"I am referring to the Chosen One, Eliju," said the old hag directly.

"How do you know about him?" Shadow Rain gasped.

"Oh, my dear child, I know him well. And I know that it matters not to you so much how I know, but that what I know will help you to accomplish what you seek, nay, what you were predestined to have…"

"What's that!?" Rain exclaimed.

"His seed, my child."

"His seed?"

"Of course! The seed which shall give you the child, the child by the man you love. You know you want to have the young man, and we both know you want to bear his child. You feel if you cannot have him forever, you may at least have his child forever. For his child shall always hold and be a part of him, by the self-same blood coursing through her veins."

"Her veins?"

"Yes, of course…*the meaning will be lost on her until the day, when her daughter's birth shows the way.*" The old woman nodded to herself, "Your daughter by the Chosen King, Eliju. Your daughter shall show the way."

The old woman just kept nodding to herself, acting as if she were letting Rain in on a special secret. "So, do you want it or not?"

"Want what?"

The ugly woman smiled indulgently, her crater face wrinkling in a dozen tiny creases with the expression. "Want to know how to ensnare the boy of course. Your inexperienced mind will never come up with it on its own. You'd be pining away forever if I hadn't come to help you. Well, do you love him or not, child?"

"I love him...with all my heart!" Shadow Rain exclaimed, bursting out with the words she hadn't fully admitted even to herself yet.

"And do you want to own this boy?"

"Yes, but I can't make him love me, and I just know he never will..."

"You're right, he won't—at least not of his own accord. And if you cannot hold his heart forever...would a single night with him suffice for a lifetime of fantasies?"

"Oh, yes, yes!"

"And would having his child, in a way, make you feel as if you would always have him? As if he were always with you...*in the child?*"

Shadow Rain hesitated. Of course, she knew what the old woman was saying was horribly wrong. But the woman was right in that they were her desires. Although it was wrong, the intensity of her emotions had a life of their own. She wanted to make love with Eliju, and she was determined to bear his child.

She sensed these strange desires were her destiny, and she could not, and *would not,* be able to quell the desires until the desires were met and fulfilled. This is what she'd seen back in the mirror of the Crystal Palace. This would be her worst act in life, but raising his daughter, she felt certain would be her best.

The hideous hag smiled. She knew she had her now. So, the experienced elder spun her yarns of secrets about the way women had trapped and ensnared men for centuries, with the use of special herbs and spells, and with well-considered timing, she could have the desires of her heart. When the woman left, all Shadow Rain could think about was how limited she was on time, how much she just *had* to see Eliju, she *must* go *now,* she must leave, she must be with him, to see and touch him, to love him, *just one time...*

Rushing from the tent the flapping skin of her door waving wildly behind her, she moved faster than she had since the last battle that'd claimed her best friend, Jonlin. Charging full bore in the direction of the chief's leather skin tent, there was no real "rushing" in their nomadic tribe, for as she was the promised Medicine Woman-to-be, everywhere she went those who saw her came to ask her questions, or compliment her, or seek her knowledge and wisdom and advice. Usually, she tried to be as slow and patient as the birthmark of the tortoise on her abdomen with her tribe, but today...

"Please help us, Shadow Rain! My son has been suffering so since his pet fox died! Oh, Medicine Woman, whatever should I do to cheer him up?" Something wild and impulsive had taken root in Shadow Rain's normally gentle and steady soul.

Biting her lip impatiently, she asked, "He has a love of animals then I take it?"

"Oh yes, Silver Lynx simply lives for them!"

"Tell him White Tiger and I will meet with him in a few months to discuss his calling as a caretaker for the animals in our tribe."

It had been something she'd been considering for the boy for some time. Watching this young man in his love for the animals, and knowing the boy for all his years, she knew well this was the perfect position for him, his family, and their tribe. It was his destiny.

"Oh, Shadow Rain he would absolutely love that! Thank you so much! I will tell him! Oh, you always know just what to do!" Smiling at the loving mother, she wondered if the expression she saw there would ever be worn on her own face, and rushing through the tribe once more, she tried to get to the chief's tent before anyone else saw her.

Chief Grey Wolf would surely be pleased when the mother came to him with this solution. It would reassure him and soothe any worries he had about her being ready to take the place of White Tiger, but at the moment it was not his concerns or the concerns of becoming the Medicine Woman which was irking her.

"Chief Grey Wolf!" she called, seeing him just leaving his tent. "Chief Grey Wolf, please wait!"

"Yes, Shadow Rain? Yes, my dear what is it?"

"I have a request; a request to see someone from the quest! We always knew the group would someday come back together…"

"And is this the time, Shadow Rain?" his eyes rose in surprise.

"No, no, it's just time…time I see someone from the group of fourteen, Chief Grey Wolf. It's very important or I wouldn't ask." Biting her lower lip again, hating to lie, still she found the courage to meet the chief of the tribe, who'd always put his utmost respect and trust in her, in the eyes.

After a nervous rattling of heartbeats, while the chief looked deeply into her slanted cloudy eyes, and studied her painfully intense expression, making her exceedingly uncomfortable, he nodded his assent. "How long will you be gone?"

"Not long," she assured him. "It may take a few moon cycles to travel, and I will not visit long, but I think it would better to see him now rather than after I take over the position of Medicine Woman to the tribe."

"So, it is a male you are visiting, Shadow Rain?" He was studying her very carefully. His eyes missed nothing. She bit her lip to keep from cursing the man. What was wrong with her? Why couldn't she get a hold of herself and her emotions? She felt like she should apologize to the chief for cursing him in her head.

"Please Grey Wolf, it's urgent and it is something I don't care to discuss." He said nothing more, merely nodded. She simply couldn't bring herself to outright lie to the man telling him Eliju was ill or something. Besides she was about to do a lot worse than lie. How many things could she do in a day to make herself feel guilty over?

As soon as he'd nodded his assent, she nearly dove from him to pack for her journey to the desert. Dashing away from everyone in the tribe as fast as she could; away from her people, away from her own family…to get to *him* as fast as was feasibly possible.

Going over and over every memory of Eliju, day after day, she turned the memories over in her mind, like a stone worn smooth by the consistent pressure and penetration of the waves. After hardening the stone of her heart, which was being molded and reshaped by the constant beating waters of her memories, she knew she would go to him in Haran, and see if he could possibly see in her, the love of his love.

Could he, would he ever consider coming back to her tribe *with her*? Would he ever consider becoming the tribe's chief, with her as the Medicine Woman? Was it foolish to dare to dream of something so fantastic? Of course, she knew deep down in her heart this was never to be, but the hope of the fantasy propelled her forward on her journey from the mountains of her people to the flat desert lands of Haran where Eliju lived, with more relentless fervor than she had thought herself capable of.

If only Jonlin had been there, as her best friend, and voice of reason, he may have helped her, may have guided her to a different path. As life no longer had him in it, she was prepared to make some questionable choices in her pursuit to have and to hold some part of Eliju, the object of her love and obsession. Even if whatever she gleaned of his was not freely given, she came to the desert prepared to steal it…

Through forests and over mountains she traveled alone, through valleys and the desert, through the vineyards of grapes to be turned into wine. Single-mindedly and determinedly, she walked through groves and abandoned fields of grape and olive vines, ever closer to the man she'd grown to love.

She could feel the energy and spirit of Eliju on the very soil of the ground she walked on, and his fire energy pulled her toward him; leading her to his very cabin door in the dead of night, feeling like a loony bird in a death flight over the waters that would inevitably claim her wildly beating wings and heart.

It was he who unbarred the door to her, and his face was like the soothing balm of aloe vera on an open wound to her frightened heart and overwrought mind. She certainly seemed wild-eyed and irrational to Eliju, as he guided her inside. Her lips were bloodied and chapped from nervous biting.

Restlessly she moved from room to room in his hut, sitting on one piece of furniture then bounding off to another, and standing at length and talking about things from her tribe Eliju had no reference for or ability to relate to. Lord knows he was trying to be patient. But she was really just rambling on, and had no concrete reason for being there.

She wasn't talking or acting like herself at all. It was as if a Phooka from the Fae Realms had taken over her body. Varawynn had told Eliju about them. They were tricksters and shapeshifters. One of their favorite past times was wreaking havoc on poor farm animals, as other animals were usually terrified of them, which was kind of how Eliju felt about how Rain was behaving just now.

Wandering Wolfe came inside at this point, from sleeping outside, as was his custom, after hearing voices inside. None too soon for Eliju, who welcomed a reprieve to take the edge off her endless blathering. "Shadow Rain!" Wandering Wolfe exclaimed gaily, sweeping the girl up and into his arms. "I can't believe you're here! Are you trying to bring the group back together!"

"I wish!" Shadow Rain laughed. "I miss you all so much!" her eyes looked Eliju's body up and down, drinking in his growing muscles from the years of hard laboring on the farm.

"Oh, we miss you too, Shadow Rain!" said Wandering Wolfe, practically bubbling over with joy at seeing her. Eliju stood apart, eyeing Shadow Rain aloofly, needing space from her clingy attentions and endless chattering. He cared about her, really, but something about her energy right now unnerved him. He felt a strong urge to find his black stallion and get the hell away from here. She almost gave him an ominous feeling, though he tried to dismiss it as being too hard on the poor girl.

She was tired from traveling, and went to bed soon after her arrival, which relieved the shepherd greatly. "She never says anything when she talks, Wandering Wolfe, have you ever noticed that?" he whispered to him, trying to make sure she wouldn't hear. "She says a lot, but never really says anything at all!"

"Don't say that, Eliju, it isn't nice. You don't want to hurt her feelings," warned Wandering Wolfe.

"No, I don't want to hurt her feelings," Eliju agreed. "I just have a weird feeling about her being here. Honestly, I don't know what's gotten into me. I should be happy to see her. Of course, I should. But I feel, rather, a foreboding…"

Wandering Wolfe looked at him disapprovingly, and Eliju decided then and there he would keep his unfounded misgivings to himself. Really, it made sense Rain would want to see them again before she took over as her tribe's Medicine Woman, and found it harder to slip away and visit any of her friends from the group.

She was probably just acting so strangely out of the exhaustion of her solitary travels. What was so strange about *that?*

It became blatantly clear to Rain all too quickly that Eliju was never going to love her, that at best she would be considered a dear, slightly crazy friend, never even a best friend. Wandering Wolfe and Eliju's animals had held the corner market on that before he'd even met Shadow Rain.

Even Alondria held a greater place of honor and respect in his eyes and heart, as she did for them all. She was divinely beautiful, but more than that, it was her kindness, fairness, and intelligence that won over both males and females.

Yet Shadow Rain could feel a future life kicking in her womb, feel a desperate impulse to claim some piece of him. She could feel her daughter's spirit as one half of her and one half of him. It was destiny for her to bare his child, as it had been destiny that claimed the life of Jonlin.

"Come outside, Shadow Rain, I want you to see Eliju with the black stallion of his dreams...remember how he told us he always wanted a horse, but one that came to him from the wild and chose him?"

"No, I don't remember that," said Shadow Rain.

"Oh, well maybe it was before you'd joined us. Either way, I want you to see Eliju with him."

She was glad she followed the Shaman outside that day to the clearing of old roots, from what had once been an olive grove. Seeing Eliju on the back of the wild stallion, with its long black hair flowing out before him, running as fast as it could against the wind, with Eliju's hands and arms raised up in freedom and abandon, was utter joy. There was something heavenly in seeing a person wholly themselves. Eliju was in his element.

That fire, that wild spirit, that horse's spirit, that need Eliju sometimes had just to run, to ride on the back of a wild thing into the sun and wind, was so very different than the essence of Shadow Rain. She was slow, methodically laboring over any problem.

His essence fascinated her. Their differences captivated her. Seeing him with his stallion, made her wish she could be more like that...more like him. More...free.

She wished she had his spirit, not just because it would make them more suited as mates, but because deep down, she really would have rather had the spirit of a horse, than the spirit of a tortoise.

~ ~ ~

About a week or so went by in her visit, Wandering Wolfe said he was going on a short journey alone, as he did from time-to-time. Eliju never minded, for as much as he relished his time with the Shaman, he still needed some time to himself. He surmised that this sudden journey was probably more to give Shadow Rain the opportunity to talk to Eliju alone about her feelings than a short sojourn. Wandering Wolfe had aptly speculated that this was likely why she'd come, and that when he returned, she would probably be gone, as Eliju would reject her advances.

That evening Shadow Rain sat alone during twilight watching the Chosen One, without the comfort and crutch of the Shaman. She was watching Eliju with his stallion again, running along the twisted old roots of the abandoned olive grove, kicking up the sand into the skies, with their wild freedom, with their reckless abandon that brought unwanted tears of longing and desire into the young woman's eyes.

Recalling the mirrors in the Crystal Palace, recalling the mirror of your worst act, Shadow Rain realized what she'd seen there was about to come to pass. Ready to steal from Eliju what he would never give freely, she went into his innocent abode whilst he was with his horse, and brewed the old hag's potion, the way she'd carefully learned from the Spearfinger, and memorized and practiced on her journey to Haran.

She'd waited and watched carefully for this opportunity, when Wandering Wolfe was away, and she was alone with the object of her desire. After the concoction was complete, she dumped the potion into the soup she'd been preparing over the stove, for when Eliju returned home. It was premeditative what she did. In her obsession with Eliju, and his closeness with Varawynn, Shadow Rain had remembered something Varawynn had said to Eliju about the first night they'd met—something about Camelot.

So, Shadow Rain had read the Legend of Camelot and the Knights of the Round Table and the Isle of Apples, and the evil, or perhaps, merely misunderstood, Morgan Le Fey, depending upon your perspective, and what angle you were coming from. The story had given Shadow Rain this idea. Really, she'd had this idea in her head even before the old hag had knocked on her tent door. The Spearfinger had shown her how to do what she'd been thinking of doing all along. She'd carried the means with her to Haran, carried the ingredients, so that just in case Eliju wouldn't give her his love, she would have the wherewithal and the means to *take* it.

Holding in her hands the special chalice etched with crescent moons and stars, laced with herbs and filled with wine and the ingredients to glean the desired and intended effect, as Eliju's senses were already dulled by the soup she'd carefully prepared, he drank the chalice of wine full of herbs like a baby drinking its mother's milk.

It was so easy, and worked so well, Shadow Rain felt a little let down. Shouldn't doing something wrong be more of a challenge? Why was doing something good so difficult, and doing something she knew was bad, as simple as taking candy from a baby?

Shadow Rain murmured the spell softly under her breath. Groggily mumbling to himself, he stumbled about the room. Falling over her, she half-carried, half-dragged him into his bedroom. Shadow Rain fell on top of him, as he pulled her tightly against him.

"Mmmm kiss me," Eliju murmured, pressing her lips firmly against his.

Shadow Rain's mouth opened hungrily to his mouth, searching for his tongue, eager for his taste. Pulling his shirt off, he made soft, sensual moaning sounds, as he stroked her body and pulled up the hem of her dress. Of course, she knew it was wrong. He didn't even realize what was happening, but she loved him, and she wanted him, and she knew this was the only way she was ever going to have him.

This would only happen once. She had just one shot at this. She wanted a baby. She wanted his baby. Her hormones raging, she thought if this was her only night with him, she was determined to make it a good one.

It turned into an unforgettable night of passion Shadow Rain would recall in her mind over and over again as the years went rushing by, in an endless replay. It was the perfect night of fantasy she would cherish until the day she died. Kissing him all over his face and head, her hungry, inexperienced lips made their way down his neck and onto his chest.

"Oh, Eliju…" she tingled and thrilled from head-to-toe with the sweet sound of his name on her lips, and her ability in this moment to express her feelings for him in the physical.

"Oh, Varawynn," he murmured, tearing her bodice apart in two with his bare hands. She knew that it was Darlillyth he loved; she'd seen it on his face when she'd exposed herself to them, and yet he was calling out Varawynn's name and ripping her clothes to smithereens?

Regardless of who Eliju really loved, she selfishly took advantage of his mindless murmuring, as if he had said her name. Her desire for him was too strong to be denied. They were so very wrong for each other, so wrong even she could see it, but she loved him for being the person she wished she could be, and felt she loved him enough in that moment for the both of them.

By the shy morning's first light, her betrayal of their Chosen King was complete. She already knew down deep inside—that his seed had taken root in her womb, and their daughter would be born of him without his knowledge, in late September or early October.

Kissing his lips one last time as he slept, she slipped undetected back to the spare bedroom, where she packed her things. She could not wait for Wandering Wolfe's return to say goodbye to him, for he would easily and readily detect the guilt and deceit within her eyes. The best-case scenario was that Eliju would remember nothing when the herbs wore off, or at least imagine it to have been a dream. She would not allow herself to consider the worst-case scenario.

The group was disbanded, and as the years passed his daughter would grow unbeknownst by him. The day would come when Shadow Rain would have to come to terms with the truth of her betrayal. But for now, she'd best get back to her tribe, and become the Medicine Woman, before anyone knew she was with child. She would have nine moon cycles to prepare for the coming and the raising of a daughter who she'd known for some time was meant to be, born of the betrayal of the Chosen King.

Autumn was the time of harvest, and though the seeds were reaped in sin, her daughter's life would be a harvest time of great joy and abundance...at least that was what Shadow Rain told herself, to ease her guilt and still her anxious thoughts, and comfort her ever restless, hormonal body that longed to give birth.

"Oh, Autumn Rain, my daughter, my hope, please show me the way…"

Autumn Rain

The summer heat gives way to cooler winds,
The fall of mankind that sprung from sin.
It was the Fall of Angel and Man,
That exiled us from the most beautiful land.

The light disperses the deep shadows,
Shadows made more prominent in the summer day,
In Autumn's gentler light, the shadows fade.
By the Autumn Rain, the dim light shows the way.

From the worst action of a life,
The light springs forth.
The destiny and fate
For these three: horse, tortoise, and bird born free.

In Autumn Rain, the land and sin is cleansed,
With the power to die, and be reborn again.
Through the shadows beyond the trees,
The burning autumn light, shall lead.

--The Prophecy of Shadow Rain

~ ~ ~

Chapter Thirteen
Along the Grecian Shores

From when and where the group disbanded on the Isle of Sky, traveling into southern Europe, into Greece—

After the group dispersed, Pharean asked Aldoran, "So where does that leave us?"

"Together," he'd assured her. That was enough for her. Aldoran and Pharean traipsed off together, excited to explore parts unknown. Aldoran didn't want to go back to his Kingdom and be with his sister. Her cold aloofness was only altered by sudden, unpredictable bouts of rage. He just didn't have the patience for her blaming and bitterness.

No longer having a home or family to go back to, Pharean had formed an intense attachment to Aldoran, who'd valiantly protected her on more than one occasion. So she was content to be his shadow sidekick on their adventures. Now they really were the two parts they'd been pretending to play upon their first meeting: they were seeking their fortunes on adventures to faraway lands, for how long and to where it would lead them mattered not, just so long as they were together.

Aldoran took the lead, and Pharean provided helpful knowledge along the way. As her father had been an advisor to King Mardavian, and a philosopher who often brought his children along with him on his travels, she'd picked up a lot about tracking.
It was second nature to her now.

It was not such common knowledge to Aldoran, who hadn't had much need in his prior life to travel, having stayed mainly in his Kingdom in the Andorra Mountains. Pharean's ability to know animal tracks from human tracks, and how the breaking of branches may mean the immediate presence of a predator, was both intriguing and invaluable on their wanderings.

Alternating equally between talking and listening to one another, Pharean enjoying sharing her knowledge about the trees, and why they grew in this area versus the desert, and why this bird sang, and this bird didn't, and why this bird lived in this region versus another. Aldoran listened aptly, actively asking her questions and filing away her precious knowledge like gold. Sometimes her communication or details were too vague, and Aldoran knew just how to ask pointed questions in order to clarify her meaning. Thus, Aldoran was like the sharpener to her wit, the ink to her pen, and together they felt like they could accomplish anything.

Aldoran would often recall his life in the Andorra Mountains, regaling Pharean about his love of adventures with his beloved twin sister, his training in fencing, his studies in religion, spirituality, and the philosophies of life.

Out of the blue one day, Aldoran burst out, "I have an idea!"

Pharean looked up at his animated expression, and smiled back at him. His enthusiasm was contagious. "Well, what is it? What's your idea?" she asked, nearly as excited as he was already, and not even knowing why.

"We could pen a book together!"

"A book?"

"Yes!"

"I love that idea, Aldoran!"

"We could even write several books! We could write a book about trekking, about trees and plants and animals, and where they grow and how they grow, and why, and we could write a book about your father's work…his philosophies! Oh, Pharean! Wouldn't he be *so* proud? Wouldn't that make him so *happy*?"

For a moment Pharean froze like a statue in place. As Aldoran picked her up and threw her around, and up and down, and danced a jig, and spryly ran off his excited energy to-and-fro, like a puppy given too many treats, he finally looked back at Pharean still clearly frozen in a quiet haze.

"What is it? He asked her tentatively. "I thought you would like the idea?" Upon his words, Pharean promptly burst into tears.

"Oh, no I've done something wrong," Aldoran sighed to himself. The last thing he'd wanted to do was hurt her.

"That's just it," cried Pharean. "It's the best idea I ever heard! My father would be thrilled! How come I couldn't come up with that myself?" Aldoran laughed at her, pulling her into his strong arms, and letting her cry like a baby into his sturdy chest.

"That's okay," he told her when she pulled away from his wet shirt, stained with her snot and tears, "It wasn't one of my favorites anyway." Flashing her one of his golden grins, just like that, before she knew which end was up, her tears had turned to laughter. Her bittersweet pain and surface anguish at missing her father had turned into the excitement of the proposition of making an incredible legacy from his death.

"But where should we write the?" Pharean asked him. "Wouldn't a study work better than the outdoors?"

"Money is no object," Aldoran assured her readily, "I have all the money we need to provide us with pen and paper, and the outdoors is more inspiring to write in then a stuffy studio. Besides, the trees and air and the birds we pass by will inspire what we write. Getting out and seeing, touching, and experiencing what we're writing about will make it that much better! And of course, as part-muse, hopefully I will also be an inspiration to you as well." He smiled.

"That makes sense," Pharean had to agree, "and I'm sure that you will be, but who'll actually be doing the writing?"

"Mainly you'll be dictating to me of course. I can add the descriptions you have a hard time with, and you can edit what I've written at the end of the day, while I catch us some prey for our dinner."

Pharean shook her head in wonder. "It's perfect. You've thought of everything." Aldoran threw her one of his wide, toothy grins again that addled her brain and sent her mind shooting off into space on the breeze.

They were both dreamers, but Aldoran provided an anchor for their dreams, a practical application for their creativity. Working well together, they made a great team. What one lacked, the other seemed to naturally or intuitively provide.

Aldoran insisted on writing the three books all at one time, so as not to get bored with the one they were on, and restlessly ponder the others. When they were restless, and they both often were restless of spirit, they switched between the three books effortlessly, and almost always on the same wavelength, they turned to the next book at the same time…their thoughts floating in and out of each other's, like air effortlessly directs the movement of water, and the turning of the tides.

One morning, about seven months into their adventures, Aldoran took Pharean's hands in his and kissed them. As the rays of the dawn flooded his face with light, he said somberly to her, "It's time."

With fluttering heart and blushing cheeks, Pharean stuttered, "Time for what?"

"It's time to go back to the Greek Isles…to your home in Ascalon. I want to see where you grew up. I've seen where your family met their end. Will you let me bring you to where they raised you, where you loved them?"

Pharean's cerulean eyes flooded with the tears of her deep pain. She couldn't speak, so she just nodded, and without words he understood. This meant a lot to her, but she was scared and trepidatious about seeing the place she used to belong…with the family she had lost.

So, they traveled to a place he'd never been, to the land she'd so loved, where beaches of white stretched over shores of soft green-blue. Where dolphins danced amongst the waters, and seafaring men sold their catches in the farmers' markets of the coastal towns. Where merchants sold gold and jewels, and necklaces of sea shells were bought and sold for pennies to the children who smiled and grinned and danced for their wares.

Where ladies and men wore robes of white, and the girls wore their hair in long layers of luscious brown, black, or blonde curls, adorned with flowers and sea shells. Where ladies wore turquoise necklaces on their long swan's necks, and flowers were wound around their necks, wrists, waists, and worn on their feet woven into sandals; colors and blooming life splashed on beds of white. Where the people loved as freely as the waves beat to and fro against the pure white shores. Where life had once been so simple, and hope had not been so hard a fish to catch.

She'd grown up feasting on olives and fishes, on berries, breads, and exotic wines, spending days lying languidly in the sunshine. She studied, walked, danced, ate, and laughed along the Grecian shores, dreaming of a future that had once seemed so bright, now dimmed with the death of the family that had been such an integral part of her happiness.

There, upon a mountaintop overlooking craggy cliffs, by the time velvety night had swept through the sky and over the shores, with the sound of waves crashing against craggy rocks, lay Pharean's high-rise home. By far, the largest home in the area, her father, the philosopher, Ruminous, had been both popular and respected.

Pharean and Aldoran climbed the cliff, and Pharean found the key in the old hiding spot for their entry. They fell asleep almost immediately upon arrival, without any exploration of the elegant estate, which stood in fairly good shape, in spite of it standing empty for going on two years now, and at dawn's first light they walked to the town square.

Pharean could've walked there in her sleep. As she walked into the heart of the town she'd grown up in, flooded with the soft early morning light, the townsfolk ran up to accost her.

"Pharean! Pharean!" The people of Ascalon cried, their faces alight with joy and excitement. For a while they reveled in the happiness of having their beloved Pharean back home, and meeting her handsome friend, Aldoran. It wasn't long before they were asking where the rest of her family was, and what had happened to them all this time.

Evidently King Mardavian had never returned to this town to inform them that Ruminous had been betraying the King for the better part of Pharean's life. She only thanked God that there hadn't been time for King Mardavian to kill all the people in this small coastal town in his wrath at Ruminous' betrayal, thanks to the timing of the group of Chosen Ones coming together to bring his defeat. Since Varawynn had killed him, he'd never have the chance to come back and kill them off, as there was no question he would have done eventually.

Pharean turned to Aldoran with a look of helplessness. Aldoran stepped forward then, not shy to speak up for her when she needed him to. It mattered not that this was the first time he was meeting her people. He was more afraid to not be there for Pharean when she needed him, than he was concerned about what these people would think of him.

"I'm sure that all of you held the utmost esteem for the Philosopher Ruminous, and personal Advisor to the King, but he was an even better man than any of you knew. When his daughter Pharean was put in danger by King Mardavian as a little girl, Ruminous vowed to thwart the King at every turn in order to protect his family and his people from his twisted and violent acts of destruction. Ruminous knew that anyone who harmed a little girl was nothing less than evil, and he could never follow, or help to advise such a man."

Aldoran's rushing in to her defense did wonders for her nerves, fueling the young woman with strength and courage she wouldn't have had without him by her side, speaking up for her. Pharean stepped into place beside him, taking a deep breath, and speaking now for her father.

"This might be hard for all of you to hear and accept, but after the King harmed me as a young child, my father had a vision of God, of the one God who would redeem his family and his people. The God of my mother who you know is a descendent of that spiritual group of Jews, the Essenes. He converted to Christianity when I was little girl, secretly. He converted to the religion worshiping Christ, the son of God, who died for all our sins."

The townspeople looked to one another in surprise. Very few people had known about Ruminous' conversion. He was afraid if King Mardavian found out, he would take it out on innocent people. King Mardavian had never been a man of God, and had resented the idea of any God or religion interfering with his ultimate power and authority.

"Christ, the son of God who I and my people also worship," Aldoran interjected to make the claim for his faith as well. "And I also," added Pharean. The townspeople gasped and murmured to each as Pharean continued to speak. She wasn't used to standing in front of people giving a speech or orating, and didn't enjoy being the center of attention, but she knew her father would want them to know the truth.

"Due to the hard work of my father, this coastal town has clearly remained thriving in our family's absence. A few years ago, when the King discovered the secret workings of one his most loyal advisors, my father, working against him, he killed a whole town of innocent people, as well as all of—"

Pharean had gotten this far, and she was trying, but the unbidden and unwanted tears welled up in her eyes, and her throat closed until she couldn't speak. Again, Aldoran came to her rescue.

"As well as Ruminous and his family, all, that is, except Pharean. Her family died to save her, as she is one of the Chosen Ones prophesied to redeem and protect us all. But you all know about that."

Pharean recovered and continued, for here was something good she could tell the people she'd known all her life, something to give them hope. "But you've not yet learned what happened soon after this. The group I joined engaged in combat against King Mardavian and his men, and one of the girls whom he had also harmed, overtook him. I come to you with good tidings: King Mardavian is dead!"

The town cheered. The crowd was beginning to get pretty riled up, but Pharean wasn't done. Pharean looked to Aldoran for help for the last bit. "Pharean is not going to be staying here. She belongs with the group of Chosen Ones. She's going to be staying with all of us. She may never return here with all you. She has come now to impart the truth, and to say goodbye."

Aldoran's eyes turned vulnerable, as he looked to Pharean for reassurance that he had not spoken out of turn. She nodded to him. For she knew in her heart that as much as she'd loved growing up here, she no longer belonged here.

"With my father and King Mardavian gone, you are free to become self-governing. This region is now free to worship and love as you would," Pharean looked at the townsfolk she'd known and loved all her life, with a shy smile. "Continue to believe in the pagan gods or convert to Christianity—you are free to choose for yourselves."

There was a lot of raucous talking amongst the townsfolk, before Aldoran interjected one last thing. "Remember," Aldoran's voice boomed out, silencing the chatter. "Ruminous died to protect you. So, honor him by making the most of living free. You know from his writings, and you know from his life, and the life he lost to protect this ideal—that this is what he would've wanted most for all of you: FREEDOM."

A moment of silence came over the open square, and then the people clapped and applauded and cheered. Gathering Aldoran and Pharean on their shoulders, they carried them up and down the farmer's market, down to a park with monuments of marble statues they'd fashioned for Ruminous in celebration of his life. Pharean couldn't help but wonder how they would honor him here in his death.

There the townsfolk left them, to pay respects to her father's memory. They went to celebrate and prepare a feast for the couple. Aldoran stayed at Pharean's side, watching her movements, looking for the slightest hint she needed something from him.

The monument was beautiful, and Pharean kneeled there silently to pray. She stayed kneeling and praying for an hour, as Aldoran waited patiently for her a few feet away, before joining with the town and their reveling once more.

"Please don't use that sanctuary as a place to worship my father," she told them, "Please make this a place to worship God." The townspeople agreed. For many hours she spoke with the people of her childhood. She reminisced with childhood friends, many of whom had gotten married in her absence, a few of which had babies or babies on the way. It was good to see them, but it made her keenly aware that she was no longer one of them. She belonged with the people and creatures of their group of birthmarked anointed ones. Now they were her family and best friends.

By the dimming light of the sunset's fading colors, Aldoran took Pharean back to her old home, back to the home she'd brought him to when they'd first arrived back to the Grecian coastal town of Ascalon, late the night before. The white mansion of glass and white marble stood out like a cross on the cliffs against the swirling colors of the sky. The large glass window in the living room and dining room overlooking the low cliffs and shores of the sea was a dramatic backlash for the white marble and blue couches decorating the interior. They went to their separate bedrooms, and fell right asleep.

The next day, Pharean spent with Aldoran in the house alone, desperately needing some quiet time away from the meandering crowds. They wandered together from room-to-room, where Pharean showed him and spoke to him about each book, each decoration, and each piece of furniture.

"I'm glad we did this," Pharean told him, as they sat at the glass dining room table piled high with a seafood feast some of the townsfolk had prepared and brought up for their dinner.

The table held all her favorite things: fresh figs and fresh pine nuts, feta cheese and broiled lobster, fried coconut shrimp and baked crab, with delicate crystal bowls of butter to dip the succulent seafood in. Grapes and fine baby spinach with black and juicy pink, green, and black olives lay on a long platter in the center of the table, with a slivered line of olive oil over the hearts of palm.

Aldoran sucked the supple crab from its shell staring intensely into Pharean's gentle turquoise eyes, watching her fair hair as she bent down to eat the delicious food of her people. She was beautiful. He could see forever with her at that table. Eternity was in his eyes as he looked at her. They were going to have a beautiful life.

~ ~ ~

The next day they decided to venture out. Exploring the Grecian grounds, climbing small, wide mountains atop crests of cliffs, the view was nothing less than spectacular. Aldoran had seen nothing like it. He'd never been to the waters this far south. Pharean had missed it.

Holding her hand to lift her up when the rocks gave way beneath her feet, he was always there to catch her. It was harder going down the mountains then up, and slower going too. But they were in no hurry. They took their time exploring the home and nature Pharean had grown up in.

The waters at the bottom of the mountain were warm, like a sauna. Aldoran wanted to bathe in the sea salt bath, until his skin and hair shone as luminously as the townsfolk did. But Pharean insisted on dragging him onto the shore first.

The Grecian shores were clean and white, and the rocks and sea shells were soft peaches and pinks and silvers. The sky was a clear, clean blue, and the air was warm and softening to their skin. Pharean felt the humidity in the air making her skin glow. She felt radiantly beautiful. And she was.

"Beat you to the water!" Aldoran cried, with a mad desire to dive into the ocean burning inside him. Diving into the water before she'd even thought to move, he felt the water rushing over him like thousands of kisses over every inch of his body.

"Cheater!" Pharean cried as she dove in after him. "You gave yourself a head start!"

For a few minutes, they were in sheer bliss. Swimming was Pharean's favorite activity, but while swimming the depths of the ocean, a dark mass moved amongst them. "Be careful," Aldoran shouted. "There's something in the water." The dark mass moved toward her.

It was a Charybidis, a sea monster in the shape of a giant mouth. Opening its mammoth mouth up to swallow tiny Pharean whole, Aldoran jumped up onto the back of the sea monster hitting it square on the top of its mouth's head as hard as he could, over and over again. The monster released Pharean and howled in pain and fury. In a frenzied attempt to get Aldoran off it, it plunged back into the waves to eat him alive.

Aldoran yanked the sea shell souvenir from the small pack on his side, piercing the sea monster with the sharpest end of it. The creature, all mouth, howled again. Yanking some seaweed up by the roots that were flowing around them, riding atop the waves of the water, he deftly wound the long, thick seaweed around the creature's two front teeth, pulling with all his might as it screamed.

After a few moments, with one violent Ker-POP, the creature's two front teeth burst out of its mouth, as blood from its gums poured through the water surrounding them. Releasing the creature jetting back out to sea, to nurse its two lost teeth, and a bitter grudge against this man-beast that'd bested him, Aldoran raised his fist into the sky triumphantly, as he leapt from the creature's back swimming off in defeat.

"That'll make you think twice before frightening a lovely young girl," he called after it.

Pharean swam as smoothly as a mermaid into his arms to thank him for saving her. Her lithe body felt supple and sleek against his chest. Again, he wanted to kiss her, but he only lightly caressed her hair and swam further out to sea, unafraid even after their attack.

How she admired his fearlessness! His courage steadied her tendency towards fear and anxiety. As her steady faith comforted him, in his endless doubts. But she wondered and worried why he had moved away so quickly after she embraced him, and just after he had referred to her as lovely too.

They kept swimming together in the warm, lucid water. All around them beautiful sea nymphs laughed and sprayed each other, and Aldoran and Pharean. Laughing with the sister nymphs, he swept Pharean up and out of the water, chasing her along the length of the beach, as the sea birds around them flew up and away, indignantly cawing at the intrusion of their territory. Aldoran was delirious on the Grecian beauty, drunk with it.

Then danger struck again, interrupting their play. On the beach, running after them now, were the Mares of Diomedes, the wild, man-eating horses. Pharean grabbed Aldoran by the hand, screaming "RUNNNN!!!" even while Aldoran was still laughing. She yanked him up the mountains and hills where the horses couldn't climb, up into a cavern where a small lake ran through the midst of it. The water was hot and steaming, like a hidden cavern sauna. Pharean and Aldoran slipped into the water, laughing at their speedy escape.

"You really challenge me, you know that?" she accused him.

"How's that?"

"I think I've experienced and explored more of this island in the past few days with you than I have in my whole life!" Aldoran grasped her hungrily in his arms, wanting to kiss and devour her. Holding back his feelings until the time was right; he took comfort in just holding her up against his chest as closely as he could.

Pharean's heart beat wildly in his arms. It felt good to be so close to him. "This is the Corycian Caves," she informed him, still hanging on tightly to her hand in his, feeling a little light-headed with his nearness. "Legend goes it's haunted by nymphs."

"There seems to be a lot of mysteriously beautiful women around here," Aldoran chuckled, pulling her closer again. The water was so soft and hot…and her skin was so supple and warm.

"Yes," she agreed, taking a deep breath, as she stared up at his mouth and lips, with a sudden urge to kiss him herself. "There are Corycian nymphs, hamadryads, oak tree nymphs, Hesperides, and the nymph daughters of Atlas here. There are the fountain nymphs the Crinaeae, the Limnades lake nymphs, the Melia ash tree nymphs, and the Oceanid, the nymph daughters of Oceanus in the ocean we just saw today, to name just a few…" said Pharean.

"Oh, is that all?" Aldoran chuckled.

"I'm sure all cultures have their magical creatures," said Pharean wisely.

"And legends are usually the history from a distant past."

"Now you sound like my father Ruminous!" she giggled, hitting him playfully on the shoulder.

"Well, he *was* the wisest man around these parts!"

"Yes, he was, as well as the bravest. Standing up against King Mardavian for most of my life is no small thing, and you are a lot like him," she looked up into Aldoran's eyes admiringly.

His heart turned over in his chest when she looked at him like that. Hoping he'd always be able to protect her, as he'd done in the past, he'd never want to see those bright eyes full of tears. He never wanted to see her hurt as badly as losing her whole family again.

"Thank you for bringing me back to my homeland, I feel like myself again," she told him earnestly, squeezing his hand tightly. "Only better and much more fun than I was before!" she laughed again, with her eyes so full of joy she might have only been a child.

Innocence and open sincerity were in her mien, and as Aldoran looked at her, so fully in that moment her true self, he knew he was in love with her, and would spend the rest of his life trying to keep her so happy and innocent. He wanted to shelter her from the world, as her father had done from King Mardavian, so he was meant to defend and shield her from evil for the rest of her life—that is, if she let him.

Aldoran lifted her up, as he'd done all day, out of the hot springs, and into the warm and breezy air of the southern seas. Holding hands all the way down the caverns, and back to the high cliff where her father's mansion stood tall and proud overlooking the Sebastian Sea, they had a light dinner, and went straight to sleep. Pharean slept peacefully in her childhood bed, to the sound of pounding surf and the tempestuous waves of Ascalon she knew so well.

Aldoran, on the other hand, tossed and turned. The restless waves stirred the restlessness of his soul. Wanting to go to Pharean, he held himself back. She deserved more than a night of passion. She deserved a lifetime of nights of passion. The Prince of Andorra came to a decision that night that caused him to steal away in the early morning light, while Pharean was still fast asleep, back to the town square, alone…

~ ~ ~

When Pharean awoke, Aldoran was gone. All of a sudden Pharean felt utterly alone—she didn't know what to do with herself. She'd become so accustomed to his presence, it was strange to be without him, almost like he was a companion of some sort. She dismissed the thought, and went to the kitchen to make a simple breakfast of fruits and olives, with tea and honey.

Yet as the day wore on, her anxieties and worries worsened. *Where was he?* Her mind began to wander, imagining the worst case scenarios, until she was in such a state of panic, she was nearly coming out of her own skin.

Finally, she threw on some clothes and decided to head into town to look for him. By now it was nearing the end of the day. Sunset was only a few hours away, and she hoped to be home before dark, as it could be dangerous to climb the cliffs alone after the sun went down.

She'd learned the hard way as a child; how easy it was to slip and fall on the rocks in the dark of night. So, if she wanted to search for Aldoran, she knew she'd better hurry. Yet as she was heading out the door, something made her turn back, and enter her parent's bedroom.

She went right to her mother's jewelry box, rifling through it until she found the beautiful pearl earrings and necklace set—the set she had always admired and coveted from her mother.

"I'll give them to you on your wedding day, my sweet daughter," her mother had said to her as a child, with a knowing smile. Pharean placed the necklace around her neck now, and clipped the delicate dangling earrings that matched it in place, before heading out the door...

She was careful, but hurried, as she climbed the cliffs down to the valley, and on to the open square, where the water fountain and the statue of her father had been decorated by entwined roses and a million sparkling lights. The town had been transformed.

It was decorated as in the times of festivals and holidays. The lights were just beginning to show up as the sun began to dim. Then at the bottom of the square, on a landing that opened up to a gorgeous panoramic view of the sea, Aldoran stood waiting, and she knew.

He wore a tailored white garb, with jewelry of gold adorning him. The townspeople stopped their bustling when they saw Pharean, and stood in place. The whole town seemed to be holding their breath, as they watched their beloved town sweetheart make her way down to the handsome Prince.

Now Pharean had always been a girl with a penchant for whimsy and fantasy, but this was enough to capture even her imagination, for the rest of her life. Prince Aldoran took her hand, as he helped her up the landing with the best view in town.

All the people she loved and had grown up with, and knew best in the world, hung close enough to watch, and listen. "My dear Pharean," Aldoran began.

"From the first moment I saw you, I knew that I was meant to protect you. I knew that I should save you. Then after I did, and I discovered you were one of the Chosen Ones, along with my beloved sister, I knew that I would be working to save you for the rest of my life."

"But there is something more than that," he continued. "When I looked into your beautiful blue green eyes the first time I saw you, having heard your story in the Prophecy, having known your loss, your pain, and your own gentle brand of strength, I knew that I loved you, and that I would need you too, to save me, for the rest of my life."

"Having gotten to know you over these past few years, having seen where you come from, I know that I have fallen in love, with who you are, and who you were, and who I hope you will become…as my wife, and the Princess of Andorra."

He kneeled before her, holding up a ring from the fancy jewelry store in town that people came from miles around to see the handcrafted pieces, and the wealthy came from miles around to purchase them. It was a princess cut yellow diamond surrounded by white diamonds, in a rose-gold band. It was very delicate and feminine, exotic and rare, just like the lady he loved. He looked up into her eyes, and with his own golden-brown eyes gleaming with love, he asked, "Will you marry me?"

It turned out that there had been no need for Pharean to worry about getting home before dark, for their engagement party the town threw for them lasted all night. They ate, they danced, they smiled, they laughed, they *lived,* as all happy fools in love live, as if they would live like this forever. It wasn't until the soft light of the morning that they dragged their tired bodies back to her childhood home up the cliffs, and collapsed into that kind of dreamless sleep that comes from sheer exhaustion.

~ ~ ~

They stayed in that Grecian paradise, in a happy state of bliss for two more weeks. He gave his fiancé some time to spend with her childhood friends, and say her goodbyes. The last night of their stay there, Aldoran slept peacefully, and Pharean shifted restlessly from side-to-side, knowing this was to be the last night of her youth, the last night in her own childhood bed.

The blossoming beauty of womanhood was before her, but she knew she'd retained what some had never had: the divine innocence of youth would never leave her, that purity some children never knew, would be a part of her nature from birth to death. For some people by nature are pure, and she was grateful to be one of them. As she lay there, on her last night of her childhood life, older, but still full of youth, her face was aglow with the joy and excitement of the life that lay before her. The sweet purity of her life would only be made more beautiful in the silver hairs found in the way of righteousness.

When Aldoran fell asleep, he slept deeply and soundly, knowing that her childhood was over. Knowing they'd done right to come to her homeland so that she could make peace with the townsfolk she'd known and loved, and with the life and the part of herself she was leaving behind.

He was comforted knowing soon the day would come he would unfold that blossoming beauty, like the opening petals of the first flowers of the spring. She would always be like that first perfect spring flower. She would always be that youthful spritely spirit, and they, as dreamers, would dream forever the simple, extraordinary dreams of true love, and a lifetime lived with your heart's twin.

Like mirror images, when she was restless, he was calm, and when she was calm, he was restless. In this way, they complemented each other. Their weaknesses were each other's strengths. They would be made whole in their destined marriage. Aldoran looked forward to the day he would take Pharean home, and marry her back home in Andorra, where all the people he loved could bear witness to their union.

~ ~ ~

Chapter Fourteen
Desert of Jinn

From when and where the group disbanded on the Isle of Sky, traveling into the Arabian Desert—

Ileona recalled Varawynn as a little girl, with her long, dark ringlets swept up and held back with bands of roses, violets, lilies, or whatever flower was in season. Green had always been her favorite color, so her dresses were usually green, to match her dark emerald eyes.

She'd always looked up to the Lady of the Lake. Varawynn's sparkling eyes had once danced with adoration as she'd looked upon her, bordering on idol worship of her magic, and enchanting beauty. So Ileona couldn't help being partial to the child, with her doll-like beauty, incredible talent for magic, set apart as a Chosen One, and most of all, she'd liked the priestess for giving her the respect due her.

Learning to walk with one leg lame had taken Varawynn longer than most. She was about three or four before she'd managed to get around as well as other children did at two or three, but she'd been doggedly persistent in overcoming the setbacks of her disability, and that had worked miracles in her ability to overcome them.

Ileona was trekking with her few belongings through the Eastern deserts, quite unlike the desert of Haran. The eastern deserts lay in stark contrast to the lush lands and shimmering waters of Caledonia, where the Lady of the Lake and the Priestess Varawynn came from, and part of Ileona knew it was wrong to leave the group for this quest, particularly when Varawynn's life and death, so to speak, hung, in the balance—but she left them anyway.

Her intuition comforted her that Varawynn would be resurrected. If anyone would, or could, it would be the obstinate, perseverant soul of the Celtic Priestess. And as her ashes rose to life, so Ileona searched the far deserts for the meaning of her own.

Ileona knew better than anyone this fighting spirit of Varawynn's, for it was similar to hers. At least she called it a fighting spirit. Perhaps others would just call it plain old-fashioned stubbornness.

They were both incredibly stubborn in their own ways. Varawynn was less vocal about it than the Lady of the Lake, but she knew Varawynn was too determined to let a little something like death stop her. Ileona smiled to herself, visualizing the young Celtic Priestess coming back to life from the glimmering embers. She knew it was meant to be.

On the other hand, there was Jonlin. His gentle spirit had always been of the embers of the afterlife, composed more of spirit than the dust and toil of the earth. A soul so tender and sensitive never fared well in the physical realm. Even the creatures of the waters who were sensitive, never lasted long among the sharks.

It was sad really. The world needed more of Jonlin's goodness to temper the aggressive violence of too many others. At least Ileona thought so. Yet the world often held down and held back the gentler folks like Jonlin, rarely understanding or acknowledging that they were the strongest and greatest of the souls on earth.

Ileona regretted leaving the group, in the midst of their quest to bury the beloved bard in Hebron, and resurrect the Celtic priestess, but she was positively consumed by the search for the box with the ring her father had given her, which she believed was the key to unlocking it. Whatever was in that box had become her obsession. Deep down, she felt if she found the object to whatever the key opened, she would somehow have her father back.

Recalling and recounting their conversation in the in-between between life and death, over and over, again and again, she sought to remember his last words in regard to the prize, as she viewed it. Merlin had said the box had been something of an obsession for him too, that he'd sought the sacred object for as long as he'd worn the ring engraved with the strange symbols.

Like her father before her, magical objects held a fascination for her. Like him, the idea of adventure and quests in search for treasures and prizes, devoured her.

Using a ring for a key...this was something clever and interesting, not to mention unique. Ileona had never heard of anything like this before, especially coming from the mind of a human, but there was no telling what creature had devised the ring to what lay in the box. No telling *why* they had either. Surely whatever was hidden would be important, and could be used to help the group on their journey together in the future. At least that was what Ileona told herself to justify her actions.

Because Ileona still held a general contempt for the human race, though to a lesser degree after she met her father Merlin in the in-between, and had experienced their own lack of esteem and common sense, she wagered the mystery was devised by a nonhuman. Pondering different sacred objects, she'd heard about in legends throughout her life, she turned the ring over on the finger of her right hand.

Her finger was getting raw with the constant moving irritating it, but she didn't seem to notice. As her mind ruminated over every sacred object she'd ever heard of—magical items, and the legends of the Celts, Saxons, Egyptians, Romans, and Greeks; her father was at the heart of her mind's meanderings.

Perhaps a stone, she thought, *not likely, but a stone set in a ring, an iridescent diamond reflecting all the colors in the shades of light. What else? What else? What else? Gold perhaps, or something that was producing gold? What would be so special about a piece of gold?*

Could it be a rare diamond? What was most likely? Think Ileona! Think! Then again, what's likely in the view of a hidden prize? The Holy Grail! Yes! That's it! That's a definite possibility at least…and it's something Merlin and King Arthur were in pursuit of throughout their lives.

~ ~ ~

Into the eastern deserts, Ileona travelled deeper and deeper into the Arabian nights as the weeks went by. Wandering in the deserts of the Far East alone had made Ileona lose some of her rationale. A strange clicking sound was plaguing her.

At odd times of the day or night, she would hear it. Sometimes she thought she saw shadows slithering around her like snakes in the sky. Being alone and virtually unprotected, she hoped it was all in her imagination.

Sometimes in the dead of night, Ileona would wake to the strange, clicking sound, and she would be overcome by cold sweats and fears. *What was that sound?*

The days passed into weeks, as Ileona began losing track of time. Between the random clicking sound, and the howling wind, she wanted to scream. But she kept going. Though she was beginning to realize she didn't know *where* exactly she was going, or even where she was *supposed* to be going.

She was lost.

She'd wake in the dead of night from nightmares of spiders crawling over her body. She'd scream and shove them off her, but nothing was there.

It was getting worse. It was getting harder. She was losing weight, as animals and vegetation here were hard to come by.

She was repulsed having to kill the small, strange creatures of the desert. Worse still was eating them. Water was scarce. And water was her element. As her water supply waned, she wondered if she was going to die here, in this ugly, dry desert, her carcass picked and eaten by dirty vultures.

It'd been a few months by now, and Ileona decided to give herself the blessed relief of the release of her emotions. No one was around anyways. So, she fluffed up her pack one night, laid her head on the make-shift pillow, and let the tears flow. She didn't believe in giving in to her emotions. But she was alone, no one was around, and she really wasn't sure she was going to survive.

It was in that moment of release that a tiny scorpion slipped from her pack. "Ahhhhh!" So *that* was the strange clicking sound that had been plaguing her!

The scorpion had been with her for weeks…waiting for just the right time to sting her with its deadly poison. Of course, she was revolted by the ugly creature, but she also felt a sense of relief that she wasn't entirely losing her mind after all.

She screamed, and the little deadly scorpion scurried all over her bag. Feeling her mind closing to reason, all she could do was shout, "AHHHHH!" and move the pack around wildly until the little devil finally fell off and slipped away into the desert, probably more afraid of her now than she was of it.

She dumped everything out of her pack. A spider had nested and made a web, and she dumped the spider's eggs, and broke the web onto the desert floor.

"I don't want to be ALONE anymore! Help me! I can't be alone anymore! Damn this horrible, dry, barren, empty desert! Damn it all to hell!" She didn't consider *who* or *what* she was screaming at. She just needed to scream!

A nearby armadillo was meandering by, and she aptly threw her dagger directly onto its back. She took out some of her frustrations on killing it. She made a fire and cooked and ate some of its meat to revive herself.

Not sleeping and eating properly was taking a toll on her body and mind. She carved a weapon from the dried bones of the armadillo to empower her survivor spirit, a foreigner in the lands of the dry desert she realized now she despised.

From the hideous armadillo's teeth, she made a weapon of fangs. Having this weapon reassured her. Of course, she had her magical weapons, but she wanted weapons taken from the elements around her. She needed to learn to survive in this hell of flying dust and endless barren lands. The next time she heard the horrible clicking sound she would be prepared for it.

It didn't take long for the sound to haunt her again. A few days later, the clicking sound started up again. Deftly, she searched for the sound. It went click, click, clack behind the cactus. There were so few animals and vegetation here. She knew the runaway scorpion would be waiting for her nearby. She would capture it offensively, catching it unawares.

Raising the weapon of knotted fangs and bones together, she brought it down, down, down unto the unsuspecting scorpion's tail. The odd, ugly creature let out a scream louder than her own. Louder than a dying human, or an ancient creature of the water like her.

"I hate it here!" Ileona screamed into the whining wind. "I hate the desert…I AM the Lady of the Lake!"

She was enraged by the scorpion. In a crazed frenzy, she tore the small predator up with her weapon of tied fangs, till both its poison and innards lay all about the desert floor, completely dissected and defenseless against her spent rage.

She rubbed the poison of the scorpion onto the fangs of her armadillo weapon, so that the next predator that attacked her would die with the scorpion's sting coursing through its veins like vinegar. Her anger dissolved, erupting into crazed laughter. She laughed until her sides and face hurt. It had been a long time since she'd had a good laugh.

The laughter spent, her volatile emotions wandered into praise and bliss as the sky opened before her, and a storm brewed in the air. A flash of electricity hit the very cactus where the scorpion had hidden beneath. She laughed again, in gleeful pleasure at the very nearness of the elements.

Something grateful filled her as the sky filled with rain, the idea of getting wet made her delirious. It was a change of scene and was some form of water, which she sorely missed.

First, she filled her water skins back up with the welcome rain pouring down. She'd taken to drinking just one small sip of water to keep her going. Now she drank from the skins over and over, drinking her fill.

Lifting her hands into the wind, as the open desert sky filled with tears, and flooded the sand with the wet, miracle of rain, she danced. She danced as if the Creator was right there with her. In the midst of the storm, by dancing, she expressed her praise and gratitude.

Dancing like a creature created just to dance, her long hair flipping about her wildly, her skirts heavy and drenched with the rain, couldn't deter her from her passionate, carefree movements, her waving arms, and her prancing feet. Skipping and leaping and twirling, she shouted up hallelujahs into the sky. With a beaming sunlit smile, she embraced the moment, embraced this miraculous moment in her life.

She raised her empty hands to the heavens, so that they might be filled. She raised her eyes toward the heavens, so that the rain would flood her face, and she would be cleansed of months of dry desert dust. As the caked sand fell off her, as the rain washed the months of sweat and grime away, it was like she was herself again, like the rainbow after the rain.

It was as if she herself was the golden prize at the end of her journey. Then at last she realized there was no greater prize than the prize of wanting for nothing, and surrendering and letting go of all worries and cares, so that in her emptiness, she was filled by the love that comes right after the moment we surrender, to take a leap of faith, and learn to fly.

As she danced, she let go. Let go of her frustrations. Let go of her loneliness. Let go of the people in her life that were gone. Let go of the hurt from the hurt people who hurt others. In the dancing, she sang, and in the dancing, the singing of her soul evolved in the evolution of humanity not every human finds. For it was the human part of her that danced and sang, laughing in the rain.

She let go of what society says ought to be. She let go of wifehood and motherhood and the things not meant to be, and the things that should have been, and the things that might have been, if the people in her life had chosen different things, chosen love and nobility, chosen purity instead of the quick fixes that eased the pain and emptiness, if only for a moment that never lasted and resulted in eternal consequences.

She let go of her limitations. She let go of her burdens and her grief. She let go of her parents. She let go of her expectations.

As she raised her hands, waving them wildly in an air full of water, the moisture in the dry desert air poured down upon her face. Her mouth opened to the taste of the fresh, sweet rain. The hallelujahs turned to weeping sobs, and she fell down onto her knees to pray for all the souls who didn't understand the power of Jesus' name…and the power of his love.

She knew her love was insufficient to combat the pain of reaching out to the people who didn't love her back. God's grace was ever so much more powerful. "I love you God…" she whispered. As her soul submitted to the Creator, the Savior saved her soul.

~ ~ ~

More months went by. Deeper and deeper into the desert, Ileona went, learning to survive. Ileona was no closer to finding the prize—or the Jinn then when she'd first begun her journey.

The heat was still affecting her mind and wearing on her body. She was learning tricks of the desert, but her body and spirit were also slowly deteriorating.

The glorious moment during the storm she'd shared with God seemed like a lifetime ago now. She rarely recalled the day before the last. The days and nights in the desert just ran together. She gave into hours of rage and then hours of crying. Expressing her emotions more helped her cope with her life here, or the lack thereof.

Lack of proper food and water, and consistent disturbed night's sleep by nightmares, the constant feeling of being in danger, and being watched, had made her overly emotional. Her normally brave attitude was riddled with paranoia and fear. The heat of the desert had worsened. After weeks and months on end without rain, want of another storm made the air tingle with the heat that was nearly physical.

Obsessively, Ileona sought the box throughout the desert plains. The wind whined angrily at the onslaught of a coming storm. Ileona furiously pushed through the raging wind. She knew she should take shelter.

Stubbornly, she pushed forward, into the eye of the storm. *Nothing will keep me down,* she thought to her herself, with a prideful whip of her long, light hair. She felt invincible, even while her body was falling apart.

Step-by-step she marched forward. The wind made shallow cuts all over her body that opened and bled in the days of sweltering heat, never quite able to scab over and turn into scars. Never quite able to heal.

She talked to herself more and more to keep herself company. By day, the desert highs of 110-120 degrees filled her mood with anger. The desert lows of 40s-60s degrees made her shake with cold each night.

Soon she lost her focus and began to walk endlessly, not knowing if she was going forward or in circles. Soon she didn't care. And as the minutes passed into hours, and the hours into days, and the days into weeks and months, she wondered if she was moving forward at all. The endless expanse of the Arabian Desert, slowly began to claim her sanity.

Until another storm finally gathered furiously around her, hanging in the air like a promise. Every storm was be a blessing, breaking the monotony of the heat and continuously beating sun. As the sky darkened, a dark shadow swept upon her, material and in the physical, no longer abstract. It was clearly material, yet composed of an immaterial substance—the stuff of shadows and nightmares.

As the storm hung in the air around her, she felt her high emotions turn to trepidation, as her eyes focused on the dusky being approaching her. Like a being from the in-between, the creature's substance was in-between: real and imaginary, physical and spiritual.

The wind whirred and blew about her, but the rain didn't come. It was only thunder and lightning that lit up the sky. Disappointment and defeat filled Ileona's fighting spirit as the hours of the night passed without rain.

When the lightning storm ended; the being which had been in the shadows, stood clearly before her, slithery and sleek. "What are you?" Ileona asked it.

"A demon of the desert sands…a Jinn," the being said, in a tone as dark and cold as the Isle of Apples in the winter, beneath layers of ice and snow. Ileona's heart skipped a beat. Merlin had told her the box she sought was held by a Jinn in the desert. Inadvertently she'd finally stumbled into one, after nearly a year of fruitless searching.

She held out the staff that would force the Jinn to do her will. But her body was weak, and she was losing her resolve. She was weary, exhausted to the marrow of her bones.

Strategies played out within her mind on how to get information from the Jinn. She contemplated what would be the best way to overtake the sacred object from it. First, she needed to know if he had it, or knew where to find it. She'd need to learn the weaknesses of the Jinn, and what they most desired—or most feared, in order to outsmart them. To do so, she'd have to think fast, speak fast, and if need be, move fast. Some of her old self and her old courage welled up inside.

"What do you want with me?" Ileona asked.

"I was about to ask you the same thing," the Jinn whispered warily.

Let's start with the direct approach, Ileona thought to herself. "I'm searching for a holy sacrament contained in…a box."

"And what makes you think the Jinn possess it?"

"My father, Merlin, told me your kind were in possession of it."

"Merlin…" the Jinn murmured, spinning itself in the darkness like a top.

"Do you remember him? Did you know my father?" Suddenly that was more important to her than the box itself.

"We have the box...but we require a sacrifice in exchange for it."

"What do you want?" Ileona asked, immediately on guard.

"A soul in exchange for the box..." the Jinn eyed her hungrily, licking its black lips expectantly. A flash of warning like the distant thunder crossed her mind. Something deep inside her soul screamed *RUN!!!!!*

Rushing across the desert plains and away from the shadowy Jinn pursuing her, there was no outrunning the desert creature. As demons, they could move a legion in a breath. Her heart constricted in fear.

What can I do? Where can I turn? There's no way to get away from it. So, she did the only thing she could think to do. She just kept running.

~ ~ ~

Silvandrin and Illumina were going south, to the great abyss of the desert lands, to find the oracle Ileona. They were going to the most remote area of the country...to the Desert of Rakiyon where they would find the Sphinx, Sphayte, and her sister, Areylinder, who guarded the gates of the great castle in Alambu.

For a human, this journey could take at least a few months, but Silvandrin and Illumina were able to make the journey in only a few weeks. Neither unicorn nor elf had ever met a Sphinx. They were not apprehensive, only expectant. They knew the Sphinx they sought knew a very important part of the Prophecy.

Darkening now in the cool, dry desert air, the wind was full of flying bits of dust. The sand was hard and pelted their faces, making small cuts on their bodies. Tumbleweeds blew, and occasionally they'd see cactus and lizards, and maybe a snake or two. Yet there was little life here, especially as they went further into the desert.

"I have to admit; I don't care much for the desert lands. I much prefer grass and forest, trees and water..." said Silvandrin, in his deep, velvety voice.

"I know what you mean. Right now, I'm thinking about the crystalline shore, and the flowers that grow along its bank and cliffs," agreed the sea elf.

"The sea is lovely where you are Illumina, so pure and unpolluted by human waste."

"Yes, thank the gods; they have not discovered our sea dwelling yet."

"But someday..."

"It is just a matter of time, Silvandrin," Illumina sighed.

"Are you certain, Illumina? Have you foreseen the demise of our kind?"

"Yes, Silvandrin, I'm sorry to tell you I am certain. I have seen the end times. Someday, the last unicorns shall return to the south, to remote areas in that majestic land of Africa, and the few remaining elves shall have to seek remote areas in the largest forests of the earth. We'll be forced to hide our minuscule numbers from greedy human eyes, among the canopy of the forests of the endless rains, just so we won't be completely annihilated by the snares of man's greed."

"Damn them!" the cursed black unicorn cursed.

"It shall be the inevitable fate of all magical creatures. Surely, you have seen it too?"

Silently Silvandrin looked up into the open sky full of countless shining stars. "If only we could find another planet to beam up to," the dark unicorn murmured. "Up and away from the destructive humans..."

"Silvandrin—I have seen what was and what shall be. King Mardavian discovered the secret of our blood—"

Somewhere in the distance, before Illumina could complete her thought, they heard a hissing voice say, "Sssssoon there sssshall be nothing left of your kind, Illuuuumina..."

"How do you know my name? Who are you? Where are you?" asked the sea elf, visibly caught off-guard, she who was usually so poised and detached.

"Show yourself!" commanded Silvandrin.

The mammoth black cobra slithered out before them. She was the largest snake they'd ever seen. "My name is Onessssa," she hissed, moving herself in quick, graceful movements up and around Silvandrin's broad black back.

"What do you want with us?" demanded Silvandrin.

"I only wissshhh to warn you."

"Warn us about what?" asked Illumina, trying to shoo the snake off Silvandrin.

"Only thattt Illlleonnnaaaa is in danger..."

"How do you know about her?" Silvandrin demanded.

"The desssserrt is noooo place to beeee travellllled allonnnne...." Onessa warned them.

"Hence, we're on our way to find the Sphinx who can help Ileona so she won't be alone," retorted Silvandrin, pulling himself up and puffing out his broad chest in stately dignity. "We do not need *your* help."

"You are goingggg to the Desert of Rakiyon corrreccct?" asked the snake.

"Yes, why?" Illumina piped up.

"Check your mapppp. You need to be going ssssouthwest not ssssoutheast. You are sooo closssee, but you must alterrr your courrsssse, and fassst. Illlleonnnaaaa needddsss you."

Silvandrin consulted his map. "Why would you want to help us?"

"You have noooo reassssson to trusssst meeee."

"Then why should we?" Illumina asked it.

"I can offferrr you a knowledddgeee of the dessserrrttt you land and water creaturrress do not posssessss. I can tell you thattt the magiccc city is hidden, and requiresss a passssword forrr entryyy."

"Okay, so what's the password?" asked Silvandrin, deciding to humor her.

"Chaos to Calm
Fear to Might
Weakness to Power
Darkness to Light"

"Therrreee issss a dooorrwayyy...in the middleee of the dessserrttt...sayyy these worddsss, and the cittyyy sssshalll apppearrr," and with that, the mysterious snake Onessa slithered away, back into the shimmering shadows of the shifting sands.

"I believe she's right," said Silvandrin. "The city has been magically hidden. That's why we haven't been able to find it! We just need to alter our direction a little to find that doorway—"

"How can there be a doorway in the middle of the desert, Silvandrin?" But the unicorn insisted there was. As if on cue, strange music that was very out-of-place in the desert, wafted toward them from the west. The elf and unicorn followed the music for several hours.

As the sun began to set, they saw before their startled eyes, right in the middle of the desert, a door standing upright, with nothing surrounding it. Illumina eyed Silvandrin cautiously. "This might be a trap you know."

Silvandrin nodded. "I know, but what else can we do?" He repeated the password poem the snake had given them.

A city appeared out of nowhere, and set before them were two tall pillars made of pure white marble, constructed to face and bend at the top towards each other. Guarding each one of the pillars were two magical creatures that took their breath away.

Their feminine faces were beautiful, regal and dignified in bearing. Their almond shaped eyes were lined with black, making them stand our more distinctly. Their thick, long hair flowed out like a mane, down to their lion's backs.

Their torsos were that of beautifully formed women, down to the legs and paws of a lion. Their long, sharp claws, and razor teeth which ready and willing to shred and devour any unwanted intruders into their kingdom. Their tails flipped around warily, as they narrowed their eyes, and studied the unicorn and elf standing before them.

Silvandrin and Illumina recognized the creatures as Sphinxes. They knew they'd found the Sphinx they'd sought—the Sphinx of the Prophecy, Sphayte.

Silvandrin sighed with relief. "We've finally found you! I can't believe it!" exclaimed Illumina. "Onessa was right!"

"What is dark and black, with white, illuminating at times, and no illumination at other times?"

"Sphayte," said Illumina. "Don't you understand? We haven't come here to solve a riddle, but to tell you that your time in the riddle has come…"

"This something also sometimes has dots of sparkles everywhere, and sometimes nowhere, when it is obstructed."

"Sphayte–" tried Silvandrin.

"What is dark and black, with white, illuminating at times, and has no illumination at other times?" the Sphinx continued.

Silvandrin smiled to Illumina. "I think I can solve the riddle."

"Then do so, Silvandrin, maybe then she'll give us what we came here for!"

"The answer is: *Night*."

Areylinder smiled at her sister, and then the great gates glowed and shone like the stars referenced in the riddle. Silvandrin had clearly deduced the correct response.

"You may enter," spoke Sphayte solemnly.

"You don't understand, we don't want to enter the castle. We want you to tell us the part of the Prophecy you know," said Illumina, trying again.

"I don't think reasoning with her will work, dear elf."

"Then what shall, Silvandrin?"

Silvandrin's voice boomed into the night, electrifying them with his powerful tones:

> *"Her golden body with the lion's tail,*
> *Her wings that take her anywhere,*
> *Her riddles old and wise and deep,*
> *Her roving eyes which never sleep—*
>
> *She is the key to what shall unfold:*
> *The beacon of our dreams untold.*
> *She shall reveal the truth with subtle grace,*
> *Like the unlined beauty of her human face.*
>
> *She is dark and light,*
> *She is day and night,*
> *She is true and full of deceit,*
> *She shall accomplish great feats.*
>
> *She, of the roving desert lands,*
> *Is the birthmark on the Lady of the Lake,*

WHILE THE ASHES RISE TO LIFE

Created for her, to protect and defend her,
From a deadly fate.

She is the nexus that unfolds
The future of magical beasts.
She is the key
To the fulfillment of the Prophecy."

Sphayte fully turned to look at them, and her sister looked astonished. "But we need you here," Areyin said. "It can't yet be time for you to leave us…"

"It is time," nodded Sphayte to her sister.

"But—"

"You can easily guard the castle without me."

"But—"

"I must go…" Sphayte insisted, moving away from the place she'd dwelled for a thousand years.

"There shall be consequences—" warned Areyin. "The Pharoah shall know you've left us!"

"I leave for us all. I leave to save our kind. I leave to protect you, my sister. I leave because it is my duty and my destiny. You know that, as well as I do."

"If you leave now, you know you can never come back…" Areyin whispered.

"I know," Sphayte answered softly. "I won't need to." The two beautiful human faces stared back at each other, crying two sets of giant iridescent tears. Like mirror images, when a tear came out of Areyin's left eye, a tear fell from Sphayte's right eye. "I shall miss you, dear sister; I hope no harm shall come to you in my absense."

"We are so sorry to ask you to leave your home," Silvandrin said, with tears of compassion in his eyes.

"Where did Ileona enter the Arabian desert?" Sphayte asked them.

"We think she entered from the southeast," answered Illumina. "But we were told that you would know."

"She needs me," Sphayte nodded to herself. "You woodland creatures are unused to the desert sands, and need my assistance. I have a sense of direction here because I am used to the ways of the desert."

"But sister—" Areyin argued.

"I am guarded by destiny, kept secure by fate," insisted Sphayte to her sister.

"Please, don't do this—not if you can never come back here!" her sister tried again. Silvandrin just shook his mane.

"Sister, there is nothing you can say to stop me. You know how I am once my mind is made up."

Areyin sighed. "Then go in peace," she whispered, with a wave of her paw, and an impatient flip of her tail.

"One last riddle I give you, and I know you shall know the answer in an instant:"

"What are born in the same ocean,
but leave it separately?
What share the same blood,
and yet are distinct from one another?
What share one vessel,
but leave it independent of each other?"

"I shall remember you into forever, Areyin, past eternity..."

"Twins," Areyin whispered the answer to the riddle sadly. Abruptly, Sphayte turned her back on all she had known, and on all she had loved. Led by Silvandrin and Illumina out of the gates guarding the Kingdom of Rikayon, her tears drying quickly. A great booming filled the land, as Sphayte stepped down from the throne, from the borders of the land she'd been guarding for a thousand years.

Neither sister said the word goodbye. The group would later learn why it was necessary she should come. The riddles she spoke with her sister Areyin were meant to help them. Her part on the journey was to teach them to understand the deeper wisdoms in the complexities of the riddle in the Prophecy.

"Please let Ileona know that Varawynn was safely resurrected," Silvandrin told Sphayte. "But she doesn't need to know she turned into the Selkie," Illumina said to Silvandrin aside. The Sphinx assured them she would relay the news to the Lady of the Lake.

The unicorn and sea elf went back to their lands, while Sphayte, the Sphinx, opened her great wings to the desert sky. Sphayte was quiet in the days she flew over the desert, sad about leaving her sister behind. She gave herself this time to grieve, for when she found Ileona, she needed her old life to be totally behind her.

Her wings crossed the span of the desert quickly. Above the desert sands, she flew toward her destiny, high above the endless stretch of drifting amber sands. So Sphayte set out alone to find the Lady of the Lake, who bore the birthmark of the Sphinx, to save her from herself.

~ ~ ~

Chapter Fifteen
Book of the Fallen Angels

From the shores of Greece, traveling north to the mountains of Andorra—

After Aldoran fell in love with Pharean in the southern coasts, from a culture he'd never imagined he would ever experience, they travelled north once more. Aldoran's magical compass guided them back towards the Kingdom of the Franks and the Andorres Mountains. They went back into their old habits of talking and listening, writing and editing. Everything they spoke about, and everything he learned, Aldoran carefully copied down in their two books imparting knowledge to the general public. The life and philosophies of Pharean's father Ruminous, went into the third book they were composing simultaneously.

He knew now, somewhere deep inside, that their journey was coming to an end, and he would soon be taking Pharean, of the beautiful Grecian shores, back to his homeland to become his wife. He missed his sister, and he missed the unique beauty and peacefulness of his culture, where their purpose was for the one true God, in a plan far greater than themselves. He wanted his sister to stand up with him when he married Pharean, and he wanted his parents to be there too.

Pharean told him all her ideas about their wedding day, the way she envisioned it. It was up to him to make her dreams come true. She was a sea-faring girl, getting married and moving to a mountain Kingdom. It would be a big change. But her family had been leaders in the seafaring town, and he had every confidence she would be up to the task.

After all the times Aldoran had saved Pharean's life, he had nearly forgotten about the time back in that dusty town near where her family had been killed, that she saved him. "Do you remember this?" Aldoran asked, pulling a book from the bottom of his pack and staring at it curiously. The book was from that time and place when she had wily tricked the clerk into having compassion for them.

"What's that?" asked Pharean.

"Isn't this the same book from that general store so long ago? I thought you put it back. I never knew you took it."

"I didn't mean to steal it," Pharean told him, a little defensively. "Remember how the men were after us and you yanked me out of there?"

"Yes…"

"I didn't have time to put it back, so I hid it in the folds of my cloak before you put me on my horse."

"Did you ever look at it?"

"No. Not really, I felt too guilty about how I'd gotten it, to give it much attention."

"In your guilt you must have accidently shoved it into my pack last night," Aldoran teased her.

"Well, why don't we look at in now?" Pharean asked him, her tone as if to say *we might as well.* Aldoran nodded, and they sat together cross-legged with the book between them.

The *Book of Mysteries,* was written across the top. A rush of wind swept past them as Aldoran opened the cover of the book to the first page. Then the wind slammed the book shut even as he held it in his hands. An eerie darkness settled over them, making it too dark for them to read the words. In the middle of the day, it appeared as night.

He took out a candle from the pack and lit it. He opened the *Book of Mysteries* to a page that spoke about the fallen angels:

In the region of Sheol, the land was darkened by wicked lust and unnatural desires. There were angels that consented to fall from heaven that they might mate with the daughters of the earth. In those days the Sons of Man were quickly multiplying, and the daughters born to them were of great beauty. Therefore, when the angels, the sons of heaven beheld them, they were overcome with desire and said to one another: "Come, let us choose wives and husbands from among the race of men, and let us beget children by them.

Now the leader of the Nephilim was Samyaza, who said, "Perchance you shall be wanting in courage to implement this resolution, and I alone shall be answerable for our fall." But the Nephilim swore to him they would in no way repent to achieve their whole design and purpose.

There were two hundred angels that fell from grace, descending onto Mount Harmon, which became marked as the Mount of the Oath, whereby the Sons of Man had sworn to their leader to take their own accountability for the Fall. The names of those angelic leaders who descended with this objective were: Samyaza, chief among them all, Urakabarameel, Azibeel, Tamiel, Ramuel, Danel, Azkeel, Sarakuyal, Asael, Armers, Batraal, Anane, Sameveel, Ertrael, Turl, Jomiael, andArizial.

These Sons of Man, the Fallen Angels, took wives and husbands from the peoples of the earth with whom they had intercourse, and to some of whom they also taught magic, such as the art of enchantment, and the properties of earthly things like roots and trees to use as an aid in spells and curses. The Nephilim Barkaial was the master of those who study the stars. Azaradel taught the motions of the moon, Akibeel manifested signs on the earth, and Amazarac provided instruction for the secrets of sorcerers.

In this region of Sheol, the land was further stained by the profanation of the fallen angels exposing this arcane and heaven-born knowledge to earthly men and women they took as their lovers. Brute force took advantage of the divine law, reigning supreme. The balance between the human and the divine had been disturbed by these unlawful revelations. Only a deluge, a great flood, a monumental torrent of water could wipe out the enormity of the stain upon Sheol, Mount Harmon, and the eternal war between heaven and earth itself.

"The timing of finding this book is a little strange, isn't it?" Aldoran turned to Pharean to see her expression. "Didn't Shadow Rain say something about a legend that had to do with her and the Nephilim, and rain and a flood or something?"

But Pharean was lost in space again, and he had a strange sensation to check and make sure she was still there. He looked back to the *Book of Mysteries* and then back up at Pharean, but she was gone. Her body was there, but she lay on the ground as limp as a doll.

"Pharean! Pharean!" he shouted. "Where are you?" Instinctively, he sensed some dark magic from the book was the reason for her disappearance. Frantically searching through the *Book of Mysteries,* the pages flipped as if by their own accord. Aldoran read the page aloud, fast and furious, ready to stand and fight to get back the girl he loved.

The Grimlocks are servants of the Grim Reaper. They are sent to take those who have recently lost a loved one, someone very close to them. Able to destroy the soul of both the recently departed and the living, they torture the the human's mind until they kill themselves. To defeat the Grimlock chant these words:

"We break this curse of death and shadows.
You cannot take this soul God made.
A lifetime now we breathe without you,
Until our appointed time, shall we greet our grave."

If the Grimlock takes the soul to another dimension, a part of that soul was already lost or taken by the deceased. That means they have only been half-alive. This is their opportunity to fight the Grimlock to regain their soul and reclaim themselves.

To do so, they must defeat the demon, or the temptation within them, to give up. They must stand up to the voices telling them lies. They must find and face the truth. For if they don't, their soul shall be lost and overtaken by the Grimlock, for eternity.

Aldoran looked up from the book in a reverie. *Pharean and her father Ruminous. That's what this is about!* Aldoran knew she'd suffered her father's loss more than any other. She'd even shared with him a lot about her quest, so he knew she'd been to Purgatory, and seen him suffering there.

As he'd opened up about his own past, and the friend he'd lost as a young child, Oric, she'd slowly begun to open up about her past. But these words made no sense. Hadn't she already faced the truth and conquered the demon encouraging her to die? What was left for her to do? What truth was left for her to uncover?

Of course, this wasn't even about Pharean…it was about saving Ruminous from the Grimlock! It was the Grimlock who had a hold of her father's soul, feeding him lies and keeping him in an endless circle of suffering and blame and guilt! Perhaps this is the way Pharean could save him!

The Angel of Death had told Pharean that the only way to save her father was to die, in order to bring him to the light and help him forgive himself, but Pharean had realized that this was a trick used so that she would kill herself and be trapped in purgatory herself. But maybe there was another way. Maybe she could use the Grimlock who had taken her into another dimension, to get through to her father.

What can I do? How can I help her? The words were only in Aldoran's mind, and yet the pages flipped by themselves again, as if they'd heard his thoughts. He read the words on the page where the book stopped flipping, even more carefully this time, reading it over and over, wanting to really understand and comprehend the ideas that seemed to leap off the page…

Astral Projection is the practice of your soul leaving your body to be in two places at one time. Your physical body is left a shell, unprotected by your soul. Thus, if something happens to your body, for example, if your body is killed while your soul is elsewhere, your spirit is trapped in the ethers without a temple to house it.

To Astral Project, the desire and need must be clear, focused, and strong. It is a willing of the mind, and an opening of the soul. Astral Projection is associated with a feeling of lifting, or flying, as your soul leaves your body. Your mind must have clarity on where it is going, that is, where your soul needs and wants to be, with whom your soul is yearning to be with.

Take exceptional care to leave your actual body somewhere safe and protected, not just from violent harm, but in case a loved one happens by, and believes you are dead or comatose and buries you alive. It is possible to take another body, but this violates the rules of Karma and disorders the spiritual balance. If you unbalance Karma thus by stealing another person's body, when your soul is eventually released from the foreign body, your punishment shall be unthinkable. Be forewarned that taking the body from another soul, is an evil graver than murder.

Also bear in mind that as a soul you have no physical force. You cannot move things, and you shall move as if by an invisible force, with invisible wings, effortlessly and formlessly. Yet you shall retain the use of your voice. You shall have your presence, your true spirit, but you shall not be able to physically help someone and keep them from being harmed in any material way. In time, and with much practice, it is possible to move things with your soul like a ghost with your mind, known as Telekinesis. But it is rare and improbable in the initial attempts. Telekinesis takes much time and practice to develop and control.

Another warning about Astral Projection is that your soul can get lost if you are not clear in your intention about where you are going, and then you may not be able to get back to your body temple. Fellow spirits can bind your soul as easily as your fellow man can tie up or chain your body. A curse on your body is less powerful than a curse on your soul. It is the soul that is eternal, thus your spirit is of greater importance, and any harm done to it is of greater consequence.

Aldoran pondered the words on these pages for a long time. Kneeling before the *Book of Mysteries,* he lifted up a prayer to the Lord, to let him astral project in order to help Pharean. *"Show me the way, Lord, show me the way to do this. Show me the way to her. Show me the way to help her, in your name I pray, El Shaddai."*

Aldoran explored the landscape, found a cave and made camp. Building a fire, he cooked some vegetables on the pit. After eating his supper, he lay down and stared into the dancing flames, letting his mind focus and wander at the same time. His eyes grew heavy, as he stared into the firelight. Willing his spirit to be with Pharean, the silence sounded loud in his ears. As heaviness filled him, his desire grew stronger. His body felt so heavy. His mind filled and emptied.

Then his body lifted, or rather, his soul lifted from his body, and he dropped the weight of his temple for the lightness of his soul. He was free! A feeling of expansiveness resonated in him. It was as if the whole of the horizon was in reach of his soul's flight. For a moment he was lost in the feeling.

Then Pharean's sweet face flooded his mind. He regained his will. He reclaimed his purpose. His spirit closed itself to the sudden desire to soar amongst the stars, and instantly he was with her. He found her in the place she had described as Purgatory, where a Grimlock had bound her, and was torturing her.

Whimpering silently, Pharean stared at her father's suffering with tears in her eyes. Aldoran watched them from a distance, waiting for the perfect moment to reveal his presence.

"You belong here with them. You belong here with your family...your father." The Grimlock's grey skin and bald head was sinister and frightening. It was a creature of the night, of the darkness, of a strange evil that twisted the minds of its victims into condemning themselves through their guilt. But God doesn't want us to feel guilty. If we do something wrong, we should repent and try again, but without guilt we can go boldly to God to ask him to help us truly change. Guilt keeps us trapped in place.

"No," Pharean shook her head.

"You think you can escape death so easily? You think you are better than they who share your blood?"

"No, I'm not better than anyone."

"Then you should be here with them."

"No, my family died to protect me, so I should honor them by whatever good I manage to do in my life, and that's what I intend to do. It's not my time yet. I know it's not."

"I shall never let you go. Nor shall *he*," the Grimlock motioned to her father. "His pain and suffering shall continue to draw you here until you give in. He needs you."

"He needs what I cannot give. He needs to make the choice for himself to see through your lies, to the truth. I've already defeated the Angel of Death. I will not kill myself, Grimlock. You are wasting your time with me."

"Then how did I bring you here?"

Pharean looked over at her father, watching him gather water from the ravine. The ground was scorched and burnt, as if from a recent fire. His face was caked with dirt and grime. "I don't believe it was you who brought me here," she whispered, imagining it must have been her father, as he'd done so before in her quest.

But from the other side, one of Pharean's sisters stood beckoning her. "Katrina! Katrina is that you? What are you doing here?" Katrina, or the ghost of her youngest sister, the idealistic optimist of the trio of sisters, continued beckoning her.

Pharean followed her to the edge of the river, as the Grimlock followed her. Aldoran was still watching, silent and unseen, from a distance. Beckoning to Pharean frantically, wordlessly Pharean crossed the river to the other side. She'd barely walked a few yards when Katrina pointed to the bottom of a valley from the mountain where they stood, out into a land of lost and tortured souls.

Writhing in agony, their screams pierced through Pharean, their bloodied bodies flooded her eyes with tears. "What can I do? What can I possibly do for them?"

The screaming and weeping were suddenly silenced, and the silence was deafening. The silence was louder than the screaming had been. It was as if the Grimlock, Katrina, Pharean, and Aldoran had entered a time warp, where there was no sound. Making more wild motions with her hands, Katrina was trying desperately to tell her sister something, but Pharean could not for the life of her figure out what.

"Help them," her sister was mouthing wordlessly, over and over again. "Help them!"

It was then Aldoran's spirit stepped forth from the shadows. "Aldoran…" Pharean's soul recognized him. "How did you get here? How did you find me?"

Looking from Pharean, to her little sister Katrina, he shouted out the words of his own making—inspired by one the poems from the *Book of Mysteries*, and prompted by Holy Spirit, his words came effortlessly, not from his own self, but from the very mouth of God:

"We break this curse of death and shadows.
You cannot keep these souls God made.
An eternity now they breathe without you,
To the light they fly, and the One who saves."

A tremendous burst of light exploded in the skies. As the light burst, the formless soul of Aldoran grasped the formless soul of Pharean. His hands covered her face and hair. Covering her eyes and closing his own, he shielded her from the cataclysmic bursts of light, as the screaming began again. But this time the screaming and writhing were not coming from the human souls, but from the demon Grimlocks who had been keeping the humans' minds and hearts burdened and trapped with lies and doubts and confusion.

It was as if the sun exploded in the darkness, as shooting stars fell from the sky, and the whole darkened world was flooded with blinding, burning light. The rocky, scorched dry ground basked in the glow of the bursting sun and falling stars. The world around them fell apart, as it came to life.

Dozens of Grimlocks shouted and screamed, as the sky was falling in around them, the ground erupting and caving beneath them. As the Grimlocks fell one-by-one, deeper into the bowels of hell, a light shone from the highest heavens, down to the innocent people who'd been killed by King Mardavian, trapped ever since in their own self-condemning shame and guilt. One-by-one the souls were taken into the light. Their expressions were lit up by love and grace, their whole bodies became light and color and energy.

Pharean's sisters came to her, with looks of pure gratitude. "I knew you would come," said her sister Katrina. "I knew you would help us."

"I'll admit I was not so sure," said her sister Lona, ever the pragmatist of the bunch. "But this is one time I am glad to be wrong." Lona smiled too. The three sisters' formless souls embraced. They were more connected in the ethereal ethers than in the warmest embrace of physical life, because spiritual love fills every crevice, from the inside out.

"Thank you both," Pharean smiled gently. "But I'm not the one who saved you—*he* is," she acknowledged, with a motion of her hand towards Aldoran.

Katrina looked over at the finely dressed prince, impressed. "He's cute," Katrina whispered, giving her sister one last kiss on the cheek. Lona rubbed her sister's shoulder, with a look expressing her wish they could all be together again somehow—if not on earth, then in heaven.

"Someday," she whispered to Pharean softly. "But not today. You still have your life to live, and there's something else, something important."

"Something important?"

"Yes, you needed to free all of us, so that mother could tell you something."

"Tell me something?"

"Yes," Katrina repeated. "Something very important."

Lona and Katrina were swept up into the light, as Pharean's mother, Penelope, stepped forward. Pharean's tender heart rejoiced at the sight of her beautiful mother, with her slinky long light hair aglow with the light, and her eyes alit with the motherly look of love she bestowed only on her beloved daughters.

"He is a good man, Pharean," she said to her daughter, looking over at Aldoran approvingly, as they embraced. "And he is a good fit for you."

As Pharean's mother released her, she looked to Aldoran, with a look of knowing twinkling in her eyes, she said, "Take good care of my daughter." Aldoran's face reddened, and as he silently nodded, Penelope gave him a sly wink.

Ruminous' face was radiant with joy, as he said, "Oh my dearest daughter, however can I thank you? Not only have you redeemed our family line in life, but you have saved our souls in death…"

"But father, it was not by I you were saved," Pharean acknowledged, looking up with admiring eyes to Aldoran.

"Nor was it by I," said Aldoran humbly, "But by the Holy Spirit moving through me, and the love I have for your daughter, and a desire to save the family she loves."

Ruminous looked into Aldoran's eyes, which are the window to the soul, and smiled. "A blessing shall I give you both: that your union to one another will be richly blessed for yourselves, as well as for all who know you. Let no man tear asunder what God has brought together." Then he whispered something softly into his daughter's ear alone.

Penelope's face creased with worry lines. "But Pharean, there is something else. Your father has given you a blessing, but I must give you a warning."

"A warning?"

"Yes, my beautiful girl. You have someone missing in your group."

"What do you mean? I don't understand."

"You have a secret enemy, but you also have someone missing in your troupe. The chosen fourteen, the troupe of the Prophecy, have *not* all yet come together."

"Someone is missing?" Aldoran face glowed, as deep down he hoped he would be the one to officially join the ranks of the Chosen Ones.

"Not everyone in the group is as they appear to be," Penelope continued. "You must be very careful, Pharean. You must be careful to remember that no one is all good, or all bad. You must be the peacemaker. You must be the one who turns an enemy into a friend." Pharean just stared at her dumbfounded.

"Do you promise me?" her mother persisted. "Will you remember this warning, and hold true to these words?"

"Yes, my dear mother. I promise you I shall never forget them. I shall remember them when the time comes."

Penelope nodded at Aldoran, and smiled one last time warmly to Pharean. Her life's work completed, she turned from them, to walk into the light.

Ruminous was the last of Pharean's family to go into the light, as he would be the first to greet her when it was her own time to enter into eternity. He gave her one last smile and embrace. Then he was gone.

Aldoran leaned down in the midst of the chaos and rubble about them. Bathed in the radiant glow of the last of the resplendent light raining down from the heavens, he kissed Pharean.

They spiraled back to their own bodies at the campsite. From that moment on, they were of one body and one mind, as their courtship was slowly refined into the holy sacrament of the marriage that was soon to come. It was time now to go home to Andorra, and for Aldoran to take his rightful place as heir to the throne beside his sister, with Pharean at his side.

WHILE THE ASHES RISE TO LIFE

~ ~ ~

Chapter Sixteen
Watermarks

Within and along the Atlantic Coast...

Swimming hurriedly through the waters, wanting to get as much distance between the ship and the Sirens as possible. Feeling sick and disturbed, I wasn't paying any attention to where I was going.

How could such beautiful creatures be such monsters? What other dark creatures were lurking in the depths of these waters? The Sirens were half-surface creatures, so what worse dangers would I encounter here, deeper in the water's depths? I suddenly very much wanted to be back on land, as a human, safe and sound.

A strange scream echoed in the waters. *Looks like I may be about to find out what other perilous beings live here,* I thought to myself.

As quietly as I could, I moved toward the dark green reefs, going into a giant open sea shell to hide inside it, willing it to protect me and make me invisible. Emerging from a coral reef, a human-horse-fish hybrid of epic proportions glowered through the waters, screaming its displeasure.

Its head was nearly human, but its slit tongue was like a snake's. Its torso was the broad back of a horse, and its legs were the fin of a merman. The Nuckelavee was so unusual as to be virtually unknown by most humans, but I'd heard of it in a tale told by an elf that was passing through the Isle of Apples when I was a young girl, so I knew what it was.

Its screaming filled the waters like a hollow echo. Swimming up and away as fast as I could towards the surface, the obvious insanity of the creature brought to mind immediately what the Kelpie had told me about the darkest creatures fearing the surface and air, and after what I'd witnessed of the Sirens, all I wanted to do was escape the waters.

The Nuckelavee continued to scream, but it didn't seem to be pursuing me. I didn't know what was wrong with it, or what it wanted or needed, and I didn't want to find out. Though perhaps some legends of malevolent sea creatures were false, such as the Kelpie, I couldn't bet on that always being the case. I certainly had never expected the Sirens to be so...barbarous.

Gasping for breath, tasting the salty air upon a rock peaking up above the waters, I was mad with the relief to be out of the sea. Perhaps I should land and rest on the shore for the night. Perhaps I needed a break from the sea and its endless dangers.

It took another two hours to swim inland, even with my body and fins perfectly conducive to quick swimming. By the time I'd reached the shore, I was beyond exhausted. Crashing with a loud thump against an average-sized grey rock on the beach, I fell asleep as soon my head and body touched the sand.

When I awoke, a wretched stench filled the air...the smell of a wet animal, the kind that didn't have enough pride to keep itself clean. My seal skin was draped over my body like a blanket, and I realized that during the night, in the cold, I must have inadvertently taken off my seal skin, and donned it as a covering. Embarrassed, I realized that the unpleasant odor was coming from *me!*

Sitting upright now, I prepared to place the seal skin over my shoulders and turn back into a seal. As instantly as my transformation would have allowed me to get back into the waters, but I didn't get the chance. A gigantic water rat, a Lavellan, scurried at me from slightly below, plunging its fangs upon my left thigh, and tearing off a chunk of my flesh triumphantly.

Having the wherewithal to gather the seal skin up into my arms and run from the beast, its short, fat little legs couldn't catch up with me, though it had certainly won itself a large piece of my flesh as consolation. Continuing to run past the shoreline, wanting to put as much distance between me and the Lavellan as possible, I paused upon the threshold of a quaint cabin near the sea. It was only midmorning, yet the fire could be seen and heard crackling and glowing upon the hearth, as something savory and sweet was being roasted upon its pit.

The warmth of the cozy home and the delicious smells from inside it, tempted me, compelling me to seek the company and favor of the house's lord and lady, if only for the day, if only for one good night's sleep away from the dangerous sea. Brushing as much sand from my skin as I could, and straightening my wild curls as much as possible, I knew just how to drape the sleek seal skin around me like a sultry dress.

Standing tall and holding my head high, I went to the cabin and knocked on the door. *Might not be as sexy as those Sirens, but I'm not exactly a Kelpie either,* I reassured myself.

A warning note rang in my ear drums, but I was still incredibly tired, and had been in need of warmth and good food for so long, I didn't listen. Surely the owner of the cabin would not mind playing host for a day or two. It was what I wanted to believe. Still hesitant, I knocked on the door again, in four carefully timed beats with the knocker.

A woman, clothed in dirty rags, opened the door. A shock of fear went all through me, as a man yanked the woman back and yanked me in. He pulled his massive hands on the tops of my hips and drooled in obvious lust, as he took in my body and garb with his small, greedy eyes.

Shaking me so hard I felt my eyes rolling around in the back of my head, as if he were trying to shake the clothes right off me, he shoved me a few feet away, off my feet and onto the floor. Staring up at him, I could see immediately that he was nothing more than a heathen, and I spit on the stone hearth at his feet, glaring up at him defiantly.

In a rage, he lunged after me, hitting me on the top of my back. I was bowled over, as if I'd been hit by a horse's hoof. With the weight of his fist on my body, I totally collapsed. I lay in a heap on the floor, unable to move a muscle.

Pulling me up by the hair until I stood facing him, he grasped my uppermost arms so hard I could feel them bruising, finally punching me in the face until I was unconscious, while his filthy wife, who kept his hovel spotlessly clean, hovered in the corner, arms crossed over her belly and crying silently, rocking herself back and forth without a sound, even on the old, sunken wood floor.

She gasped when he hit me. I could hear her crying in the background as I lost consciousness, and she cried when he turned his rage-filled eyes towards her the following day. It seemed his rage was never spent. Always there was something, someone to rage about— and he took out his rage on those who loved him, and were closest to him.

"Please I didn't do anything..." she stammered. It was true she hadn't, but what fun was it to torture the new girl when she was still asleep?

So, like an animal, he turned his angry fists on her. Saying nothing more, only silently crying, she continued to cover her belly with her hands, praying in her mind for his rage to cease, so that there could be a moment's peace. Not until she was bruised nearly from head-to-toe, did he fall laboriously into his chair by the hearth, as if he'd put in a hard day's work, instead of a hard day beating up his wife.

~ ~ ~

The next day I was barely awake before he was beating me unconscious again. His wife, Sara, I heard him call her, just cried and cried. Sometimes it seemed like all she did was cry. She certainly knew well enough not to speak.

Her husband didn't touch me or look at me sexually again, and in this alone I drew comfort. Already I was plotting my escape, but how could I leave this poor woman alone with her beast of a husband? After the first day I knew their names, but I didn't say a word to either one of them.

"Cainon," Sara's voice trembled frightfully one evening, nearly a week into my captivity. "Your potato soup is ready. Is ye ready to eat it?"

"When am I not ready to eat, aye?" he growled, seizing a large pewter ladle and dishing up a hearty helping of the steaming soup into one of his large black bowls of mortar. In days past, he would have hit Sara on the back of her head for good measure, but potato soup must have been one of his favorites, for it seemed to have lulled him into the first tolerable mood I'd seen him in.

Sara was working on knitting a small blanket, but her hand was faltering, and her eyelids drooped as she fought her exhaustion. Waiting for his poor wife to go to sleep, he turned his hungry eyes to me. *No, I won't go through this again.*

"Aren't you tired? Time to go to sleep, Sara," Cainon practically demanded. Nodding, she gathered her pieces of yarn and went into their bedroom.

I could feel it coming, and I steadied and readied myself. As he was greedily gobbling down his fourth helping of the potato soup, I slyly stole Sara's carving knife from the table, holding it tightly in my fist against my chest.

After Cainon had finished his final helping, in want of the fulfillment of another type of appetite, his savage grey eyes turned to me. They were homely and unintelligent eyes, and yet they were the same color as King Mardavian's, and for that, above any other more logical reason, I hated him.

Without bothering to hide it, his eyes roamed up and down my body, settling upon my blossoming chest thinly concealed within a worn old dress of Sara's she'd let me borrow. Drool emerged and dripped from his mouth, as he licked his chops, like a dog at a table about to be given a choice piece of mutton. Clearly, he liked what he saw. He rubbed the top of his belt, making to take it off. His eyes narrowed as if in anticipation of the coming ecstasy. Pretending to be into it, I moaned and rubbed my hips.

His eyes widened and lit up, surprised and excited that I might be a willing participant in the affair, and not a forced conquest. Rape was all well and good when looting and pillaging, but when he'd been lusting for the whore for days as she moved like a horny ally cat around his house, even letting out her pheromones and sticking out her 'arse temptingly in front of his wife…no with that kind of whore he wanted equal give and take.

"Stand up," he ordered. "Face me, chest out." I did as he demanded. Holding the knife behind my back tightly, with my chest puffed out, as if I were on display, and wanted to be seen in the best light and positions. He inspected me for a few minutes in order to get his anticipation and excitement up.

As he was now in the most compromised of motions, in the process of taking off his belt, about to remove his pants, I lunged the cutting knife deep into his abdomen. He let out a yowl, falling forward.

Whereupon, I grabbed two towels from the table to protect my hands, and grasped the still smoldering cauldron of soup from the hearth, slamming the sizzling pot onto the barbarian's shoulders and back. The soup went flying off his body, some of it flying halfway across the room, some of it rolling down unto the floor, strewn across the floor and walls.

"You damn slut bitch; you'll pay for this you will!"

"There's where you're wrong!" I shouted back. "I've bested better than the likes of you—and it's YOU who'll pay," I glowered, taking the red-hot poker into my left hand, which was still protected by the towel, and shoving it directly into the center of Cainon's forehead.

Screaming bloody murder, and hobbling around the room, he was in a pain beyond imagining. The hot poker was still in his head; all the way through I'd wielded it. For a few more minutes he hollered and shouted, and ranted and raved, making noises like an injured animal, until he finally fell over dead as a door nail. I stood over him, smiling in pleasure.

My pleasure startled me. It frightened me a little too. Was it okay to take pleasure in a man's death, even in men as evil as King Mardavian, and as abusive as this husband was to his wife? Was I more like the Sirens then I realized?

I did feel my body tighten as he took his last breath. Was I more human now, or sea creature? What part of me took pleasure in his death?

Unexpectedly, another cry rang out from the bedroom. "Sara?" I called, as she tentatively rushed from her room. Clutching her abdomen, Sara cried, "Water, hurry, fetch me some hot water! He's coming!"

"Who's coming?"

"My baby!" A baby! Oh! How had I not known? Of course, she often clutched her stomach, but she was so thin. It was hard to believe Sara had carried the baby to full-term, and if not…

Hurry! Please!" she cried.

There was no time for such questions now. Going back into the open living room, I moved past the bloody mess to the kitchen, grabbing another big pot from the cabinet. By now I knew where most everything was kept.

Running outside I pumped the pot full of water from the well, carrying it as quickly and carefully inside as I could, replacing the pot on the hearth where the cauldron had played its part in killing Sara's husband, had sat. Pulling the red-hot poker from Cainon's head, which had surely finished him off, I coaxed the coals to bring the fire and flames back to life, trying to ignore the gore and caked blood hanging off of it.

While the water heated up, I went back into the bedroom with Sara. Sweat was pouring from her too pale brow. She looked flushed and wan. I worried that her frail body couldn't bear the pain of an early labor.

"Do you feel weak?" I asked her, concerned. "Grip my hand as hard as you need to." I was surprised by Sara's strength, as she nearly broke the veins in my hand with her grip.

"All...that...noise...my husband...what...happened...is he...dead?" I shook my head at her, now was not the time for such concerns.

"Please...before...my baby...comes...I need...to know...how much...danger there...is." Suddenly I understood. Sara hadn't just been hiding her pregnancy from me...but from her husband. With the way he hurt her all the time, she'd been worried he could kill the baby in her womb, and once the baby was born...she was afraid...

Kneeling on the bed beside her, as she gripped my hand like an iron trap, I bowed my head to her humbly and answered, "You need not worry about your husband anymore, my lady. He will never hurt you again, nor will your child ever know of its father's violence and cruelty."

A light of hope and gratitude passed across Sara's eyes. Her cheeks cooled slightly and filled with color, as a fresh glow of radiance swept across her whole mien. "God forgive me for saying so, but you must be an angel sent from on high."

Before I'd had a chance to answer her, she screamed, and I ran to get the hot water as she cried, "Hurry, he's coming!"

Catching the baby right as it crowned, I pulled the innocent babe from his mother's womb. I took it to the hot water and washed it, cutting the umbilical cord, and wrapping it in one of the blankets Sara had woven. I'd attended the birth of several children in Avalon. So I understood the delicacies of child birth.

"Thank you," said Sara, with the shadow of a smile, in a mouth full of chipped and missing teeth.

"How did you know it was going to be a boy?"

"I don't know. I just did. A mother's instinct I suppose," she answered honestly.

"Is there anymore of the potato soup? I'm afraid I'm awfully ravenous after all that." The poor young woman had only eaten half a bowl of the soup she'd made, before her husband had screamed and shouted that she was making a glutton of herself and he would never tolerate a fat wife.

Smiling sheepishly, I shook my head. After all, I'd thrown what remained of the boiling soup in the hearth all over her husband. Sara nodded, "That's okay. I'll just rest then, rest and hold my little man without any worries of the big man coming in and throwing him across the room."

"Don't worry, I'll try to put something together for when you wake up," I assured her. She smiled gratefully. "That would be nice," she whispered weakly.

I watched them together for a few sacred moments more, as she gently caressed her baby's tiny, innocent face; counting and blessing each and every little finger and toe. There was guilt and remorse in my heart as I looked over at the dead father, just a few mere feet away from them, but at the same time, I felt relief as I looked back to the mother and child.

Murder was wrong, and I did still have a conscious I recognized with relief, but I was glad that they were safe from Cainon, just as I was glad for all the people who were protected from King Mardavian's dictatorship because I had killed him. This was the way it had always been in the untamed lands of the Celts: kill or be killed. Only the strong survive.

This had been the way of man long before I had come down to the earth. And this brutal way of life was bound to continue long after I left it. Surely there would not be much I could do to change that. Still, I had done a lot to change the future of the little boy Sara held. I felt deep down that I had saved them both.

For a few more weeks I stayed on to help with her transition into motherhood. The first thing I did, as Sara and her son slept deeply and soundly together, was clean up the soup and the "mess." I baked some biscuits, and made a simple vegetable soup, full of nutrients that would be good for the mother and her milk.

After Sara ate something and got a little strength back, we had a small burial outside of the hovel for Cainon. It took me the better part of a day to make the grave deep enough for him, but I felt it was the least any human deserved.

"What he deserved was not to be buried at all...just cast off into the sea, to be torn apart and eaten by the sharks and other sea creatures," Sara said, as if reading my mind. Fidgeting uncomfortably, I wondered what she'd think if she knew that I too was one of those sea creatures she was so callously referring to.

We exchanged a few trite words of sorrow for her husband's passing that neither of us really meant, and as the baby let out a soft coo, we rolled and dumped his heavy body into the grave. It took me the rest of the day to cover his body with the piles of dirt I'd uncovered. Sara breathed a sigh of relief as I tossed the last of the dirt over her husband's grave.

Sara was a new woman once her husband was out of the picture. She'd taken on a newfound strength and resolve: she laughed more, talked more, smiled more, and cried much less.

As the days and weeks passed, I felt the time was drawing near for my return to the sea, until one day the sea's call made it clear to me. Standing and looking out the window at the soft, early morning light of dawn, I turned to Sara with a half-guilty, bittersweet smile, and said, "It's time I go back to where I came from."

Finally, it was time to say goodbye. I was surprised at how hard it was for me to leave her and the baby. Nodding to herself, as if she'd always known this day would come, she asked me no questions about where I was from, or where I was going, or nagged or bothered me with guilt trips, beseeching me to stay, when she already understood that I couldn't.

Bouncing the crying baby on her hip, she looked at me beseechingly, asking only, "But please, what can you do for him before you go?"

"What do you mean?"

"Surely you are a goddess, or in some way have clearly been blessed by the gods. This innocent baby has his father's violent genes running through his veins, what can you do to ensure him a better destiny?"

Looking deeply into her open eyes, absent of guile, I saw she only wanted to protect the innocent babe from growing into a man like his father. I thought about if I'd fostered a baby from King Mardavian's violation of me—as Darlillyth had. I thought about how Darlillyth had suffered, and how it had twisted and changed her.

I did not blame Darlillyth for what she had become. I did not blame her for turning me to ashes. How could I hate her, when I understood her so well, having been through the same brutal violation from the same ruthless man? The hardest thing for me to forgive about Darlillyth, was that she was the woman Eliju really loved and wanted to spend his life with.

Turning my attention back to the broken family at hand, I studied the howling baby screaming bloody murder on his mother's knee. More than likely his father would have killed him before he'd ever become a man. If he had somehow lived, I had saved him from knowing such a father, who would only have taught him the best ways to hurt another.

His mother was right; his innocent blood still coursed with his barbarian of a father's blood. So, what blessing could balance, or even tip the scales to his favor? I knew that it was only justice that she sought, for her son to not have to pay for the sins of his father...

Justice! That was it! Justice...and Clemency. Justice and mercy, and the joy of a mother's unconditional love. "The boy's name shall be Justille Clemence."

His mother nodded, as if this had always been so. The baby had gone weeks without a name. I realized now that Sara had been waiting for me to name him all along.

"His name means Justice and Mercy. He will live in justice and mercy, work toward justice and mercy, and will be a beacon in the community for good. I'm going to impart to you a very special gift now."

Sara nodded placidly, with utter acceptance of what was to come, and utter trust and gratitude in her eyes, as she watched me with her beloved son. Donning my human form for my seal skin, I transformed right before the woman and babe, into the Selkie.

Sara's eyes widened in wonder, but she seemed to accept the transformation as a gift from the gods. As a seal, I lay my fin upon the baby's forehead. Sara helped me by leaning the baby down for me to reach. My fin left a watermark on the boy's forehead.

In the sea's sonar language, which sounded very different out of the waters, I offered the child a blessing in the form of a prayer. "May you never lose the joy and innocence of this moment of the first few weeks of your life. May you know the honor of justice, tempered by the refined grace of mercy—this opposes your father's legacy, so that you may tip the scales of justice towards good, and live a far better life than he did. Justille Clemence, I leave you in peace and love. Always stay true to this moment's perfect purity and innocence..."

I had let someone in. I had let the woman know my secret. She knew I had killed a man, her own husband even, and she now knew that the legend of the Selkie, was real and that I was one.

The legend of the Selkie would be told to her son, and passed on in stories throughout the generations. Without question, I knew she accepted me, and was grateful for what I had done. Without knowing what I'd said, because I spoke the blessing in the sonar language, the woman understood and believed that I had blessed her son, with perfect trust. Nodding goodbye, she opened the door and let me return without another word, to the sea...

~ ~ ~

July, and several Julys to come—

As the years passed, not all of the creatures I met were dangerous and threatening, or beautiful and deceiving. Some were merely delightful and fun. Like the endlessly shape-shifting water spirit, called a Tangie, moving seamlessly through the waters that I'd been following and watching secretly for days.

He'd turned from a water sprite, to a fish, to a tiny little sea horse, to a polar bear, to a nail, to a treasure chest, to a whale, to a dolphin, to a lovely turquoise coral reef, to a sea shell, to a clam, to a snake, to a frog, to a lily pad, all in the course of three days, making me laugh excessively with each comical transformation.

"What's your name?" I finally asked it.

"Yellywla," the creature laughed, making spinning circles around me. "And I know you've been tailing me for days!" Laughing back at it, I did somersaults through the waters. He taught me tricks on how to catch fish.

We ate and played together at the same time. Flipping and somersaulting through the waters, he amazed me with the ingenious and quick transformations he concocted. We were having such a grand time, when…

Madorna, the elusive female water spirit called the Melusine, a mermaid adorned with a head dress woven not with feathers, but with sea shells, stared at me in blind fury. My very joyfulness seemed to infuriate her. In her anger, she turned into her malefic form of a winged serpent.

Her wings were vivid sea-foam green, and matched her lovely sea-foam hair. Her scales were a darker grey-green, and as she hissed, they opened and flapped at me threateningly. She was as fiercely beautiful as her fury was fiercely frightening. In her blind fury, she dove at me and knocked my side. The wound immediately gushed out blood.

Letting out a cry, I swam away from the mermaid, turned snake, turned utterly snake winged crazy. She continued to pursue me. Flying about in the water, her now slithery, leathery wings propelled her through the waters…

"*Noooo!!!!*" my silent sonar scream sounded through the waters. In my mad attempt at escaping the Melusine, a horrible cousin of the sweet and beautiful merpeople, I met with all forty-five razor sharp fangs of the hungry, salivating mouth of a dragon!

The Melusine left me to it with a wild scream, as if to say, *you've got dibs on this one—she's all yours—just leave ME alone!* My little Tangie friend Yellywya was long gone too. I couldn't blame the happy little sea creature for leaving me. I would be on my own with this one.

A Knucker, the green and red water dragon the Kelpie had warned me about before, furiously pursued me to the edge of all hope and reason. He bore his fangs on me again. He was so close, I could count all his teeth.

There was no hope. Something in my spirit flagged. There was no getting out of this one. I didn't have the strength or ingenuity to escape the massive dragon, king of all sea creatures.

So, I took a good long look at the creature that was going to kill me. It was magnificent. That none could deny. Its scales were luxurious in the air and even in the water. Their texture was sleek and scaly. His whiskers were long, and acted as an extra sensor to smell out his prey. There was no hiding from the great beast. If I was to die now, with the Prophecy unfulfilled, this would be an honorable way to go.

It was not stupid or unfeeling. Its intelligence was as refined as any human, and I believed so was his heart. Though it spoke a different language, I believed it held some of the same thinking patterns and schools of thought as I did, and when these creatures lost their mates, I believed their feelings were as keenly hurt and felt as most humans.

If I had learned anything from my time in the sea, it was the higher frequency the sea creatures vibrated to. Their thoughts and emotions, though different, were often of a higher octave. I would almost be glad to die in the jaws of the red-green water dragon.

Just as my body gave way, and I'd started slowly floating with the currents of the waters towards its mouth of venomous fangs, I felt the words of the Shaman Wandering Wolfe and Eliju. I couldn't make out their words, but I heard their murmurs, like a prayer. Eliju's face filled my mind, and the sky of the sea I was submerged in, as if he were all around me.

Another Knucker emerged through the currents, a luminescent white like the mother-of-pearl of a clam shell, glimmering so brightly I was temporarily blinded by the iridescent scales. I was not the only one to lose focus and nerve.

The red and green water dragon cowered before the magnificent white dragon before it. Clearly there was a pecking order among the dragons as well, and this great white beast was of some significance. I felt a peace that passed my understanding, and knew that I would survive this encounter.

"Sifeornor," the once vicious and imposing red-green dragon now simpered pleadingly.

"What is the meaning of this, Akomite?" the old white dragon's grey whiskers twitched warningly.

"Just a bit of fun..." simpered Akomite.

"I'm sure," said Sifeornor sarcastically. "Just as I'm sure that 'fun' would have entailed ripping this poor Selkie apart from limb to limb, had I not arrived in time to stop you."

"Sire..."

"Enough!" the white dragon's sonorous voice boomed and echoed amongst the shells and coral reefs.

"Leave this creature be. You know as well as I do that, she does not list on our menu, and this Selkie in particular is of grave importance in the human realm."

"I did not know this."

"And that is the point!" Sifeornor's voice boomed. "To think before you feast!" Akomite cowered and shook in the echo of the master dragon's great, booming voice.

"Now come here, creature," he beckoned me forward with his paw. Now it was I who felt like cowering before this powerful beast.

"Don't worry, I wish you no harm," it beckoned me again, its voice as warm and inviting as a feast of berries and nuts in the Forest of Camelot. Deciding I had nothing to lose, and since he clearly had all the clout anyway, I flipped my body towards him.

Placing his right paw upon my back, I felt a whirring and burning. A white burst of light exploded beneath the waters, as millions of tiny particles of burnt seaweed, sea shells, coral reefs and bits of fish who had been near us at the time of the explosion, floated past us.

"What happened?" I asked, my sonar voice cracking.

"I have branded you, young sea creature, with an imprint, so that you need not swim in constant fears through these waters anymore. You will still encounter malevolent beasts, I cannot protect you from that, but they will fear you, and you shall fear them no longer. Those beasts who wish you no harm will make fast friends of you."

"With what did you brand me?"

"A watermark of the ancient name of the sea," said Sifeornor significantly. "It is the most powerful piece of magic I could wield for you. It is the oldest of the olde magicks, and with that great mark, none may hurt you whilst you swim, or slumber, or plunder the seas."

"Why is that word so powerful?"

"You must know. Names have a resonance, an influence. The original name of the sea, from a time when all creatures and humans spoke the same language, is incredibly potent. When one speaks the ancient names and words of this language, it makes one virtually undefeatable. When one bears the name of it in a mark on the body, it brands you as one-of-a-kind, and impervious by any other water creature. You are, in essence, above the pecking order here now."

"Is there one name that is more powerful above all others?" The great white dragon eyed me warily. "Yes, of course...the name above all names...the secret name of God."

"God?"

"Yes."

"But which god? The pagans have many gods..."

"As do the dragons..."

"So which god..."

"THE God..."

"THE God...?"

"The God: the creator of the heavens and the earth, and all creatures moving upon it, and of the seas and creatures swimming in it, of the sky and all creatures flying in it, of the universe and all the stars and planets spinning in it."

"And who is this God?"

"THE God."

"One God?"

"THE God."

"Do you mean to tell me that all the hype is true?"

The White Knucker shook its massive head. "It is not hype. It is truth."

"Then why do you worship gods other than THE God? Why do we Celts worship many gods?"

"Because it is easier to worship the light than the sun; it is easier to worship a reflection, than the source itself. I myself worship this one God. But once I was like you...drifting along with every undertow, being pulled under and being brought back up, again and again, and never thinking to ask *why*."

"When I discovered the Order, that we each are part of a Great Plan, and I saw the Light and the source of that Light, I stopped worshiping the light OR the sun and worshiped instead the Creator of the Sun and the Light, and I learned...more than I ever knew possible about life and eternity. This is why I am revered and respected, and also feared by other dragons."

"Why?" I asked him curiously. "I'm not sure I understand."

"I was once a dragon red and fierce, breathing fire thirty feet into the sea every time I opened my mouth to breath, but when I saw the true light, my mind was opened, my eyes were opened, and my color changed to what you see now before you. I became the King of the Sea Dragons. For what one does not understand, one will destroy if they are more powerful, or revere and worship if they cannot overpower it."

I felt a strong urge to leave now, my mind exploding a little with the conversation. Nodding, as if he knew how desperately I longed to swim away and was dismissing me, I turned back to say, "Wait—one last thing!"

"Yes...?" asked the Great White Dragon languorously.

"Do you know if anyone knows the secret name of God?"

"Of course," Sifeornor nodded. "The first man and woman know."

"You mean the Creation Story of Adam and Eve? They knew the name?"

Shaking his head, he said, "No, not Adam and Eve. Adam and Lilith. Lilith knew…that's why God isolated her and threw her out of the Garden of Eden."

"Oh…"

"Goodbye now, you are safe. Blessings Selkie seal of the waters, human Priestess of the Isle of Apples, and raven bird of the skies." With his blessing, he plunged his great head and bulldozed into the waters, leaving a gigantic wake in his stead that took many minutes to calm.

Plunging towards the shore, I swam as fast as my fins could propel me into the safety of the caverns. I couldn't comprehend the conversation I'd shared with Sifeornor, or the magical mark of protection he had left on my skin.

Once I found an old mirror at the bottom of the sea, I moved to and fro, and every which way, to see the watermark on my back. It looked like the mark of a pine cone. How odd. Now I bore this on my skin, as well the mark of the raven.

What had the dragon meant by calling me the raven bird of the skies? Was he referring to my mark of the raven in flight?

Still barely believing I had escaped the dragons, and not just *a* dragon, but *the King* of the Dragons, the King of the Sea Monsters; it took me some time to calm my nerves with steady breathing on the cavern floor.

I needed some time apart from the other sea creatures. Even though Sifeornor had branded me with a mark to protect me, I needed to reflect and process our conversation. I knew this was only the beginning of my adventures in the sea, and the coming years would uncover many more mysteries…

~ *** ~

Chapter Seventeen
Marriage of Scholar and King

In the Andorra Mountains—

Aldoran's relationship was still strained with his sister, but he asked her to stand by his side when he married Pharean once they'd returned to their Kingdom. Bearing the crowns from the poor people who had been killed, both crowns were glowing as they said their vows, as if fate had predestined their rulership over the lands desecrated by King Mardavian.

"I wish my father were here," Pharean whispered sorrowfully, holding back tears. "And my mother and sisters, and my whole family. It really doesn't feel right getting married without them."

Alondria hugged the frail girl tenderly, as the sister she'd never had. "I'm sorry for what happened with your family. But you have Aldoran now, and our parents, and me...we'll be real sisters after tonight!" Then she smiled her angelic smile that flooded wherever she was, with light.

Pharean laughed to keep from crying, and kissed Alondria sweetly on the cheek. Pharean felt so grateful to have a sister again. Alondria's sentiments meant the world to her.

Aldoran's parents Theodore and Selena treated her with the utmost kindness and respect. They saw her as a talented young writer and that pleased them, as creative talent was their most important measuring stick for the value of a person's character. Selena also felt that as long as people kept up their passion for their gifts and their life, there would always be passion in their marriage.

Aldoran presented Pharean with the wedding band he had taken from the Queen from the poor kingdom who had been killed along with her family. After they said I do, Aldoran presented her with the crowns from that kingdom as well. Her elegant engagement ring was from her hometown, and their wedding bands were from the land where her family was lost. Now Pharean entered into a new family with the royalty of Andorra.

Pharean had explained to Aldoran soon after their engagement that the legend of the crowns for that Kingdom was that they glowed atop the heads of its rightful rulers. In this way, the crowns chose who ruled the small city, not the blood lines.

The crowns glowed atop their heads once more, as they had when they first put them on over a year ago now. So Aldoran and Pharean would also visit that Kingdom and take care of it, as well as their territory in Andorra.

At the end of the wedding ceremony, Pharean read an excerpt from the book she and Aldoran had proudly finished about her father's life. The speech her father had written only a few months before his death, Pharean bravely recited in his honor.

"We must not stay stagnant in any moment of life. We must move on. We must move forward. We must not keep looking back to days gone by, for moments of joy and pain were experienced to teach us something about life. Once these lessons are learned, we may be transformed from the grimy, common caterpillar into the beautiful butterfly, colorful, bright, and free.

So let us learn the lesson of the butterfly. Let the butterfly teach us its lessons about love. If you cling too tightly, you will choke love out, and if you hold love too loosely without the nourishment of consistent care and affection, it will fly away, forgetting to return. We must hold love open in the palm of your hand, open to learning how fly. Fly together.

We cannot help the caterpillar along. If we break open its cocoon too soon, it will never learn the lesson of the struggle it needs in order to break through, opening its wings to the air and sky of abstractions unknown and unseen.

We each are met on our journeys by unique temptations, trials, and tests tailored especially for us, to break our hearts, crush our spirits, and destroy our souls. In the midst of the pain of the worst of our fears coming to fruition, in the middle of the most difficult, the most impossible of circumstances, we may have, even then, especially then, a choice—to let disappointments break our hearts, crush our spirits, and destroy our souls, or to learn to endure our hardships by the guiding light of love.

Whether or not we are healed, whether or not we are redeemed, whether or not we have to wait forever for our promised destiny that never comes, we can choose to rise above our own temptations, we can choose to accept our circumstances, through the path of peace that leads to love. Remember the lesson of the butterfly, a microcosm of all of life itself.

Only by love does the caterpillar have the will to struggle against its cocoon. Only by hope does it transform into a butterfly in order to grow wings and break through. Only by faith does it fly. Only by believing and trusting in the mighty power of the powers unseen, like love, may we walk by faith in the darkness, holding tightly to that still, small voice inside our hearts, telling us to keep moving forward, telling us to never give up, telling us love never dies, and all that matters in life is love.

If and when we crack beneath the weight of our pressures, if we give in to immorality or despair, or whatever it is that tempts us, we can yet choose to forgive ourselves and begin again. Accepting the frailty of our humanity and rising up again and again, vowing to do it better next time, may be the greatest glory any human being can ever possibly know. We can learn each day to be better than the day before. If we never give up.

So, don't quit. We all fail. No one is without faults. But love never fails. To learn what it means to truly love, is the only way we may fully live. To love unconditionally is the greatest measure of a man, or a marriage."

Selena held onto her to daughter Alondria during the speech. Alondria was fighting back tears. Her mother had known from the start how her daughter felt about the gentle bard Jonlin. She knew how hard it was for her now to be at her brother's wedding, wanting him to be happy, but also brokenhearted, and fearing she would never have true love for herself.

It was unorthodox for a bride to give a speech at her own wedding, but her dear father Ruminous had taught her well to think and act for herself. The speech was met by tears and cheers from their guests, but many more than Pharean's family were absent and missed from her wedding to Aldoran.

Eliju and Wandering Wolfe had come, but not Varawynn or Shadow Rain. Varawynn was somewhere at sea, Eliju had said, and while they were glad to hear of how she'd been resurrected, with her leg healed, it was sad to think she was somewhere so alone and apart from them that she could not be reached for their wedding. Shadow Rain had given word by the Shaman that she was too needed now as the Medicine Woman of her tribe to leave them without a spiritual leader.

At the reception, Aldoran presented his wife with three gifts, *In Your Footprints*, the research book they'd written together about trekking and travelling, *Trees, Plants, Flowers, and Animals: How, Where and Why They Grow*, an encyclopedia thereby, and *The Turning of the Tide: The Life and Death of the Philosopher Ruminous*.

There was an inscription on the first page: *This book was written by his loving daughter for her larger-than-life father. His last words were, "Do not let my death be for nothing. Live, so that in death, my life might have meaning."*

Ruminous died to protect the kingdoms from King Mardavian. His life and efforts were not in vain. King Mardavian was killed by the group of Chosen Ones his daughter joined. So, King Mardavian will hurt no one ever again. May this great man rest in peace, knowing that the futures of the innocent are protected by his daughter and their group.

Aldoran gave Pharean these weddings gifts in front of their small group, and his new bride broke down in tears for what they meant to her.

"When the time is right, the group shall come back together," Wandering Wolfe told Pharean as way of an apology. "Though I'm very sorry so many of us aren't here for your big day."

Ileona was still off searching for something in the desert, but Illumina and Silvandrin had come. Orzenith and Flint did not attend such things as weddings or funerals, so they too were absent. There was a sadness; a heaviness over the proceedings that did not seem natural for such a celebration of life as a wedding. Alondria did her best to shower her new sister with gifts and affection, but Pharean was sober at the reception. Aldoran was attentive and understanding as always.

Many of the fairies from Astarra came to the reception, and lit up the night with their sparkling clothes and wands. The royal bard Larsius broke out his fiddle and sang for them song after song with lovely, enchanting melodies, and recited poem after poem, regaling the crowd with several funny stories making the guests laugh and clap, gayer than a few in the wedding party were.

Lord Larsius was one of the guests. The bard's handsome, windswept dark hair was combed just so, and his deep blue eyes told romantic stories all their own. His voice changed from character to character as he acted out his tales. The range of his voice was enthralling, as it lowered and rose when he sang, in dreamy ballads that swept the whole courtyard up and into his bedroom eyes and gorgeous tenor voice. At least all the hearts of the women thrilled when he sang, and perhaps a few of the men's hearts did too.

Pharean nudged Alondria about him gently, for Larsius was more than a mere bard, he was a nobleman: Lord Larsius, of excellent title, breeding, and standing in the community. Not that Pharean, Aldoran, or their parents cared about such things as status, but Lord Larsius seemed perfect for Alondria, they felt. Many of his songs had been written by her father, Theodore, himself.

He was handsome and dashing, as talented as Jonlin (indeed much more so truth be told—though they never would have admitted that to Alondria), intelligent and bright. He seemed kind and thoughtful too, but Alondria was utterly oblivious to her brother and sister-in-law's prodding toward him.

Selena and Theodore were often there for their daughter, hugging her, kissing her, and drying her tears. But it was Luquinn who accompanied her to the wedding, taking her arm and squeezing her hands, as she cried in happiness for the happiness of her brother. It was Luquinn who had stayed with her and never left her side after she had disbanded from the group. And it was Luquinn who most often comforted her in moments of loneliness and despair.

Within the first year of the marriage of Aldoran and Pharean, their first child was born, Hope. She was frail and weak, barely able to cry or make a mewing sound, and so they worried and fussed over her, but she lived.

Luquinn visited often, as their personal doctor, he went above and beyond to care for little Hope, and his extra attentions and remedies did wonders. Aldoran and Pharean were over the moon with happiness, and the whole kingdom seemed to ring like one giant bell of merriment at her birth, after she'd pulled through her rocky start in life. Yes, *Hope lived!*

Alondria was both excited and saddened by the birth, always having believed growing up she'd be the first to marry and have children. Dismissing the feeling as selfish and childish, once she'd seen the sweet babe, the only thing she could possibly do was to love it, and the sadness dissolved into joy.

Hope did a lot to bridge the open wound between her and Aldoran. Though without any communication over their resentments, it would have been expecting too much for the child's birth to have healed their relationship entirely.

Of course, Alondria sympathized with Pharean, having no family at all, and helped care for the little girl as lovingly as if she were her own. Her brother was so happy, Pharean was so happy, the Kingdom was so happy, and yet her own life lay out before her like a long, empty stretch of desert; blank and open and meaningless, with no love for her, but the half-love and the half-life of her brother's family, who were not fully her own.

Luquinn, or Luq, as he allowed only Alondria to call him, was a constant comfort and companion. Over time he'd developed and grown into her, so as to know her every need and thought before she'd articulated it. In this way, he was always capable of fulfilling her wants and needs, just before she'd recognized them herself.

Luq was the one who lovingly nursed Aldoran's daughter back to health when she born so tiny and weak. Through his constant care and vigilance, he kept Hope alive. Just as his love and tenderness kept Alondria, in the intensity of her unending grief, alive.

Thus, time passed. Luquinn became the best and most well-renowned doctor of the Kingdom. He often went to the houses in the land and made people better who would surely have succumbed to death without the skills of his anointed healing touch. He put his entire being into being a doctor and servant of healing to the community. Alondria, being half-muse, inspired him to save lives.

But the bedside of the princess Alondria, was the one he visited most often, daily administrating to her healing remedies, lotions, and balms for her skin. He made a lipstick he applied to her lips with his own steady fingers. He brewed perfumes, and oils that he massaged into her sleek and lustrous curls. He could not do enough for her. His patience and caring for her seemed to have no end.

Alondria had set him up with his own research lab, wherein he created potions and remedies for the townspeople and children. Researching and experimenting were his special forte. He kept constant watch over the Kingdom, like a shepherd with its flock. In his research lab, he studied the properties of plants, studying constantly, always researching and inventing things to help and serve the people more.

He had Pharean and Aldoran's *Encyclopedia of Plants* in a place of honor on his mantle. It was a sort of Bible for him, and he read from it daily, and had whole pages of it memorized.

The placement of their book wasn't just in homage to their work. It was practical to have it there, as he so frequently used it as a research source. Pharean's knowledge of plants and the book she'd written about them, were invaluable to his projects, and in coming up with medicines to treat the ailments in their land.

Alondria herself learned to curb her constant ache over Jonlin by keeping busy serving the community through using her own gifts. She nurtured little Hope and went out amongst the townspeople to hear their stories and act as a mediator.

She and Luquinn were like Hope's second parents, and Aldoran and Pharean asked both of them to be the Godparents a year into her little life. It only made sense. Alondria was the sister and Luquinn was the doctor who had saved their daughter's life. They were also both a part of the troupe.

Alondria lent her ears, and most especially her heart, when the townspeople complained, and she gave them her sympathies, always trying to make things right in a way that was fair to all parties. She became more than their Queen, she was their Judge, but only in the cases that were most difficult was her fairness and wisdom called upon to make the perfect judgment.

Most nights she forced herself to feast in the open hall. She danced at the balls and parties to raise the spirits of the townspeople. But she barely paid any mind to the gorgeous bard, Larsius, who told his stories at the evening banquets, who sang and danced with her at every ball, and who held the title of Lord from a mother of royal descent.

Lord Larsius was a bard because he could afford to be, he could afford to do whatever he liked. He was a gentleman. He held a title, good standing in the community, owned lands and had the sort of fine looks which sent every woman except Alondria into a swoon.

Even her father and mother grew impatient with her constant lamentations over Jonlin. They too pushed her towards Lord Larsius, as talent was the most important thing to them, he was the one they wanted as their son-in-law.

Luquinn was the only one who let Alondria be herself, and say what she was really thinking, how much she was still hurting over Jonlin. Luquinn, in his quiet and unassuming way, was often overlooked. He was a very handsome young man, but Lord Larsius had the attention-grabbing personality that left the mild-mannered doctor's polite, stiff manners in the dust.

Luq's practical nature, penchant for scientific research, and duty as a doctor, was very different and foreign from every other person in Alondria's creative family, who, as creative as they were, didn't see outside the box of the arts, for the mate of their children. They only placed marital value on the inspiring of souls. They didn't leave room for the idea that a muse can inspire any gift or talent in the people around them, including the scientific development of medicine to save lives. Luquinn had saved the life of their precious first grandchild, Hope. Still, no one in Alondria's family recognized his true worth.

It was Luquinn's nature to push and nag those he loved, however. He worried over Alondria, and fretted about her sometimes, but most of the time he allowed her to grieve. He admired the gracious way she handled her people. She was a wonderful co-ruler with Aldoran. Even though bad blood lay between them just beneath the surface, they made an excellent team, and the love between them was as clear to the world as a cloudless blue sky.

Aldoran worried about his twin sister Alondria incessantly as well, but his worry came out in bursts of sudden anger, as did Alondria's resentment. "You both cannot go on this way," Pharean told her husband one day. "Not when I am with child once more."

She stared up into her husband's eyes with a dreamy grin. His eyes were alit with sheer, gentle tenderness, and he flashed her that irresistible golden smile that still made her feel weak at the knees.

"Aldoran," she said, trying to regain her composure. "You know very well I can't count from 1 to 10 when you insist on looking at me with that smile of yours."

Grinning back at her, he replied, "And you know very well that you make me far too happy *not* to smile like this every day, all day for the rest of my life."

"Oh, well, very well then. We are in a sorry state! How do you expect us to keep writing books when I can't even string a coherent sentence together whenever you look at me like that?"

"It's easy," he smiled a little clownishly. "Just don't look at me when you're trying to get something accomplished."

"And when I'm *not* trying to get something accomplished?"

Deviously mischievous, he replied by taking her up into his arms, "Then don't stop looking at...or touching me." Kissing her furiously, she shoved him away from her, laughing and giggling like a school girl.

"Aldoran stop it now! This is how I got in this sorry state to begin with!" she said, looking down at her stomach, and rubbing her belly. "Besides, I was in the middle of saying something about your sister."

"You were?" he laughed. "You could've fooled me!"

"Well, *anyway*," she said primly, straightening her skirts and hair. "You need to speak with your sister. Really speak with her—heart-to-heart, Aldoran. It's too important to keep pretending nothing is going on when the whole Kingdom can feel it. It's evident how much you love each other—but the resentment and anger you're both trying to ignore is also evident. It isn't good for them to see it, and isn't good for us, and isn't good for our family," Pharean said, rubbing her belly again unconsciously.

"And most importantly—it isn't good for you or your sister. Aldoran, Alondria has been so good to me. Please make amends. Please heal your wounds with her, and help her to move on. She deserves some happiness in life too."

"I'll try, but it's not that simple, Pharean," Aldoran answered her honestly. "She blames me somehow for the death of Jonlin, and that's not an easy problem to fix. She's my twin, before you came into my life; she was the closest person to me. We could've been one person we were so close. And now, now I don't even know how to begin to fix things between us. I really don't know how to help her get over Jonlin. God knows, I could never get over *you!*"

"What about Lord Larsius?" Pharean mentioned tentatively.

"Darling, you know I agree with you about him being perfect for her, but neither one of us has been able make *her* see how perfect they are for each other!"

"Well," said Pharean, as she tied a yellow ribbon in her hair, and stared into the mirror critically. "That's no reason not to *try*. And I'm afraid I'm putting my foot down dear, something you know I never do. It's time. Darling, I'm telling you it's time to lay this burden down, and put your problems to rest."

~ ~ ~

"It's time. I'm telling you it's time," Luquinn told her.

"No nagging today, Luquinn, really, I'm in no mood for it! Mrs. Harris is up in arms over Mr. Hutchison's pointer breaking through her fence, and killing one of her hens again. Boy, who knew the ruling of a Kingdom could sometimes be so...provincial."

"Alondria, I know you're busy. We're *all* busy. I'm simply asking you to care as much about your own problems, as you do about helping with everyone else's."

Alondria sighed, staring into the mirror at her sleek brown curls, full of natural highlights. She took up a brush, and brushed out her curls into long, wavy tresses.

She was in no mood today for perky curls. Waves would do better for Mrs. Harris and Mr. Hutchison's dispositions.

"Alondria, are you even listening to me?" Luquinn nagged.

"Yes, yes, I hear you Luquinn, and you make a good point, you really do; only...I don't know how to fix things between me and Aldoran. He was always the one there for me. He was always the person I went to for everything, every happiness, every problem. But he really wasn't there for me after Jonlin died. *You* were. My mother was. My father was. But not him."

"I know that's how you feel."

"It's not how I feel, it's the truth! You know as well as I do, it was wrong for him to stay and take my place in the group of fourteen, right when I needed him the most!"

"Yes, I agree. You know I never approved of him doing that either. But did you *tell* him you needed him?"

"Did I have to tell you?"

"No, but—"

"And he's my twin, my twin, Luquinn! How much less should I have had to ask for him to stay with me than you, you who were at the time someone I barely knew...a virtual stranger?"

"You know that I agree with you. Lord knows I understand your position, but you still have to talk to *him* about it, Alondria. One thing is for sure; I can't make things better between you two. Pharean can't make things better between you two. Fixing the problems between you can only be fixed by both of you. It's time. Alondria, I'm telling you it's time. Please, for the Kingdom's sake, for Hope's sake, for his sake, and for YOUR sake...?"

Alondria took in a few slow, deep breaths, to steady and ground herself. Looking at her reflection in the mirror, the long waves of disentangled curls suited her, she thought. But evidently the row between Mrs. Harris and Mr. Hutchison would have to wait. She had her own row to take care of today. She hoped that it wouldn't be the end of her relationship with her twin brother.

Setting the brush down, she looked up in the mirror and nodded at Luquinn, in consent of his request. Twisting around in her chair to look at him directly, she warned, "All right, I'm going to try. But I am warning you now: this won't be pretty."

~ ~ ~

Chapter Eighteen
Marriage of Bard and Queen

In the Andorra Mountains of the Kingdom of the Franks—

The bard Larsius, Lord Larsius, bright and talented and dangerously gorgeous had infiltrated Alondria's life with his dashing ways and winning charm. Attempting to court Alondria for the past few years, she'd been too drawn within herself to even notice his dutiful efforts.

"You can't waste your life pining over Jonlin," Aldoran said to his sister softly.

"Why not? Varawynn will pine her life away over Eliju," Alondria countered.

"It's not like you to act this way, Alondria—you of all people. You've always been the most loving, sweet and happy person I've ever known. I know how much you loved Jonlin—"

"No, you don't."

"But I want my sister back. Can't you give Lord Larsius a chance? He's hopelessly smitten by you, in spite of your blatant rudeness to his advances."

"It isn't rudeness if I haven't even noticed his advances, Aldoran," rebutted Alondria, frustrated and frazzled. "Don't I give the Kingdom everything they want in a princess? Don't I force myself to dance at balls and feast almost every night in the banquet hall, when I would rather sit alone in my room and cry, singing sad music to myself and reading poetry? Don't I constantly go out among the people and work to improve our laws to better serve them? What the hell more do you want from me, Aldoran?"

"I just told you—I want my sister back!" he shouted, pounding his fist against the top of the nearest table, breaking it into smithereens, its table legs splintering and then falling into a sorry heap on the floor.

Alondria drew a deep breath and let her eyes rest significantly on the mess he'd made due to his anger, in the same way she'd done when they were children growing up together. When his pent-up hormones and the necessities of being perfect for the Kingdom would become too much for him, Aldoran remembered how he and Alondria would steal away, and she would watch him pound away at things, until a look would come into her eyes that let him know he'd better go no further—or he would go too far.

"Time is not going to heal my wounds, Aldoran. I wish it could."

"Then work towards healing Alondria! You are a healer, my dear sister. You have the ability to devise a way to heal yourself. Luquinn is a doctor. He is constantly devising ways to heal and help you."

"Don't I know it? You need not remind me how Luq is wasting his life away with his loyalty and friendship to me. I bare a lot of guilt in regard to him, brother. Feelings you may not be able to relate to."

"And what does that mean? If Luquinn is so incompetent to help you—"

"Don't blame him, Aldoran. I don't blame you either. I'm the only one to blame for the miserable state I'm in."

Aldoran sighed. "I'm only trying to help you."

"And I know that. But how will marrying Lord Larsius help any of my problems?"

"Perhaps you could learn to love him—all the women rave about him. He could have any one of them!"

"Then why doesn't he take one of them? Why does it have to be me? Could I learn to love the bard Larsius, at the same time learning to stop loving the bard Jonlin? There is little chance of that, Aldoran. I know myself!"

"If nothing else, it is expected of you to marry, Alondria…for the sake of our Kingdom."

She moved away from him as if he'd slapped her. "I never considered you to be the type of person to use duty as a manipulation. I may have grown bitter over all that I've been through. But what's become of you?"

"You care more about the power of being a king and the power in taking MY place in the group of fourteen than your own twin sister? We, who come from swimming in the same water of the same womb? We, who together, up until recently, have done everything as one…you guilt trip me now for how I've changed…*but what has become of you?* Pharean has not brought out the best in you, Aldoran."

Aldoran's eyes flashed dangerously. "Don't you dare drag her into this! And don't blame *our* problems on her. This is between you and I."

"Yes. It is. You failed me, Aldoran. Luquinn was right. The worst thing you can do to someone who is in grief is to leave them alone in it. And that's just what you did to me."

"You're right, Alondria. I abandoned you."

"So, you finally admit it! *Why?* How could you do that to me? How could you abandon *your twin?*"

"Because I felt you were wrong in how you handled it."

"I was wrong, so you abandoned me?"

"Yes. Perhaps I was wrong to abandon you, but you abandoned me first."

"What?!"

"You've been wrong to let go of life. You had more going for you in your life than Jonlin. My God, Alondria, something as simple as the spring blossoms used to send you over the moon! You say my love of

Pharean hasn't brought out the best in me. Well, what of your love for Jonlin? Has it brought out the best in you?"

"How dare you! How could you say something like that...twist it all around! And it's not the same thing!"

"So, what is love supposed to do, Alondria? Consume us over the one romantic love we crave in exclusion of everyone and everything else we used to love...other people, other talents we have, our beliefs, the ruling of a Kingdom...and in your case does losing love absolve you of all responsibility?"

"You used to love *me,* Alondria. *Me.* You used to know how to comfort me the same way I knew how to comfort *you.* Not only comfort, we used to share in each other's *happiness,* not just share in the responsibilities of this *Kingdom!*"

He raged on, the past few years of resentment exploding, "You used to sing your *own* songs before Jonlin came around to sing you his. *I* used to play for you when you sang!"

"We used to enjoy the beauty of nature. We used to enjoy feasting and drinking and playing, and just being together! Now there's only room for your obsession over Jonlin. That is your life. That's who you've become. That's all the love you have room for in your heart."

"And you expect the people who love you the most to watch you do it, watch you *lose* it—you who were once the most vivacious, full-of-life and love person I've ever known—I'm supposed to just watch tolerantly as she casts all her love and precious life away over for the death of the man she loved."

"Well, I *won't* stand idly by and watch you do it! I deserve your love too. Luquinn deserves your love. My *wife* and *child* deserve your love! Our parents deserve your love! We deserve your love, and we *are* sorry for your loss."

"But we love you and we need you too! Jonlin was a good man, and he wouldn't want you acting this way. He wouldn't want you to stop living, wouldn't want you to stop loving. I never stopped loving you or praying for you, but your obsession and lack of love for all else, for me, yes, Alondria. It felt like a betrayal. It felt like you'd abandoned me even when I was right there next to you."

A pregnant pause passed between them. "And worst of all, I know you blame Eliju and me somehow over Jonlin's death. I know you do. I'm your twin, I can sense it. How do you think it makes *me* feel to know that *I'm* to blame for this half-life and this half-person you've become?"

"I'm supposed to fix the way you hold *me* responsible? Eliju didn't kill Jonlin! I didn't kill Jonlin! I DIDN'T KILL JONLIN!" Hot and angry tears poured over Aldoran's eyes and down his face, but he kept bulldozing on, not taking time to wipe them away.

"Aldoran—"

"I didn't want him dead! For your sake I wish he were still alive! But I can't be around you, while you're blaming me! You're blaming me for your unhappiness! And so, I thought maybe if you married Larsius, maybe if I could be the cause of some *happiness* in your life, then you could finally forgive me…"

Standing before her, panting and sobbing, he fell to his knees, all the energy from his anger spent. In his weakness he fell to his knees and knelt before her. "Forgive me, forgive me my sister," he begged, burying his head at her waist. At last she understood his side.

Taking his head into her hands, there was nothing she could do, but forgive him. Kissing the crown of his head, she said, "Aldoran if me marrying Lord Larsius means that much to you, if it will reunite us somehow…"

"Do you forgive me then?" his face was full of tears.

"I forgive you," she pledged, falling into his arms, as she had done of old. "But I don't want to discuss this anymore, never again."

"But will you please give Lord Larsius a chance, sister?" Aldoran begged her.

"I'll agree…to give him a chance." Grinning as he clasped her delicate head against his chest, he nearly crushed her skull with the force of his happiness. He wanted it so much, for his sister to be happy.

"I want to make you happy, Aldoran," Alondria said into his chest, her face covered with tears. Aldoran's heart filled with relief, he let her tears convince him of her release of Jonlin and her hope for the future. He misinterpreted her tears and submission, not realizing her surrender was for his happiness and not her own. They were not tears of joy or healing, but of resignation.

~ ~ ~

Another two years passed before Alondria's wedding day. Now it had been five years since the death of Jonlin. Somehow it felt like it'd only been a day, and yet a lifetime simultaneously, since he'd been gone.

Her misgivings about Lord Larsius had been met with impatience from Aldoran. He thought her objections were merely due to her obsessive love over Jonlin.

It was true, the night before the wedding, Alondria dreamed of Jonlin. Crying out in her dreams his beloved name, she reached for him from amongst the shadows. He was shouting something, but she couldn't hear all his words.

She heard only, "Don't, don't, don't, *don't do this…*" Was the ghost of Jonlin trying to keep her from a life of happiness…or warn her about a life of misery?

When morning came, she set the nightmare aside, and prepared for her a day of upcoming festivities. She wore a long dress of white; the white lace corset cinched in her tiny waist; her hair was long with romantic auburn tendrils falling well past her waist, carefully swept up around her delicate, heart-shaped face, and full, cherry blossom lips. Pharean and her mother helped with her corset and hair, as Alondria's fingers were shaking all the way through the wedding day primping.

Pharean's face was radiantly happy for her sister-in-law. Alondria's face looked drained and pale. It took half an hour of Pharean pinching her cheeks to give her any color at all. But her hair and dress were perfectly beautiful, though the look of terror in Alondria's eyes would not have been the ideal expression for a lovely young bride on her wedding day.

Lord Larsius wore brilliant dark blue and royal purple robes to match his twilight-colored eyes. His gleaming eyes sparkled, and his jet-black hair shone.

He looked more handsome than ever, but all Alondria could see when she looked at him, was the ghost of Jonlin. "Don't do this," echoed from his lips the night before. A memory flashed through her mind of Jonlin in a suit of gleaming white. She didn't know where the image came from... It was from her wedding day with Jonlin in his quest in the Land of What Might Have Been...

When Larsius took Alondria's hand in his, and they said their vows to each other, her body flinched. At the reception, he sang a song written about his love for her. But the notes to her sounded gratingly out of tune. As he sang the song at their reception, she felt she was now living out a life not quite her own.

She was living in the shadows, as once she'd been a star shining brightly in the night. She hated his song, and his good looks, and she hated his voice, and his talent, and she hated most of all the love he showed her as he sang his version of the "Song of Alondria," which paled in comparison to the voice of Jonlin, who had sang in the Land of What Might of Have Been…a life still playing out in some furthermost recess of her mind and heart.

There was a melody God gave to me
With words I heard an angel sing
Creating the song of our life,
A living dream.

Feelings expressed best by the notes
Of reds and indigos and blues
Yellows, white, pinks and greens
The colors and notes of me and you.

All I need to live is you
Let the world just be
All I need to make it through
Is the love between you and me.

When the waves are crashing over us
Hold onto me to make it through
The storm will pass just so long
As I'm in the storm with you.

Together we create a life
Of beautiful dreams coming true
We weave colors and notes into a tapestry
And with our love we'll create a family.

All I need to live is you
Let the world just be
All I need to make it through
Is the love between you and me.

After the reception, where Alondria barely ate or drank or danced, when he made love to her, she felt like the wind, elusive and ever out of his reach. He pulsed and throbbed and beat her with the waves of his passion, but she was the one woman his passions seemed to cool, even repulse.

She knew on some level that Larsius was a better bard in every aspect than Jonlin; that his songs were better, and his voice was better, and his musical ability was better, and his looks were better, and yet he was not better, and yet he was nothing but a shadow in the dying light of Jonlin. And she hated his shadow, and she hated his light, and she hated every moment of her life…more now that Lord Larsius was in it, than when she had been living it alone.

She knew beyond a shadow of a doubt by the time the sun set on her wedding day that she had made a grave and irrevocable mistake. The night of her honeymoon, she dreamed of foreboding men in ominous cloaks of black, she dreamt of suns that didn't rise, and moonless nights that never ended. She dreamt of death. And when she woke up, she lived a nightmare.

~ *** ~

Chapter Nineteen
Creating a Monster

In Darlillyth's main stronghold, a castle in Caledonia—

Darlillyth remembered...the first time...*I heard my father's heavy boots coming down the hall towards my bedroom. He entered my room with such a strange look on his face. It was as if he were in a trance, as if what he was doing was not entirely of his own accord. At least that was what I wanted to believe.*

When he got into the bed with me, he climbed on top of me. When he started pulling off my clothes roughly, I started crying. Then I disconnected myself almost entirely from my own body.

I was looking outside myself as it happened. I looked above, and up, outside my window, at the stars. I imagined myself to be flying amongst them.

It was as if I were floating above myself, looking down at what was happening, looking down at my eyes crying buckets of tears. I was in shock, so young and inexperienced. This was my first experience with astral projection and disassociation. And sex.

Later, years later, when my brother came into my bedroom late at night, I fought him back. That brought a whole new level of terror and trauma, because it confronted me with my own powerlessness. The fact is, as powerful I may have been in magic, physically, I was overpowered by my half-brother, Mardavian. Facing the powerlessness that is being female, was something I never forgot, and could never get over. It may be why I was always trying to take the power from others, as if in taking their power, I was regaining my own.

But the first time, with my father, I just lay there, in total shock, frozen. I could never forgive myself for that...for not fighting back with him—at least trying to stop it from happening.

Then, when my father started coming regularly into my bedroom late at night, I felt my body flying amongst a galaxy of stars, flying higher than the sky outside my window, into the cosmos. My soul went into the void itself, into the emptiness, into the source of all pain.

After he'd finish, I was pain itself. I was dirty and ashamed and sullied. The light was lost. There was only darkness. He had stolen something innocent and pure from me, and I knew I could never get it back. I would choose the darkness now. For how could anything lovely, or pure, or sacred, ever touch me again? When my father raped me, I believed I'd been condemned to a loveless life, for how could anyone love me after that?

When my father finished with my body the first time, he raped me, there was a strange gleam in his eyes, like he'd entered a whole new level of evil. After he left, a part of me stayed amongst the stars, stayed within the void, so that I wouldn't have to face the guilt and shame of what had happened. I blamed myself, deep down, and hated my father, stepmother and brother. I blamed them too. I hated my family, but they held all the power.

So, I bided my time, and I waited my turn, and when the time was right, I called upon the forces of darkness, now my only allies, to overpower my parents, so that darkness like theirs would cease to exist from the earth. I would make sure that I was the last person who was destroyed by their evil, the last person whose life was ruined by their perversions.

~ *** ~

"You good-for-nothing! You're worthless! You can't do ANYTHING right! Incapable! Incompetent! You're so ugly, who'd want you? Why do you make me yell at you this way? Why do you make me hurt you? Because you're so rotten! You're a rotten piece of filth."

"You're a freak. You'll never amount to anything more than the boy who killed his father. That's the most I can hope from you. Now whose fault is that? NOW! Answer me! Whose fault is this?"

"Mine."

"Yours and who else's?"

"My father made you do this to me," he said the necessary statement she required, devoid of emotion.

"I should just kill you right now. You don't deserve to live. You probably don't even have the wits to kill your father."

The whip came flying through the air, and down onto the boy's bare back, raw and bleeding and bruised from constant beatings. His screaming was trapped within the walls of the dungeon. The walls were insulated so that no one could hear his cries.

He was never released. He was never seen, for no one knew of this dungeon, and no one was permitted near it but Darlillyth herself. Only she even knew of the boy's existence.

Chaining the boy to the chair, she pulled out a bowl of water she had ready. Placing her son's feet in the stirrups and into the water, he quivered with fear. Like her father before her, Darlillyth devised creative and original ways of her torturing her child. The boy could always tell when a new special kind of torture was coming, which was often. She had a look in her eyes like she was graduating to a higher level of evil.

She placed an electrical charge in the water, and watched as her son writhed in pain as he was being electrocuted. Using the device a few more times for good measure, to tease his senses; alternating between calming, and then reigniting his fears.

Inevitably, she would ask the question at the end of all her torture and abuse, "Now whose fault is this?"

"It is mine and my father's—and I deserved it," was his well-trained answer.

"Very good," Darlillyth nodded. After every beating, she brainwashed her son by forcing him to put the blame on himself and his unknown father. Thus, whipping him at least once a week, devising machines to torture him with water, fire, earth and air, she taught her son through her abuse of him, to hate his father.

After his trained answer, she left him to collapse upon her exit, still chained and fried and broken from the inside out, his feet still in stirrups and water. After a few more hours there, he peed in his wooden seat and remained in his own filth, completely unable to do something as small as move or keep himself clean.

"You good for nothing boy! You can't even wait to use the bathroom I, see? You have no control. Twelve-years-old and you still need your mother to do everything for you. What a momma's boy!" she laughed and ridiculed him cruelly.

He was her punching bag. She used him to get out all her frustrations over the people who had hurt and destroyed her. She blamed him for things that had happened before he was ever even born. She did the things to him that had been done to her.

She would use him to destroy any hope that still burned in her soul. For hope was a cruel and dangerous thing—it had to be destroyed and rooted out before the disappointment came when things didn't work out, as they inevitably never did. She knew what would come after that.

The despair. The pain. The futility of living. The sadness. The tears. The feelings. The emotions. Like love: the greatest weakness of humanity.

"It's time for your lessons now, boy. Only dark magic for the likes of you!"

Since the boy was never taught to read, everything she taught him was verbal and physical. Necromancy, the study of controlling the dead; alchemy, the studying of transmuting objects into gold; obscure predictions of the future by killing animals, and studying the patterns of their blood; the study of the stars without the intention of understanding others better, but of how to control others and predict the future; as well as hidden texts of the Kabbalah and numerology, in order to control people through use of words and names. The intention of their study of magic was power, dominance, control, asserting of authority, bullying, threats— nothing positive; nothing good.

Benoni had no choice but to bow to his mother's supreme authority. There were no outside influences. There was no sound except his mother's voice. There was no air except the cold, stale air of the dungeon's walls. There was no light except candle light. There was no warmth, except the tattered, worn blankets she would give him when the air outside turned cold. There was no sustenance, except the scraps of bread and moldy cheese she fed him.

Her abuse was severe, and her control over him was complete. She didn't touch him sexually. That she couldn't, wouldn't do. She still believed what her father and brother had done to her was wrong. Instead, she followed the twisted advice of her stepmother. She used her power over men—either her "feminine wiles," or, over her son, she used the whip.

He was a prisoner of the darkness, the darkness where he lived, and the darkness of his mother ruling over him. In the secret recesses of his mind, he planned to escape, but fear kept him from making any attempts, for he had no knowledge of the outside world, and no capacity to support himself in a world in which he knew nothing.

He was afraid all people would be as cruel as his mother. He wanted to seek vengeance upon his father, as his mother had ingrained and drilled into him daily.

He didn't know who his father was, or where to find him. He knew his father was important—a king of some sort or other. But his utter lack of knowledge about life in general, made escaping his imprisonment a daunting proposition.

Every day Benoni tried to understand his mother and her ability to hurt him; her inability to love him. There was no one to turn to. There was nothing good to believe in. There was only pain in his life—pain and torture. There was only despair. There was no use in his life for anger. There was no good reason to hope.

Yet this feeling he had no words to articulate, lit a spark of humanity in his soul. There was love in his heart that no malice could kill, a love for his mother that came from the blood of his father.

Blind and faithful, without logic or reason, unconditional and gently imperishable, like the inextinguishable flame of hope dimly burned in his spirit. An inner knowing that there was more to life than this, and that the world held more than this dungeon, kept him going.

The earth just had to be warmer than the cold stone floor beneath his bare feet. The air outside these walls just had to be cleaner than the stale and trapped underground air he breathed. There just had to be more fulfilling sustenance than hardened bread and moldy cheese. Somewhere, there were people in the world kinder than his mother, who would have the ability to love him. *There just had to be.*

"You stupid, simpering, foolish boy!" his mother screamed, in an endless, untamed rage that was never spent. Whipping her son Benoni, until his back was raw and bloodied, he didn't shed a tear.

He'd learned long ago that crying only further angered her. He wasn't quite sure what had set her off this time, but he went away in his head. It was a game he played with himself when her abuse was so painful, he mentally disconnected with his body and the pain of the reality of his living hell.

He tried to escape into other worlds of his creation. He used his imagination to birth worlds of color, like the different shades of purples and blues and greens from his mother's dresses. He could fly in these other worlds. He was a bird. He was free. He was majestic and beautiful, bathed in color and light, clothed with vibrant feathers. Time did not exist, nor suffering. The world was only good.

He would try to imagine what the real world was like, where people were very different from him mother. He imagined his father was not as awful as his mother claimed. Imagining a new life, he fantasized how the world looked from the outside, far away from the walls of the dungeon. It was a world where people could be kind, and there was love and belonging, even for him...

~ ~ ~

Arakiel was the first of the female Fallen Angels. She was the first of the female Nephilim. As such, she did not feel like humans did. She was of those fallen, who lost themselves in pleasure, which became their God on earth. After Arlillyth died, the mother of Darlillyth, she saw her chance to raise her magical status even higher, to the earthly status of Queen.

Arakiel came to stay in Amen-Ra's realm. She knew how to adorn herself in the most flattering of ways. She knew how to incense jealousy in a man by entertaining the flattery and come-ons of other men. She knew how to use her beauty to capture a man, like a spider into a web, or a rat into a trap.

So, it wasn't long before Amen-Ra lusted after the fallen angel Arakiel, who still retained some of that heavenly beauty. She had a certain charm, and a unique beauty, which she used to manipulate her way with men. Thus, she assumed that all women were like her, and as Darlillyth was part Nephilim herself, her assessment was not altogether untrue.

Darlillyth, as another female, even as a child, was in her way. Her way of manipulating all men for herself. Consorting with any man who would have her, or whom she wanted, reveling in the decadence of feasts and opulent surroundings, gaining favors everywhere she went, for her charm, magical powers, and otherworldly beauty.

There were a strength and authority in Arakiel's regal bearing. Her dark red hair held streaks of black. Her eyes had strands of deep brown with red in them. Her lashes were long and black. Her body was perfectly formed. She was beautiful, and she was used to getting all the attention for herself. Darlillyth was a threat to her power, for she was beautiful and magical too.

Long ago, Darlillyth's stepmother had abused her in the same way she now abused her son Benoni. *"Get over here, girl!" Queen Arakiel screeched. Darlillyth's dark hair lay limp and unwashed across her face. She kept her dark hair in her face as a way to try to be invisible.*

"I told you to get over here!"

Darlillyth's eyes welled with tears; pridefully, she struggled to keep her tears in her throat. The lump felt like a dam blocking out the natural flow of water. Darlillyth moved to her stepmother, immediately prostrating herself at her feet in the kneeling position, with her head down to the ground.

"Arise girl," her stepmother commanded. "Your brother has informed me that it was you who killed our prize horse in the stables."

"It wasn't me—it was him," Darlillyth said honestly.

"Silence!" Queen Arakiel shouted. "How dare you, insipid, FOOLISH child place blame upon MY SON for your own violent behavior! You do know the horse was hung from the rafters? My God, you are a sick and twisted creature! You must have used magic, and you know I have forbidden you to use your magic openly!"

Darlillyth lifted her head insolently at her stepmother, her hair parting from her face a little. "I told you before, and I shall tell you again—it wasn't me who killed the horse. It was YOUR SON."

She spit on the floor at Queen Arakiel's feet. Her dark eyes stared up at her, full of burning hatred. "And you might ask yourself what kind of mother YOU have been to cause him to so violently kill that stallion." The steadiness and sureness of Darlillyth's eyes, and the confidence with which she raised her head, made it clear she was telling the truth.

But Queen Arakiel was not interested in the truth. She was only interested in punishing Darlillyth, and so she did. Over and over and again and again.

~ ~ ~

It was always when she left him, when the danger of her whips and curses were gone, that the hope would dissipate, and his dreams would fade, and the dark, empty despair of his reality would envelop him like the eternal darkness surrounding him, and he would give in and cry, and scream, and rage against the walls, against his life, against the absence of anything good or pure. His mother said it was his father's fault she hurt him, so he hated his father, with the passion of all the pain his life of abuse had given him.

He wanted to love his mother, but she wouldn't let him. Love was a weakness, and she gave him no solace in her motherhood. She had loved her daughter, Shadonai, for being a girl. She held no sympathy in her heart at all for her son.

Benoni longed to be held, as he never had been. He longed for the comfort of a gentle touch. He longed for a kind word. He longed for the love he had never known, the instinct of all humanity: created by love, for love, and to love and be loved in return. He loved without knowing how or why. He loved, ineptly, and with little knowledge or experience—with pure instinct borne from his father's blood that coursed through his veins, he loved.

The emotional roller coaster he felt, from anger to despair, from grief to rage, to peace, to escapism, was the necessary release of his heart, from the severity of his mother's abuse. He could never be normal. Benoni didn't even know *how* to smile. What did *he* have to smile *about?*

Terrified he could never be happy and whole, that nothing good could exist in his life, and absolve him of his shame and suffering, he tried to imagine the world outside these dark walls. He tried to imagine a better life. He knew more than most others know about the spiritual realm, for that was where his spirit dwelled.

As his life had always been covered by darkness, he lived more in death sometimes, in the in-between than life. He had never seen the sunlight, and yet he could see his mother's, and his own aura. He could see the halo surrounding all things, the etheric.

He could see it always with his naked eyes, for he was more of the ethers and shadows than the light. The etheric and auras were the only light he had ever known.

No part of him could develop. His mind, his language, his communication skills, his heart, his feelings…all were cruelly thwarted. He had only been born to kill a father he had never known. And yet he was not a machine. And yet he was not a monster—for he shared the same deep feelings as his mother.

Of course, he strove to hide them, shoving them aside. Though he was powerless against her abuse, the resentment occasionally rose up in him, and he fought back when the torture became too much for him to bear. It was always worse for him when he did. That's when she would devise wholly new ways to break his body, totally new ways to torture his heart and soul.

He wondered all his life how his mother could do this to him. Somehow, he sensed a mother was not supposed to behave this way. Sometimes he tried to make himself lovable to her, in twisted ways, like being quiet and obedient to the abuse.

Yet this too, only angered her. She wanted him angry and strong. She wanted him hellbent on revenge.

Anger is an emotion too. Where there is emotion, even out-of-control rage, there is hope. It is the lack of love, it is indifference, that is the truest danger and the opposite of love.

Sometimes when Benoni escaped in his mind, he would see somehow, somewhere in his mind's eye, an angel; radiantly bathed in the light that would come and save him from the dungeon of his life and his own mind. She had the words he needed, a magical way of speaking that was filled with truth, encompassing him with a supernatural strength that could dissolve a lifetime of such extraordinary brutality. She was...the "Light of God," and he had this feeling in the core of his soul—she was the key to his salvation.

~ ~ ~

She had never wanted it this way. When her father first married Arakiel, she was a normal young girl. She was special yes, magical beyond any human, yes. But she longed, like any girl would have, for her dead mother, and hoped like most any girl would have, that her father's new wife would like her, maybe even learn to love her. But Arakiel was jealous of her from the start. And her father made it clear from the start where his loyalties lied.

The path of evil for Darlillyth was like that corridor, the hallway outside her bedroom where she would hear the footsteps of her father's heavy boots every night down the hall coming into her bedroom. It was like getting out of bed in the morning afterwards, hurt and sore, and with every step she took, it was chosen day-by-day. It was like a falling star, burning, sparkling bright. It was without form, without end. It was an ever-descending spiral of chaos, confusion, and hatred that began within the self.

"How could my father do this to me?" She asked herself each night. Her mother had died when she was very young. She wanted to believe that the only mother she'd ever known, Queen Arakiel, didn't know what her father was doing to her. She wanted to believe that she would be outraged and come to her defense if she knew. But instead, one morning when her father had stayed the

night, and he was sneaking out of his daughter's bedroom, and out again into the hallway, his wife saw him leave his daughter's room in the delicate morning light.

Instead of following her husband, she went into her stepdaughter's bedroom. Darlillyth pulled up the bedsheets around her bodice to hide her gentle curves when the Queen walked in. Darlillyth looked at her, with a question in her eyes, and a glimmer of hope shimmering.

"So how long has this been going on?" Queen Arakiel asked her. Darlillyth realized she had been holding her breath and gripping the bed sheets so hard her knuckles were white. She took a steadying breath, and answered, "Two years now, my Queen."

Queen Arakiel stood at her stepdaughter's window and looked out at the dawn, choking back tears of horror and shame. Darlillyth waited. She didn't hear, or see, or sense the Queen's feelings, but she was hoping to.

Queen Arakiel knew then that this was a defining moment. The guilt and grief washed over her. The feeling of inadequacy enveloped her. Then a rage entered her spirit, a rage that needed a voice; that sought an outlet.

You can't attack the perpetrator because they're the strong one, she thought to herself. She didn't want to lose her husband, or her standing in the community. She didn't want to lose her son, Mardavian. She wanted her son to be the King, and she had always wanted Darlillyth out of the way. Now she viewed Darlillyth as competition with her father. Not just politically, but sexually.

"You've been after him for a long time. It's a wonder he resisted this long," Queen Arakiel said.

"What?" Darlillyth asked her, shock registering over her young face.

"You heard me," Queen Arakiel snarled viciously. "Your father is only a man. A man—a God to be sure, above other men, but still a man."

"I don't understand what you're saying..." Darlillyth stuttered.

"Oh, don't you?"

"No."

"You are a woman, my dear, do not pretend to deny you understand how to use your feminine wiles on a man." Darlillyth couldn't believe she was hearing this, and she really didn't know what she was talking about. What in the world were feminine wiles?

"A woman's sexuality is her source of power. You want the throne for yourself. You want to take it from your brother—from my son, Mardavian—from me even, but it won't work, my dear. I am too clever for your little games."

"What are you saying? I have no idea—"

"Oh, don't you? Two can play at this game, child. No, you're not a child, anymore, are you? You've probably had this in your head all along. From the very first day I stepped over the threshold of this castle, as your father's new bride, **this** *is what you had in store for me"*

"No!" Darlillyth eyes welled over with tears.

Queen Arakiel's heart constricted in her chest when she saw her pain. She needed to get out of that room where her own husband had—or she would break down into tears herself. This was the moment of truth—or lies.

She would have to find something particularly cruel and cutting to say now. Something that would change her stepdaughter forever. Something that would destroy her. So that she would not herself feel so defeated. That with all her feminine wiles, and ageless beauty, and heavenly charms, it had not been enough for Amen-Ra to keep his fidelity.

"You're not the only one, and you won't be the last. But don't you ever think you were the best. I AM THE BEST. Use your femininity to trick men, to weaken them, to trap them, but don't you forget I set the trap for your father first—and if you go up against me, I'll squash you like a worm beneath my heel. I'll make you regret turning your father's head, but you shall never have his heart."

"No…" Darlillyth whispered. "My mother shall always have that."

Arakiel slapped her stepdaughter hard across her face, and stormed out of the bedroom with a last haughty flip of her hair. As soon as she was well past the bedroom doorway, and far enough away not to be heard, she rushed into the quiet library, and fell into a crumpled heap beneath a bookshelf and wept.

Darlillyth realized that deep down she'd been hoping her stepmother would save her, would be her saving grace. Even though the Queen had always been jealous of her and abusive of her physically, she had harbored a deep desire to be close to her all along. After Queen Arakiel's actions and words, that last hope in Darlillyth died. Her greatest pain, was that Arakiel was unwilling to be her mother, and to protect her. It was that that destroyed her.

Darlillyth sobbed for exactly three minutes after Queen Arakiel left her bedroom. She waited until her clipped, angry footsteps had long passed. She spent the whole day lying in bed and not eating. She thought and contemplated the rest of her life. The only way she was finally able to manage the energy to get out of bed, was to contemplate her revenge against her family.

She devised a plan to avenge the innocence they had taken. The betrayal of her stepmother's reaction hurt even deeper than her father's abuse had. She contemplated what her stepmother had told her about using people.

Now that she was sullied, who would want her? What else was there for her to do? These were her thoughts after a day of wasting away. As the shadows descended into her room, and the sun set over the horizon, a new idea formed in her mind, as dark and sinister as the evil that had been inflicted on her.

After the stars came out again, she called upon Satan himself, and she sold her soul to the forces of darkness and shadows. Many demons entered her bedroom, demons of greed and vengeance, of nightmares and curses. She saw them as clearly as day, and she spoke to them as her new friends and comrades.

WHILE THE ASHES RISE TO LIFE

She lit candles around her bedroom, and laid ritual items about her bedroom strategically. She slit her wrist, and let the blood drip onto the candle's wax. It felt like a lifetime ago, when her father's heavy footsteps had first come for her down the hall.

It seemed like a lifetime ago that she had believed in anything good at all. She let go of her pain and despair, she let go of her human emotions and vulnerability, and took on the strength of the demons around her. She cursed her parents, and bid her time to destroy them.

She let the demons and the powers of darkness empower her. She let them come inside of her. She avoided the light of the sun, and sought the darkness only, the night. The moon and stars were her only illumination. She truly believed there was no hope now of redemption or salvation. Truly, she no longer sought, or thought about salvation. Only vengeance...

Then the day came, years later, when Darlillyth took the life of her father, Amen-Ra, and her stepmother, Arakiel. Their blood stained more than her hands; they stained her soul.

She was happy. She was satisfied by their deaths. But only for a moment. For revenge can never really satisfy for long, because it cannot take things back, and it cannot make things right.

So Darlillyth began to turn her unending, burning rage on others, on innocents. Until the dark day came when she locked up and abused her son with Eliju, Benoni. Until the dark day came when she became the very monster she had sought to destroy...

~ ~ ~

Epilogue
The Battle for Souls

The angels watched the humans from a distance, interceding on their behalf whenever they could. They watched the human struggles, their failures, and the realization that victory lied within. The war had been won with the Cross. But the battles for human souls were waged every moment of every day, all around the world.

The demons also watched, waited, plotted, planned, attacked, stole, and destroyed the plans of God, whenever they could. They lied to the humans. They used the children of the darkness to attack the children of the light. They possessed humans, oppressed humans, and blocked humans from the blessings God had in store for them, from the moment of their creation.

The fight for souls tipped the balance from darkness to light, from evil to good, from despair to hope. The angels were empowered by the prayers of the humans, by acts of love, and the faith of all the human souls that fought the good fight.

Most humans had no awareness of the spiritual battles waging all over the earth by the angels and demons. The principalities each had their territories.

The demon's territories were won by evil deeds and words by the humans that they possessed because they had let them in. Humans let the demons in, in many ways. Some let the demons in by drinking too much, by using drugs made from the things of earth that God had never intended to be consumed. Or by using their body as currency.

Others succumbed to the pressures of life. They sold their souls for creature comforts, money, success, and notoriety. Still others lost their souls when they were attacked violently, raped, and abused. In their inability to forgive, they took on rage and vengeance, and let the evil in. Sometimes these souls ended up committing the same acts of rape and abuse that had destroyed their own purity, and original innocence.

Each human had a guardian angel that protected them. Some people had many angels who protected them, even archangels. Just as angels had their assignments with humans, so also did the demons have their assignments.

The demons plagued mankind. They fed on the human's light. They especially delighted in feasting on innocence, so children were often the target of their attacks. But there were also adults, strong and righteous, who they especially longed to possess, and if they couldn't get in to possess them, they destroyed them.

They tried all the strategies tried and true. They inflicted pain and disease on them. They played with their minds, made them doubt themselves, hate themselves. They inflicted pain and ailments no doctor could cure.

They took away homes, and livelihoods. If possible, they turned the hearts of the ones they loved, towards evil, so that those closest to them turned on them, attacked them. Yet some humans were so faithful they remained true to God even still.

If the demons were not able to possess these noble souls, who held on to their love of God, even when their circumstances were unendurable, then they worked to destroy their lives, and thwart their hopes and efforts towards good, every step of the way.

Most humans only looked at what was right in front of their eyes. They only believed in what they could see, touch, hear, smell and feel. Only holding truth in what was right before their eyes. But everything that was right before their eyes was temporary. Reality was a delusion that passed away before the etheric, auras, chakras, the spiritual states of faith, hope, and love, and all that was eternal.

In the flesh, most humans perceived all of life, so that the spirit was lost. When it was the spirit that lived after the flesh had rotted and fallen away. Most humans never lived the life of spirit and purpose they were born for, lost in the material world, they were born, and died, as if they had never lived at all.

The angels watched the humans from a distance, waiting for the recognition of this truth like a silent promise. Waiting for their prayers to give them permission to intercede on their behalf.

The demons tempted and tortured the humans to the point of despair. The angels fought for them, the human prayers empowering their every blow, and protecting them like a shield, for the battling of souls on the sides of Good versus Evil, in the Eternal Conflict, the Eternal War between pride and humility, love and hate, unforgiveness and grace. Only God knew the souls that would be saved, and those who would be lost, condemned to the shadows of darkness forever.

Every person on earth had their angels and demons fighting for their souls. Every piece of earth had been trod by the spiritual forces. There were territories won by the angels, and territories marked by the Devil and his demons.

Darlillyth had her angels and demons too. Even though she had sold her soul to the Devil long ago, God still sent angels down to earth to fight for her in the spiritual realm, because God had created, and Jesus had died, for every soul on earth. Every being mattered to God, whether or not the humans knew it, or believed it.

And so, the angels continued to fight for the sorceress. They, who knew better than she did herself, how the wounds inflicted on her in her childhood had changed and warped her, had hurt and damaged her.

They knew what she would have been, without the abuse. They knew that with all she had endured, if she learned her lessons, and she turned to God, she would be even better than before. Because there is something akin to divinity, when a soul that's been covered by wounds, still turns to the light, still loves, even covered in scars.

For that was what the creator had done, when he came down to earth. Jesus demonstrated what love is, showed the humans what love looks like. Not perfectly formed and beautiful, not a hair color, not in a shade of skin, but broken, bruised, and scarred, yet still shining with eternal light.

"She's mine!" the demon Azazel cried. "Darlillyth has committed too much evil to ever be cleansed!"

Archangel Michael drew a flaming long-sword from his side. "You convinced Arseth long ago that Darlillyth was dead, but the truth has come to light! And Eliju's prayers for her empower us in our fight!"

"Everything can be pardoned and redeemed," Balthial, the angel of unconditional forgiveness interjected.

Mammon, the highest demon of Avarice and Greed, hissed at Bathial. Belferith, a demon associated with curses, and also assigned to Darlillyth, stood on the side with Azazel. "She was offered to us from her birth by her father."

"People have to choose to be evil," Archangel Chamuel retorted.

"And she did choose evil after our greatest demon of lust, Asmodeus, entered her father and brother Mardavian, and raped her. She was enraged by our demon, Zombar, and sold her soul to our Master long ago."

The Archangel Gabriel stood next to Michael, his robes of silver and sapphire like a night full of stars, billowing out several feet behind him. His voice was deep and serene, with a quiet confidence that held not a single note of fear, whilst being devoid of arrogance or self-righteousness.

"Shadonai has chosen to remain in the in-between, praying for her mother and brother, and Eliju, and all the Chosen Ones, even Vorseth, her grandfather. She is the only one who even knows of Benoni's existence. Her prayers hold a power, like a bridge between heaven and earth, like a beacon of light over all the fires of hell."

Archangel Michael added, "We know a legion of demons have been after Darlillyth since birth—she is far too important to have escaped your notice, but neither has she escaped ours. We've had more angels assigned to her than you've had demons after her."

"But our demons Apolin and Maras have been called upon by Darlillyth to haunt her prey in dreams and nightmares," Mammon growled. "We did not enter her spirit unwillingly—she invited us in. She's used us to further her own agenda—of greed and selfish vengeance. She has used us to destroy others—many others, including the innocent."

Zaphiel, nicknamed "God's spy," spoke up, "But there have been moments in Darlillyth's life she's spoken and prayed to God."

"In anger!" a demon of war, death, and destruction, Ycanohl, shouted.

"Often yes, but there have been times she broke down in tears. There is still hope for her because she feels so deeply," countered Zaphiel. "Feelings are an essential aspect of the humans!"

"There is always hope," agreed the angel Haniel.

"But we also use human emotions as a weapon against them—to poison their minds, and torture their souls!" shouted Belzubub, the Demon of a Thousand Names.

Archangel Phanuel came swooping down upon them, in flowing robes of white and gold, fanning out on the ground underneath him. "Varawynn has joined in the prayer! Her prayers for Eliju and Darlillyth cause her much grief and pain because she longs so much to love Eliju herself, and thus her prayers hold even greater power!"

Then Phanuel held out his arm, and in his hand was a scroll with words inscribed with gold. The words on the scroll jumped off the page, becoming three threads of gold, for a cord of three is not easily broken. The cord wrapped itself around the throat of Azazel, choking him and incapacitating his power, so that Darlillyth, the woman he'd been torturing all her life, could have a moment's peace.

Azazel threw his head back in a howling scream. "She's mine!" he shouted again, pulling the cord even tighter around his neck, and up into his mouth—to bite it, and loosen himself with his gnarled, rotted teeth, like old oak roots, strong and thick.

"Get him!" Archangel Raziel cried. "Bind him!"

Suddenly a shadowy army of demons stood above them on the horizon, in the dimension where the battles for souls were ever-waging, in a constant storm. As the demons descended upon the army of angels and archangels that had been fighting, and praying, and working on the behalf of Darlillyth for centuries, the angels knew that the war itself was already won, and that always steadied their resolve.

The battle for Darlillyth's salvation was essential to the race of Magickind, and the Devil knew that. If Satan himself had to fight for Darlillyth's soul, he would.

And the legions of demons that served him, would always be ready for a fight, in the everlasting battles for the immortal souls and their eternal life.

"Now!" Archangel Michael charged first before them, his flaming sword held out and burning. Archangels Gabriel and Phaniel swept up above them, their wings beating fast, their swords drawn, as the demons descended down upon the angels, and the battle for Darlillyth's soul waged on…

~ *** ~

................To Be Continued In..............

The Creation Series
Volume Four

When the Lines
Of Lilith Unite

By Crystal Wolfe

Key for Characters and Places

Adam—the first man in the Garden of Eden.

Aengus—the prince in the royal Celtic line of Morgan le Fey, and Varawynn's brother. He was murdered in Volume One, *Where the Shadows Meet the Light*, by a sorceress.

Aldoran—the Prince of the Kingdom of the Franks, and the twin of Alondria.

Alondria—the Princess of the Kingdom of the Franks. Member of the group of fourteen chosen ones. Her birthmark is of a *cross* in the right palm of her hand.

Anak—the land of the Cyclops.

Andorra—the name of the city where the twins Aldoran and Aldoran come from.

Apolin—a demon of dreams and nightmares.

Arakiel—the first female Fallen Angel. The stepmother of Darlillyth, who married King Amen-Ra after Arlillyth died, and the mother of Mardavian, becoming Queen.

Areyin—one of the sister Sphinx.

Ariel—one of the highest Archangels.

Arlillyth—the daughter of Lilith, the first woman in the Garden of Eden, and the first fallen angel, the Nephilim Samyaza. She is also the mother to Darlillyth.

Arra—the daughter of Lilith and Adam, and the twin of Ra, who were both born immortal when their mother ate of the Tree of Life while they were yet in the womb.

Asmodeus—greatest demon of lust.

Astarra—the land of the fairies.

Astori—one of the two Birds of Eden, and the former mate of Celestria, who was killed in the Garden of Eden by Lucifer, after Celestria struck a deal with him.

Atreeynne—an elder sea elf on the Council of the White Sinore.

Avalon—a magical land in England where Varawynn is from.

Azazel—an ancient demon.

Balthial—the angel of unconditional forgiveness.

Beelzebub—"The demon of a thousand names."

Beiarnon *(Red Beard)*—a warrior dwarf and friend of Eliju.

Belferith—a demon associated with curses.

Bellerica—a young peasant girl that King Mardavian raped in *Where the Shadows Meet the Light*.

Brindyr—an elder sea elf on the Council of the White Sinore.

Catranore—an elder sea elf on the Council of the White Sinore.

Cecil—a fairy from Astarra.

Celestria—one of the two Birds of Eden ever created from the Garden of Eden. Her mate was Astori. One of the group of chosen ones, her birthmark is of the *apple* on her throat.

Chamuel—an archangel.

Cleo—a cyclops from Anak.

Dagda—the Priest of Avalon, and the father of Varawynn.

Darlillyth—the Queen and sister of King Mardavian, whose mother was Arlillyth, and whose father is Amen-Ra. Her grandmother is Lilith, and her grandfather is the Nephilim, Samyaza.

Deedee—a fairy from Astarra.

Drakkin—the King of the Dwarves.

Dresden—an elder sea elf on the Council of the White Sinore.

Eleethion—the infamous unicorn killed by a sorceress, which was the indirect cause of the Curse of Silvandrin.

Eliju—the King of both Mankind and Magickind, formally a shepherd and farmer in Haran. One of the chosen ones. He has the birthmark of a *stallion* on his right thigh.

Enoch—walked with God in the Garden of Eden. He never died, but lived so righteously that he became the angel *Metatron,* and the Keeper of the Akashic Records.

Eve—the second woman in the Garden of Eden, made from Adam's rib.

Finnien—an elder sea elf on the Council of the White Sinore.

Flint—a wolf, and a member of the group of fourteen, who bears the birthmark of a *fox,* the trickster, on his left side.

Forest of Eleethion—home of the unicorns.

Forest of Namoth—where the last of the wood elves were

annihilated by King Mardavian.

Gabriel—one of the highest ranking Archangels.

Garden of Eden—where the creation of the earth, and all the magical creatures and mankind originated.

Gellywug—the leprechaun who stole the "Ring of Solomon' from Narith.

Glenshaw—an elder sea elf on the Council of the White Sinore.

Grifficon—the great-winged bird, a Roc, with a wing-span of twenty-five feet.

Gwinnie—a fairy from Astarra.

Haniel—an angel of hope.

Haran—the town where Eliju comes from.

Hazel—an ancient demon.

Hebron—the place where Jonlin comes from.

Helynra—an elder sea elf on the Council of the White Sinore.

Ileona—the Lady of the Lake. She rules over the Crystal Palace in Lake Avalon in the Isle of Apples. She is half-human, and her father is the famous wizard, Merlin. Her mother was the Lady of the Lake in Avalon before her, Vivienne. A member of the group of chosen ones, she was born with the birthmark of the *sphinx* on her spine in the middle of her back.

Illumina—an elder sea elf. One of the fourteen chosen ones, she has the birthmark of the *selkie* on her left ankle.

Isadore—Eliju's mother, who is Hebrew.

Isidore—Illumina's deceased husband, who was murdered while sailing a ship on the high seas.

Isle of Apples—an Island in England where Ileona is from.

Isle of Skye—an isolated Island in Caledonia.

Jacob—Jonlin's little brother, who died tragically in a sword fight.

Jaquoire—an elder sea elf on the Council of the White Sinore.

Jasmina—a fairy from Astarra.

Jinn—demon spirits of the desert.

Jonlin—the "Bard of Hebron." One of the chosen ones, with the birthmark of a *lamb* over his heart.

Kenju—a trainer of Aldoran.

Kenneth—the father of Eliju, with Celtic origins.

Kinlindore—an elder sea elf on the Council of the White Sinore.

Krinshaw—an elder sea elf on the Council of the White Sinore.

Mammon—the highest demon of Avarice and Greed.

Mardavian—the King of Caledonia. His half-sister is Darlillyth. His father was Amen-Ra, and his mother was a fallen angel.

Maras—a demon of dreams and nightmares.

Lady Boann—the Priestess of Avalon, and the mother of Varawynn.

Larsius—a Lord and Bard in Caledonia, who Luquinn met briefly before King Mardavian conquered their village.

Leah—one of Eliju's favorite lambs.

Lilith—the first woman in the Garden of Eden, equal to Adam, and originally called a Ra, not a Woman. Lilith and Adam together were called a Man-Ra. Since Eve was taken from the rib of Adam, after the woes Adam had undergone with his first mate, she was called a Wo-Man.

Luquinn—a physician and one of the chosen ones. He has the birthmark of the *beaver* over the back his left hand.

Merlin—the greatest wizard of his generation.

Metatron—once the human *Enoch*, who walked with God in the Garden of Eden. He was so righteous, he never died, but when it was his time, he was lifted up into the heavens, transformed into the angel Metatron...the Guardian of the Akashic Records, the Lord of the Void, the Scribe of God, the King of the Angels, and so much more...

Michael—the highest-ranking Archangel.

Miko—Aldoran's horse.

Mora—a Star Fairy from Astarra.

Mordorn—Pharean's talking owl.

Mountains of Morne—the kingdom of the dwarves, who live in the caverns beneath this mountain range.

Narith—a wood elf, who once was entrusted to guard the 'Ring of Solomon.'

Nephilim—the Watchers and the Fallen Angels. They were

once angels who fell from grace when they left heaven to mate with humans.

Norgorian—a Dwarf warrior, and a friend of Wandering Wolfe, who once saved his life.

Noryn—A fairy from Astarra.

Onessa—a talking Queen Cobra.

Oric—Aldoran and Alondria's friend. He was a stable boy who killed tragically by a spooked horse in their childhoods.

Orkin—the Cyclops swordsmith who made Eliju's magical sword.

Orzenith—a trickster. One of the chosen ones, who bears the birthmark of the symbol of **unity** on his neck.

Penelope—the mother of Pharean, and the wife of Ruminous.

Phanuel—an archangel.

Pharean—one of the fourteen chosen ones. She is a scholar and daughter of the philosopher, Ruminous, who was the former advisor of King Mardavian. She was born with the birthmark of the **owl** on her right foot.

Amen-Ra—the son of Adam and Lilith, and the twin of Arra, in the single line of the first two people ever created on earth.

Rachel—one of Eliju's favorite lambs.

Raegar—Varawynn's talking raven.

Ramuel—one of the first fallen angels, and a leader of the Nephilim.

Raphael—one of the highest-ranking Archangels.
Mardavian.

Raziel—an archangel.

Ruminous—the Greek philosopher and advisor to King

Samyaza—the first of the fallen angels, and the top leader of the Nephilim.

Seadreama—the daughter of the sea elf, Illumina, who temporarily replaced her mother on the Council of the White Sinore, after she left for her adventures as one of the fourteen chosen ones.

Selena—the Queen and the mother of Aldoran and Alondria, half-muse.

Serfire—the horse of Aldoran's that spooked and killed Oric when he was a child.

Shadonai—the "Shadow of God." Her mother is Darlillyth, and she has two biological fathers, King Mardavian and Wandering Wolfe.

Shadow Rain—a Medicine Woman/Shaman. One of the chosen ones, with the birthmark of a **tortoise** on her abdomen. The source of the *Legend of Shadow Rain.*

Silvandrin—an ancient unicorn with a cursed black mane and silver hair, hooves, and horn. One of the fourteen chosen ones, with the birthmark of a **Roc**, the great-winged bird engraved in the spirals of his horn.

Sphayte—Sister Sphinx.

Theodore—the father of Aldoran and Alondria. A descendant of the magical sect of Jews, the Essene line, and a gifted artist who was inspired by his muse wife, Selena, to create beautiful works of art throughout Andorra and the Kingdom of the Franks.

Varawynn—the Priestess of Avalon. One of the chosen ones, who has the birthmark of a **raven** on her left thigh.

Viviennene—the Lady of the Lake in the Isle of Apples in Avalon, and the mother of Ileona.

Vorseth—one of the most powerful wizards throughout time. The author of the Prophecy, and the mentor of Darlillyth, Shadonai, Mardavian, and many years ago, Wandering Wolfe.

Wandering Wolfe—the greatest Shaman of the day. The leader of the group of chosen ones, with the birthmark of a **wolf** on his left shoulder.

Ycanohl—a demon of war, death, and destruction.

Zaphiel—an angel nicknamed "God's spy."

Zayin—an elder sea elf on the Council of the White Sinore.

Zombar—a demon of rage.

About the Author

Crystal Wolfe attended college at Purdue University in Indiana and a Suny College in upstate, New York. Wolfe has been published in newspapers across the country and is an award-winning writer.

Wolfe currently lives in Queens in New York City, where she's done freelance reporting for newspapers and magazines such as the New York Press, the Queens Ledger, and the Juniper Berry Magazine. She's had hundreds of articles published in newspapers and magazines nation-wide. She's also written political biographies for encyclopedias published specifically for libraries in High Schools, Colleges, and Universities.

Wolfe has raised hundreds of thousands of dollars for nonprofits like the ASPCA and the NRDC, as well as political organizations, such as the ACLU and Amnesty International. As one of the organization's top fundraisers, she became a trainer for the company in Los Angeles, CA and Denver, CO.

Wolfe has participated in service projects throughout the nation; some of which include: beautification park projects, planting trees, literacy programs, Adopt-A-Highway, volunteering in nursing homes, sending care packages to soldiers in Afghanistan, and working in food ministries feeding the homeless across the country.

Wolfe has put her time and resources into serving the homeless by founding her own nonprofit, The Solution to Hunger, Inc., to feed the homeless and hungry with the food excess from catering companies, schools, and restaurants—serving hundreds of thousands of homeless every year. A portion of all book proceeds goes towards this mission.

The author began researching thousands of books from science, to religion, to history, to geography, to mythology over the course of a lifetime, to pen *The Creation Series*. Volume One of the Creation Series: *Where the Shadows Meet the Light,* Volume Two of the Creation Series: *Within the Origin of Time,* and Volume Three of the Creation Series: *While the Ashes Rise to Life.*

Wolfe is also the author of *The Resurrected Dream: A Collection of Poetry and Prose from an Awakened Soul,* and a comprehensive book on homelessness, *Our Invisible Neighbors: Accounts, Causes, and Solutions to the Epidemic of Homelessness.*

You can keep up-to-date with Crystal Wolfe's nonprofit work serving the homeless, upcoming novels, author talks, and other creative endeavors at her personal website:

www.thesolutiontohunger.org
thesolutiontohunger@gmail.com

Other Novels by Crystal Wolfe

Devotional: *You Shall Know Them by Their Fruit: A 365 Daily Devotional for Cultivating the Fruits and Gifts of the Holy Trinity*

Poetry: *The Resurrected Dream: A Book of Poetry & Prose from an Awakened Soul*

Non-Fiction: *Our Invisible Neighbors: Accounts, Causes, & Solutions to the Epidemic of Homelessness*

Positive Thinking: *The 9 Principles of Positivity*

Children's Book: *Different*

Children's Book: *With Teddy Forever*

Fantasy/Sci-Fi: The Creation Series—

Volume One: *Where the Shadows Meet the Light*
Volume Two: *Within the Genesis of Time*
Volume Three: *While the Ashes Rise to Life*
Volume Four: *When the Lines of Lilith Unite*

Fantasy Romance Spin-Off of The Creation Series:
Age of Camelot: The Legend Comes to Life

The Jimmy Hardwin Mystery Series—

Volume One: *Killer of the Voiceless*
Volume Two: *Murder of the Jewel of NYC*

If you enjoyed this novel, please consider putting up a good review for it on Amazon and Goodreads! Thank you so much!

Please buy novels from the shop page on the website, so a portion of book proceeds can feed people in need: http://www.thesolutiontohunger.org/shop/

www.ingramcontent.com/pod-product-compliance
Lightning Source LLC
Chambersburg PA
CBHW030405030726
47497CB00002B/483